Mantis Preying

A Daniel O'Dwyer Oak Island Adventure (Book 2)

Lance Carney

DEDICATION

For my wife Kathy, with love and gratitude. She edits me, adds intelligence and humor. She completes me.

CONTENTS

ACKNOWLEDGMENTS

Cover Illustration Copyright © 2018 Jacob Howell

Editing (plus humorous additions)-Kathy Carney

Oak Island, Caswell Beach, Southport, Wilmington, Fort Fisher and Kure Beach are real places, faithfully described, but used fictitiously in this novel. The same is true of certain businesses frequented by Daniel O'Dwyer, Willie and pals.

In all other respects, however, this novel is a work of fiction. Names, characters, places (Boiling Grove Community Hospital, No Egrets) and incidents are either the product of the author's imagination or are used fictitiously. Any resemblance to actual persons, living or dead, or to actual events or locales is unintentional and coincidental.

ALSO BY LANCE CARNEY

Ripped Tide: A Daniel O'Dwyer Oak Island Adventure

No Egrets: A Glenn and Glenda Oak Island Mystery

With David Moss

Fin and Tonic, Talon and Tombstone (short story collection)

Pirates for a Day (short story)

.

1 - PIRATES AND WANKERS

"I don't know if I can spend eternity with this guy when he goes. I mean—just look at him."

"Aye mate. I know what you mean. He's only been on our vessel for what seems like a fortnight and yet his voice scrapes on me like barnacles. Witness the parley between these two; I'd rather dance the hempen jig than listen to more."

"In our day it would have been easy to get rid of a scurvy landlubber like him. Drop him on a deserted island, make him walk the plank, keelhaul, wait 'til the rum flows and bump him over the side."

"Sounds easy 'nough, except for two problems. No water, thanks to this fool. And the best we can do is move a glass or knock over an empty bottle of his grog."

"Yes…yes. Tis hopeless. We're doomed."

Fiddling with my ear, I stared at the wall. Something was missing. I had only glimpsed it through the cabin door before, but now the bare wall looked out of place. Something was definitely missing.

"What are you doing with that Q-Tip?" Willie shrieked. Then he gasped in that way that teeters between overacting and a teenage crisis.

I stopped mid-twirl, looking at him like I always did when he asked a stupid question—incredulously. "What's it look like?"

"Like you have no regard for your ear canal or otic health."

I removed the Q-Tip and purposely tossed it onto an end table that looked like an antique nesting table but appeared as sterile as an operating room. Willie responded to my callous action with another gasp and a fast exit into the galley, returning quickly with forceps and a small plastic bag emblazoned with the fluorescent orange biohazard symbol. With extreme caution, he used the forceps to extract the Q-Tip from the end table and place it in the plastic bag. You would have thought my ear canal contained

1

radioactive wax.

Germophobes are a unique breed and Willie could be their king.

When he had disposed of the toxic waste and wiped up its remnants, he returned to his chair and looked at me sourly.

"What?" I asked, preparing for a lecture.

Instead I got a "tsk-tsk" and a head shake. I waited him out, my way of torturing him slowly.

Finally, he broke. "I don't care what you do in your own house, but this is my home and I will not have you throwing caution to the wind."

Willie's "home" was actually an old houseboat he had fixed up (with the help of handyman extraordinaire Moses and my money). He had dubbed it the Silent Cow and planted it in the middle of the wooded lot I owned behind my house. Living on it in the water had been out of the question—too many waterborne illnesses. (I had asked him to prove it and he brought up the CDC website and started ticking them off: Legionella, Vibrio cholera, Norovirus, typhoid…)

This was actually the first time I had been allowed inside the Silent Cow—and thanks to my dirty aural openings, perhaps the last. Could I help it if it was something passed down through generations of O'Dwyers? Back in Ireland, my great-great grandfather and namesake was often called Daniel Derdy Ears.

"Um…caution to the wind?"

"Yes," Willie answered indignantly. "Don't you ever read the cautions on product packaging?"

"Heck no! Those are only for—" I started to say "morons" but caught myself. "Uh, lawyers."

Willie walked into his bedroom and returned with a rectangular Tupperware container.

"What's in—"

Ignoring my question, he popped the lid and began reading from something within. "**Warning: Do not insert into ear canal.**" (Written in bold letters, he read it that way.) "**Entering the ear canal could cause injury,**" he finished.

"Oh, come on!" I started.

He silenced me with his hand and continued. "Keep out of reach of children."

Keep out of reach of morons, I thought. "You mean to tell me you've never used a Q-Tip to clean your ear? The whole world uses Q-Tips to clean their ears!"

He shook his head. "I value my ear drums and do not wish to puncture them with a stick."

"A stick!" Willie had done it again. I was visibly upset—over Q-Tips for God's sake. I leaned over and looked in the Tupperware container and read from the Q-tip box myself. "It's a cotton swab; has soft cotton on the end." My eyes went back to the box. "It's the Ultimate Home and Beauty Tool."

"It's a dangerous lance," Willie said matter-of-factly.

Not wishing to give in, I offered one last jab. "And why do you keep the box sealed in a Tupperware container?"

"Cotton."

"Cotton?"

"Yes, cotton is a breeding ground for deadly bacteria."

My hands were raised in front of me; I let them drop, surrendering. But I had to ask: "Then why do you have Q-Tips in your—" I looked around the Silent Cow. "Home—house—houseboat?"

"I dip them in isopropyl alcohol and clean the keyboard of my laptop twice a day. More often if necessary. The Q-Tip was invented in the 1920s by Leo—"

"Stop," I interrupted. "I don't care. So why did you leave three Q-Tips out of the box, within my reach, if the cotton was absorbing all the nasty bacteria floating through the air?"

"Madame asked for three Q-Tips. Oh, that reminds me, she also asked for something else." Willie carefully placed a third Q-Tip on the remaining two and returned to the galley in a hurry.

Madame? He had told me he had a surprise in store. Had he invited Ginger, his lady-friend bartender from the Oar House Lounge? His mother?

I looked around the living room, er...lounge. Salon perhaps. Stateroom? (No wait, I think the stateroom would be Willie's bedroom.) Well, whatever it was called, the room was immaculate. Our ultimate handyman Moses had worked his magic on the Silent Cow, as well as my house (which I refused to call the Prescription Pad as christened by Willie and my friends). I looked closely at the flooring. It appeared to be planks off shipping pallets but they had been cut, planed and sanded to fit perfectly together. Some of the boards were stained and some not, creating a beautiful one-of-a-kind floor. I touched the surface, noting it had enough of a top coat sealer on it to give it an ice rink appearance. If there were any bugs or germs in the wood, they were trapped as tight as a wooly mammoth in the La Brea Tar Pits. Over in the corner was a marble-topped bar, complete with octagonal mirror behind. A small but intricate stone fireplace with logs filled out the far wall from where I sat on the plastic covered couch.

Willie returned with a Fat Tire bottle for me, an organic beer for him and a rose-colored drink in a tumbler glass.

"How in the world do you burn wood in that fireplace without burning down the Silent Cow?" I asked.

"Those are electric logs."

I didn't need to ask him where his electric came from; coming down the path I almost tripped over two of the heavy-duty extension cords snaking from the back of my house to the houseboat.

"Oh yay," I said weakly. "Do they produce heat?"

"Of course. Electric fireplaces have the highest heating efficiency of any type of fireplace. When I crank it up on cold nights, the whole underbelly of the Silent Cow stays warm. Without having any nasty, dirty wood laying around."

"Let me guess. Cut wood is a breeding ground for insects and disease."

He gave me a blank look, like I had just said a truth as simple as "The sky is blue".

When Willie looked away, I examined my "adopted" friend (a school mate from junior high in West Virginia, he had magically materialized on Oak Island in almost the same way his houseboat had appeared on my land). Willie—pale, squat and muscular, with a flat-top haircut he had kept longer than most of his coiffures—actually looked better than he had last week. He smelled better too, as he no longer walked around with a tallow poultice wrapped around his upper body in a flannel cloth. ("The fat from a cow," he had explained, "Applied in a poultice around the chest will keep a deep cough from becoming pneumonia." Picture a silent cow lying in the pasture with four stiff legs skyward for months—that's what Willie smelled like.)

I tilted my Fat Tire bottle toward him and he clinked the top with the neck of his Eel River Organic Amber Ale.

"Where'd you get the beer?"

"The Fat Tire is from your refrigerator—"

"Not the Fat Tire! The organic beer." I had long given up getting mad at Willie for rummaging through my refrigerator—and kitchen cabinets—and mail.

Willie glanced at the red and white label with a picture of a bridge in a black circle in the middle. "I finally convinced the Food Lion manager to stock organic beer. I can be very persuasive."

I nodded. Persuasion, in a Willie-type way, meant the manager hoped if he stocked organic beer he would never have to have another tiresome, exasperating, make-you-want-to-claw-out-your-eyes-and-feed-them-to-the-seagulls conversation with Willie ever again.

My eyes found the bare wall once more, and suddenly it dawned on me. "Ian Anderson!" I cried.

"Where? Where?" Willie jumped to his feet and ran to the porthole. "Where?"

"Yes, Willie. Ian Anderson is on Oak Island," I said sarcastically. "And I invited him to the Silent Cow." Ian Anderson, the face of the band Jethro Tull, as far as I knew, lived on a farm in England and maybe had a house in Switzerland. Chances he was on Oak Island ranged from remote to nil.

"Hey!" Willie shot back, picking up on my tone. "It could happen!"

Willie owned a picture of Ian Anderson, which, until recently apparently, had hung on that wall keeping watch over the Silent Cow from his 8 x 10 frame. Willie's eyes shot to the empty place on the wall, he looked away quickly, and he actually shuddered. I decided to ask about Ian's whereabouts later.

"So, what's this surprise?" I asked instead.

Willie's countenance darkened as his eyes darted around the cabin. He actually looked terrified. Like he had been lowered into the middle of a room full of strangers who all turned toward him and coughed at the same time.

I placed my hand on his arm and he didn't pull away from my touch. Another sign this was something serious. "What is it? Did your cold from last week turn into pneumonia, despite the tallow? A relative from home passed away? Did you discover that organic beer is only a marketing gimmick?"

His eyes were wide, flickering all about the cabin. In a hushed voice, his lips barely moving, he said, "The Silent Cow is haunted."

"I—wait—what?"

I stared at Willie, waiting for the punch line. He said nothing more, just continued to scan the cabin nervously. I followed suit—aft, stern, port, starboard, there was no movement, nothing out of place. If there were ghosts on board, we were going to need a bigger boat. My eyes fell upon the tumbler with the rose-colored drink. Something about it looked familiar.

Bam! The cabin door exploded inward, knocking over a chair before hitting the wall. Instinctively, I jumped up from the couch, banging my head on the low ceiling. I rubbed the spot furiously and despite the immediate pain, determined I would live. It was probably only a skull fracture.

The being in the doorway was a tiny figure, dressed head to toe in black. With the sunlight behind, the vision was surreal, eerie. I shivered (or perhaps it was a slight seizure from my head trauma).

"I always imagined ghosts to be much…taller," I whispered to Willie.

I leaned forward to get a better look. Based on the wardrobe, it appeared to be a woman. Black dress to the floor, black shoes, black lace veil pulled down over her face (which looked more like a black half-slip with the waist band tied in a knot). I noticed the top of a white, flat box sticking out of a huge, black bag hanging at her side. The top of a bottle was also visible. Gin? Did ghosts drink gin?

The lace rustled as her head turned back and forth, surveying the Silent Cow.

"Madame!" Willie cried, relieved. "Welcome."

Madame?

Willie turned to me. "I have asked the Madame here," he said. "To rid the Silent Cow of ethereal beings." He locked eyes and issued a warning. "Behave and believe, Daniel."

What? What did he mean by that? Why, my mind is as open as the next guys. I mean, I don't really think ghosts are real, but today should turn out to be—

She took one step into the Silent Cow and stopped, extending her arms out and up, pope like. (She was either trying to summon the spirits or bracing for a phantom rogue wave to hit the Silent Cow.) Her hands were obscured by an oversized black shawl; a thin, gnarled, trembling finger found an opening through the dark garb. Like the Grim Reaper, she pointed it at Willie.

"Where's my Rose Kennedy Cocktail, Germ Boy?"

I laughed and clapped my hands. As I was saying, today should turn out to be most entertaining.

Willie ran over, grabbed the drink and took it to the old woman. She threw back her veil, revealing the familiar weathered face with thin, stringy white hair falling all around it. She grabbed the glass with both hands.

"I really need a damn drink," she said.

"Miss Matilda!" I cried, running to hug her. "How come you're here? Won't Glenn and Glenda miss you at No Egrets?"

I should have recognized the rose-colored drink as soon as Willie brought it into the room. I had been at the local bar, No Egrets, on enough Sundays to see her down close to fifty. (She only drank Rose Kennedy Cocktails on Sundays, having a different drink for each day of the week.)

Matilda pushed me away. "Keep your distance, Pill Man," she said, referring to my previous life as a hospital pharmacist. "Get ahold of your carnal urges. I have a job to do." For the first time, I noticed she was wearing jewelry. Matilda never wore anything more than a grimace or sneer, so I was quite surprised. (I could only assume the extra bling would serve as some kind of conduit to "the other side".) She dripped with Mardi Gras beads, somebody's old prom ear rings (circa 1962) and finger rings that looked like they came from a gumball machine.

"Besides, it's been too uppity at No Egrets since the anniversary party," Matilda continued. "Too many people and it's 'Mind your manners, Tilly', 'Be nice, Tilly', 'That's not for polite company, Tilly'." She paused in her mocking of the owners long enough to growl (I had to admit she had Glenda's voice down pretty good). "Glenn and Glenda think they're hot shit now. If it weren't for the smoking hot firefighters next door, I'd be long gone."

I couldn't suppress a laugh. This was too much. I was in a landlocked houseboat with Matilda, the local barfly, known all over the island. Whether riding her Vespa through town or in her usual seat at the end of No Egrets' bar, her sarcasm and razor-sharp tongue would cut people to shreds. She was also quite blue for an elderly woman, and I don't mean the color of her hair. Vulgar may be a better description, so I wondered how much Glenn and Glenda were actually missing her today.

"Tilly, Tilly, Tilly," I said, smiling.

"It's Madame Matilda today," she snarled.

I started to laugh again but noticed Willie shooting me a nasty look. Instead, I bowed to her and swept my arm into the interior of the houseboat. "Madame."

Madame Matilda slowly walked into the living area (Lounge? Salon?) of the Silent Cow, slowly turning and surveying the hull of the vessel. She stopped suddenly, shivered and pulled her shawl tight around her thin body.

"I just felt a cold chill. Has anyone died aboard this boat?"

Willie took two steps back and seemed to pull into himself. He looked around, horrified. I imagine any type of blood spill, even imaginary, would be enough to send him into a full-blown panic attack. I could hear him now, ticking off the list of bloodborne pathogens.

"Well," I said. "Last week Willie wore a tallow poultice and it smelled like someone had died."

Willie shot me another dirty look, but at least the distraction seemed to ward off his panic attack. "Daniel, if you aren't going to take this seriously, I'm afraid you're going to have to leave."

"Oh, no!" Matilda cried, grabbing my arm and leading me to a chair at the small round table Willie used for a dinner table. "We must have the Power of Three."

The Power of Three? Are you kidding me? Wasn't that from some witches show on television? An episode of Dr. Who?

I started to make a snide comment, but Willie, sensing it, smacked me in the back of the head with the handle of a nearby Swiffer Wet Jet mop.

"Ouch! What's that for?"

Willie looked at the cleaning gadget in his hand. "It's a wonderful all-in-one mopping system. The best I've found because of the disposable cleaning pads. Traditional mops just spread the bacteria around and are breeding grounds—"

"Shut up, you wankers!" Matilda screamed. "Cut out the Abbott and Costello routine and make me another Rose Kennedy Cocktail." Her eyes seemed to roll back in her head, leaving only the white. "Time to get started," she added in an otherworldly voice.

I jumped back. Willie scurried into the galley to mix another drink. I looked closer at Matilda. Maybe I had misjudged her, maybe she really did have psychic ability. I really didn't know a whole lot about her past (except she had been crowned Miss Ring Girl at a Charlotte Toughman Contest sometime in the 80s and she had banged a Rolling Stones' roadie backstage to the rhythm of Bill Wyman's bass).

Matilda cackled, showing crooked teeth through a crooked smile. "You like that? Scared the little guy silly. I've been able to roll my eyes back in my head since I was a teenager. If I didn't like a feller, used to do that after I faked an orgasm. They'd think I died and would run from the house!" Her whole body was shaking with laughter at the memories. "God, those were good times!"

I grinned and took a slug of my Fat Tire. Yep, this was going to be entertaining.

Willie entered, placing a fresh Rose Kennedy Cocktail in front of Matilda and taking the third seat at the table. Matilda attacked the drink like a lizard with a long, sticky tongue ensnaring an insect. It was somewhat disgusting to watch (and very messy).

"Willie" I said, trying to keep the skepticism out of my voice. "What makes you think the Silent Cow is haunted?"

His eyes flicked about the cabin again. He shivered. "Drinking glasses move on their own—on this very table. And just yesterday, my empty bottle of Eel River Organic Amber Ale was knocked over four times! Every time I set it upright it was knocked over again." He ran his hand over a spot. "I had to scrub the tabletop five times."

"Maybe ghosts don't like organic—"

He silenced me with an upraised hand. "And…they knocked my autographed Ian Anderson photograph from the wall and broke the glass in the frame."

I gasped. So that's what happened to Ian. And the picture was signed? The way Willie worshiped Jethro Tull's music left no doubt that an autograph from its flutist front man would be his most prized possession.

I could see Willie's eyes were beginning to tear. "It crinkled the edges of the photo," he wailed. "It's ruined."

I placed my hand on his shoulder and again he did not pull away. He really was out of sorts.

"Maybe—" I scanned the floor of the houseboat. "Have you gotten out your…er, my level recently? Maybe the Silent Cow has shifted and she is no longer flush, um plumb. We did have some big winds from Hurricane Matthew."

"A skewed deck could not produce what I saw," he said simply. "And then there's the toothbrush."

We waited for him to continue but all he did was crinkle his nose and begin retching. Matilda looked to me for guidance; I shrugged my shoulders, letting him cough and sputter. When Willie was repulsed and nauseated by something he considered revolting, there was no reeling him back in. Best to let him flounder around until he bobbed back to the surface.

Willie carefully dabbed the sweat on his brow with a folded lint free cloth and leaned back in his chair. With a trembling hand, he raised the Eel River Organic Amber Ale to his lips.

I gave him another minute before asking, "What happened to your toothbrush?"

Willie shivered and I thought he might start the whole process again, but he managed to gather himself.

"Every morning—" He paused to clear his throat, almost retching again. "My toothbrush is already wet when I pick it up."

I gasped. Matilda snickered.

"I've only got one toothbrush left from the 10-pack I bought last week," he said sadly. With a sudden wave of his hand he continued, "I can't talk about it. Please! Madame Matilda, can you help me?"

Matilda twitched. (I think she may have drifted off.) She pulled the large black bag from her shoulder and placed it on the table with a thud. What did she have in there (besides the gin)? A crystal ball? Tarot cards? Holy water?

She struggled to pull the long, flat rectangular box out of her black shoulder bag and unceremoniously plopped it on the table. What the heck? The box was white, or used to be white; one corner was gone and old, yellowed tape held the other end together. It had a red cartoonish devil displayed—with a wand! The Sensational Game, the box proclaimed. Entertainment for Everyone!

Matilda tore the lid from the box, removed a flat, wooden board from the bottom and slammed it on the table. Before flinging the box off the table, she took out a triangular piece of wood with a small, round window near the point.

It really wasn't all that surprising "Madame" Matilda intended to ward off Willie's spirits with an Ouija board. My guess is it would work better than a Magic 8 Ball.

"My, that's an old one" was all I could think of to say.

Matilda stroked the wooden board lovingly. "It was the one thing my father gave me before he runned off with the baby sitter. Well, I also got his raging libido."

I shuddered. It was almost impossible to guess Matilda's age after years on a barstool. She could be anywhere from sixty-two to ninety-two. She probably didn't weigh more than ninety-two pounds either.

"Well?" Matilda hollered at Willie. He looked at her dumbstruck.

"The magic sticks! You moron."

Willie hopped up and ran over to the end table, bringing back the three mysterious Q-tips. Magic sticks?

"Okay, my interest is piqued. What are the Q-tips for?" I asked.

"Not," Willie stated emphatically. "For use in the ear canal."

Oh, goody. Willie was feeling better.

Madame Matilda had her eyes closed (had she drifted off again?) and after a few seconds she answered. "Besides my natural abilities, I was taught the art of hoodoo by a witch in Harlem. It was there I learned that cotton can absorb more than earthly matter."

Hmm, chalk up another unusual use for the Q-tip website. (As long as you don't use it to clean a ghost's ear canal.)

"Mr. Big Stuff," I sang. "Hoodoo you think you are?"

Willie and Matilda stared at me blankly. "Daniel," Willie said. "This is no time for a wordplay game. What is wrong with you?"

The number of times I had been in the middle of something, either serious or intense, only to be interrupted by Willie demanding a wordplay match probably numbered in the hundreds. His eyes would light up and there was no turning him away. The first time Willie and Matilda had met at No Egrets, they had locked in a killer game of wordplay revolving around wine and liquor names.

Now they both looked at me as if I was the childish one. "Whatever," I said, rolling my eyes.

Matilda placed the heart-shaped planchette on top of the Ouija board and handed a Q-tip to Willie and me. "Time to get started, before I need another Rose Kennedy Cocktail."

I watched as she and Willie placed the end of their Q-tips on different sides of the planchette. What the heck. "That's not going to work," I claimed. "Without human touch the pointer won't move."

"Au contraire, non croyant," Matilda said.

I looked at Willie. "Did she just call me a croissant?"

"It was French," he said in an exasperated tone. "She called you a nonbeliever."

French? Matilda? Did she learn it from the Harlem Hoodoo Queen? The only French I had heard her mutter at No Egrets was "Merde". I had thought Matilda was only multilingual in "The Seven Words You Can Never Say on Television" as made famous by George Carlin. (She did seem to know that particular word in seven different languages.)

"Please," Willie begged. Feeling somewhat foolish, I picked up the third Q-tip and placed one cotton end on the third side of the planchette.

We sat there motionless for a full minute—the heart-shaped piece of wood did not move. I noticed the color of the wood planchette had faded to a dull gray, reminding me of the color of my spare bathroom. Jaclyn had brought me paint chips from Oak Island Hardware and we planned on painting the bathroom walls soon. I looked at my Q-tip and imagined dipping it in paint, swabbing the faded planchette with a nice buttercream yellow to spruce it up. Or maybe a nice lemon chiffon.

"Someone!" Madame Matilda bellowed. I flinched and my Q-tip dropped, spinning a little and coming to rest near a word on the Ouija board. "Someone is not concentrating! At least not on the spirits."

As they both glared at me, I started to pick up my Q-tip. "Hey look!" I said excitedly. "My cotton swab is trying to tell us something." My Q-tip was pointing to the word "Goodbye" at the bottom of the board.

Willie actually growled at me. I remembered the last time he had made me so mad that an inhuman "Grrr" escaped my lips. I felt bad for a second, a second and a half maybe, and then I smiled. Chalk one up for Daniel. Score: Daniel-one; Willie-five hundred and fifty-three.

I picked up the Q-tip and placed the end back on the planchette. The other two followed suit.

I tried my best to concentrate on the spirits, wondering what they looked like. The only spirits I had seen recently were on the shelves of the Oak Island ABC Store.

Madame Matilda's head slowly lolled back until she was staring at the ceiling. I had to look away because it reminded me of the day she brought a test tube into No Egrets, leaned back on her barstool and tried to get Pinhead Paul to give her a Zombie shooter (it was Thursday).

When a low moan escaped her lips, I gave sudden thought to fleeing out the cabin door. The last thing on earth I wanted to hear was Matilda moan. That would be the granddaddy of all nightmares.

Her head shot forward again and she called, in a crusty voice, "Spirits of the past move among us. Is there anyone here who wishes to speak with us?"

I almost dropped my Q-tip as the planchette jerked. I eyed Willie to see how he had made the wood jump, but he had a shocked look on his face.

Madame Matilda spoke again. "Is there anyone from the spirit world who wishes to speak with us?"

I had a strange feeling in the pit of my stomach. It seemed to be a mixture of fear and…hunger? Had I eaten breakfast this morning? My stomach let out a weird, prolonged gurgling noise.

Willie gasped. "Yes," he whispered. "I hear the spirits."

I was about to open my mouth to debunk this particular development when the planchette jerked again.

"Is there a spirit present in the Silent Cow who wishes to speak with us?" Madame Matilda cried.

The planchette, which had been in the middle of the board, began moving slowly to the left. Amazed, I watched as it came to rest over the first letter on the top row: "A". Now it was moving again to the right and toward the bottom row. The next letter was "Y". Back to the top row on the left, the planchette stopped on "E". We all waited breathlessly for it to continue moving.

When the planchette didn't move again, I asked, "Aye? Who says aye nowadays?"

"They're here," Madame Matilda proclaimed in a high-pitched voice, staring, for some reason, at Willie's blank television screen in the corner.

"Who?" Willie asked, shivering.

I couldn't contain myself. "Why Captain Ahab and his great, white whale. We're all in here together. In the Silent Cow." Muttering, I pondered again, "Who says aye?"

Willie looked at Madame Matilda. "Can I ask them a question?" As she nodded, the black veil/half-slip fell back over her face.

"Oh, great spirit!" Willie nearly shouted. (I had a sudden image of the Peanuts gang in the pumpkin patch summoning the Great Pumpkin— Willie did look a little like Linus.)

"Oh, great spirit," Willie repeated. "Is it you that has been...um, touching my toothbrush?"

I looked sideways at Willie. One question to ask the netherworld and he chooses that one?

A quick spasm in the planchette and it began to move again. First letter: "C". A quick left to "A" and finally to the right on the second row: "T".

"Cat!" we all three exclaimed, somewhat perplexed.

"That doesn't make any sense," Willie said, shaking his head.

"Sometimes," Madame Matilda offered. "The words are too long and the spirits can't gather enough energy to finish."

We pondered this for a moment, waiting to see if the planchette would move again.

"Maybe they were spelling a name and didn't finish," Madame Matilda finally said, the black veil still hiding her face. "Have you been banging somebody named Cathy and she's been using your toothbrush when you're not looking?"

"What?" Willie screamed. "No. A thousand times no! And even if it were true, if I found out she was using my toothbrush, I would throw her over the stern and into the woods, just like all of the contaminated toothbrushes."

I was only half-listening, thinking about the first spelled word, the beer bottle, Ian Anderson photograph, drinking glass and toothbrush. How could they all be tied to the word "aye"? The logical mind of the pharmacist tried to fit them all together

"I've got it!" I cried. They both looked at me expectantly. "Who says aye?"

"Johnny Depp in those Disney Pirate movies," Willie answered.

I grimaced. "Close. However, I don't think the Silent Cow was built that long ago; I don't know how pirates could be haunting it. But I do think it's seamen."

Willie looked around his home, aghast. "You mean there's seamen—" His eyes flicked from floor to ceiling. "Seamen all over the Silent Cow?"

I could sense a cackle building deep within Matilda and a lewd comment just around the bend. I waggled my finger at her, saying, "That would be very un-Madame-like." It was all I could do to hold my own tongue with a Monica Lewinsky one-liner on the tip.

I tried to steer the conversation in a different direction. "So, how does the word cat fit into a seaman—er, seafarer's world?"

They both looked at me stupidly (or at least I imagined Matilda did through her veil).

"Seamen were often flogged with a cat o' nine tails!" I said triumphantly.

"Huh-what?" Willie stammered. "I don't get it."

"It's simple," I said slowly, as if explaining to kindergartners. "The Silent Cow is haunted by seamen. They are using...um, some kind of invisible whip, a cat o' nine tails to knock over your beer bottle, move your glass on the table, knock Ian Anderson off the wall—"

"Sacrilege," Willie exclaimed. "But what about the toothbrush?"

I thought about it for a minute, then had an idea. "Easy. I assume your toothbrush is secure in some kind of wall holder?"

"Yes," Willie answered.

"Then the ghost seamen can't knock it off the wall with the invisible cat o' nine tails. But—apparently, they can use the cat o' nine tails to flick it and apply a coat of some kind of ectoplasmic slime to the bristles."

Willie eyes grew wide and he started retching again.

"I might be wrong," I said loudly, over Willie's gagging and coughing. "It's just a theory."

A sudden low, guttural moan silenced us; it sounded inhuman, seeming to reverberate off the walls, building in the room until we had to cover our ears. I glanced at Madame Matilda and her head was tilted back at what seemed a ninety-degree angle, the black veil still covering her face. The sound was coming from her!

The lights flickered. Willie let out a girly scream (or maybe it was me). The Ouija board flipped from the table and landed on the floor. I watched as the planchette pirouetted through the air in slow motion, heading toward Willie's head. Too stunned to move, the point of the planchette struck Willie just below the left eye. His hand went immediately to his cheek and I could see blood leaking down between his fingers. I watched in horror as my Fat Tire bottle moved a little on the table and then fell over. It was three-fourths full!

The lights began flickering so fast I thought I was back in the disco era, dancing my cool white-boy dance ("Do the Hustle!"). The strobe effect finally died and the Silent Cow was immersed in darkness, with only a slim ray of light coming from the other room.

Willie let out a little whimper (or maybe it was me, mourning my spilled Fat Tire). The inhuman moan from Madame Matilda became louder. I leaned closer to get a better look. Her head was still tilted back and—she seemed to be rising out of her chair. Now when I say rising, I don't mean standing up. She was floating! Her bony behind was at least a foot off her chair.

I was terrified, but I couldn't help wonder how much Glenn and Glenda would pay to have the ghostly technology available to float Matilda off her barstool and out the door of No Egrets on occasion.

I was still looking at Madame Matilda when a fireball of light seemed to shoot from beneath her veil, blinding me. The moaning stopped. The Silent Cow was silent. After a few seconds, I heard the sound of Willie rubbing his eyes (or maybe the table, trying to sanitize it).

My eyes were still adjusting when a deep, masculine voice began spatting an unending string of curses. I could only make out a word here or there, but there was no mistaking the intent. I heard strange words like "quim", "quiffing", "doxie", followed by more familiar words like "feck", "arse" and "shite".

Finally the spots were gone from my eyes and I concentrated on focusing on Madame Matilda's face. Her face was shimmering beneath the veil and it looked like...she had whiskers! A foul smell emanated from her, unlike any I had smelled before (even worse than the time she had eaten cooked cabbage at No Egrets—the rest of the day an olfactory sensation I will never forget).

The floating form of Madame Matilda reached out two bony hands, one grabbing Willie by the throat and the other latching onto my windpipe. She had the strength of ten seamen.

A growling voice came from beneath the veil. "Fecking arses!" My eyes, popping, beheld a sneering, bearded, masculine face shimmering in place of the old woman's.

"Not pirates," the voice growled. "Privateers!"

I tried to break the hold on my neck but Madame Matilda gripped it like she was hanging on to a ship's boom during a storm (or the last Rose Kennedy Cocktail on earth).

"Shite," the voice said, starting to weaken. "A cat—" I could see the shimmering face beginning to fade. With a final burst of energy, the voice shouted, "Is a fecking cat!"

The Silent Cow went dark. Madame Matilda's hands loosened and fell from our throats.

A loud sound, like fingernails scratching the inside of a coffin, filled the interior of the Silent Cow.

2 - POMEGRANATE GATOR PÂTÉ

My hair streaming behind me, leaning into the wind, I felt like I was flying. Exhilarating. Freeing. The Oak Island Beach Villas obscured my view of the Atlantic Ocean, but I could sure smell it. I briefly closed my eyes and inhaled as much of the delicious salt air as my lungs would hold. Ah—*don't worry, be happy* (to quote Bobby McFerrin). I pedaled faster, loving the feel of my new Cannondale CAAD12 Disc Dura Ace beneath my bottom. It felt like I was twelve years old again and I didn't have to be home until the street lights flickered on. I had splurged on the bicycle a few months ago, the cost putting a dent in my savings. It cost a bit more than my Schwinn 10 speed from back in the day (okay, thirty times as much), but that was a worry for another day. *Don't worry, be happy.*

I jammed on the bike's handbrakes, nearly flipping over the handlebars like I did that time on my Schwinn when I hit the rock at the bottom of 21st Street hill. (I left a little of my purty teenage face on the concrete that day.) Up ahead, a radar speed sign! Cool! Wonder how fast I can get my new wonder bike to go? Without a car in sight, I pedaled as fast as my legs would turn, accelerating down the straight stretch of Caswell Beach Road, the lighthouse looming in the distance. Flying by the radar sign so fast, I couldn't make out the numbers, so I guessed sixty-five or seventy miles per hour. At least! Nervously I scanned the area for a police car. They took speeding seriously on Caswell Beach.

The small town on the northern end of Oak Island, Caswell Beach was beautiful, packing more into a small space than a hoarder on crack could ever hope to achieve. The stunning, lithe Oak Island Lighthouse sported its gray, white and black right next to a United States Coast Guard Station. The Oak Island Golf Club sprawled between the beach and Intracoastal

Waterway. Fort Caswell encompassed the northern tip of the island, at the mouth of the Cape Fear River. I stopped pedaling as I remembered hearing pirates had once frequented the fort area, including the notorious Blackbeard, Edward Teach. Fort Caswell changed hands four times during the Civil War and a final time in 1946 when the Baptist State Convention of North Carolina purchased the land. The fort still stands, making me wonder if the Baptists are preparing for holy war, maybe with the Methodists. I had heard an unconfirmed report recently that the Baptists would allow tours of the fort, but only for a half hour. ("Okay folks, Fort Caswell was named for the first governor of North Carolina and Revolutionary War hero, Richard Caswell. Over there is the original fortification, right here is one of the seven cement batteries, to the left is the horse barn, straight ahead the prison, and near where you entered is the hospital/morgue. If you have really good eyesight, you can see the tombstones of the cemetery rise just above that ridge. That's all the time we have. Thank you and have a blessed day.")

I slowed at the base of the lighthouse, craning my neck to look upward. I *had* taken a tour of the lighthouse right after I arrived on the island. If I remember correctly, it was completed in the late 1950s. And talk about a great workout! The lighthouse wasn't built with the usual spiral staircase inside, but an ascending series of ship's ladders. The tour only went to the second level—what I wouldn't give to sneak in once a week for the Ultimate Lighthouse Fitness Run. Click the stopwatch at the bottom and see how long it takes to make it to the beacon. The bolt to the beacon. Better yet, invite a friend. Race to the top—first one there gets the Fat Tire and the best damn view on the island.

I jumped off my road bike and walked it alongside the asphalt to the bike rack. After a last look at the impressive structure, I made my way down the wooden steps to Caswell Beach. Near the bottom, a black cat leaped out of the vegetation and crossed my path. I had to sit on the last step, my heart racing. The cat and thoughts of pirates ("Well excuse me—privateers!") brought back the whole crazy episode in the *Silent Cow* yesterday.

At the first sound of scratching, Willie stood and I had followed suit, moving away from the table. As the scratching became louder, followed by a banging, Willie jumped into my arms.

"You have a lot of faith that I don't have cooties," I gasped, as I struggled to keep my balance. His flat-top haircut tickled my nostrils and I couldn't contain a sneeze. I tried to turn my head as far as I could, but it didn't matter. Willie dropped to the floor and turned to confront me.

"You—you—you sneezed on me!" he cried. Apparently, my germs were more terrifying than ghosts.

"I turned my head!"

"I need to get into the decontamination shower, PDQ!"

In spite of the situation, I chortled. "Yeah, right. Where you going to find one of those?"

Willie pointed back through the doorway, where a small sliver of light still shone. "I have one. A Hughes Emergency Shower; I had Moses install it instead of a regular shower."

"Let me guess," I said, sarcasm dripping. "You bought it off ParanoidWeirdoEndoftheWorld.com."

"No," he stated matter-of-factly. "Amazon. Your account."

Before I could respond, Madame Matilda moaned and her head flopped forward. I could just make out her face as she brushed the veil back.

"Wow," she exclaimed, a little groggily. "I feel like a centuries old, smelly man with brown, crooked teeth and bad breath was inside me."

I could just make out a twisted smile as she wrapped her arms and hugged herself. "Damn! That was good. He made my eyes roll back on his own. Much better than the big 'O'. I'm tingly all over."

Before I could shudder at the thought, the banging intensified, causing me to shudder.

Willie squealed. Matilda picked up her Rose Kennedy Cocktail and downed it, ice cubes and all. "Damn," she said. "I wish I had a cigarette."

Scratch—scratch. Bang!

"It sounds like it's coming from the other room," I whispered.

"The head," Willie whispered in return.

"What head?" I gasped, picturing a three hundred-year-old pirate's (I mean privateer's) disembodied head banging around in the next room.

"No, it's coming from the head—the bathroom."

I tried to push Willie ahead of me through the doorway, but he wouldn't budge. I did the next bravest thing—I whisked Matilda from her chair, supporting her like a rag doll in front of me, and walked through the door. She was the Madame mystic after all (and we were about to walk "into the mystic").

"Hey, why do I have to go first?" Matilda cried.

"That's what Willie is paying you for," I answered bravely.

Willie, behind me, whispered, "Paying? Who said I'm paying her?"

"What?" Matilda shouted, twisting in my arms.

"Don't worry," I told Matilda. "We'll order you a custom horn for your Vespa." (Off my Amazon account, no doubt.)

"Well, okay," Matilda agreed. "Don't want one of those wussy horns that go 'Meep' though. Want a full-throated one that sounds like Isaac Hayes singing the 'Theme from Shaft'."

"*Who is the man that would risk his neck for his brother man?*" I sang deeply, holding the old woman in front of me as I approached the door of the head.

"Shaft!" Willie answered, singing in falsetto from somewhere behind us.

"*You damn right!*" I crooned, opening the door and thrusting Matilda through.

"*This cat Shaft is a bad mother—*"

"Shut your mouth," Matilda commanded.

The old woman wiggled in my arms until I had to drop her to the floor. "Put me down! This is no time for you to cop a feel!"

Scratch—scratch. Bang!

Just within the door, we all stopped in our tracks. The bathroom light, which had been off, began blinking. I was mesmerized by the light. *Dot, dot, dot—dash, dash, dash—dot, dot, dot.* It seemed like some kind of message. If only I knew Morse code, I might be able to figure it out. Could be important.

The light went out followed by a huge bang. I turned to run...I mean check on Willie. He was holding his swelling cheek, the planchette injury, and his eyes were wide. I swiveled back and saw Matilda looking up. The ceiling of the head seemed to be moving!

Bang! Bang!

Matilda went into full Madame mode, chanting, "Is there anyone from the spirit world who wishes to cross over? Please cross over. Is there anyone from the spirit world who wishes to cross over? Please..."

BANG!

The walls shook and I could see Willie's toothbrush teetering in its holder.

"I sense a presence," Madame Matilda mumbled. Uh, no shit Madame Sherlock. I *hear* a presence.

The ceiling opened with a blinding light and something fell into the head with a flash of white. My mind immediately flashed to the movie *Poltergeist* and the spirits crossing over into the light. Willie screamed. I let out a little whimper and tried to appear brave (as the egress from the head was blocked by my terrified friend).

Madame Matilda's eyes rolled back in her head and she collapsed in a heap on the head's floor. Willie screamed again. The toothbrush began spinning in the holder, faster and faster until it made a whirring noise. Willie hyperventilated during his last attempt at a scream. The light flashed on—I expected to see a one-eyed pirate sodomizing Willie's toothbrush. What I saw—what I witnessed astounded me and left me speechless. Willie fainted, falling backwards like a deadened tree. I could hear his head hit the wall and then the floor with a thump.

The black cat wrapped around my legs, kicking up the sand of Caswell

Beach, scaring me; I pulled my legs up quickly onto the wooden step before realizing what was happening. I chuckled as I bent to pet it.

"Hello fellow, or are you a miss?"

The cat looked at me sideways and did not answer.

"I've got a beautiful calico cat you'd like to meet. She's the bee's knees."

I looked out at the Atlantic, smiling, thinking of Willie passed out on the floor and his toxic toothbrush.

The otherworldly presence that had "crossed over" turned out to be my calico cat, Pickford (named for silent film star, icon and movie mogul Mary Pickford). She had been scratching at a small hinged trap door on the cabin roof, trying to open it. No doubt, she had managed to insert a paw under the trap door and lift it several times. (I had seen her open kitchen cabinets and drawers many times in search of fresh fish.) Finally, she had lifted it high enough to squeeze through and all we saw was a blur of white, black and brown fur, falling from another dimension (a.k.a. the roof). The feline landed on her feet on the floor, apparently not at all surprised to see humans, and immediately jumped to the bathroom vanity. Pickford's long pink tongue snaked out and began licking the bristles of Willie's toothbrush.

Later, after carrying Willie to his plastic covered couch (bumping his head on the sterile end table in the process), splashing Eel River Organic Amber Ale on the non-planchette injured side of his face, administering oxygen from his portable O2 cylinder (and sticking a Q-tip in his ear canal—I couldn't resist), Willie groaned.

Matilda appeared above us. Apparently she had recovered from the traumatic scene and had gone to the refrigerator in the galley. She was holding a three-fourths full pitcher of Rose Kennedy Cocktail by the handle and drinking from it like it was a beer stein.

"Rouse Willie," I told her.

"I *beg* your pardon?" Matilda replied between swigs. "I don't care if you pay me an extra five hundred dollars, I don't do three-ways. At least not anymore."

"*Rouse!* Wake up!" I gave her a sideways look. "Not *arouse*."

She shrugged and turned up the pitcher.

Willie's eyes fluttered open; when he opened his mouth to scream I poured in some Eel River Organic Amber Ale. I needed him calm so we could sort out this mystery.

When he stopped sputtering and coughing, I asked, "Why would Pickford—um, like your toothbrush?"

Matilda snickered. "Like? Did you see that cat's tongue? That animal licked the hell out of those bristles!"

19

Willie started retching and I gently lifted him to a sitting position. I had just got him back to consciousness; it wouldn't do for him to asphyxiate on his own vomitus.

"The cat had probably been out there in the woods hunting first," Matilda continued. "Probably bit the head off a nice fat vole and pulled out all its intestines before eating it."

"Matilda!" I cried. "Stop it!"

"They lick their butts, too," she couldn't help adding.

"This—is—a nightmare," Willie managed to say between retches. At least he was talking and taking breaths—less of a chance of him being seasick all over the floor of the *Silent Cow*. That might send him over the edge.

"I've never known Pickford to…take a fancy to *my* toothbrush. What's so special about yours?" I asked.

Willie shook his head. "I don't know. They are just cheap toothbrushes from Thomas Drugs. I boil them in between brushings and use them until the bristles fall out."

As if on cue, Pickford sauntered into the room on paws as silent as the films of her namesake, licking her kitty lips. Willie groaned. I snatched up the cat quickly and headed toward the door. I stopped short, sniffing. Besides the usual feline smell, there was a sweet scent.

"She—" I took another sniff. "She smells sweet," I said, holding the cat in front of me.

"Oh, you are a sick man," Matilda croaked. "First you grope me and now you're going to play out your feline fetishes right here in front of us."

Ignoring Matilda, I presented the cat to Willie. He leaned back into the couch, trying to escape. "Do you recognize this scent? It's kinda fruity. I've never smelled it on her before."

"I recognize it!" Matilda cried. "Pomegranate. I've got a pomegranate douche."

Realizing I would never be able to consume that particular fruit ever again, I soldiered on. "Willie? Pomegranate?"

"Oh no!" he cried. "Two weeks ago, I started using a new organic toothpaste. It has neem and pomegranate in it!"

"Neem? What is that? Is it another name for catnip?"

"Catnip! You really think I would brush my teeth with catnip?" he answered. "Neem is a traditional botanical used to clean teeth."

I snarled a little, wanting to ask why he didn't just go out in the woods, rub leaves on his teeth and be done with it.

"Matilda," I ordered. "Go into the head and find that organic tooth balm."

"I will," she murmured as she got up and shuffled through the door. "As long as someone makes another pitcher of Rose Kennedy. I'm thirsty."

She held up the empty pitcher.

Pickford gave me a funny look, usually meaning pet me or suffer the consequences, so I gave her several strokes and scratches to the head and neck area.

Matilda returned with a strange looking tube, which looked more like hemorrhoid ointment than toothpaste. Guess that explained why Willie was a butthead sometimes. (Cue the snare drum and cymbal, *Ba-dum-tish*!)

I took the tube and squeezed a small amount on my finger. It looked like congealed Red Bull pâté (or something that leaked out of a real bull).

Pickford immediately perked up and began squirming in my arms. The last time I had seen her act that way was when I returned from Haag and Sons with a plastic bag filled with five different fresh fish varieties. I held out my finger to the cat and she licked it frantically. I swear I saw her eyes roll back like Matilda's.

"Willie! You've been poisoning my cat!"

"What?" Willie looked perplexed as well as sickened. "Your cat has been contaminating my toothbrush!"

"Will somebody *puh-lease* mix my Rose Kennedy Cocktail!" Matilda screamed.

It had finally happened. I had descended into the depths of delirium, the inner circle of the inane; fallen into the fiddlededee of folly. Boy, did I feel stupid.

"I'm leaving!" I tucked my cat under my arm and slammed the door of the *Silent Cow*.

A small, brown Seaside Sparrow landed in the thick vegetation and the black cat turned slowly, hunkering down for the impending attack. The human, no longer needed, was ignored as natural instincts took over.

It was high tide; the ocean waves, unusually rough, pummeled the shore. My original plan was to swim a couple miles after biking, but not being in top aquatic form yet, I reconsidered. I had lived through an encounter with a jellyfish to a rather embarrassing body location and had only recently garnered enough courage to get back on that particular horse and start swimming again. At the thought, my pelvic region began to itch and I had to cross my legs.

Funny how the encounter with the jellyfish had led to danger, excitement, romance. Quite the adventure. I could have done without most of it, but I did meet some great people along the way, including Jaclyn. I took a deep breath, content with my current situation, pledging to keep a low profile, remain calm and be as boring as possible. I laughed. All I needed to do was avoid marine life, or any creatures from the animal kingdom for that matter, and it would be smooth sailing.

Two teenaged boys, sprinting down the beach, stopped near me. Breathlessly, one shouted, "Gator! On the—beach!" He pointed in the direction they were running.

Ooh—an alligator on the beach! This I had to see. I ran up the steps to my Cannondale CAAD12 Disc Dura Ace.

Ahead, I could see a gathering of cars and people. I cruised in near them, depositing my bicycle in a nearby rack. I followed a family of five down the path to the beach. Amazing how fast word spreads on the island. As Jimmy Buffett so eloquently stated, "You can hear it on the Coconut Telegraph." Of course now you can hear it on the Coconut Facebook or Coconut Twitter.

We joined about thirty other people near the surf. A pre-teen was going from one side of the semi-circle to the other, telling everyone, "At first I thought it was a log. But it had eyes! It was really crazy. It was scary. I have pictures of it on my phone, want to see?"

An older woman in a sarong stepped up. She had a tiny, puffy Pomeranian dog, with a pink bow on its head, on a leash that looked like kite string. "How come the police aren't here taking care of this? They are useless. Defend and protect indeed!"

"Where is it?" someone shouted.

The young girl pointed to the waves where we could just make out a long, dark shape in the water. I could see the stripes on its tail. A breaking wave moved the shape closer to shore. The woman next to me screamed.

"Why is it in the ocean?" the woman asked her husband.

"Must've come off the golf course," he told her. Then he grinned evilly and slapped his pale wife on the behind. "But don't worry, alligators only like dark meat."

She didn't slap him; I was considering doing it for her when we heard a siren.

Wait a minute! Off the golf course? Could it be the same gator on the fifth hole of Oak Island Golf Club—the same gator hiding down by the water hazard—the same gator where my golf ball ended up right beside its tail? Playing that day with Jaclyn, she had convinced me keeping my hand was more important than retrieving that particular golf ball.

The alligator washed into the shallow and I got a good look at him. Close to six feet long, dark with stripes, swelled body, long snout, longer tail. By god, I think that's him! I would recognize him anywhere.

"That gator owes me a golf ball!" I told the woman beside me. Thankfully, my voice was drowned out by the siren and squealing of police car tires on the gravel. We all turned to look at the Oak Island Police officer jogging down the path.

I recognized him immediately. Hans Rodriguez stopped by the crowd, scanning the water for the alligator. Hans (whose name had morphed into

Hands on the island) was of Mexican (father) and German (mother) descent. He turned his blues eyes (his only German features) back to the crowd.

"Okay, who saw the alligator first?" he asked.

"Me!" the girl squeaked. In rapid fire she added: "At first I thought it was a log but it had eyes, it was really crazy and scary, I have pictures on my phone, want to see?"

The policeman looked at the animal in the surf. "Um, maybe later. Did you see where the alligator came from?"

The girl shook her head. Officer Rodriguez scanned the crowd, his eyes stopping when he saw me.

"Daniel," he said, with a slight nod of his head.

"Hands."

"I need to speak with you when this situation is under control."

I nodded, my curiosity piqued. Was it something serious? I often shared a drink and a yarn with Hands and his partner Sphinx at No Egrets. Maybe he had heard a good joke he wanted to tell me.

"Officer, what are you going to do about the man-eating crocodile?" the older woman clutching the Pomeranian asked. She had on a large floppy hat and had to keep pushing back the brim to look the policeman in the eye. "The police should have these animals under control and not let them run wild!" The dog yipped in agreement. "I expect," she added acidly. "You to do your duty."

"First," Hands said. "It's not a crocodile. That is an alligator. Second, it's not man-eating—as long as you leave it alone." The woman harrumphed. Hands made a point of staring at the little foo-foo dog the woman was now holding in one hand. "However, they have been known to snack on pets so I wouldn't get too close."

"Especially ones with little pink bows on their heads," I added, figuring it was something Hands had wanted to add but couldn't.

"Well—I never!" the woman exclaimed, storming off.

Hands put his hand to his face and mouthed the words "thank you" where only I could see them.

"I have called Oak Island Animal Control and they should be here shortly." Hands said authoritatively, returning his attention to the crowd.

The crowd calmed at this point, the murmurs mostly positive. Hands turned to me, but before he could speak, someone shouted, "They're here!"

All heads turned to the bank (good thing the alligator stayed in the surf); I could just make out the top of the Oak Island Animal Control vehicle pulling in beside the police car. When the animal control officer exited the vehicle, a cheer went up.

The large animal control officer carefully made his way through the thick sand on the path, picking up his feet and cautiously placing them down, as if making his way through a giant box of kitty litter.

"Shoot," Hands whispered to me. "It's Jed Frid. I was hoping Gus would get the call."

Jed Frid received another cheer as he finally made his way to Hands' side. He seemed to swell at the attention, pulling in his ample beer gut, and standing as tall as his five-foot, six-inch frame would allow.

"No applause necessary, folks," Jed Frid replied, smiling and making a weird, palate-to-nose snorting sound. "Just point me to the porpoise with a purpose."

"Jed," Hands said. "Where's Gus?"

Jed smirked. "Gus? He's on a rabid coon call at the other end of the island. Don't need Gus for this."

"Uh-huh," Hands responded. "What did dispatch tell you?"

With enthusiasm, Jed hitched up his drooping pants; as an apple falls from a tree and hits the ground, the gigantic jeans settled back to the same low spot.

"I can handle this, me-self," Jed told the cop, with a touch of disdain. "Ain't nothing to hauling in and tagging a dying dolphin." With a self-satisfied smile, he pulled a metal hook from his vest.

"Uh-huh," Hands repeated. "Animal's over there." Hands pointed to the surf before turning and giving me a secret smile.

Jed Frid, Oak Island Animal Control officer, turned and haughtily proceeded toward the surf, stopping only once to adjust the waistband of his colossal khakis.

"Asshole," Hands whispered, pulling me aside. "He always gets Gus to do all the work; I'm surprised he's here on his own. Somebody at dispatch must be playing a trick on him. Secretly, I think he's afraid of animals."

I glanced at the huge animal control officer making his way toward the dark object in the waves.

"Listen," Hands said. "I was looking for you. You really need to get a cell phone."

I thought of my cell phone—on the bottom of the Intracoastal Waterway—and felt nothing. It had been over a year now and I didn't miss it. There was a time my cell phone made me feel like a galley slave chained to the oars.

"Jaclyn called the station," Hands continued. "She's been trying to reach you. Willie is in the hospital."

"What?" I cried. "What's wrong?"

"I don't really know. I got the information secondhand. I think he's bleeding."

Willie? Bleeding? It would have to be really bad for him to go to the hospital. It would be pathogen-central as soon as he walked through the doors.

"Can you give me a ride back to my house?" I asked.

"I wish I could, but I have to stay here and help Tweedledum," Hands said, pointing back over his shoulder.

"But shouldn't you tell him it's a—"

A full-throated scream filled the air.

"He knows," Hands answered.

As I ran up the sandy path to my bicycle, I was passed by a sweaty, fat man in uniform like I was standing still.

3 - "ACK"-ISTAXIS

Boiling Grove Community Hospital—I couldn't seem to escape its grasp. Always the last place I wanted to be. And yet, the hospital seemed to suck me back in—like a shellfish, slurped out of the shell and right through the automatic, double sliding glass doors.

I stood in the lobby, feeling gelatinous.

The huge mural of the Oak Island Lighthouse on the back wall still welcomed patients and visitors, but I noticed a few subtle changes. Lots of plants, real and otherwise, had been sprinkled throughout and a few pieces of abstract art added to the other walls. (The art couldn't hide the fact the same brick on the outside walls covered two of the four walls of the lobby—nothing like yellow brick and mortar to calm the fears of anxious patients.) Staring at one particularly strange piece of art, I imagined the comments of passersby: "Hell, I could do that!"; "What is it supposed to be anyway?"; "Is that a face or a piece of cheese?"

Heading toward the reception desk, I passed a couch with a bare wall across from it, suddenly recognizing the spot. After my employment at the hospital ended, administration had splurged for a 90-inch HDTV for the lobby and, since it was the largest screen in the area with the exception of Surf Cinemas, it became a gathering place for the community after visiting hours. Unfortunately for administration (and especially hospital security), the television was mounted and turned on during the crucial final episodes of *Dancing With the Stars*. Jaclyn told me about women (and men) showing up in country dance attire, poodle skirts with 50s accessories, dressed as salsa dancers and flappers—the DWTS soiree was on and the news spread like wildfire. Each week more and more mirror ball trophies appeared, in all shapes and sizes. The crowd would break into "teams" and cheer for their favorite dancers. Security met with administration each morning, trying to figure out how to diplomatically shut the party down (however, cafeteria sales were up which contributed to the conundrum).

My head swiveled toward the area as I walked, trying to remember the straw that had broken the dancing camel's back (forcing administration to remove the television). Out of the corner of my eye, I saw a white-coated medical student/resident, neck bent, eyes cast downward staring at a cell phone, heading straight for me. I tried to step back and pivot but tangled my feet. He plowed into me; I hit the floor face down, the air whooshing out of me.

I rolled over. "Call 9-1-1," I groaned. "I've been mowed over and immobilized by a mobile phone."

The white eyes staring down at me were huge, about to pop out of their skull. This kid could give the late comedian Marty Feldman a run for his money. ("He's got Marty Feldman eyes…")

He tried to talk. "Ack—um, aww—ack."

Not much more than a boy, it looked like he was about to stroke out. Sweat had broken out on his brow; he nervously looked from side to side. He clutched his cell phone tightly, shaking it like he was preparing to throw a pair of dice. Orange Cheetos' dust coated his fingers.

I jumped up. "It's okay. I'm okay. I was only kidding about calling 9-1-1."

He swayed and I thought he was going to fall over. I reached out and tried to steady him; he emitted a strange "neep" sound when I touched him. As I guided him toward the lobby couch, I supported him by clutching his white coat, feeling like one of the balloon handlers in the Macy's Thanksgiving Day Parade, fighting the wind. If he started tottering to the right, I would pull back on the left side of the coat, followed by a knee to his right side, guiding him like a horse. He continued to make strange noises. I was afraid if he fell I was going to have to shoot him. (Whoa, where did that come from, Pilgrim? It's not like he had a shattered leg—he just kind of gurgled and bleated.)

I plopped him on the faux leather lobby couch and he slid to the back with a squeak (or maybe he said "neep" again, I couldn't be sure). Eying the bare wall across from the couch, I suddenly remembered why the television had finally been removed. Two of the DWTS teams got into a brawl (I can't remember the dancers, so let's just say Team De Niro and Team Queen Elizabeth) and the fighting had spilled over into the elevators, stairwells, cafeteria and gift shop. Several dance fans were admitted to the emergency room with severe mirror ball trophy lacerations and contusions.

The medical student's head lolled back against the wall and I took a good look at him. He had dark Hispanic features topped with a wild mane of blonde hair. A strange mixture, not unheard of, but the fact he was a full head taller than me made me curious about his ancestry.

"What's your name, son?"

"Neep," he answered.

His eyes were fluttering, his head at an uncomfortable ninety-degree angle against the wall. Still perspiring heavily, I decided loosening his white lab coat might help. I saw his name right above the stitched "Université d'Etat d'Haïti Faculté de Médecine".

"Carlos!" I called loudly. When he didn't respond, I got closer to his ear. "Carlos!"

His eyes continued to flutter but didn't open. A small crowd had gathered behind us. I noticed Edna, the elderly volunteer receptionist in her pink smock, standing front and center. She was clutching a plastic bottle of water, her name written on it in black magic marker (no doubt an attempt to keep those other "thieving volunteers" away from it).

"Edna," I said, turning to her. "Remember me? I worked here for a little while."

"Of course," Edna replied. "I wouldn't forget you, William."

Ah yes, I remember now. A little hard of hearing, she had thought my name was William. Well, as long as she didn't call me Willie.

"Edna, can you give me your water?" I asked, pointing to her hand.

A puzzled look crossed her face. "My daughter? You want my daughter's hand?"

Carlos had stirred and I turned back to him as I said, "Water. Water!"

"My daughter lives over in Bolivia," Edna continued. "But she's happily married. She's got two kids and four cats. Sometimes she brings her cats to stay with me."

Thankfully, a man walked over and handed me his bottled water. Putting my hand behind Carlos' head, I pulled it forward, squeezing the water bottle with my other hand in order to splash a small amount of water on his face. A large stream shot out, nearly drowning the poor kid. They don't make plastic water bottles like they used to.

Carlos spluttered and his eyes opened—wide. If I didn't know it was physiologically impossible, I would say they were about to shoot from his skull like that cartoon Big Bad Wolf when he saw Red Hot Riding Hood. ("He's got Marty Feldman eyes...")

"Ack!" Carlos said quickly.

A larger crowd had gathered behind us and suddenly, hospital security appeared out of nowhere to shoo them away, anxious to quell another visitor uprising. (No doubt, the *Dancing With the Stars'* fracas still fresh in their minds.)

"Easy there, big guy," I said, trying to calm Carlos.

"Neep!" he responded.

I could tell he was getting agitated again, so I said soothingly, "I'm not hurt, Carlos. But you need to look up from that gadget and watch where you're going. It's how aliens are going to take over Earth without a fight."

Not sure how it was possible, but his eyes grew wider. A look of confusion crossed his face and he uttered an intelligible word: "Aliens?"

In explanation, I acted like I was holding an invisible cell phone, with my head bent and my thumbs pummeling it with imaginary text. I used a deep, narrator voice out of a 1950s sci-fi movie. "The flying saucer will emit the beam to abduct human beings, and distracted cell phone earthlings will walk right into it."

"What the hell is going on here!" a voice boomed from behind us.

Carlos seemed to wither. I turned and recognized a physician I had the pleasure of crossing paths with when I worked at the hospital. Cincinnaticus Pearson, MD, all six foot seven of him, towered over us. He looked like he had packed more pounds on his huge frame. An elder statesman of the hospital staff, he was as much a part of the hospital as the plaster and 4x4 gauze. The straggling members of the crowd behind him had scattered—out of respect, fear, or loathing, I did not know.

Carlos whimpered and somehow managed to slide the lids over his bulging eyes. His body actually quivered.

"Dr. Pearson. How nice to see you again," I said, attempting to diffuse his anger.

The snarl froze on his face; slowing melting, it was soon replaced with perplexity.

"Do I know you?"

"I helped you with the computer once. You were trying to order Lasix."

He frowned and suddenly a big smile appeared. "I remember you. You worked in…housekeeping?" The frown reappeared.

"Yes!" I reached out my hand. "Daniel O'Dwyer, Environmental Services." My hand disappeared into his big paw for a manly greeting. He shook it once and dropped it. "I am blessedly unemployed at the current time, though."

Carlos made a small "neep" behind us.

The doctor moved forward, invading my personal space, and peered down behind me. "What has my medical resident done now!" he sputtered (spraying me with spittle).

"Who, Carlos?" I asked.

"Ca-Ca-Carl," came a weak voice from behind me.

"Um…yes, Carl," I corrected. "You see Dr. Pearson, I was walking along like this—" I paused to mime myself walking along (I threw in some "invisible wall" hand motions for effect), gazing from side to side, never looking straight ahead. "And then—" I snapped my head to the opposite side. "I saw something shiny." I slapped my hands together. "And bam! I knocked over poor Carl."

Carl "neeped" from behind me in the affirmative.

"It was totally my fault, Dr. P.," I said cheerfully, trying to be chummy.

He gave a grizzly growl, eying first Carl, then me. Under his glare I felt like I was in the middle of a lie-detector test. I regulated my breathing—slow in, slow out. I nodded to him, mouthing the words "my fault".

"It's a good thing!" the doctor exploded. "One more stupid stunt and our student from Haiti is history!"

With that he swiveled and we couldn't help but watch his massive derrière dance from the hospital lobby.

I helped Carl/Carlos to his feet. "Thank you," he said, eyes averted down. "I've—I've done some things—" His voice was so low I could barely make out the words. "Dr. Pearson is not happy with me."

"You're assigned to Dr. Pearson?" I asked incredulously. Who played such a horrendous joke on this poor young man? No wonder he made such strange noises.

"Ack," the young man answered. He glanced at the screen of his phone. "Oh no! Late for rounds!"

As he ran off at an awkward gait, I couldn't help notice his large shoes. Size 16? 17? He looked back as he rounded the corner and I heard a breathless, "Thanks again. Neep."

Lord have mercy. I shrugged and walked to the Information Desk, trying to remember why I had come to the hospital in the first place. I silently prayed for Carl/Carlos. I hadn't known him very long, but it seemed he may need divine intervention to survive his rotation at Boiling Grove Community Hospital.

Edna was smiling behind the desk, surrounded by two silk ficus trees. "Hello William."

That was it—Willie! "Hiya Edna. Can you give me the room number of Willie Welch?"

It took her an excruciatingly long time. As volunteers weren't allowed to use the computer system, Edna slowly traced her finger down a printed list of patients and room numbers, looking for Willie.

"I know her," she said, her finger stopping on a name on the confidential list. "Deb." Her finger continued downward. "Grace? I didn't know she was in here. She goes to church with me. Well, she's really there to meet a man…and I don't mean Jesus." She cleared her throat. "Uh, what was that name again?"

"Willie Welch."

Edna finally found the room number—306. I thanked her and turned to leave when she said, "I've got a granddaughter that's not married. But she's too young for you. She's only twelve."

"Umm—thank you, Edna. You have a really nice week."

She looked down and pulled at the fabric of her volunteer smock. "Yes, it is," she said, smoothing her hand over the sleeve. "It *is* fleece. How nice of you to notice."

I entered room 306 with trepidation. In the community, if you tried hard enough, you could find most of the common bacteria and viruses; in a hospital, all you had to do was pop your head in regular rooms to get the common flavors and then run over to the isolation rooms for the exotic ones. In other words, this was Willie's purgatory.

The first thing I saw was Moses sitting in the bedside chair, his elbows on the chair arms and his chin propped upon his interlaced fingers. His ageless face was blank, but he gave a small shake of the head.

Moses had pretended to be Jamaican when I first hired him to fix up my house. It turned out he was from the Southside of Chicago and had a past more interesting than five of mine, including civil rights sit-ins and racism while he served in Vietnam.

"Hail up, mon?" I said to Moses, dropping back to what I thought was a Jamaican greeting.

Moses grunted. He was a man of few words.

"Did you bring him here?" I asked.

Moses nodded.

"Good friend betta dan pocket money," I told him in my bad Jamaican accent.

"Get a damn cell phone," Moses said gruffly in response.

Willie groaned from the hospital bed. I walked over, expecting to see IV tubing, machines, oxygen. All I saw was a haggard Willie with gauze packing in both nostrils. He didn't even have an IV line inserted.

"What happened, Willie?" I asked.

Willie's eyes fluttered open and the whites of his eyes were more bloodshot than I had ever seen them—even worse than after the time change of daylight saving time, which seemed to put him in a month-long funk.

"Daniel," Willie gasped in a nasally voice. "Is dat you?"

"Yes Willie. I'm here."

He reached out and grabbed my arm. "I want you to have all my earthly possessions."

I thought about his proclamation, the items he had just bequeathed me: The *Silent Cow*, a galley full of organic food, an ice chest full of organic beer, Jethro Tull albums and an Ian Anderson signed photograph.

"Willie, it looks like you're going to be okay."

His grip on my arm tightened. "Daniel, I'm—I'm dying."

I looked over at Moses. He pursed his lips, closed his eyes and shook his head side-to-side.

"What happened?" I asked Willie.

"I was on the roof of the *Silent Cow*, installing a padlock on the trapdoor." He paused to take several breaths, having to breathe through his mouth. "I felt a cold, piratical presence and then—blood spurted everywhere!"

I looked him over, lying on the hospital bed, and tried to muster some empathy. Failing, I said, "So, you had a nosebleed."

"Blood was everywhere—everywhere." Willie started gagging.

"Certainly all over my car," Moses muttered from behind.

I turned to him, aghast. Not throughout the interior of the coolest car on the planet! Moses had a late 60s Pontiac Parisienne that embodied War's song, "Low Rider". The hood alone was larger than my bedroom.

"One of the worst drives of my life," Moses said. "And I've lived a long time."

"I'm sorry, Moses. I'll help you clean it."

"Get a damn cell phone," he repeated.

When I turned back to Willie, he was (blessedly) asleep. I saw his chest rising and falling, so he hadn't died yet. I don't want to make light of nosebleeds which can be critical in patients on blood thinners, anti-platelet meds and aspirin, but I had never heard of a healthy male on an all-organic diet being taken down by a nosebleed.

Moses arose and stretched. He passed me on his way out the door and I barely heard, "Goin' fo' coffee."

Willie was softly snoring. I noticed the television on, but muted. Finding the remote tied to the bedside rail, I turned up the volume. WECT News Anchor Bill Murray finished one story and introduced another.

"An alligator was spotted today on Caswell Beach. Agnes Marzella, a 12-year-old girl on vacation from Logan County, West Virginia snapped these photos of the gator."

(The 12-year-old appeared on the screen.) *"At first I thought it was a log. But it had eyes! It was really crazy. It was scary."*

The anchor continued: *"She was playing in the surf at Caswell Beach, when a nearby jogger alerted her to the gator in the water. Agnes ran out of the water and grabbed her cell phone to snap pictures."*

The screen showed more still pictures of the alligator.

"Shortly after, Oak Island Animal Control and Oak Island Police responded to the call to try to trap the beast." I grimaced; the huge form of Jed Frid filled the screen. He looked like he was backing away until he noticed the camera—then he hitched his giant pants up and pretended to move toward the water.

"Officials weren't able to trap him and the gator moved into deeper water."

There was a sudden picture of a police officer on the screen with the name Officer Hans Rodriguez displayed on the screen. Hands looked furious. I imagine if he carried a billy club, the cameras would have caught him beating an animal control officer about the head and neck area.

"Officials estimate the gator is six feet long. Nicknamed "Wally" by the locals, he usually moves between Oak Island and Caswell Beach."

The camera shifted back to the anchor desk where Bill Murray was smiling wryly. *"Authorities said since the initial report there have been several alligators spotted—about 12 blocks away, Oak Island public access 70, public access 6 and another on the far end of Oak Island at The Point.*

Always the professional, the anchor gathered himself. *"While only the first sighting has been substantiated, please be careful. If you see a gator, you're asked to contact Oak Island Police right away."*

Willie emitted a loud snore and I turned away from the screen momentarily. When I returned my attention to the news, there was a story about North Carolina leading the nation in copperhead bites. I was mildly interested when the physician on the screen claimed antivenin use was controversial. Once the story ended, they teased sports before going to commercial. Hey, was that roller derby?

I turned off the television and sat in the bedside chair, surveying the surroundings. One hospital room looked like another, especially when I had cleaned most of them under my previous "special" undercover employment assignment. I noticed some build-up in the corner where dirt had settled. I would have to take care of that before Willie woke up. Old habits die hard. Housekeepers work extremely hard and are an integral part of the healthcare team, if not always treated as such, and I had been proud to work along beside them. (My mother would have been astonished at how many beds I made during that time, considering it "punishment" for never making mine as a kid.)

Willie snored away.

I found Willie's food menu for the next day on the bedside table—he hadn't filled it out yet. I would probably have to help him when he woke up. The finicky wacko's not going to be happy if there are only a few organic items to choose. I scanned the menu. The finicky wacko's not going to be happy by the complete lack of organic items to choose.

I looked around the room, bored. I considered waking Willie—but wasn't that bored. As my aunt always said, let sleeping loonies lie. (Course Uncle Davey was known to walk around in his long johns at all hours of the night, chirping like a cricket.)

Willie had always been a bit "off-center". We met in junior high school in West Virginia, although he moved away before high school. Come to think of it, I had vivid memories of the junior high school cafeteria; while the rest of us were content to amuse our peers by making armpit "fart" noises (having graduated from making milk squirt out of our noses in elementary school), Willie sat at the far end, carefully arranging the food from his *Space: 1999* lunch box in alphabetical order.

I remembered something else from the junior high school cafeteria. Still clutching Willie's menu, I began tearing it into long strips of paper. It took me a couple of tries, but I finally folded the perfect triangular football. I folded a second—and a third for good measure. Now all I needed was a goal post.

Willie moaned in his sleep, drawing my attention to his bedside table. That's when I saw the two half-size ginger ale cans with straws sticking out of them. Perfect! I positioned them parallel near the end of the table with straws extending up as straight as I could get them. I took an unopened straw and draped it across the tops of the cans.

I gazed at my creation with pride. Much better than the milk carton goal posts we had in junior high school.

I placed the triangular "football" on the other end of the table, point down, teeing it up with my finger. With the middle finger of my other hand held back by my thumb, I released it and "kicked" the paper football toward the goal posts. Ooh! Wide right and onto Willie's bed.

I figured out the problem—it wasn't the wind; the crowd at the game was much too quiet. I made the classic crowd cheering sound while kicking my second football and it sailed directly between the two goal posts. Three points! The crowd roared.

I tried a third field goal which was wide right again, ending up near Willie's head. Frantically, I began ripping up the rest of the menu and making footballs.

"Excuse me."

I turned to find a dietary aide standing behind me.

"I came to pick up Mr. Welch's menu for tomorrow. Do you know if he's filled it out?"

I looked down at the five triangular paper footballs in my right hand, quickly closing it into a fist.

"I—umm—well, I'm afraid the menu was used for other purposes," I stammered, turning red. "If you can leave another one, I will make sure Mr. Welch fills it out as soon as he awakens."

After she left, I quickly kicked five more field goals in quick succession. Three were good and two were wide right onto Willie's bed. I thought of gathering all the paper footballs, but since I was a bit hoarse from all the crowd cheering, I decided to forgo the second half.

I sat back down in the chair and it didn't take long before I was bored out of my skull again.

Willie snored on.

Slowly, I took in the rest of the room, my gaze stopping at the white board. I remembered the white board from my time working the rooms as there was a place to write the housekeeper's name on the board with a black erasable marker. Also written on the board were the nurse and nursing assistant's names for the day, as well as the last pain med administration. At the top was the patient's diagnosis and allergies. Willie's diagnosis was listed as *epistaxis*, a fancy medical term for blood spurting out the nasal passages. His drug allergy was listed as *penicillin*, but my eyes couldn't help be drawn to "Other Allergies". They were written smaller than the others because there were so many. I had to get up and walk to the board to read them.

Other Allergies: Leather shoes, coins, sunglasses, bodies of water, disco, flea markets, potting soil, Bud Light, and cats.

Cats! Since when was Willie allergic to cats? He had been around Fairbanks and Pickford and never complained... Ah, Pickford. To be more exact, it should be listed as an allergy to cats who lick his toothbrush.

I looked around the room to make sure there wasn't anyone else around. There was one more allergy that should be added. I picked up the black dry erase marker and added "pirates" to the end of the list.

I heard a huge sigh from behind me. I turned to find my girlfriend, Jaclyn, standing in the doorway, shaking her head sadly.

4 - DR. OZ CURES THE BLACK DEATH WITH DANDELION TEA

Jaclyn sighed a second time. She had been doing that a lot around me lately. Now, I'm a guy and not privy to the inner workings of the mind of the female of our species, but I reckon that's not necessarily a good sign.

"Hi Jaclyn" I said excitedly, moving my body in position to block the white board.

I had met Jaclyn after my…um, jellyfish accident. The Emergency Room Clinical Director, she had a problem with an ER nurse "borrowing" my pain medication and exchanging it with saline. It was not an exchange program the hospital supported.

She did not move from the doorway. Her red hair was mussed, her white uniform looked soiled and her face looked flushed. I had never seen her more beautiful.

"Jaclyn," I said, moving toward her. "You look terrific."

"I look awful," she said wearily, blowing her hair out of her face. "It's been a banner day in the ER and to round out the hours, I've had to run up here." She narrowed her eyes at me. (Another bad sign?) Flopping into the bedside chair, she continued her recap. "I also had to stop what I was doing this morning to deal with Willie—he called me in a panic and I had to find him a ride to the hospital. Good thing *Moses* has a cell phone."

"Oh—sorry."

"Daniel, you really need to get a cell phone."

Geez, talk about peer pressure. Or in the case of my phone at the bottom of the Intracoastal Waterway, pier pressure. (You should have seen the beautiful dive my old Samsung made as I crossed the bridge onto island living—a sensational back two-and-a-half somersault with thirty-four and a half twists.)

I started to answer but she held up her hand. "I know," she said. "Your cell phone is sleeping with the fishes." I couldn't help notice she didn't try very hard to get the Sicilian accent down.

I laughed anyway, hoping to pull out her sexy smile. Not a chance.

"It was funny the first couple of times. But it's not funny anymore," Jaclyn said. And—she *sighed*. A deep, expressive sigh. Definitely a bad sign.

I gave up my position of blocking the white board as I moved toward her. I was in deeper doo-doo than I realized. Placing my hand on her upper arm, I said, "I am really sorry, Jaclyn. I'll, um, think about a phone." I felt her relax a little. "I really will."

Willie started muttering in his sleep and thrashing in bed, obviously nowhere near his "happy place". If he thought his dreams were bad, just wait until he opened his eyes and realized he wasn't at home anymore. Jaclyn pulled herself up and walked to Willie's bedside; I couldn't help watching the lithe movements of her body. I was still admiring her curves when she stopped suddenly and turned back to me. My eyes shifted guiltily to her face. She pursed her lips, but one side slid up into a little smile.

Finally, a good sign. It wasn't much but it was enough to give me a little ray of hope.

Willie groaned and his hands, which were on top of the sheets, began clutching and pulling at the fabric. "No," he said quietly, his eyes still closed. His head began twitching side to side, as if trying to ward off invisible foes. "No, no...NO!" His voice became louder but he didn't open his eyes.

Jaclyn looked to me with surprise and concern. I must admit, Willie did look a little pathetic and I was beginning to feel a little unsettled myself.

Willie began thrashing his whole body back and forth, fighting an invisible foe. Before Jaclyn could subdue him, he yelled, "Catbrush, planchette pirates!"

Jaclyn firmly placed her hands on Willie's shoulders, trying to calm him. "Willie. Wake up, Willie," she said in a low velvety voice, meant to calm him. (It had the opposite effect on me, as it was the voice she used to whisper in my ear when we were alone—I crossed my legs and tried to behave.)

"Catbrush, planchette pirates," he cried again.

"He's talking gibberish," Jaclyn noted.

"Well..." I said.

She looked at me. Then she looked at my addition to Willie's allergies on the white board.

"Explain," she demanded.

"Oh...my, it's a long story." I moved closer to Willie's bedside. "You see the laceration on his cheek?"

She removed her hand from Willie's shoulder and slowly turned his head toward her, examining the wound.

"That's a planchette injury."

"A *what?*" she asked, undoubtedly baffled (and it wasn't easy to baffle a long-time emergency room nurse with a new injury).

"A planchette," I explained, shaping the index fingers and thumbs from both hands into the shape. "It's a triangular piece of wood used in a board game."

"I see," she said. "So, you and Willie were playing *Jumanji* and got transported back to pirate days."

"Not exactly."

"And why did you hit him with the planchette?"

"I didn't!" I cried, petulantly. "It flew through the air on its own and the point struck him on the cheek." I used more visual effects to show the invisible, finger-formed planchette approaching Willie's face, stopping just short of his wound.

She eyed me suspiciously.

"Hey!" I snapped my fingers as the realization hit me. "'Planchette injury' should be a secondary diagnosis." I looked longingly at the white board. "Can I write that on the white board under epistaxis?"

Her steely glare pierced through me. I guess that would be a "no". I collapsed into the bedside chair, dejected.

Willie's eyes fluttered like a slot machine, coming to a stop with a small slit of white visible for both eyes. His pupils slowly swam into view, surveying the surroundings. In a few seconds, his eyes became as big as saucers—flying saucers. Seeing he was on the verge of panic, Jaclyn leaned in, saying, "Hello Willie" in that velvety voice again. She sounded like one of those phone sex girls. (Not that I had ever called one—I…um, watched a documentary about the industry once.) I squirmed in my seat, trying to get comfortable.

Willie blinked and seemed to focus on her. "Hello Jocelyn." (An I.Q. off the charts and a photographic memory, and yet Willie couldn't remember names—amazing.)

"How do you feel?" she asked, soothingly. (In my mind, she had asked for his credit card number.)

Willie didn't answer her; his eyes were flitting around the room and the look of panic returned. "Hospital? Hospital!"

Instinctively, I knew what was coming next, as did Jaclyn. Willie tried to throw the covers off and escape, so I moved to one side to hold him down and Jaclyn pinned him on the other. He looked like a squirrel caught in a cage, and if we opened the door, he would shoot out like a squirrel cannon. (Not that I had ever trapped a squirrel—okay, *the* diabolical Cube pummeling squirrel—in an opossum cage and released it on the canal bank.

FOOM! It shot from the door and flew about thirty feet in the air. Attention PETA: No animals were hurt in this catch and release scenario.)

"Willie, calm down!" I cried. Short and compact, Willie had more strength in him than I thought. When an animal is cornered, it is at its most dangerous, and we struggled to hold him down. Jaclyn was in the unfortunate position of being between Willie and the door, his perceived freedom, and I wasn't about to let him mow her down. I thought of smacking him, but between his gauze-packed nostrils and his planchette injury, there wasn't much real estate left to strike.

"I'll never get out of here alive," Willie croaked.

I tried to suppress it, but a small laugh escaped, causing Jaclyn to shoot me another look. "Oh, come on," I said to Willie. "You had a nosebleed."

Willie looked at me sadly. "I wish," he said. I was surprised to see a tear forming in the corner of his eye.

"Willie," Jaclyn said calmly. "What is it?"

Willie shifted his gaze to Jaclyn. His voice was low and we could barely hear him. "I am infected. Bad. It's bad."

Infected? Had the lab even had time to send someone for a blood sample, let alone run it and get the results? I glanced at Willie's bare arms, not seeing any punctures or adhesive bandages.

Before we could ask, Willie blurted out, "I am infected with the bacterium Yersinia pestis."

Jaclyn looked at me, frowning. I shrugged. *Yersinia pestis*, where had I heard that before?

"Willie," Jaclyn said, true concern in her tone. "Where did you pick up this bacterium?" Jaclyn turned to me and whispered, "I've never heard of this one."

"The pirates infected me with Yersinia pestis," Willie said mournfully, pressing the palms of his hands into his eye sockets.

Yersinia pestis? I know I have heard that somewhere recently.

"Um…pirates?" Jaclyn asked suspiciously, her eyes darting back to the white board. "Do you mean the Pittsburgh Pirates?" she asked hopefully.

"No," I replied absently, still thinking about the bacterium. "The swashbuckling kind—you know, Errol Flynn and the like. The *Silent Cow* is haunted." (Yersinia pestis…Yersinia pestis—why did it ring a bell?)

Jaclyn stood there stunned, looking from Willie to me, waiting for one of us to break and start laughing. When we didn't, I could actually see the red spread up her neck and throughout her face to match her flaming hair. But my mind was elsewhere.

Suddenly it came to me. A couple months ago, I was watching UNC play Duke in the last regular season basketball game (there are only two shades of blue in North Carolina—Carolina blue and Duke Blue Devil blue) when I fell asleep on the couch. When I awoke, the television had been mysteriously changed to the History Channel. Fuzzy and confused, I watched European citizens running around in the 14th century instead of coach K's and coach Roy Williams' boys battling it out on the hardwood. Turning blearily to my left, I saw Willie sitting on his stainless steel stool beside the couch, watching the television intently. He entered my house whenever he wanted and I had long ago given up locking my doors to keep him out (which never worked anyway).

"What the heck! Who won the game?" I asked.

"It's not a game," Willie replied. "It's the greatest epidemic in human history."

"Duke or UNC!" I cried.

Willie, ignoring me, continued. "The Black Death. Wild rodents running rampant."

I looked to the screen, seeing black rats piled four deep, squirming.

Now I appreciate history as much as the next average man, but at times like this, I have a one-track mind. "UNC or Duke!" I cried again.

A physician came on the television next, explaining the disease process behind The Black Death. Which included the bacterium—

"I've got it!" I exclaimed loudly, scaring Jaclyn. I grinned at her triumphantly.

Thirty seconds of my smug, stupid smile was all she could take. "Well?" she asked huffily.

"Yersinia pestis. It's the plague."

"So…" She looked down at Willie who was nodding his head morosely. "Willie has the—plague?"

Willie started ticking off the symptoms, which I remembered the physician on the History Channel stating almost verbatim. "Fever, chills, extreme weakness, abdominal pain, bleeding from mouth, nose or rectum, shock, gangrene."

"Uh-huh," Jaclyn said doubtfully, almost as if she had bubonic plague victims in her ER every week. She grabbed Willie's chart and starting riffling through it. Laying the chart down, she felt Willie's forehead, palpated his abdomen and checked his extremities.

"It seems to me you only have one of the symptoms of the plague," Jaclyn said.

"It's in the early stages," Willie shot back. "The gangrene's beginning on the tip of my nose. See, it's black."

Willie was looking cross-eyed at the tip of his nose when Jaclyn reached out and flicked the black speck off his nose. Willie gasped and passed out.

"Fleck of dried blood," she said, shaking her head.

"Hey!" I said excitedly. "Can we bandage his whole proboscis so that when he wakes up, I can tell him the gangrene spread while he was out, his entire nose blackened—" I paused for a second because of the disgusted look on Jaclyn's face. "And his nose fell off," I finished with much less enthusiasm.

Jaclyn sighed.

I gulped. "Jaclyn, have I…did I, um, do something wrong?"

She shook her head sadly. "It's okay, Daniel. I think I'm just worn out. The nursing shortage has me working shifts to fill the schedule and my management duties are woefully behind. I may never see the light of day again. And the conference is in a week and a half, which will put me behind even more."

I reached out to take her hand in mine, to comfort her, but her hands remained at her side. She sighed. "Maybe we should talk soon," she said, as she turned and walked out of the room.

Walking back through the hospital lobby, in a daze, it was a good thing Carl/Carlos wasn't in my way or I would have bowled him over for real. I felt like I had been kicked in the gut; like I had all the symptoms of bubonic plague. Edna called out to me as I blew past her, saying something that sounded like "widowed sister", but I just kept walking, head bowed, until the sliding glass doors opened into the afternoon heat.

I had been dating Jaclyn for almost a year now and, like most naïve, moronic male simpletons, I thought it was going pretty good. We enjoyed our time together, laughed, acted a little goofy…and the sex. The sex was— beyond description. Behind the…on top of the…in the middle of…Cool Whip and anchovies… (Oh come on, you didn't think I was going to kiss and tell, did you?)

Even though Moses had returned and I had promised to meet him at the Oak Island Auto Wash to help clean the inside of the coolest car ever made, I found myself wandering through the parking lot. My Nissan Cube, on the hot asphalt, looked like a steamy boxed lunch on wheels, and I passed it without so much as a glance. At first I wasn't sure where I was walking until I turned the corner, realizing I had unconsciously gravitated to a place I had spent many happy breaks with my co-workers.

"Hey! Watch where you're walking, pretty boy," called out a husky female voice.

I stopped and realized I was standing a couple yards away from a huge hunk of uprooted concrete. I looked up in time to see one of the basketball backboards come crashing down. Seeming to fall in slow motion, it was like a really bad dream, a black and white avant-garde film about the death of basketball. Dr. James Naismith rolled over in his grave.

"You can stand there, but don't come any closer for your own safety. I like having eye candy nearby. Makes me work—harder."

The woman in the hard hat gave me a wicked wink. She was well over six feet tall and looked slightly ominous in her work clothes and boots. I noticed her muscular biceps; she could pound me like yesterday's beef.

I waved weakly at her and turned to walk back to my steamy boxed lunch on wheels.

Pulling the Cube under my house, I exited and paused at one of the pilings. I leaned into the wooden piling, placing both hands on it, and stretched my aching back and calves. Cleaning the inside of Moses' giant Pontiac Parisienne had been a chore. The leather seat of the passenger side looked like the scene of a Sergio Leone spaghetti western shoot-out. There was blood in every little nook and cranny of the leather, on the seat belt, the floor, the dash board. I asked Moses why Willie didn't stick a tissue up his nose to stem the bleeding and he told me Willie wouldn't do that because it wasn't sterile. I asked Moses why there was blood on his dashboard and floor and he told me Willie had heard on Dr. Oz the way to stop a nosebleed was to put your head between your knees, count to three thousand and then drink dandelion tea. Dandelion tea? ("Moses, you have dandelion tea in your glove compartment?" I asked, reaching for it. "Trust me. Best not to know what's in there," he said in a low, gravelly voice, causing me to stop mid-reach.) Head between your knees? Amazing! Even little kids know to sit up straight and pinch the soft part of their nose shut to stop a nosebleed. We should have called Dr. Mehmet Oz to come down to the Oak Island Auto Wash "stat" to scrub the blood out of the coolest car ever made.

I walked up the deck stairs slower than usual and when I opened my front door, the orange cat entering at my feet barely registered. I hadn't opened the blinds that morning and the interior was bathed in shadows. Halfway across, I flicked on the kitchen light switch.

If Moses' car looked like the *Gunfight at the O.K. Corral*, my kitchen looked like Quentin Tarantino had teamed up with horror directors' Wes Craven, John Carpenter and George A. Romero for a project. *Halloween Night of the Living Pulp on Elm Street*, perhaps. (Or maybe it was the return of Bela Lugosi.) I screamed.

My mostly white kitchen had blood spattered everywhere. I could almost picture the scene. Willie running from the *Silent Cow*, down the path and through my back door, no doubt screaming my name as the blood flowed. There was a pool right inside the door where he must have stopped to call out again. But why was there blood on my white cabinet fronts, my counter top, my refrigerator door for God's sake? Had he stopped for a snack and organic beer?

I gasped as I discovered the bloody trail leaving the kitchen. Just as I turned on the light for the living area, my wall phone rang. (Jaclyn called it my "landlubber-line".)

The phone rang a second time. Creepy. I picked up the receiver in a trance, looking around the bloody room, expecting the voice on the other end to say, "Have you checked the children?" or "I saw what you did, and I know who you are."

Instead the voice said, "Daniel. Daniel? Can you hear me? Daniel, are you there?" The voice got louder with each word.

"Yes, Mom. I'm here."

"Can you hear me?"

"Yes, Mom. I can hear you."

"Oh good. I got me a cellular telephone," she said proudly.

Oh no! My mother has gone over to the dark side.

"It's one of those Jitterbug thingies. It's got big buttons and large print."

I heard a beep which caused my mother to pause. "Did you hear that?" she asked. "That beep? It started doing that after I talked to Helen for two hours. At first, I thought someone was 'beeping in', but there wasn't anybody there. It happened after I talked to your father and Jerry next door, too. I don't know what it means. I swear I'm going to take this phone back. Do you think it's a lemon? How can I talk if it keeps beeping?" She paused briefly, but before I could answer she started back in, louder this time. "Good lord! Do you think someone is listening in to our conversation right now? Politicians in Washington? Oh my gosh! The Russians? How dare you people eavesdrop on a mother who just wants to talk to her son. It's not like we get to talk every day. He's *so* busy. That's what I told Helen, 'Daniel is a good boy, he's just been busy.'" *Beep!* "There it is again! Did you hear it?"

"Mom, it just means the phone's about to die and you need to charge it."

"Charge it? You know I never charge anything—I paid cash for the phone. You are going to get into financial trouble, dear, if you keep charging things."

"Mom, charge the battery. The beep means the phone's battery is dying."

"Charge the battery? They didn't show me how to do that."

She went off on a tangent about Helen and I slowly surveyed my great room. Great is was not; there was a trail of blood in a straight line down the tan carpet before shooting off toward each piece of furniture. What the heck? Did Willie feel the need to search for me behind the couch and under my recliner? There was blood spattered on my wall!

Fairbanks, the large orange tabby who owned me, entered the room just as my mother said, "Daniel, can you hear me?"

"Yes, Mom"

"I asked if you were eating?"

"Yes, Mom. Lots of fresh fish."

"Oh, I can't eat seafood anymore. Not since I got choked on that fish bone."

My mother had gotten choked on a fish bone when I was in elementary school. Something didn't look right about Fairbanks and I started toward him, but the outstretched phone cord stopped me.

"What, Mom?"

"I said, are you dressing better?"

I looked down at my biker shorts and faded Toots and the Maytals t-shirt. "Well…"

When she started talking about how sloppy "kids these days" dress, I bent down to get a closer look at Fairbanks. He was coming toward me and seemed to be swaying to one side. Was he limping? I reached out my hand trying to get him to come to me.

"You aren't going barefoot, are you?"

I looked down at my bare feet; I had kicked off my shoes at the door as usual. With Willie's blood staining my feet, this was one time I wished I had listened to my mother.

"Well…"

Placing a hand under Fairbanks' chin, I lifted his face upward, and gasped. He had blood on the side of his head and from the looks of his swollen eye, I had to surmise it was his and not Willie's. He let out a pitiful meow. He looked like Rocky Balboa after his first fight.

"I said are you seeing anyone?"

"I'm sorry, Mom. My cat—"

"Stop being silly for once, Daniel. I'm talking about a girl. Are you seeing a real, live girl?"

In spite of Fairbanks appearance, I had to snicker. As opposed to a real, plastic girl?

"Yea, Mom. I'm seeing someone."

Fairbanks was stumbling around the room, meowing loudly. I could only guess he was calling out to his lady cat friend in the same loud, punch-drunk voice that Rocky called out for his woman, Adrian after the fight. "Pickford! Pickford!"

"Are you treating her right?"

I reached out for Fairbanks and stopped. Was I treating Jaclyn right? I was no longer sure.

My mother was rambling about how bad her sister's husband treated her when I finally snagged Fairbanks. He screamed when I touched his leg and I could see a hole in his head near his eye.

"My lord, what's going on?"

"It's my cat, Mom. He's been in a fight and it sure looks like I'm going to have to take him to a vet."

Fairbanks gave me a nasty look with his one good eye.

"But Mom, I really do want to tell you about Jaclyn. I may need some relationship advice. And I promise I will come home to see you soon. I love you, Mom."

"You're a good boy. I love you, too, Da—" *Beep!*

I hung up the phone, wondering if my mother would figure out how to charge her Jitterbug or would take it back to the store. I almost felt sorry for the wireless sales representative I would never meet. Fairbanks meowed loudly, "Pickford! Pick—ford!" In a near perfect Sly Stallone imitation I screamed, "Jaclyn! Jac—lyn!"

5 - ET TU, NEW TRAY?

As I pulled the Cube into the parking lot, the first thing I noticed on the sign was a cool logo of a black dog's head silhouette with an overlay of a white cat silhouette. Then I saw the name: Neutre Veterinary Clinic.

"It's okay," I told Fairbanks. "Surely it's an old family name and not a play on—well, you know." I winced and unconsciously lowered my hands to protect my privates; Fairbanks appeared to do the same with his front paws.

The lovely fragrance of barely disguised cat urine wafted from the cat carrier I had borrowed from a neighbor (it smelled like she had tried to mask it with cheap parfum or eau de toilette spray). A prisoner in the smelly box, Fairbank's tail beat double time.

"You got Restless Tail Syndrome?" I asked him, trying to lighten the mood. His tail beat triple time.

Taking the key out of the ignition, I glanced at my sleeve. Before leaving, I had grabbed a baseball cap and thrown on a windbreaker jacket; it was a good thing. It was wrestle mania trying to get Fairbanks into the cage (to any onlookers, it must have looked a lot like a steel cage match). Even though he was saddled with a limp and vision out of only one eye, I was no match for the large tomcat. Fairbanks shredded my windbreaker like a cheap, television slicer ("It's the Ronco Veg-O-Matic! It slices, it dices. It will turn any piece of clothing into fabric scraps and remnants. Order now for only three easy payments of $19.99.") Thankfully, the material kept my arms and torso from getting scratched, but I hadn't covered my hands and they looked like I had been punching barbed wire.

Opening the passenger's side, I tugged Fairbank's funky-smelling feline prison off the seat. From the corner of my eye, I picked up a flashing light.

When I turned toward the front door of the clinic, I saw the source—a LED sign in the front window. In Las Vegas style glitz it announced: *Fifty Shades of Spay.*

I turned Fairbanks' cage away from the sign and told him to avert his eyes. He was already mad enough at me for bringing him to the vet.

I entered the vet's office struggling with the heavy cat and carrier, my sweat-stained baseball cap crooked on my head, the tattered windbreaker flowing like a vintage suede fringe leather jacket, black biker shorts riding up painfully, and hands that left a trail of blood spatters to the receptionist's desk. Fairbanks shifted around in the carrier, causing me to bang into a chair, a table, and knock over a magazine rack. A low, guttural sound came from within the carrier, transitioning at the end to a higher and louder whine. After a slight pause, the noise would start again. It sounded just like the alarm from my school years to shelter-in-place due to chemical leaks— perhaps I should dive under the receptionist's desk and kiss my ass goodbye.

"Can I...help you?" the befuddled receptionist asked, frowning. I watched as her eyes scanned my appearance. I placed the reeking cat carrier on the desk with a bang, letting her get a good whiff of Eau de Cat Pee. She curled her nose and rolled her desk chair back a few inches.

Her look of disdain couldn't help but bring out my inner wisenheimer. She obviously thought I was some kind of bum, living in a cardboard box on the banks of the Intracoastal Waterway, so I decided to play along. I sniffed loudly, wiping my nose all along my tattered sleeve. "Is this the Brunswick County Sperm Bank?" I asked in a phlegmy voice.

The look on her young face was priceless. Fairbanks however, was not amused and hissed loudly from his confined quarters.

"Look, I'm really busy," the receptionist said. She noticed me looking around the empty waiting room. "We happen to have a reptile emergency in the back," she said haughtily.

"Yes ma'am. I know it's late in the day and I apologize for my sense of humor. It's been a long, trying day." I held up the cat carrier to eye level so she could look in at a steaming mad Fairbanks, who glared at her with one eye. "My cat's been in a fight and I was hoping the vet could have a look."

Her annoyance with me melted at the sight of my feline Muhammad Ali. (He may "float like a butterfly" but it looks like he got stung by a bee.) She put her fingers through the bars and tried to pet Fairbanks. "Oh, poor wittle kitty. What happened?"

Now, the only time I ever talked baby talk to Fairbanks, he turned and bit me in the calf. So I was surprised when he lowered his head to be scratched. He always did have a way with the ladies.

Still looking at Fairbanks, she asked, "Have you been here before?"

"Are you talking to the cat or me?" I asked.

She shot me a nasty look, then turned a smiling face back to my cat.

"No ma'am, *we* have not been here before."

She gave Fairbanks one last scratch. "I'll see what I can do. Fill this out." She plopped paperwork on a clipboard down in front of me, stood and walked toward the door to the back.

I turned the opening of the carrier around to face me. "Dang Fairbanks, you is one suave dude when it comes to the opposite sex." He snarled and spittle flew through the bars.

I quickly filled out the paperwork and left it on the desk. I walked over and took a seat by the front window, beneath the LED sign. Looking around, I noticed a television near the left of the receptionist's desk. An animated feature had started and the opening title had just appeared.

"*All Dogs Go to Heaven*—what do you think, Fairbanks?"

The cat gave a chirp, a yowl and a hiss, which I can only interpret as "Cats rule—dogs stink like expressed anal glands".

I picked up a magazine from a table beside my chair. "If all dogs go to heaven, where do cats go?" I couldn't help pondering aloud. "Egypt? Mars?"

Fairbanks meowed long and loud.

"I agree," I answered. "Hopefully not China, Korea or Vietnam. I'd hate to see you in a soup bowl or on a plate."

I don't know how he did it, but Fairbanks actually rattled his cage.

"I'm sorry, buddy. I promise there's only fresh fish on *my* plate and I'll grill an extra-large piece just for you when we get home."

That seemed to calm the large alley cat, so I focused on the magazine in my lap. Spying the name of it, I quickly threw it back on the table, feeling dirty. I looked around the waiting room—still empty—before letting my eyes drift back to the cover of the magazine. *Cockhandlers: The Cockerel and Hen Farmers Magazine* (Spring/Summer Issue). The picture on the cover was a man holding a large rooster. I couldn't look away. The main cover line, "Cock-a-Doodle-Don'ts: Top Advice Revealed". Additional cover lines, "Poultry Show Preening" and "The Best of Carolina Cocks". I quickly buried the fowl publication beneath other magazines on the table.

"Whew! Here's a better one," I said, picking up a copy of *Modern Cat*. "You and Pickford certainly aren't modern," I told Fairbanks. "But I don't think they make a magazine called *Roaring Twenties Cat*."

The door to the back examining rooms banged open and I looked, expecting to see the short receptionist reenter the room. Instead an extremely tall man ducked and stepped out. I couldn't see his face but I recognized him immediately.

"Bobby!" I cried. He turned, smiled and walked over.

I had met Bobby at No Egrets through Glenn and Glenda. Bobby had been through a lot in recent months, including three attempts on his life.

He had recovered from his injuries, became engaged to be married, and looked better than I had ever seen him.

At six feet eleven inches and over three hundred pounds, Bobby towered over me in the waiting room chair. I stood and still felt like Fay Wray looking up at King Kong. I was about eye level with the white plastic painter's bucket in his hand.

"Daniel!" Bobby shouted as we embraced in an awkward bro hug. "What's in the cage?" he asked.

"One bad-ass cat who got his bell rung," I said. "What's in the bucket?"

Bobby tipped the bucket so I could see in. "One horny reptile," he said.

I bent closer. It looked like the red-eared slider turtle I had owned at a young age. Except my turtle's shell had been the size of a quarter; this turtle's shell was the size of a small dinner plate.

"Tito had a rough morning," Bobby said.

Tito? I remembered Glenn talking about Bobby's five turtles and how he had named them after The Jackson 5.

"He got a bit randy—"

"If Tito bit Randy, how come you had to bring Tito to the vet?" I asked.

"No, no, no," Bobby said. "Randy wasn't a founding member of The Jackson 5; they brought him in later." He counted off the original members on one hand while balancing the painter's bucket in the palm of the other. "I don't have a Randy. I suppose if I ever get another turtle it will be Randy." Bobby chuckled, shook his head and looked to the ceiling. "But I don't see that happening, as the future Mrs. thinks the turtles stink, are too much trouble, and should return to the great outdoors from whence they came."

Bobby glanced a bit sadly at Tito. "The Jackson 5 may have to break up and go solo."

Bobby looked over at the receptionist who was sitting again at her desk. "So anyway, Tito got a bit randy." He dropped his voice. "You know, sexually aroused."

He reached into the bucket, took the turtle by the shell and turned him over.

"Whoa!" I cried.

There seemed to be a recurring theme for my visit to the vet but I just couldn't wrap my fingers around it...not sure it holds up... (I suppose if we threw in a jellyfish emergency room visit we'd come full circle.)

I couldn't help asking, "You been giving that turtle Viagra?" The receptionist was looking at us now, slyly grinning.

"No," Bobby said, his voice barely a whisper. "He's got a protracted pecker. Can't get it back in."

My mind drifted to the Viagra and Cialis commercials: "If your erection is painful or lasts for more than four hours, seek immediate medical attention".

I couldn't help myself as I looked in the bucket again. "How come there's blood."

Bobby grimaced. "It turns out Michael's not a guy."

I imagine that debate ranked right up there with JFK conspiracy theories or evolution vs. creation, but I didn't see what it had to do with the matter at hand.

"Soooo," I finally said.

"Well," Bobby replied, actually blushing. "Like I said, Tito got randy, er, aroused and came at Michael…I mean, who knew Michael was female?"

"I imagine Tito knew."

Bobby burst out in a belly laugh. When he finally quieted, he continued. "So, Tito came at Michael fast. Sort of…sword first. Turtles have this little seduction dance they do." He paused to demonstrate. He weaved to and fro, holding his arms in and his palms out, like turtle flippers. Now I've watched a lot of nature shows on cable in my time, but I've never, ever seen turtles dance the horny hula.

Bobby stopped swaying and continued his story. "I happened to walk by the tank at the same time Tito went into action. And I remember thinking, 'There's no female in there. What's he doing?' So, I watched and I guess I was too stunned to stop it. Michael took offense to the poking…waving…and—"

Bobby made a chomping motion with his mouth, clicking his teeth at the end.

For the second time, I cringed, lowering my hands for protection.

"Jermaine, Marlon and Jackie were sunning themselves on the island by the sunlamp. They had no idea," Bobby said sadly.

I couldn't bring myself to look back in the bucket. Poor Tito. (I'll bet this particular adventure wasn't on Tito's bucket list.)

"Maybe he, um she, you know, Michael, thought it was a worm…food waving in front of his, I mean, her, snout," I stammered. The lyrics to an early song was running through my head: "ABC, as easy as 1-2-3, as simple as do-re-mi". *Chomp!*

"Don't know," Bobby said gloomily. "All I know is it was the most horrific thing I ever saw. Now poor Tito can't get it back—it's all swollen and stuck out." I thought of another early song, "I Want You Back".

"What did the vet say?" I asked.

"She said the swelling would go down in a couple of days. She gave Tito a steroid shot and told me to keep him separate from the others for a while. Oh, and she gave me some cream to rub on it."

"What?" I cried.

"It will make Tito heal faster," Bobby replied sheepishly.

"Well, I have no doubt it will make him feel better."

The receptionist called out to Bobby. "Mr. Portis. I have your Silvadene cream here and I have your bill ready."

Bobby walked over to her as I sat down. I looked over at Fairbanks; he winked back at me with his good eye. "I love ya, man," I told the cat. "But there are some things I just won't do for you."

I had just flipped open *Modern Cat* when the front door opened and another customer entered. The article I turned to was "13 Secrets Your Cat Wants You to Know". I scanned down through the numbers, stopping at number 13, "I have psychedelic super vision."

"Maybe you're not from the Roaring Twenties," I said absently to Fairbanks. "Maybe one of your previous lives was in the Psychedelic Sixties. Reefer, L.S.D.; perhaps you were Timothy Leary's cat. Ah, the stories you could tell."

Scanning back up the page, I stopped at number 7, "I see you as a large, useless cat". Reading below, the article stated, "Cats view humans as large, useless cats, not another species, and thus will treat you as such."

I looked at Fairbanks. "Well, that sure explains a lot."

The front door banged open, followed by a shriek from the reception area, in a range that hurt my ears. And from the looks of Fairbanks' grimace, it was sonically unpleasant to cats as well.

"I have to see the doctor now! My precious has been traumatized!"

"Now, Mrs. Rowasa—please," the receptionist begged.

I looked up to see Bobby hurrying away from the scene. "Later Daniel," he said, waving to me as he exited, swinging his painter's bucket full of enlarged and humiliated turtle.

"You aren't listening to me!" Mrs. Rowasa whined, close to the upper limit of the human hearing range. Somewhere in the back, dogs started to bark.

When the receptionist shrugged, Mrs. Rowasa stamped her foot. "But I'm telling you, there was an alligator on the beach!"

Oh no! It couldn't be. I looked closer. Yes, it was the woman with the foo-foo dog.

"And then a man talked nasty to my precious, telling Fifi the alligator was going to eat him!"

It was the woman with the foo-foo dog named Fifi.

"And Fifi has been shaking ever since. I took her home and finally got her to rest, but she just kept whimpering in her sleep. And now she's shaking again. I tried to feed her but she hardly touched her Fifi Crockpot Chicken Stew and it's her favorite. And she barely drank any of her Dasani water."

The young receptionist seemed flustered, but to her credit she held her ground. "I understand Mrs. Rowasa, but this gentle...this man's cat has been in a fight and he was here first to see the doctor."

I pulled the sweat stained brim of my UNC-Wilmington Seahawks cap down low (hashtag WingsUp!).

"But Fifi has been traumatized," the woman whined, barely looking my way. More dogs joined in the chorus of barking.

The receptionist picked up a chart folder she had prepared, opened it and called authoritatively, "Fairbanks O'Dwyer." (I had read where both Mary Pickford and Douglas Fairbanks were buried in the Hollywood Forever Cemetery in Los Angeles; I imagined a tandem roll over.)

I picked up the cat carrier by the handle, pulled my cap down even lower and walked past Mrs. Rowasa and foo-foo Fifi. In a deep voice, I said, "Thank you, ma'am," causing the receptionist to give me a funny look. Mrs. Rowasa was studying me when Fifi started growling. Fairbanks hissed from his prison. When the woman's attention was drawn to the dog, I stuck out my tongue at Fifi and received a sharp bark in return. I'm sure it had been the most exciting day the little dog had experienced in a long time, actually getting to run around and be a dog. Tomorrow she will probably yip and brag about it to all her foo-foo friends.

The receptionist opened the door of Exam Room 2 and I was ordered to "stay". I gently placed the cat carrier on the slightly scratched stainless-steel examination table and sat on the wooden stool nearby. I stared at Fairbanks. He stared at me.

"You ready to come out of the cage, slugger?" I asked Fairbanks. After fumbling with the spring lock, I finally opened the door of the carrier. The large orange tabby slunk out carefully, giving me the evil closed, puffy eye. As he started sniffing the exam table, I couldn't help noticing the wound above his eye had swelled, looking worse. Bringing him to the vet was the right thing to do, even if he would hate me forever.

Watching Fairbanks explore the room for five minutes was mildly entertaining, but when he curled up in a corner of the floor, I grew bored with the show. I spent another five minutes reading all the posters on the wall. While the life cycle of heartworm in dogs was particularly educational and scary, after the fourth reading, my hind end was beginning to ache on the wooden stool. I stood to see what else I could find.

I was elbow deep in the bottom right cabinet when the veterinarian entered the room.

"Ahem."

I turned to face a really painful looking pair of high heels. Pretty green, though.

"Have you lost something?" asked the voice above the shoes.

"Oh, uh, doctor, I was just...organizing," I explained as I worked my way upright. But I was awestruck when we met face-to-face. Her eyes were a stunning blue; they sparkled like sapphire.

"I'm Dr. Neutre." She said her name like it was French—pronunciation "new-tray". "Mr.O'—?"

"Dwyer," I finished, in a Scottish brogue.

"Are you a compulsive organizer?"

Still lost in her eyes, I became confused. Did she just ask me a question? What should I say?

"No, I didn't move anything," I blurted. "And I didn't get on your computer," I said, pointing to the small desktop in the corner, where the screen had turned to the Blue Screen of Death. "It's just that I'm curious..."

"As a cat?" she asked, blue eyes flashing. "We all know how that ends."

I looked to Fairbanks for help; he just turned away and presented his hindquarters, as if to say, "Talk to the butt".

"Truth is," I said, trying to recover. "I've always been fascinated with veterinary drugs. For instance, that one—" I pointed to a box in the cabinet. "Torbutrol."

She frowned. "I see. Are you a drug seeker?"

"What? No! You don't actually think I beat up my cat to come here to find drugs," I cried. "I love the big lump of fur. Fairbanks, tell her."

Fairbanks flicked his tail, as if to repeat, "Talk to the butt."

"It's just," I said, calming. "Take that drug. Generic name butorphanol. It's a synthetic opioid analgesic, having both agonist and antagonist properties. Used for pain in humans, it went by the tradename Stadol."

She took a step into the room, bent and closed the cabinet door. "I see. So...you are a knowledgeable drug seeker."

I took a deep, cleansing breath. "No, I'm a—I used to work in a hospital."

She put her knuckles to her chin, nodding slowly. "And that means— mister used-to-work-in-a-hospital—that I shouldn't suspect you are a drug seeker."

"No, not necessarily." I laughed nervously. She certainly had me boxed into a corner. "I just find veterinary medicines very interesting. Especially ones used in humans *and* animals. And I had some time to kill—"

"I am sorry about that." She sighed. "I had to disinfect the other exam room thoroughly. We don't often have reptiles."

"Tito," I said, smiling. She looked at me wide-eyed.

I started singing in falsetto. "Because Tito's bad, he's bad, come on." I followed with some background "bads" fading out, before finishing with a clumsy Michael Jackson twirl and a solid, "Who's bad?"

Her eyes were still wide. She opened her mouth to speak, but slowly closed it.

I thought about Tito at the bottom of his painter's bucket. "Actually, Tito's *bad* in every sense of the word, as defined and altered through the generations."

She shook her head, her strawberry blonde hair falling over her eyes.

She used both hands to pull her hair back and she seemed composed again. "Anyway, I am sorry it took so long. My vet tech called in sick today." As she moved toward the exam table, she mumbled under her breath, "Didn't stop her from posting a Facebook selfie on the beach with an alligator in the surf behind her."

"Yeah, about that," I said, sticking my hands in my pockets. "Please remember you are only going to hear Fifi's side of the story."

She stared at me wide-eyed and open-mouthed again. After giving a slight glance in the direction of the waiting room, she said, "Do you know all of my patients personally?"

I shrugged. "I guess I have a kind of animal magnetism." Fairbanks chirped, which in this case could be interpreted as a kitty chortle.

"Yes," she said slowly. "Well, let's turn our attention to *your* animal, shall we?" With ease, she scooped the cat out of the corner and placed him on the examination table, ending with a long body stroke. "So, Fairbanks, are we here for castration today or something else?"

Fairbanks turned around and backed against the carrier, hissing and spitting in her direction. I covered my gonads for the third time. I was not happy the recurring theme of my visit had resurfaced.

She giggled, a cute little feminine titter. "See, I can joke, too."

"A veterinarian with the name Neutre—I'm sorry, *New-tray*," I said, thinking Frankenstein-Fronkensteen. "Should never joke about such things."

She moved (catlike?) to the counter by the sink, plucked some gloves from a box and pulled them on her hands. Approaching Fairbanks, she used a soothing tone. "You're a good looking fellow. Let me look at your head and I promise to give you a nice, fishy treat."

I swear, at the word "fish" Fairbanks relaxed and actually moved toward the doctor. He's just a gigolo when it comes to seafood.

"Oh my, that's a nasty abscess." When she pressed her thumbs on either side of the head wound and squeezed, nasty smelling brown pus oozed out. I had to turn away, my hand over my mouth. No need to impress the veterinarian with my hurling ability. I could toss cookies at a moment's notice, anyplace, anytime.

I chanced a look back and saw Fairbanks trying to pull away, but he wasn't making any noise.

"You know, Fairbanks," she continued in her soothing tone. "Just a little bit lower and you would have lost that eye."

"Oh wow!" I said, turning back to the table. "That would have been awful." I put a hand on the cat's back and stroked him. "If he had lost an eye, would he have to wear a little kitty eyepatch? Then he really would be a swashbuckler, like his namesake."

Applying hydrogen peroxide to the wound with a long, cotton-tipped applicator, she stopped and looked at me. "Yes, a kitty eyepatch. And if his leg needed to be amputated, a nice wooden peg leg."

She resumed applying the peroxide with the wooden cotton-tipped applicator. "Do you have a pirate fetish, Mr. O'Dwyer?"

"Not exactly. But I recently attended a pseudo-séance on a houseboat supposedly haunted by pirates."

She finished with the cotton-tipped applicator which looked just like a—

"You don't use those in ear canals, do you? Inserting those into the ear canal could cause injury."

"I can't tell you," she said. "Trade secret. I could be kicked out of the secret veterinarian society. And..." She paused to pantomime a handshake, followed by bringing her hand to her face to lick the top, and finishing by dropping the hand while flicking it several times. "I just learned the secret handshake."

"Oh-ho," I laughed. "I didn't know DVMs were so funny."

She smiled. "It doesn't stand for doctor of veterinary medicine. It stands for dung-vermin-and maniacal owners."

I laughed. She laughed. Fairbanks was not amused.

"So, what does RPh stand for?" she asked, a sly smile on her face.

Ah, busted. My fifteen minutes of fame must not have faded yet. "I see. All the talk about me being a drug seeker—"

"I was just yanking your chain. I recognized your name immediately."

"In my case, it stands for retired pharmacist."

Her eyebrows shot up. "Awfully young to be retired."

"It's a long story—enough to fill a book."

She looked me up and down. "You don't resemble your newspaper picture though—what is that?" she asked, pointing to my ensemble. "Early American hobo?"

"No, it's from the Fairbanks O'Dwyer 'Shredded' collection, called Cat Carrier Blues." I held up my scratched hands—thankfully the blood had congealed. "I am *so* looking forward to getting him back in the cage."

"Ouch! I'll show you a little trick when it's time." She moved to the cabinets and pulled out a vial and syringe. Noticing me straining to read the small print on the vial, she said, "Ceftriaxone. After the antibiotic, I will need to give him a steroid for the swelling, too."

"Thanks. Good luck sticking him, though. He bit me, twice, when I tried to put the little vial of Revolution on the back of his neck for fleas, and that's topical."

She swooped in, distracted Fairbanks and gave the shot before he knew what hit him. He didn't have time to screech.

"I'm impressed," I said. "I've got a friend in the hospital right now who is going to absolutely freak when they try to draw blood. Are you available for a road trip?"

She smiled, her blues eyes twinkling. "Love to, but did you forget Fifi?"

I groaned. "Will the therapy be for Fifi or the maniacal owner?"

"Little of both." She gave the steroid injection just as fast, before Fairbanks could blink his one good eye.

She addressed Fairbanks. "How bad does that mean ole gray cat look?" Fairbanks appeared to smile.

"What?" I asked. "I didn't see the other cat. How do you know its gray?"

She pulled up the right paw of Fairbank's foreleg, turned it over, pressed lightly on the toe pad and removed a tuft of gray fur from the between the claws.

"*Francis*," I said vehemently in a low voice, drawing out the syllables. Francis was the big, tough, gray tomcat with the sissy name who couldn't seem to coexist with Fairbanks.

The doctor gave me a questioning look, so I felt the need to explain. "It's not the first Fairbanks-Francis fight. The first one was historic, 'Rumble in the Undergrowth'. This must have been the rematch."

She smiled, taking a pad of paper from the counter. "Catfights keep food on my table."

"And neurotic canines and maniacal owners keep gas in your car," I added.

She touched the tip of her index finger to her nose. "All right, I am writing down what *daddy* needs to do for the wound to heal properly."

Daddy—that's a good one. I'm more like Fairbanks' indentured servant.

She continued: "There shouldn't be any problem with Fairbanks' eye; the swelling should go down pretty quick."

She tore the paper from the pad and handed it to me. "Thank you very much, Dr. Neutre," I said. "The rematch was more than I could handle; I couldn't have done it without you." Her smile made her eyes flash—I was momentarily lost. I tried to look down to break the spell and my eyes came to rest on her green high heels. Damn, those were some sexy shoes.

"Well, you haven't seen my bill yet. And please, call me Valeree."

"Okay Valeree. About that trick…" I raised my head, looking forlornly at the smelly cat carrier.

She pointed her index finger and began to waggle it around. In time to the waggling, she began making a "pop" sound with her mouth. As the finger moved faster, more "pops" followed (I swear, it sounded like the tune to "Popcorn", a 70s novelty song, which consisted of one "lyric", the synthesizer sound "pop"). She was a little weird. I liked it.

As her finger danced, she motioned me to get the carrier open and ready. Then she motioned for me to pick up Fairbanks, which I did with a growl (the cat, not me). Following her orders, I admit I became a little hypnotized by the dancing finger and the "pop, pop, pop-pop, pop-pop-

pop". Fairbanks was not even slightly entertained as he squirmed in my arms. I could sense Dr. Neutre was going to fail and my stomach sank. I didn't want her to be embarrassed.

"You know, Fairbanks…he's not like other cats," I said. "He has his own sense of—"

It was an amazing sleight of hand—er, finger. Chalk one up for the human race. So often cats come out the winner in any kind of battle with people, but not this time. The doctor started tapping Fairbanks' nose with her index finger, distracting him. Confuse a cat! Fairbanks could not turn away, remaining focused on the tap-tap-tap distraction on his snout. I easily slipped him into the carrier and shut the door.

"Wow! That was great! I owe you," I said, thinking in the back of my mind that Fairbanks was a quick study and would probably shred me finer than grated cheese the next time.

"Well," she said hesitantly, looking down. "I would like to meet with you sometime…"

Uh-oh! An alarm went off in my head and the face of Jaclyn flashed before me.

"This is hard for me to say aloud." She looked up, troubled. "But when I read about the drug ring you busted at the hospital, I was impressed."

Her startling blue eyes pierced and befuddled me.

"Umm…thank you. I had some prior experience, obviously, but none of it prepared me for what hit me (or stuck me) at the hospital."

She stood up straighter and a look of determination crossed her face. "I think I have a similar problem here," she said. "But I can't be sure. Could we meet and discuss it sometime?"

"Sure," I said enthusiastically. The return of Rx-Dick!

I thanked the doctor again, hefted Fairbanks and carried him out the door to the receptionist's desk. As I finished paying the bill (Ouch! I'm going to have to have a long talk with myself about finances soon), Mrs. Rowasa, Fifi riding on her arm like a flying carpet, charged the desk.

"It's Fifi's turn now," she screamed. "I demand we see the vet!"

I had taken a step back, not realizing anything was amiss until Fairbanks hissed. I turned to see a horse with his nose against the wires of the cage, sniffing, looking in at the cat. Okay, it wasn't really a horse. It was a giant black dog, an English Mastiff if I remember correctly from that famous dog show that comes on after Macy's Thanksgiving Day Parade.

"Hel-wo."

A small boy was holding the dog's leash, a boy shorter than the dog, perhaps four or five years old.

"Hi," I replied. "That's a big dog. What's his name?"

The boy pulled on the leash; the dog didn't budge. "Brutus."

"That's a good name for him. Is Brutus sick?"

"Nope. He's gonna have his pee-pee cut off."

Of course. Et tu, Brute?

6 - EDGAR ALLAN CROW

A few miles from my house, I could see the sun nearly touching the horizon, preparing to kiss the day goodbye. Breathtaking orange and red hues streaked the sky. A bold fashion statement from Mother Nature. If I had more time (minus a furious feline in a carrier in the Cube), I would bolt to The Point and stand reverently on the beach, admiring the incredible beauty of Oak Island.

Instead, my mind drifted back to "doctor's orders", keeping Fairbanks inside for at least two days (the same degree of difficulty as performing a quadruple on the flying trapeze or a triple Lutz on the ice). I wasn't sure whether to laugh or cry. (One of us would eventually be crying—maybe both of us, of that I was sure.) I recalled the one time Fairbanks had been trapped inside, when I thought he had gone out. I awoke at 4 a.m. with him pacing on my bed, before he plopped down on my face, attempting to smother me. Death by cat. I decided my only hope was to bribe him.

Dodging some rather large pot holes, I pulled into a side parking spot at Haag and Sons. Fairbanks protested loudly, until I opened the door and the smell of fish wafted into the car. His nose twitched, as if to say "I can name that fish in three sniffs". He sat down in the cage in what I call the "chicken" pose—front paws curled up under him and back paws tucked in under his body—waiting patiently. Let's hope my plan didn't lay an egg. When I jumped back in the car with a large, paper wrapped package of golden tilefish (caught by Yankee Dave), I could almost hear him salivating. So far, so good.

Exhausted, I fumbled in my pocket until I found the house key, opened the front door and placed Fairbanks just inside, still in his pee-prison carrier. Fat Tire and golden tilefish—no other plans for this night. Closing the door, I paused when I heard a scratch; a calico cat, on two legs, was stretched up the outside screen as far as she could manage, paws extended. Isn't that sweet. She's concerned about her man. Letting her in, Pickford passed the cat carrier without a glance as she tried to crawl up my leg to get to the golden tilefish package. Aw, true love.

I flicked on the light and stood there, stunned. I had forgotten my floor looked like Leatherface had run amok with his Texas chainsaw.

I leaned down to release Fairbanks. "Don't worry guys. Dinner first, then cleanup." Pickford barely gave battle-scarred Fairbanks a glance as she skipped to the kitchen at the word "dinner".

As I heated my skillet, I thumbed through the Brunswick County Yellow Pages (yes, they still make phone books). I was surprised to see a listing under "Crime Scene Cleanup" for a company named "No Blood for You!" I marked the place with a piece of fish wrapping paper as I leaned over the skillet. The soft sizzle of oil meets fish is always so…comforting. (It should be on one of those ambient music therapy recordings used for relaxation.) The smell of the fish and spices was heavenly and my feline companions took ringside seats in the floor by the stove. I flipped the fish, put down my spatula and took a big swig of Fat Tire. It had definitely been a full and interesting day.

As I added more thyme to the golden tilefish, I nearly dropped the glass bottle into the skillet when the wall phone rang. "I bet we all know who that is!" I announced to the cats as I hurdled them to make my way to the phone. Mom always seemed to know when I was getting ready to eat, heading to the bathroom, etcetera, etcetera. It had to be my mother— Jitterbugging again. The older she got, the more she liked to play with toys.

"Yo mama," I answered on the fourth ring.

"Oh Daniel!" the voice on the other end cried with relief. "Thank God, I finally reached you."

"Jaclyn! What's wrong?" I clutched the phone tighter.

"I've been calling every hour." She sounded beyond tired, like she was barely able to speak.

"I'm sorry. Fairbanks was in a fight and I had to take him to the vet. What is it?"

"I need you." She sounded as if she had been pushed to the brink.

I breathed a sigh of relief. "I need you, too. I know things have been a little off lately—"

"No, no, no." There was irritation in her voice this time. "I need you *here*. There's a full moon, the ER is packed and they keep calling me to Willie's room." She sighed heavily into the phone. "I can't handle Willie and everything else."

As I pulled into the Boiling Grove Community Hospital parking lot, my stomach growled. The golden tilefish had been cooked to perfection but I only had time to wolf down a small piece, sacrificing the bulk to Fairbanks and Pickford. Since I had to keep Fairbanks inside, I had left the new CDs by Ziggy Marley and Stephen Marley playing on shuffle, as I had discovered the Marley offspring seemed to have an unusual calming effect on the big cat.

The full moon was yellow and bright, off to the side of the hospital; it seemed to move and follow me into the building. "Full moon madness" in an emergency room has occasionally been studied, documented in journals, including statistical analyses of data, but never proven. But ask anyone who has ever worked in an ER and they will invariably describe the increase in admissions and strange happenings.

I expected to be stopped by a security guard at the desk, but it was unmanned. Strange. The lobby was deserted. I took the elevator to the third floor and hurried to room 306, expecting the worst. Willie's bed was empty. Had they taken him to surgery? Maybe he coded? Did he—*gulp*—expire? (Was he now floating around the *Silent Cow* with his ghost pirate buddies, lobbing planchettes about the cabin?)

"It's about time you got here, Daniel." I could hear the voice, but I did not see a body. Perhaps Willie's ghost was floating around the ceiling. I looked up.

"Take me home—now!" Willie was balanced on a three legged wooden stool in the far corner of the room. With his billowy hospital gown, he looked like a flamingo standing on a single stick leg. The stool wobbled precariously.

"Hi Willie," I said, moving toward the stool. "Whatchu doin'?"

"Very funny. Get me out of here." His arms were extended at shoulder height for balance, but his hands were balled into tight, white fists.

"Let me guess," I said, scratching my chin comically. "They told you they needed a stool sample—"

Willie flapped his wings for balance. "And I look more like a stool pigeon. Hilarious." He paused to concentrate on his equilibrium. "This is no time for word games," he said through clenched teeth.

I gazed as far below his hospital gown as I dared. "You got some fine lookin', pasty, spindly legs for a pasty, thick-bodied white man."

"Get me—the hell—out of here!"

I decided I'd had enough fun for the moment. "Willie, why are you standing on a stool?"

"Duh," he said, as if that explained it all.

I walked over to the bedside chair and collapsed into it. "Boy, am I tired. I think I'll be okay after a quick nap." I yawned widely.

Willie huffed. "I am on the stool—" he said, stopping as he threw out his arms for balance. When all three stool legs were back on the floor, he continued: "Because over there—" He pointed to the hospital bed. "Are numerous strains of bacteria. And there—" (in the direction of the bathroom), "Is a viral brothel."

"The floor?" I asked.

"Spores."

"I see," I said. I slowly gazed around the room. "Having worked in a hospital housekeeping department, you want to know the one part of the room that's never cleaned?"

He shook his head and tried to look away.

I pointed *up*.

Willie slumped, a beaten man. He scanned the room quickly, but realized there was nowhere safe. I could almost see his mind working, determining the height of the stool, the wind velocity, the puff of spores if he had a bad landing. He jumped down off the stool, treading quickly over the tile floor like he was walking over hot coals at a Tony Robbin's self-help seminar. (Funny how the only "self" helped in his seminars was born with the given name Anthony.) Willie leaped into bed and pulled the covers tight.

"Come on, Willie. Jaclyn told me on the phone that you could go home, if you let them draw blood."

Willie submerged under the covers so only the top half of his head showed. He emphatically shook his head.

"When was the last time you had blood drawn?"

The muffled reply came from beneath the covers. "1989."

Crap! This wasn't going to be easy; a difficult end to a difficult day. My mind zoomed through a hundred ways to trick, coerce, hog-tie, or browbeat Willie into giving blood. I could get him so drunk he would pass out, but I was pretty sure there wasn't an organic beer vending machine in the lobby. I could push him down a flight of stairs to draw blood, but the security camera footage would probably not reflect well on me. I was wondering where I could find leeches when I heard a knock on the door.

"Mr. Welch, my name is Lenore. I'm from the laboratory and I'm here to take your blood."

A lab phlebotomist! What luck! She smiled and prepared her collection tubes. (Obviously, it was Lenore's first time in Willie's room or she wouldn't have been so chipper.)

Willie still had the sheet pulled over his mouth and I had a sudden idea. "Hi Lenore, please call me Willie," I said, throwing my voice. Unfortunately, it sounded a bit feminine (okay, a lot feminine—like a cross between Gracie Allen, Betty Boop and Richard Simmons). I had purchased a "Ventriloquism for Dummies" book from Amazon and had been practicing throwing my voice. (My ultimate goal was to make it look like

Pickford and Fairbanks were trading quips.)

Willie's eyes grew wide. Lenore's mouth flew open. I continued to throw my voice (expertly, I might add): "I'm not scared to have you draw my blood, Lenore. In fact, nothing scares me at all." I paused for effect. "Well, except maybe nuclear weapons of mass destruction. That's pretty scary." I threw a creepy, squeaky laugh in at the end.

"Oh…okay," Lenore said with a shrug, pulling a tourniquet out of her basket.

There was movement under the covers and I think Willie's arms actually retracted into his body like a weird, retro toy.

"That was awful," Willie squeaked (not unlike the voice I had provided for him). "Were you trying to throw your voice? I could see your lips moving from here."

At first I was crushed. But I had only made it halfway through chapter two before falling asleep, so I shouldn't be too crestfallen. I'm sure Edgar Bergen didn't get Charlie McCarthy talking in two weeks' time.

Lenore stood there, confused, tourniquet and needle in hand. Willie looked directly at her. "You will *not* be introducing any infectious bacterium into my bloodstream today, thank you."

I thought of my long, trying day. I wanted nothing more than to curl up in a corner and go to sleep, just like I was sure Fairbanks was doing after his long and trying day. Fairbanks! I thought of the cat carrier and the vet; suddenly Plan B popped into my head.

I turned to Lenore and whispered to her, before saying out loud, "Thank you very much, Lenore. I guess we won't be needing your services today." Whistling, I turned back and lazily gave Willie thumbs up, before I screamed, "Cowabunga!" and pounced on Willie's bed with my knees on either side of him, pinning him to the bed. He managed to shoot one of his arms from beneath the covers in an attempt to push me off.

"What are you doing, Daniel? Get off me! You're invading my personal space!"

I used my knee to pin his flailing arm and moved my face closer to his. I held up my right index finger and…

"What are you doing?" Willie cried. "Stop it! Daniel, are you crazy?"

I continued tapping Willie's nose with my finger, just like Dr. Neutre had taught me to do with Fairbanks. When he whipped his head to the left, I used my right index finger; when he moved it to the right, I adjusted and used my left index finger. *Tap, tap, tap, tap* (a favorite poem came to mind: "…suddenly there came a tapping, as of someone gently rapping, rapping at my chamber door.")

Willie became so disoriented, he stopped talking and squirming. I felt a tap on my shoulder (The Raven?) and flinched at the touch. I climbed off Willie.

Willie glared at me with malice, until he noticed the tube of blood in Lenore's hand. With horror, he looked down at the puncture mark in his antecubital vein.

"I need to put a Band-Aid on it," Lenore said.

Willie growled. "You will not be touching me again, Lenore." (Quoth the Willie "Nevermore".)

I gently took the Band-Aid from her hand. I thanked Lenore and she left, muttering how she couldn't wait to tell her co-workers about this one. Willie growled at me from deep within as I placed the bandage on his forearm.

I was only half-listening as Willie said, "You smell really bad, Daniel. Didn't you take the time to shower today?" I collapsed in the bedside chair and immediately dozed off.

A sound awakened me. I opened my eyes; the room was dark, the lump in the bed made me believe Willie was still there. I glanced at the large white clock on the wall. Midnight. It looked like I might as well spend the night. I could take Willie home in the morning once his lab results were reviewed. And then I heard the sound again.

There really was a tap-tap-tapping at the window pane.

"'Tis the wind and nothing more," I muttered.

Tap, tap, tap.

I stood on shaky legs and made my way to the window. My hand trembled as I pulled back the blind. There on the window ledge, in the bright light from the full moon—a raven!

My first instinct was to run down the corridor screaming, but I once worked at the hospital, and while I had a dubious reputation, it was a reputation nonetheless.

Tap, tap, tap.

I looked closer. The black bird wasn't rapping the window pane with its beak, it seemed to have something on the ledge it was pecking. It looked to be a small package of some sort. The bird turned the package over, exposing the product's name and I gasped.

"Sunflower seeds!" I cried. The last time Jaclyn and I had played golf at Oak Island Country Club, a large black bird had swooped down off the clubhouse on the first hole and stolen my unopened package of sunflower seeds right out of the golf cart. I looked closer at the bird.

"You aren't a raven! You're a crow! And a thief!"

I banged my fist on the window, rattling the pane. "Give me back my sunflower seeds! Take thy beak from out my heart!" The noise startled the crow and it dropped the package of sunflower seeds into the darkness. With a mournful caw, the crow flew off.

Sitting down in the chair again, I tried to forget the black tail feathers, the beady black eyes of the bird. Soon the rapid beating of my heart subsided (my tell-*tail* heart?) and I drifted off to sleep.

"Daniel. Daniel! Wake up." Someone shaking me.

"Stole my sunflower seeds," I mumbled, eyes closed.

More shaking. I opened my eyes. A weary Jaclyn stood by my chair.

"Do you remember the crow that stole my sunflower seeds the last time we played Oak Island?" I asked.

"Y-yes," she said slowly.

"It was on the window ledge last night," I said, pointing. "Right there with my sunflower seeds, trying to get the package open."

"Daniel, crows steal lots of things from golf carts every day. If it's shiny, they take it."

"But it looked like my brand of sunflower seeds," I whined.

"That was over a week ago. It's highly unlikely. And what makes you think the crow stole the seeds from the Oak Island course? There may be close to a hundred golf courses in a fifty-mile radius. There's a really nice one near the South Carolina border they named after the little thieves, Crow Creek."

And…she sighed.

"Maybe it was a delayed hallucination," she said, referring to the whopper I had when a not-so-nice co-worker injected me with a potentially lethal cocktail of an opioid and benzodiazepine.

I wanted to argue with her, tell her the crow was real and I did not hallucinate the incident. Geez, it wasn't like Bela Lugosi had appeared and started taunting me with my missing bag of sunflower seeds.

And…she sighed.

I stood and lightly guided her to the chair. When she was sitting, I went behind the chair and began massaging her shoulders. This time the sigh was more of the contented kind. I continued kneading the muscles until I felt her relax.

"Better?" I asked.

"Mmm-hmm." Her head had lolled forward and it seemed she didn't have the energy to raise it.

I knelt down beside the chair. "Bad day at the office, dear?"

She rolled her head to one side so she could look at me with one eye. "You have no idea. I was supposed to leave at six—p.m. not a.m. Call-ins, full moon, it was absolutely nuts. We actually had a guy who thought he was a werewolf."

I had repositioned behind her chair, and I paused, my thumbs deep in her trapezius muscles. "If he was a werewolf, why hadn't he turned? It's a full moon."

A small grunt of pleasure/pain escaped her lips before she responded. "That's what I asked him. He said he was experimenting with different mixtures of drugs in order to negate the lycanthropy." She sat up straight, turning to face me. "Hey, maybe he's a pharmacist."

"Antidote for a lycanthrope...cool." I couldn't help smiling. "Did you cure him?"

"Not exactly." She turned back so I could continue the massage. "We did consult psychiatry, though."

Willie moaned in his sleep; Jaclyn raised her head to look in his direction. "I heard you devised a way to let lab draw Willie's blood."

I started to ask how in the world she had heard about it, but stopped. The hospital grapevine works in strange and mysterious ways.

"Yeah, I don't think you're going to find my technique written up in the medical literature though," I said. "Maybe a veterinarian journal."

Jaclyn closed her eyes for a full minute. Suddenly her neck muscles tensed, in spite of the Swedish massage strokes I applied. I prepared for the worst.

Reaching behind her head, she grabbed my wrists. I moved beside her, kneeling. "Daniel...I don't know. I just don't know anymore." She sighed.

I couldn't help myself. I uttered the classic masculine response: "Did I do something wrong?"

"What?" She looked me in the eye. "No—I don't know—maybe."

For some reason, her words weren't comforting.

She blinked back tears. "I've always loved that you can make me laugh. But lately...well, your humor seems infantile."

A small amount of air escaped me, like I had taken a scalpel to the trachea. Infantile? Me? What right did she have to accuse me of being—and then I thought of tearing Willie's menu into pieces to make paper footballs, writing pirates" on Willie's allergy list on the white board, sticking my tongue out at a little foo-foo dog named Fifi. Okay, *juvenile* maybe, but infantile?

"I'm sorry," she said, seeing the hurt look on my face. "I've been working too much and I think I'm burned out."

"Well," I said, standing and moving around to resume massaging her shoulders. "I know all about burned out. How do you think I ended up on Oak Island?"

Her head had lolled forward again. "Umm," was all she could get out.

"Hey, we can take a vacation!" I exclaimed, suddenly inspired. "We can go to Charleston—"

She perked up. "I haven't been to Charleston in a long time. I love the city market and Magnolia Plantation and Gardens."

"Oh, yeah." I stopped massaging for a minute. "I meant the *other*

Charleston. You know, Charley West."

"Huh?" she managed to ask. It appeared she was slobbering down the front of her scrubs. (In Sweden, that is considered a compliment to the masseuse or masseur.)

"Charleston, West Virginia! My old stomping grounds."

"Oh, I see. Daniel, are you asking me to meet your parents?"

What? (gulp) How did that happen? (gulp)

I decided this was not the time to appear infantile or juvenile, it was time to be worthwhile (or even Gentile).

"Sure," I said cheerfully.

"That's nice," she said softly. I had increased the pressure on her shoulders, so I wasn't sure if she was talking about meeting my parents or the massage.

When I finally stopped to rest my hands, she looked up at me and said, "Don't take this the wrong way, Daniel, but when you worked here you seemed a little different—I don't know, you carried yourself differently."

"I…don't think I follow you."

She took my hand—and sighed long and deep. "You seem…rudderless. Like you're floating through life…on a lazy river. Slowly, in a circle." She made a weak twirl of her finger.

I didn't know what to say. Her words stung me, a worse pain than diving into a fluther of jellyfish.

She noticed my stunned expression. "It's okay, Daniel. I'm sorry. I'm just tired. Let's forget it."

I helped her to her feet and we embraced. "You," I said, lifting her chin so I could look her in the eye. "Need to go home—and get some sleep."

I leaned in to kiss her; she put an index finger to my chest and pushed. "You," she said, pulling away. "Need to go home—and shower. Pew!"

Willie slept on. (I guess he had been suffering from insomnia lately— underlying cause: phantom pirate pranks.) I thought about sitting back down to digest and dissect the conversation with Jaclyn, but decided my personal hygiene took precedence. I was turning to leave when a rugged man in green scrubs popped through the door. He brushed back his salt and pepper hair and smiled mischievously.

"I heard through the grapevine that the great Daniel O'Dwyer was back in the building."

"Greg!" I yelled. I ran to my friend to give him a hug, but stopped short. He looked at me curiously.

"I've been told I smell offensively," I explained.

Greg laughed. "Whew, since I've been working in surgery I've been introduced to a whole bunch of interesting smells. Makes the odors from housekeeping smell like roses. Come 'ere."

After a long bro hug, complete with laughter and back smacking, we separated. Greg Burman had been my co-worker during my undercover housekeeping stint; he now worked as an orderly in the surgery department. I hadn't seen him in about six months.

"It's great to see you, Greg. Look at all that hair!" When I worked with him, his hair was quite short.

"Yeah," he said, whipping it back like a model. "It's starting to recede and fall out more, so I figured it was time to grow it out one last time."

"Looks good. How have you been?"

"Clean and sober, man. Living the good life." Greg was a recovering addict and faithful Narcotics Anonymous member.

"That's great to hear."

"How about you?" Greg asked.

"Apparently, I'm up the creek without a paddle," I answered, thinking about Jaclyn. "Or a rudder."

"So, you're normal," Greg said, walking to Willie's bedside. "What's up with Wild Willie?"

Willie's eyes fluttered open at the mention of his name.

"Possessed," I said.

"What? You mean like the little girl who levitates off the bed and her head spins around?"

"Not him, specifically," I answered. "The *Silent Cow* is possessed by pirate ghosts who are making Willie's life miserable, thereby adversely affecting his health. And when Willie's miserable—" Out of Willie's line of vision, I poked myself in the chest, shaking my head sadly.

Willie seemed to be following the conversation as he shook his head in the affirmative.

Greg frowned. "The *silent* what?"

Greg had been to my house a few times but I didn't realize he didn't know about the *Silent Cow*. "Sorry. Willie's houseboat he lives in, out back of my house. He named it the *Silent Cow*."

"Hmm," Greg said. "Spell it."

After I had spelled the houseboat's name for him, he frowned again. I felt the need to explain the inexplicable. "I don't know why he named it that, other than it was something his mother called him."

A grin broke out on Greg's face. He turned to Willie. "Let me guess. You never told your mom nothin' that was going on in your life or at school when you were growing up. Probably never talked to her much at all."

Willie shrugged and nodded.

"She wasn't calling you a silent *cow*—she was calling you *Silent Cal*." Greg laughed long and loud. When he finished, he saw the confused looks on our faces. "Calvin Coolidge!"

I still wasn't following; I looked at Willie and he shrugged back. Greg liked to read books about U.S. presidents but not the popular ones. He preferred to start at the bottom and work his way up from the inept and corrupt. I had no idea where Calvin Coolidge fit—seemed like he was president during the Roaring Twenties.

"Just finished a book on our illustrious 30th president," Greg said. "Very interesting."

I thought for a minute. "I seem to remember a show on TV, or maybe a magazine article, claiming Coolidge caused the Great Depression."

"Yeah, some believed his actions in office contributed to the Depression after his elected term, but I'm not convinced. His administration was riddled with scandal, but a lot of it he inherited from his predecessor, Warren G. As with all of the guys I've read about, there were some good things. He was in favor of civil rights, rejecting KKK members for government appointments, even appointing African Americans to posts."

Willie finally spoke. "Excuse me! Normally history interests me, but in case you haven't noticed—I'm in the hospital here! I'm starving and I want to go home—to my houseboat—the *Silent Cow*."

Ignoring Willie, I addressed Greg. "So, Willie's mom wasn't calling him a mute bovine?"

Greg laughed again. "Calvin Coolidge was a man of few words. He rarely said more than was necessary."

I thought of the politicians currently in office. Boy, could they learn a thing or two from ole Calvin.

"The public nicknamed him Silent Cal," Greg continued. "He embraced it, once saying 'I've never had to explain something I didn't say'."

"That's it!" I cried. Turning to Willie's bed, I told him, "That's why the pirates knocked down your Ian Anderson photograph. You need to put up a picture of Calvin Coolidge instead."

I could almost see the wheels churning as Willie frowned, thinking. Finally, he spoke: "No, I reject your hypothesis. She called me a silent cow." And that was that; end of discussion.

It was Greg's turn to shrug. He started to head toward the door but stopped. "Oh, almost forgot Daniel." His next words got my wheels churning, making *me* frown. "Our buddy Scott Unites wants to see you at ten. He asked if you could come to his office."

7 - THE PIT AND THE TWEEDLE-DUM

Walking around the hospital parking lot with coffee cup in hand, I let the warm, morning sun dry my wet hair. Greg had sneaked me into the male surgery locker room where I had showered and groomed with whatever implements and products I found scattered about. Mostly shower gels and body wash—items I would never buy for myself. (Whatever happened to good, old fashioned bar soap? The kind Granny Clampett made out back of the mansion with lye?) I sampled most of the products: one boasted "fresh, spicy and oriental" (Can you advertise "oriental" these days without offending someone and inviting a lawsuit?); many had wood smells ("I'm a lumberjack and I'm okay"); the Versace Eros had fresh aquatic notes; there was a Bath and Body Works Bourbon Strawberry and Vanilla (I kid you not); another had Calabrian bergamot and grapefruit, with fig leaves at the top (I prefer my fig leaves at the bottom, thank you).

I readjusted my oversized shirt. Greg had loaned me the t-shirt he had worn to work (on the front it had printed, "Hugs not Drugs" and the back, "Got Naloxone?"), but his jeans were too large so I had on an old pair of green scrub pants. Flip-flops adorned my feet. I raised my arm and sniffed my pit—smelled like a detonation at a flower garden, but much better than before.

Good ole Scott. I couldn't help wonder why he wanted to see me. Scott Unites was the Human Resources Director and I had done him a favor by rooting out the rampant drug diversion at the hospital. The drug ring had been snuffed out and I hoped there wasn't an isolated case he wanted me to investigate.

I still had an hour to kill so I wandered around the hospital grounds. It seemed like a better idea than going back to Willie's room and listening to

70

him whine. He would most likely be discharged later and I could take him home (whine-whine-whining, all the way home).

I heard the backhoe before it came into view. The basketball court was gone now, just a memory; the huge metal backhoe bucket deposited the soil and broken concrete into a pile off to the side. I sniffed back a tear. My right hand began twitching at my side and I looked down, realizing I was unconsciously dribbling an invisible basketball. Bending at the knees, I dribbled behind my back, pretending to feel the dimpled leather of the ball as it reached my left hand. Transported back to high school practice, I took the invisible ball through my legs and around, completing five figure 8 drills before stopping. I popped the (unseen) ball onto my fingertip, spinning it better and longer than any deceased or living member of the Harlem Globetrotters. But wait! There's only five seconds left in the game and the home team's down by two. Quickly, I jabbed left, rolled off a screen and shot the prettiest fall-away three-pointer in the history of the game, my sneakers just barely behind the line. Swish! The invisible crowd goes wild!

"That was a damn fine show, Eye Candy."

I slowly turned (on my pivot foot) to see the Amazon construction woman standing behind me. I realized I was still making the noise with my throat which sounded like a crowd cheering, perfected by nine-year-olds on playgrounds everywhere.

"Sounds like you sprung a leak," she said.

I felt the need to explain. "I just made the game winning shot."

I could see her eyes sizing me up; suddenly she shot forward cat-quick and wrapped her arms around me. She squeezed so tight I couldn't breathe, raising me a few inches off the ground. While I tried desperately to draw in air through my nose, a scent wafted down. What was that? Eue de Toxic Diesel Fumes?

I tried to extricate myself from her bosom but she squeezed tighter. My right ear was near her chest when she let out the strangest sound I had ever heard. It was long and loud, rapidly changing pitch from low to falsetto. It made me feel like I had been transported to a weird, 1940s western (John Wayne stars in *She Wore a Yellow Vest (and a Hardhat)*).

Amazon Hardhat pushed me back, smiling.

"What the hell was that?" I blurted.

A male hardhat walking by said, "You just got yodeled, man. Means she likes you."

"Just following the directions, Eye Candy," she said, pointing to my shirt. I looked down, reading "Hugs not Drugs" upside down. Thanks a lot, Greg. And what's with eye candy? With my mismatched ensemble, wet hair and dark circles under my eyes, I looked more like an eyesore.

She was smiling at me when the backhoe hit something hard, causing a jarring, scraping sound.

The smile disappeared as she turned. "Dammit Tank!" she screamed. "Ya gotta treat that equipment like it's your pecker—not your ex-wife!"

When she turned back, she was smiling again. She was somewhat attractive, in a Joan Jett/Wendy O. Williams/k. d. lang kind of way (okay, scratch that last name from the list—I plead temporary insanity). Staring at her well-developed biceps, I guessed she could out-lumberjack even the burliest of loggers.

Amazon Hardhat apparently thought I was staring at other body parts. "You like what you see, Eye Candy?" She turned to face me straight on, striking as sexy a pose as she could in her durable workwear. (It didn't do a lot for me, but I figured it could make the cover of *Concrete Contractor Quarterly*.")

"Oh no! I wasn't...I was looking at your..."

She arched her back and stuck out her chest, all the while smiling. Could be she was not wearing a bra, but who could tell under all that gear.

"Um, yes," I said, giving up. "They're very nice and seemed really soft when you smashed my face into them."

Her laughter sent a chill down my spine (mostly because I sensed she could snap my spine like a twig).

"You're funny, Eye Candy. I like you."

I tried to appear indignant. "If I could just add one thing. The eye candy connotation, you know, has a bit of a derogatory edge to it. I'm sure you meant well, but while it means pleasing to look at, it also infers a lack of intelligence, lack of merit." I thought of my conversation with Jaclyn and actions of the last few days. Hmm, maybe it wasn't too far off the mark.

She just stared at me like a playful dog, waiting for its master to shut up and throw the damn ball already. "And you smell good, too," she added with a wink.

"Thank you," I said, giving in. "It's silky Sicilian Mandarin notes—the surprising combination of masculine Wood and Leather—with an unprecedented Violet accord." The labels of the products had flashed through my mind.

Another metallic scrape from the pit caused her to whip around. I moved beside her. "What are you building?" I asked.

"Hell if I know," she answered. "Some kind of new addition." She seemed emboldened by my closeness, reaching her arm around my waist and pulling my pelvis to hers. She purred while she looked me up and down. "I'd need more than a two-minute jam with you, Eye Candy. More like a two-hour jam. I'd roll your world."

What? I didn't understand a word she said, yet I felt violated. She reared her head back and a low rumble began in her chest until she opened her mouth and it erupted. As the sound grew louder, it changed to falsetto. Her voice shifted, warbled and ululated (I shit you not).

The same male hardhat walked by. "You've been double-yodeled, man. Run!"

Out of the corner of my eye, I spotted a tall, lumbering, white-coated individual moving toward a car in the parking lot nearby. He looked familiar. When he made his way around the front of the car and tripped over the concrete block, I knew it was his turn to save me.

"Carl! Carlos!" I yelled. I tried to break the grip around my waist, but Amazon Hardhat held tight.

The young medical student craned his neck, dropped his head and hunched his shoulders as he stared my way myopically. (I could only guess he was alternately chanting "ack" and "neep" under his breath.) When he started to turn and run, I had to resort to full lifesaving measures. ("Lifejackets on; man the lifeboats; women, children and Eye Candy first!")

"Carl! Carrr-los!" I cried desperately. He had his back to me; I had to think fast. "I have a message for you from Dr. Pearson!" That stopped him dead in his tracks. It's a wonder he didn't melt into a large puddle, the only thing left a white lab coat and two large eyeballs.

I wriggled and tried unsuccessfully to extricate myself from Amazon Hardhat's grasp. Carl/Carlos was walking toward us slowly, wobbling as if he had been on an all-night bender. He showed signs of being ready to bolt at any second.

When Carl/Carlos finally reached us, I attempted introductions. "Carlos—"

"Carl," he squeaked.

"Carl, this is...um..." I certainly couldn't call her Amazon Hardhat. I searched her hardhat for a name but came up empty.

A yell came from the pit: "Sparkle!"

She let go of my waist and gave Carl a quick punch to the deltoid. "Hiya Carl."

"Sparkle!" the voice called excitedly from the hole. "You better get down here quick!"

Sparkle? Seriously? I nudged a hardhat on the ground near my feet. If her real name was Sparkle, then I'd eat this hardhat.

Carl was doubled over, holding his upper arm. "Ow," he said nasally. "Why'd she hit me?"

"'Cause she likes you; thinks you're cute."

Carl's eyes bugged out (no small feat) and he turned beet red.

"Holy shit!" came the chorus from the hole. I grabbed the hardhat and slapped it on. I took a step toward the pit and stopped when Carl cried, "But what did Dr. Pearson want to tell me? Please don't torture me!"

"Later!" I told him. I grabbed Carl by his sore arm and pulled him along until I found another hardhat sitting on a lump of busted concrete. I snagged it on the run and smashed it onto Carl's head.

"Ow!" Carl cried.

"Time for some excitement in your life," I said, dragging him roughly by the arm through the stalled construction zone. I jumped over every rock and obstruction in our path while Carl tripped along.

There was a deeper hole in the middle of the site and we stopped to survey it, like we were tourists at the Grand Canyon. The man-made opening appeared to be about thirty yards wide and we were near the path leading downward. Below, in the hole stood Sparkle and four men, looking down and gesturing excitedly.

I had to know what was going on. "Would you look at that, Carl. She violates me in front of God and everybody and now she wants me to go hang out with the boys."

"What?" Carl scrunched his face and tried to pull away. "What are you—look, I don't belong here," he protested. "You tell me right now what Dr. Pearson said, or I'm gone!"

"C'mon," I said, not giving up his arm. Stepping down in the hole, whether we had hardhats or not, would break hospital policy, countless rules and be in direct violation of interim life safety measures. But hey, I wasn't an employee. I looked over at Carl. He seemed to be weeping. I'm not sure why, but I held on to his arm and dragged him down the path after me.

"Neep," Carl whimpered.

When we pulled in behind the five construction workers, I bent to pick up Carl's hardhat that had fallen off. "Ack," he said as I slapped it back on his head. They all stood looking down into a newly unearthed section. I poked my head between Sparkle and the man who had advised me to flee earlier. He gave me a look that could only mean he thought I was crazier than a soup sandwich.

"What is it?" I asked.

Sparkle pointed to the far corner. The end of a long dirty-white bone could be seen poking through the dirt. Beside it, a smooth, round white object.

"Is that—a skull?" I asked breathlessly.

Carl, who initially appeared to be turning green and on the verge of losing his breakfast ("I shouldn't be down here, neep," he had protested while I pulled him deeper into the pit), noticeably perked up and moved to the edge of the workers.

"Damn," said the man at the far end of the line, obviously agitated. He took off his hardhat and slammed it against his thigh. "This is bad. Gonna delay us for weeks." He looked down the line at the faces. "We got to be done in two months, it's in the contract."

The workers shifted from foot to foot, readjusted their hardhats; one lit up a cigarette. Sparkle appeared to make a move to reassure them, but hesitated when she looked back over her shoulder at the bones in the pit. I wondered if her crew had encountered a situation like this before.

"Hey boss, you gonna send us home?" one of the men asked her. "We gonna get paid for the whole day? Not our fault someone made this a body dump. Hey, maybe it's some poor son of a bitch the hospital buried here. You know, like a Boot Hill, or a, um—"

"Potter's field," finished the worker beside him. All hard-capped heads slowly turned toward the man in surprise. He shrugged. "PBS." It was his only explanation and apparently good enough for the crowd, as they nodded their understanding.

I noticed the man, next to last, seemed extremely anxious; he was wringing his hands and looking around the top of the pit, as if to see if anyone was watching. "I think they're animal bones," the man said, a little too loudly.

I looked back at the bone and skull. Animal bones my boney arse.

"Yes, I'm positive those are animal," he said, looking around the top of the pit again.

"Bullshit, Tank," Sparkle said.

Tank glared at her with pure contempt. "Those are animal bones and I'm going to clean them out." He threw out his arms and pushed back the men on each side of him. He leaped the four feet down, his steel toe work boots landing with a puff of dust in the dirt.

"No Tank!" cried Sparkle and one of the other men together.

Carl grabbed me, hard. "You have to stop him! That could be a crime scene. A cold case!"

I gave Carl a classic "Who *me?*" look.

Tank, just below me, turned and scowled. "I'm taking care of it," he said vehemently. Turning toward the bones, he said either "Kiss my fat ass" or something about sassafras.

"No!" screamed Sparkle.

Oh, what the hell. I backed a few steps and took a running leap, soaring through the air like a Flying Wallenda. I hit him square in the back just as he reached down for the long bone. As we hit the dirt, I heard the air whoosh out of him. I groaned as I rolled over. When the dust settled, I wiped my eyes with the sleeve of my t-shirt. Less than a foot away, the two large orbits of the skull seemed to stare through me.

Moaning and cursing, Tank rolled back and forth in the dirt near my left side, but I paid him no mind—my eyes were transfixed on the skull. Far from an expert, I was 99.9% positive the only species the skull belonged to was Homo sapiens. Suddenly I got the heebie-jeebies, with just a touch of the screaming meemies.

"You sonofabitch," Tank muttered near my ear, causing me to look his way. Unbelievable! His hand was actually reaching for the skull. I looked around for a rock, a clod of dirt, anything. When I realized there was nothing in reach, I unleashed the only weapon I had on me.

"Ow, shit!" Tank cried as I slapped him with my flip-flop. His hand drew back, away from the skull, to protect himself from the flying rubber. With my right hand brandishing one weapon, I pulled the footwear from between my toes on the left as well. As he started toward the bones again, I used both hands to slap him silly (right jab-flip; left hook-flop!). Red welts were starting to form on his cheeks and he was cursing a blue streak. I felt like Muhammed Ali, Sugar Ray Leonard, Rocky Balboa as I landed blow after blow with my rubber thongs. A sudden steel toed boot to the groin ended my round and (having a glass groin) I toppled to the dirt like the Great White Hype.

My eyes watered, I had trouble with air intake. I hadn't felt this bad since Rich and Thomas Mack Gamble beat the crap out of me behind my house. Someone was holding me, cradling my head. When my vision had almost cleared, I looked up into the sparkling eyes of—

"Jaclyn, is that you?" I squeaked.

She was stroking my hair. "Nope. Guess again, honey pie."

"Annie?" Had I passed on to the other side to finally be reunited with my fiancée? Would they write on my tombstone: "Here lies Daniel O' Dwyer: A jellyfish, a boot and a groin afire"?

The woman stopped stroking my hair. "Three strikes and you're out, Eye Candy."

"Sparkle?" I said, my voice a full three octaves higher than normal.

She tipped her hardhat to me. "The one and only."

"I think I could give you a run for your money on hitting those high yodel notes," I squealed. "Can't hit the low ones anymore, though."

She gazed at me sympathetically. "Got one of my men running for ice."

I closed my eyes and tried to pull out of the fetal position. I groaned. It hurt way too much to unfold.

"Would you like me to rub it for you?" Sparkle asked sweetly.

"Ha-ha," I said, not wanting to guess if she was joking or not. Instead, I changed the subject, trying to take my mind off my lower region. "Sparkle? That's a strange nickname; how'd you get that?"

She looked indignant. "Not a nickname. That's my real name. My poppa named me, after I came out of the womb all glistening and sparkly."

I grunted. "Not gonna ask your middle name then."

She smiled. "Leigh. It's my momma's name."

Of course. "Well Sparkle Leigh, let's see if I can stand up."

When she pulled me to my feet and I tried to uncurl, a wave of nausea swept over me; if I had eaten anything that morning I surely would have lost it in the dust. Slowly, an inch or two at a time, I was able to straighten (even though I was still hunched worse than Quasimodo).

Sparkle supported me so closely, I thought maybe we were going to slow dance (I could almost hear the opening notes to one of the classic slow dance songs, Percy Sledge's "When a Man Loves a Woman"). Through the space under her arm, I could just make out the long bone and skull, still in place in the dirt.

She hemmed and hawed before giving my left bicep a mighty squeeze (I thought it might pop, like in one of those old Popeye cartoons). Finally, she said, "If you hadn't tackled Tank, I'd be in a heap of trouble right now, with more people and agencies than I can count. Thank you. You can't move stuff you find like that. Got to call it in and play the waiting game."

"You're welcome. I think I got the worst of it, though." I pinched my legs together to alleviate the pain.

She squeezed my other bicep (*Pop!*) "Yeah, but you gave me enough time to get there and lay a J-block on him. Knocked him silly and kept him from disturbing the site."

Even though I had no clue what a J-block was, I could picture Tank sprawled in the dirt after the contact. "Wouldn't Tank know not to disturb the site?" I asked.

"Should know the rules," she said, picking up my hardhat and placing it on my head. "Hasn't been with us long, though. Come to think of it, he is a bit strange, always looking over our shoulders and asking questions if we come across anything out of the ordinary on the job." Glancing down at my dirty, bare feet, she let go of me (I weebled and wobbled but did *not* fall down).

As she placed each flip-flop on the ground and slid my feet into them, I asked, "What time is it?"

She tugged at a chain hanging out of her pocket, which I assumed had keys attached; instead, she extracted an old pocket watch. "Ten o'clock on the nose."

Oh crap!

There was something different about the Human Resource Director's office, but I couldn't place it. I looked up and down the outer office, trying to figure it out, but all I found was my old, frumpy nemesis, Scott's secretary. I couldn't recall her name but she had a sense of humor like a piece of naval lint. She shrugged her large shoulders and twisted her head on her thick, manatee neck. "Oh, goodie," was her greeting.

"Why Miss…Mrs…." (She had the audacity to cover up her nametag while I tried to read it.) "Er…I'm pleased to see you again as well." I cleared my throat importantly. "I have an appointment."

"You're late."

I sighed dramatically. "Yes, I *am* tardy. I'd like to tell you it was my first offense, so I could get off with a verbal warning, or my second time so you could write me up. But in truth—" I paused to stick out my lower lip and blink back tears. "I am well past the number for termination. I think this is number seven. And the seventh offense means—" I risked a horrified look at the inner office door, cowering. "The Chamber of Horrors—the rack, thumbscrews, the Iron Maiden!"

"Humph," she said, flattening her lips and closing one eyelid. She looked me up and down with her open eye. "Steel spikes from every direction. If only."

Wait! Was that a hint of humor from my gal? I observed her closely. Her mouth looked as flat as a frog's on an insect free day. No, I think she was deadly serious.

"Well, your boss asked to see me. But if I'm late, I'll just be moseying along—"

"Just a minute," she said. "I'll see if he still wants to see you." She pressed the intercom button. "Mr. Unites. O'Dwyer is here."

"Oh good!" came the tinny voice from the intercom.

"Do you still want to see him?" she asked.

"Sure. Why wouldn't I?"

She looked me up and down again. "He's very dirty—and he still thinks he's funny."

I heard the intercom click off as the door to the inner office opened.

"Daniel!" Scott cried.

"Mr. Scott!" I cried jubilantly. "My favorite people person pusher!" (I noticed his secretary rolling her elephantine eyes.)

Scott Unites was a head taller than me, with a long neck, pale complexion, thinning hair and the beginnings of a little paunch around the midsection.

"Scott," I said, patting his tummy. "Put on a few pounds since I last saw you. Either you're expecting or you better lay off the Mai Tais."

Scott grinned a little sheepishly. "Hey Daniel, did you see the new addition to my office," he said, taking me over to a five-gallon aquarium on a book shelf, right next to a picture of him wearing a giant grass skirt, standing in the midst of Hula dancers on a Hawaiian beach. "I'm trying to relate more to my employees, be more interesting."

In the water at the bottom of the aquarium was a coral outcropping, dark hole in the middle. I could just make out two weird eyes on a blue insect-looking head; the eyes moved independently, seeming to study me. Freaky.

"What the—" The rest of the words hung in my mouth as a large, green shell shot out of the hole. It was a breathtakingly beautiful creature—

coming right at me—*bam!* It had raised the front of its shell, curling up and striking the front of the aquarium glass with tremendous force, causing me to take two steps back. Scott laughed and clapped his hands.

"—hell is that?" I asked, finishing my initial thought. Two long, segmented antennae, ringed in vivid blue, red and green, ending in long red feelers, extended just beneath the eyes of the crustacean. Beneath its green shell floated numerous red, blue and green appendages; some looked like legs, others flapped to and fro like fish fins. It was almost as large as a lobster, but its brilliant color made it look like Zsa Zsa Gabor to the lobster's aged Bette Davis (in a film like *Hush...Hush, Sweet Charlotte*).

"It's a peacock mantis shrimp," Scott crowed. "Isn't it cool?"

Shrimp? Compared to the jumbo ones from my last plate at Jones' Seafood House, the mantis shrimp was ginormous.

"Not cool...dangerous," muttered Scott's nameless secretary.

"Now Bertha..." *Bertha!* "There's nothing dangerous about Ebenezer."

Ebenezer! (I should have guessed the mantis shrimp's name; the 1951 black and white version of *A Christmas Carol* was Scott's favorite Christmas film.)

The mantis shrimp, which had retreated to the top of the coral, suddenly shot forward again and I could just make out two club-like appendages, which looked like they belonged on a praying mantis, before—*bam!* The glass of the aquarium vibrated and the water sloshed up over the top, spilling a little on the picture of the world's tallest and palest Hula dancer.

"You were saying, Bertha," I said, addressing the secretary.

"Looked it up on the internet," she said to me grudgingly. "They can strike at the speed of a .22 caliber bullet."

"You've got to be kidding me," I said.

Scott stepped forward, dismissing us with hand motions. "That's just for attacking prey, cracking the shells of crabs and mollusks and such." He looked at the tank lovingly. "Ebenezer's not dangerous."

"Bah humbug," I said.

For the first time since he walked in the room, Scott seemed to actually look at me. "Daniel, you are soiled." His gaze stopped at the scrub pants. "Are those our scrubs?" BGCH was stamped in black on each leg; guess there was no use denying it.

"If I answer yes, am I in trouble? Do I get the rack or the thumbscrew?"

He frowned. "The hospital loses a lot of money when scrubs disappear. We just spent money on a scrub dispensing machine so that every employee who wears scrubs has to sign them out with a password. And yet..." He pointed to my scrub bottoms.

"Actually, I've been retained to sport the hottest new arrivals for this scrubs season." I put one leg forward, returned it to its original position and then put the other leg forward. When I shook it all about I couldn't help singing, "You do the hokey pokey and you turn yourself around. That's what it's all about." I finished my big number by stating (in a deep announcer-type voice), "Fashionable, yet functional," followed by a Jimmy Durante, "Hotch-cha-cha-cha-*cha*!"

Bertha's countenance was unmoved. "I say he gets the rack *and* the thumbscrew."

Scott's face was pinched. "Someone important will be here in a moment," Scott said. "How did you get so—"

"Soiled?" I answered for him. "It's a long story. You familiar with the construction site, the one near the parking lot, the one that ate up your employee's basketball court?"

"Sure. I can see it out my office window." He gestured with his hand toward the outside wall of his office, which was in the general direction of the construction site. I considered taking him in his office to see if the bones could be spotted from this height.

"Let me ask you something. Do you have any missing employees?"

"What?" He looked at me incredulously. "What in the world are you talking about?"

"You know, an employee who hasn't shown up for work in say…five years. Maybe ten or twenty." I started the downward motion of sitting on the outer-office couch when somehow, Bertha materialized out of nowhere and, with a pretty strong shoulder, shoved me off the mark and back upright.

"Not on this furniture, you don't," she warned. I took that as a challenge and walked across the room toward a big stuffed chair that matched the couch. Bertha scooted by her desk, picked up a newspaper and landed it on the chair seat before I could soil it with my dirty, yet fashionable, scrub bottoms. "Ha!" she called out in victory.

"Look," Scott said. "I don't have time for jocularity right now. Someone important is coming to the office and we have to get you cleaned up. Bertha, can you help Mr. O'Dwyer—"

"I will not!" Bertha stated emphatically. "I've raised three sons and two daughters; I don't do soiled anymore."

Scott was looking at my feet. "Are those…flip-flops?"

Even though my feet were dirt-brown, the same color as my footwear, the toenail of my big toe was clearly visible, giving me away. "Si senor. Muy erótico?"

"Mr. Unites," Bertha said blandly. "It's ten-thirty."

"Oh poop!" Scott cried.

"Scott, on behalf of all the employees of your organization, I'm afraid I'm going to have to enforce page thirty-three of the Employee Handbook dealing with foul language. Do you prefer the rack or Iron Maiden?"

He frantically pushed me into his inner office, trying to dust me off on the way. When we were inside, he grabbed a long-handled Swiffer from behind the door, first dusting my front ("Hugs not Drugs") and then my back ("Got Naloxone?"). Enveloped in a cloud of dust (think Pigpen dancing at Christmas play practice in *A Charlie Brown Christmas*), I couldn't help but sneeze, several times.

Scott was approaching hysteria. "I wanted to get you here early so I could explain the situation before Dr.—"

Bertha's voice could be heard on the intercom, "He's here," just as the huge form filled the inner office doorway. He had to duck to enter, stopping just inside the door to adjust the massive waistband of his pants.

"Another wedgie there, Doc?" I couldn't stop myself from asking.

Cincinnaticus Pearson, MD looked down on me, scowling. Suddenly smiling, he said, "The most common side effect of being a big man."

Scott was trembling as he offered the doctor a chair. Dr. Pearson had been at the hospital more years than anyone could remember. An elder statesmen and surgeon (every once in a while), it was like the parting of the Red Sea when he walked down the hospital halls; employees and visitors alike seemed to scatter like flies.

Scott sat behind his desk, so I took the other chair in the room, dust puffing up from the seat of my dirty scrubs (take that, Bertha!) We all sat and looked at each other (Dr. Pearson was eyeing my dirty feet). Scott seemed at a loss for words, so I decided to help him out. "Dr. Pearson, I've called this meeting today to discuss your medical resident."

"What?" the doctor and Scott cried in unison.

"Carlos—I mean Carl," I said. "You scare the living bejesus out of him."

"Bull-fart!" Cincinnaticus Pearson, MD bellowed. "Fear is the best motivator!"

"Not for every kid," I replied. "It's not a one-size-fits-all, cookie-cutter approach. You can't play bad doc/bad doc without throwing some good doc in there somewhere."

Scott's jaw had dropped somewhere down below the top of his desk. He struggled to close his mouth and gain control of the meeting. "That's *not* what this meeting is about," he said, his voice quaking. "Dr. Pearson has total control of his medical residents and the Human Resources Department has no oversight of the program, other than to make sure they are oriented, vaccinated and follow the rules of the institution."

I thought of my visit to the vet's office. "Sounds like they also need to be spayed and neutered."

Scott shot me a dirty look. "Please, *please*," he pleaded. "Dr. Pearson asked to meet with you."

"Yes," the doctor said, a little calmer. "The hospital is getting another new, dang-blasted computer system. Why they think we need another new computer system is beyond me—just plain idiotic. We all just learned the other one and are finally able to take care of our patients!" He was getting worked up again.

"How long have you had the other system?" I interjected.

"I don't know!" Dr. Pearson was shouting again. "A couple of years!"

I looked at Scott and he held up nine fingers.

"Dr. Pearson told me how you helped him with the computer when you worked in…when you were last employed here," said Scott.

"Yes," said the doctor. "And I just had the training on the new one, and the whole computer—*especially* the pharmacy part—is a P-O-S!"

Thinking back to my West Virginia hospital days and medical abbreviations, I responded, "Polycystic ovary syndrome? Physician order set? Psycho-organic syndrome?"

"Piece of poopy," Scott whispered. I nodded my head in understanding.

"Although it may make me go psycho!" Cincinnaticus Pearson, MD roared. "Believe me, they wouldn't like it around here if I get mad!"

If he gets mad? We haven't seen him mad yet? In my mind's eye, I pictured a cross between a Black Mamba, a wild boar and a velociraptor.

"In the training, I couldn't even find Cipro!" the doctor yelled.

Cipro is one of those rare drugs in which the generic name, ciprofloxacin, contains the brand name, Cipro. If he couldn't find Cipro, the hospital was in for trouble when it came to Cincinnaticus Pearson, MD.

"And that's why Dr. Pearson would like for you to set up the pharmacy part of the computer system," Scott said, interrupting my thoughts.

If he couldn't find Cipro, I would be in for trouble when it came to Cincinnaticus Pearson, MD. Wait. *What?* Oh no, I didn't like the sound of that at all.

Scott and Dr. Pearson kept talking but I didn't hear any of it. There was no way I was going to get sucked back into working again. That would be plain stupid on my part. I felt like I had fallen through the looking glass; I felt dumber than Tweedledum. Dumber than a box of rocks, sharper than a marble, thick as pig shit. In other words, a real dumbard. Then I thought about Jaclyn calling me infantile; heard her saying, "You seem…rudderless. Like you're floating through life…on a lazy river. Slowly, in a circle."

Ten minutes later, when I stumbled out of Scott's office, the only things running through my head were *rudderless—lazy river—in a circle*. I didn't even flinch when I passed the aquarium and the peacock mantis shrimp charged at me. *Bam!*

8 - FOWL SENIOR SOOTHSAYERS

"Earth to Daniel. Earth to Daniel," Ray called, holding his hand over his mouth and nose, modulating his voice like he was communicating with Apollo 13. The old man gave the gaming table an open-handed smack, causing everyone at the Oak Island Recreation Center to snap to attention.

Huh? How the heck did I end up here...playing a game called Rummikub I never knew existed? My intention had been to come to the rec center to lift weights—clear my mind while pumping iron; to sort out relationship problems and make a decision about my recent job offer. Instead I sat across the table from Ray, with two elderly ladies, Irene and Jean, to each side of me. This was the last place I needed to be, wasting my time with strangers. (How was I to know I had surrounded myself with an unlikely trio of wise Oak Island sages, kind of like a senior citizen, saltwater version of the Jedi council?)

I glanced at my game tiles and my mind wandered back to Willie. When I returned to his room after the meeting in Scott's office, Willie had been practically bouncing off the walls (in spite of the potential infection risk). He was ranting, raving and practically frothing at the mouth. Not surprisingly, he signed out Against Medical Advice and there was nothing anyone could do to convince him otherwise. "Lab work be damned!" he shouted. I had tried to find out what that meant, but there was no talking to him, and the nurses had fled.

Ray banged a game tile rapid-fire on the tabletop, bringing me back to the present. I blinked at him slowly, like a turtle (Tito the turtle, before his "accident", to be more precise). Ray smiled and with his silver hair, white mustache and long, thin face, I'll be damned if I didn't feel like I was sitting across the gaming table from a present day Dick Van Dyke.

"Hey Ray, anybody ever tell you that you look like Dick Van Dyke?" I asked.

He took his cane leaning against his chair and banged the end on the floor. Then, in a perfect imitation of Bert the chimney sweep from *Mary Poppins*, he said, "Winds in the east, mist coming in. Like somethin' is brewin' and bout to begin. Can't put me finger on what lies in store, but I fear what's to happen all happened before." Many days later, when I recalled what he said, I had shivered. A sage *and* a soothsayer.

"You're full o' chimney soot, you are Ray," said Irene, who I began to think of as Mary Tyler Moore.

Ray waggled his eyebrows. "Maybe you'd like me to clean your stack."

Poof! The Mary Tyler Moore resemblance disappeared in a flash as Irene jutted her middle finger in Ray's direction.

I looked down at my hand and realized I was holding one of the small white tiles from the game. I really had no clue what I was supposed to do. From what I could tell, Rummikub was a confusing mesh of the card game rummy and the tile-based game mahjong. "Invented by a Jew," Jean had told me with a smile, as if that cleared it up.

Ray shook his head and gave a comic look to the others. "Daniel, I'll go over it one more time. The object of the game is to place all of your tiles—and you start with fourteen—on the table as part of a set." He pointed to the numbered tile in my fingers. "See, they got numbers *and* colors. Anyway, you got to place them on the table as either a group or a run."

"The runs?" I questioned. "I thought that's what sidelined Alvin from the game?"

Ray sniggered and Jean kicked him under the table. The three of them had been sitting at the gaming table when I entered the Oak Island Recreation Center, with the fourth chair empty. When they flagged me down, I ran over, thinking they were in need of medical attention. Imagine my surprise when they roped me in and forced me to sit—in Alvin's vacant chair—to join in their reindeer games.

"It's no joking matter," said Jean. "Alvin has IBS. He can't help his gastrointestinal problems."

Ray's voice got louder, echoing through the room. "I know there's nothing funny about the shits! I've had 'em plenty of times myself. I bet Alvin hasn't left the bathroom all day—I feel sorry for him. But dang…Alberta, you didn't have to kick me!"

"Jean."

"What did you call me?" Ray shouted.

"I didn't call you anything, you old fart! You called *me* Alberta," Jean said emphatically.

While Ray mumbled he hadn't called anyone Alberta, I glanced down at my fourteen tiles, arranged on little blue plastic "bleachers" and scanned the numbers. The quicker I learned the game, the quicker I could make my escape. There were numerous upside down white tiles in the center of the table, the "pile", which looked more like a boneyard to me. My thoughts drifted back to the bones found on the hospital grounds. The remains of some poor soul. How did they get there? Perhaps they were buried by their family long ago. Maybe the hospital was built over a graveyard or burial ground. Or maybe it was murder.

Ray took a piece of paper out of his pants pocket and crumpled it theatrically, before throwing it in the middle of the table. I looked up at him.

"That's my bucket list," he claimed. "Come on! We don't have that much time left!"

"Sorry," I mumbled sheepishly. I studied my fourteen tiles like I knew what I was doing. "How do you say the name of the game again?" I asked.

"Rummikub," Irene answered. "Like 'rummy' and 'cube'."

"Well," I said, brightening. "I should be pretty good at this game. I love me some Cruzan rum and I drive a Cube."

Jean chuckled, to make me feel better. "I'm assuming a Cube is some fancy, smancy sports car," Ray said.

"Yeah, something like that."

"I used to have a crotch rocket," Ray bragged.

"And now you ride in the rec center van," Irene countered, silencing him.

The game continued and I learned each player had to start the game with three tiles that added up to at least thirty, either with the same number but different colors or a sequence of numbers of different colors. Since the numbers ranged from one to thirteen with four color schemes, it wasn't easy to start. I couldn't lay down any tiles my first two turns and had to draw from the pile.

"Come on Daniel, you mean you don't have any sets that add up to thirty? Why, even the age of my first three girlfriends added up to thirty." Ray gave his head a haughty shake.

"Oh, you're such a ladies' man, Ray," Irene cooed. She turned to me. "He can hardly walk down the street without being swarmed by his harem."

"Shoot," Jean added. "He can hardly walk down the street anyway, what with his gout." And both old ladies cackled and gave each other a high five.

I laughed along with them and when I looked back at my tiles, low and behold, there were three different colored "elevens" I had missed. I laid down my group of three tiles triumphantly to the cheers of the others.

"What about you, Daniel?" Irene asked, while she placed four tiles on the table. "You're a hottie. You have a special lady?"

"Yes—well, at least I think so."

"Ah, women," Ray said. "Women will never be as successful as men because they have no wives to advise them." Ray glanced at each of us and smiled. "Dick Van Dyke said that."

"Hmph!" Jean cried. Then it was her turn to smack the table and cause the group (and game tiles) to jump. "I call bullshit. Mr. Van Dyke's quote is outdated. Women can marry each other now. I imagine in the next generation we shall rule the world." Another high five from Irene. Three women around the room applauded.

"Well, you'll still need spermatozoa in order to procreate," Ray added snippily.

"Who knows," I said, wanting to add to the conversation. "By then, science may have some amazing developments in that arena. Probably discovered by female scientists." I winked at Irene and Jean.

"Whose side are you on?" Ray grumbled, giving me the evil eye.

"You gonna talk or play?" Jean asked Ray. Then she turned to me. "So…tell us about this I-Think-So woman."

I don't know why, but I laid all my cards on the table (instead of my tiles). I told them everything; how I met Jaclyn (minus the exact location of my jellyfish sting), to the wonderful times we had shared (minus the sex with Cool Whip and anchovies), to our last couple of tense exchanges. I even told them about Annie, my fiancée who had died on the operating table in West Virginia. It actually felt good to lay it all out for my three attentive senior psychoanalysts.

Irene placed her hand on top of mine. "You know, Daniel, a relationship is like an oyster. When the heat is on, either it opens up and displays its velvety lining and possible riches, or it remains closed and you have to throw it out with the trash."

Jean took up the pep-talk from there. "There is always some madness in love," she said. "You just hope it's not the full-blown psychosis, rip-off-your-gonads kind of love."

Their words made me feel better (and for some reason, a little violated).

"Ah hell," Ray said. "Maybe you just need a break from each other. If she comes back and still offers her velvety lining, then it's for real."

They were the three wisest beings I had ever met. Three angels fallen down to earth; perhaps Zeus, Hestia and Hera come down from Mount Olympus. Irene ripped off a long, loud burp. Or, perhaps three octogenarians with the usual array of health issues.

The game was moving at a faster pace now. Tiles were being thrown down quicker than a brick mason with a new trowel.

"Rummikub is like life," Irene said, just as Ray stole one of my tiles to add to three he was laying down (he called this a "meld"). "You have groups, you have sets. Someone can swoop in and steal from you. Life, as in the game, can take any number of twists and turns. Through all the changing circumstances, we learn to expect the unexpected and make the most from what we have." She looked me in the eye. "You have another quandary you would like to discuss." It wasn't a question.

"Wha-what?" I stammered. Then I proceeded to tell them about working as a hospital pharmacist in West Virginia, escaping to Oak Island after Annie's death, my stint as Rx-Dick in the housekeeping department at the hospital, ending with my recent job offer.

"Is that it?" Jean asked.

"Well," I answered. "I worked at Weiner King when I was in high school."

"No," Jean said. "I mean, is that the quandary?"

I nodded.

Irene placed down three of her remaining four tiles. "Are you qualified?"

"I guess," I said, eying my remaining nine tiles and drawing from the pile.

"Taking a new job is like taking a dump with hemorrhoids," Ray said. "It may hurt at first, but it all comes out okay in the end."

"Wow!" Irene was looking at Ray disgustedly. "You can really be appalling at times."

"But foretelling," I said, scratching my chin. How much could it hurt to take the job? I certainly could use the money and it could only help my relationship with Jaclyn. Rudderless indeed. "I'll do it!" I cried.

"Do what?" asked a new voice over my shoulder.

I turned just as Irene placed down her last tile, winning the game. "Rummikub," she called happily. She clapped her hands as Jean produced a spiral notebook to write down scores, date and time, and I think wind direction and temperature.

"You lose," the woman behind me in a wheelchair said, surveying the table.

I looked around at my three new friends. "No, I win," I said, smiling.

Before leaving, I shook Ray's hand and kissed the hands of the ladies. "You have been more help than you will ever know—you guys are kind of like The Lone Gunmen from *The X-Files*."

Ray shook his head, frowning. "I don't know who that is," said Irene.

"Three guys who helped Mulder and Scully solve cases," I added.

"Still don't know who it is," Irene said. Ray shook his head again.

Jean looked bemused, winking at me. "We aren't *that* nerdy, are we?"

I laughed. "Okay, you're Dick Van Dyke, Mary Tyler Moore and…Rhoda." They all smiled, nodding.

Turning and waving as I approached the front glass doors, I heard Ray say, "If you need any more guidance, we are always here."

I reached the front walk, looking back as the glass doors shut. The bright sunlight glinted off the glass, but I could still make out the

Rummikub gaming table. It may have been a trick of the light, but all four chairs appeared empty.

I eased the Cube into the driveway, coasting to the end of the dirt drive and up to the edge of the concrete which began under my stilt house. It had become a game to see how close I could get without the bumper going over. If only they had competitions for parking, beach community division, I would be champion. I would prefer that to Rummikub. At least I wouldn't need anyone feeding me the rules every time I played.

I jumped out of the Cube to gauge my success. Damn near perfect! He drives, he coasts, he scores!

Checking my watch, I started toward the stairs, deciding I would go out for food in a little while, before the evening sun turned the Cube into a fire pit. But walking up the front steps, the last two days caught up with me and I almost had to reach down and pull my leg up the last step. I put my hands in the small of my back and leaned back, cracking my spine. I ambled toward the front door, pulling out my key.

Thunk!

I froze. It couldn't be.

Thunk! Thunk!

I turned slowly, staring into the pine tree. A fat gray squirrel stared back defiantly. No, not *a* fat gray squirrel but *the* fat gray squirrel. It taunted me with a pine cone, eating and stripping the scales like an ear of corn. Once stripped clean, the squirrel held out the husk to me, like it was presenting me an Oscar statuette. Then—

Thunk!

Dropped right down on the top of the Cube. The diabolical squirrel never missed! How in the world did the annoying little rodent find its way back from the canal where I released it?

I growled. That was a pine cone that would live in infamy—my Cube suddenly and deliberately attacked. This—means—war.

I yawned. But first I needed sleep. I stumbled to the door, unlocking it.

Blood. Blood everywhere. I groaned. I had told myself I would clean it up when I returned from the rec center. Damn! I pledged once again to scrub the house down…right after a catnap.

Cats? Uh-oh, no greeting committee as I entered. They had been left in the house, so nap on hold until I could track them down. At the direction of the vet, Fairbanks was to remain inside for two days, a task as easy as caging the wind. I searched the great room and kitchen; a slight motion near the top of the kitchen cabinets caught my eye. A black, disappearing tail was all I saw until two yellow eyes arose over the top of the cabinet, floating, defying gravity.

"Been licking any more toothbrushes?" I asked the calico, wondering if the orange Fairbanks was up there as well.

I grabbed a Fat Tire from the frig, aligned the bottle cap with the edge of the counter and carefully popped the top. Beer sprayed onto the kitchen floor, mixing with the blood. My momma would be so proud. Boy, did the beer taste good though. I hadn't worked out like I had planned to *earn* the Fat Tire (I don't think lifting tiles in Rummikub counted), but it had been a hell of a last two days. Another drink. Ah! It wasn't the beer that made Milwaukee famous, but it was the beer that made an O'Dwyer very happy.

I briefly thought of removing my shirt as I turned down the hallway toward my dark bedroom, instead collapsing on the bed fully clothed and passing out.

The last ring of the phone awakened me from my nightmare. I had been trapped; no matter which way I ran it had been a dead end. Sprinting through the motherboard, tripping over the CPU, skinning my shin on the hard drive, ramming into the (you guessed it) RAM. I screamed, but no one could hear me (the sound card had been disconnected). There was no way out.

Repositioning, I felt a lump of warmth near my feet. Fairbanks, I thought, as I began the gentle glide back to slumber. The dream this time was warm, safe, passionate. Jaclyn. A fire on the beach at night. Smooth skin. Sinking down into the sand, shedding our clothes, grasping at each other in unbridled passion. I reached out to pull her closer and—

A scream and a screech filled the air. Apparently, the screech was Fairbanks who may or may not have hit the ceiling when he was surprised by the sound. The scream belonged to...

"What the hell, you perv!" Willie cried.

I was wide awake now. I jumped off the bed, switched on the light and turned to confront him. Willie was stretched out on a piece of plastic on the far side of the bed, an unfamiliar pillow under his head. He had on a yellow Jethro Tull "Too Old to Rock n' Roll: Too Young to Die" t-shirt with Ian Anderson giving the forearm jerk. I couldn't stop my eyes from going lower. Thank goodness! Below the waist, Willie was wearing black boxer shorts adorned with large, yellow rubber ducks.

"Me perv? You perv!" I shouted back at him. "What are you doing in my bed?"

Willie tried to sit up on the edge of the bed, but the plastic sheet came with him, stuck to his bare legs and arms. He crinkled as he moved.

"Oh man, c'mon. Your guest room is a dusty mess," he said, as if that explained it all. "In fact, I had to take your pitchfork and toss all the clothes and junk in *your* bedroom into the closet before I could even relax in here."

He gave a disdainful look to my bedspread. "And I wasn't about to lay on that…it's hard to tell what is on it."

I looked down at my decorated maroon bedspread. "Those are palm trees for your information. And I just washed it," I lied.

"Cold or hot water?" he asked.

"What the hell does it matter? This is *my* bed in *my* house!" I shouted, almost to the point of jumping up and down. "Why aren't you sleeping in the *Silent Cow*?" I managed to get out through clenched teeth.

He slumped and kind of withered (and crinkled). "I tried," he said softly. "The ghost pirates won't let me sleep." He jumped up and stalked across the room, the plastic sheeting billowing behind him like a cape. "Drink coasters and my grandmother's doilies were spinning in the air, like a haunted mobile. I couldn't take it anymore." He gave me a pained look. "I brought my own pillow," he said weakly.

I noticed the dark circles under his eyes, could see his bruised forearm where the blood was drawn. I should have empathy for my friend. He's had a rough few days.

"Someone needs to clean up all the blood on the floor," he said.

With some people, no matter how hard you try, it is difficult to find compassion.

"Speaking of blood, did you get your lab test results—"

"I don't want to talk about it," he said quickly, cutting me off. He twirled away in his rubber ducky boxers, the plastic cape flowing behind him (He squeaks, he whines—he's Rubber Ducky Man!)

"Okay, lay back down. I've got some leftover golden tilefish to fix for me and the furballs if you want some, and then I'm going to play Cinderella and scrub the floors. And tomorrow, dear friend, you can make yourself useful and wash the dishes." (As if—not gonna hold my breath for that one.)

Willie jumped, doing a half twist before landing on my bed. He began wiggling his way down in my mattress, the plastic wrapping around him like a cocoon. He looked like a plastic duck burrito.

I pointed to his boxer shorts. "Where'd you get the rubber ducks?"

"Ginger," he answered. Ginger was the large, friendly bartender at the Oarhouse Lounge who made sure Willie never ran out of organic beer and always had his stainless-steel stool.

"Didn't know you two were still an item."

"We have an understanding," he said. "Satisfaction of carnal urges is basic human instinct."

"So, you're on call for each other?"

"Exactly."

"Why rubber ducks?"

Willie smiled. "She calls me her wittle duckie wuckie."

9 - WHAT'S IT ALL ABOUT, ALGAE?

My eyes opened wide and I stared around the dark room, not recognizing it. *Beep, beep, beep.* What was that noise? Smoke alarm? I rolled to my right on the bed and looked at the clock. 5 a.m.! *Beep, beep, beep.* The noise was coming from the clock! An alarm? Here now, what for? Suddenly it came back to me. Had I really called Scott on his cell phone last night and accepted the job? Way to go, dweeb. I banged off the alarm. Next, I heard Willie sawing logs across the hall in my bedroom. Since he had been curled up like a bug in a plastic rug, I had left him and moved to the guest room. I threw back the sheets, got up and walked to the window, using my fingers to pry open the blinds. I sneezed. Willie was right, the room was quite dusty. I stared at the darkness through the forced openings between the slats of the blind. There was an eerie quietness to the world. Was 5 a.m. really considered daytime? Who made these stupid rules? The world is a much nicer, happier place at 8 a.m. when the sun has risen and everyone has had their first cup of coffee.

In the bathroom mirror, while brushing my teeth, I noticed my red and swollen knuckles. My back and knees hurt; was I working in housekeeping again? And I had only managed to clean half of Willie's blood from the floors, walls (and even ceiling). I sneezed, blowing toothpaste in a tie-dye circular pattern on the mirror.

After tiptoeing through my own bedroom to retrieve work (*arg!*) clothes from my closet (page twenty-three of the Employee Handbook—no flip-flops), Pickford descended from the top of the kitchen cabinets. Fairbanks joined her at the front door as I prepared to leave. Ah, domesticated bliss. Fairbanks' eye looked much better and after he passed a quick eye test ("Okay Fairbanks, how many fingers am I holding up?"), I let him back outside. But not before making him promise he would play nice and get along with Francis.

The cats nearly tripped me going down the front steps, but I was entranced by the special coastal glow delivered by the dawn. Orange, yellow, pink, vivid blue—spectacular. God's way of putting a positive spin on the day and urging us to make the most of it. Almost made getting up this early worth it—almost. I kicked a few plucked pine cones out of my path as I made my way to the Cube. I got behind the wheel and sat, reflecting on going back to work at the hospital. Truth be told, I had been more excited to go to work in housekeeping than to be employed sitting in front of a computer all day.

Thunk!

Are you kidding me? Right on the hood! What time do squirrels get up in the morning? I turned the key and backed quickly out of the driveway. On the street, as I put the Cube into drive, I rolled down my window and shook my fist to the heavens (or at least the upper limbs).

In spite of God's beseeching with the fantastic sunrise, I found myself souring as I drove along Oak Island Drive. A quick left into the Flying Pig Coffeehouse for a Green Swamp Latte would take care of that problem. The Flying Pig is home base for the slightly older, local crowd. The early birds gather for jigsaw puzzles, discussions of daily news (fake or otherwise), and lighthearted banter. The same gray-haired, local smart aleck as last time, cheered when I told the gang I had another job. In retaliation, I picked up a puzzle piece from the floor, surveyed the half-finished picture, and placed the piece into his jigsaw puzzle with a distinct pop. The crowd gave a small, but audible gasp.

"Old Andy has been looking for that piece for twenty minutes!" a bald man announced as he clapped his hands.

"Guess you can't say you worked it all by yourself now," laughed a white-bearded man, his long, thin white hair on his head pulled back into a pony tail.

"Sorry, Andy," I said, feeling suddenly bad. "It was on the floor."

"Hey Andy," someone shouted from the back. "It's just like all the missing pieces in NC State's offensive line!" Laughter. "Even old Ron there…" The bearded, pony-tailed man perked up. "Could run through their line and tackle the quarterback!"

Andy looked at me. "It's okay. I can take it as good as I can give it. We're all friends." He shook my hand, then turned to the man in the back. "NC State? You bonehead! I'm a Clemson man. Remember the national championship? The orange and purple, baby! Besides, I can still kick all your asses on the golf course!"

I left The Flying Pig feeling better, to the sound of raised voices, laughter and verbal jousting. Made me miss Willie just a little bit. Okay, a smidgeon.

I pulled into the "Employees Only" parking lot behind Boiling Grove Community Hospital. I used a straw to suck up a big mouthful of whipped cream from the top of my Green Swamp Latte. A bad time for another sneeze. I looked at the speckled passenger seat and door—another mess I would have to clean. On the positive side, Willie wouldn't want to ride in the Cube with me (unless he had another sheet of plastic handy).

Before approaching the back entrance and once again diving into the labor pool, I meandered around to the construction site. Surrounding the perimeter was bright yellow, plastic caution tape, warning in bold, capital black letters, "SHERIFF'S LINE DO NOT CROSS". All the heavy equipment had disappeared. I could just see the middle of the pit which was deeper than yesterday, dirt piled on the sides. There was no one around.

I turned to go and ran right into Carl.

"Neep-oomph!"

"Sorry Carl," I said. "It's so nice running into you again. Anybody tell you that you are light on your giant feet?"

He looked excited, like he wanted to tell me something, but he held back.

"They must have shut down the site after they found that poor soul's bones," I said.

"It wasn't just one set of bones," Carl said excitedly. I had never seen him like this. He seemed almost...normal. "There were ten skeletons—"

"Ten!"

"Yes! And from the looks of them, they could be several decades old!"

Carl's eyes were intensely bright, his expression one of discovery. I had seen that look on many a physician's face when they were chasing the mystery illness. Although the odds (and Cincinnaticus Pearson, MD) were stacked against him, maybe Carl would make a doctor yet.

"After you left, the police came to investigate. I had to go back in the hospital and finish my shift, but when I came back out the Medical Examiner was on the scene." Carl pointed to a large dirt pile. "I watched from behind that."

He had a dreamy, far-off look, like he was reliving the experience and enjoying every moment.

"Later, at dusk, the State Archeologist arrived. I overheard them talking; the Medical Examiner called it an Indian burial ground. The guys from Maintenance set up big lights so the team could keep working. It was sometime after midnight when they brought the first set of bones out. They set them on a tarp and when they went back in the pit, I sneaked over and examined them."

"Wow! That must have been something."

"It was!" Carl starting talking faster, becoming more animated with every word. "I got to see every skeleton they removed. Based on the size of the bones and the skulls, I don't think they were adults and there was something strange about the skulls—"

"Wait a minute," I interrupted. "You were there when they removed all ten of them?"

"Yes," he said, his speech slowing. "I was there all night. They didn't finish until just before dawn."

I looked at Carl closely. With just a hint of dark circles under his eyes, he looked no worse for wear. "You sure that was wise? No sleep and spend the day with Dr. P?"

He smiled sheepishly. "I couldn't help it. If you hadn't tricked me that day when they were uncovered, I never would have seen the bones."

"I don't know if tricked is the right word."

He grinned. "I didn't mean it in a bad way. I tend not to venture out of my comfort zone."

"Is that your mom's words or a therapist's?" I asked.

His voice dropped to a whisper. "Therapist…I've never told anyone that before."

I gently placed my hand on his shoulder; he pulled away involuntarily. Placing my hand back on his shoulder, I said, "First, I won't tell anyone. Second, there's nothing to be ashamed of. Lots of people go to therapists these days. I've never been, but a lot of people tell me I need it."

He gazed longingly into the pit. "So," I said. "Did you talk to the ME, get his card? It's always good to make contacts?"

"No," he said shyly. "I was afraid to talk to him. He was shouting and storming around the site, like he was mad at everyone because bones were found. I stayed hidden in the shadows."

We stood quietly for a moment, staring into the pit. I pondered the enormous question of life and death, eventually shaking my head to clear it.

"Do they think there's any more bones in the pit?" I finally asked.

"They seemed to think that was all of them, but I heard the State Archeologist say he was coming back with a crew today to make sure. They'll bring their tables and sifters. I can't wait to see that!"

"Indian burial ground, huh?" I asked.

"Well, that's what the Medical Examiner kept saying over and over. The State Archeologist wasn't convinced." Carl abruptly stopped speaking. He took one step closer as his eyes darted in all directions. He finally looked me in the eye. "I'm not either," he said quickly, looking away at the last minute.

Carl hung his head and started walking off slowly. I clutched the back of the lab coat as he passed, stopping him in his tracks.

"I think maybe you found your niche, Carl. Pathologist, medical examiner, there's a whole array of fields surrounding those."

He raised his head, his face beaming like he had just won the lottery. "You really think so? But don't you have to be really, really smart for stuff like that?"

"What you need to be is really, really good at spotting clues," I answered. "Solving medical mysteries, being extremely interested in what you are doing. And you seem very interested in this discovery."

"Who wouldn't be intrigued? Ten people. Ten people buried, for whatever reason, right here. Maybe there are ten more over there." He pointed across the parking lot. "How could anyone not wonder who they were or how they got here?"

I couldn't help but smile at Carl's enthusiasm. "Well put. Now, why don't you think it's an Indian burial ground?" I asked.

"Well, my favorite part of medical school on Haiti was the field trips. Cadavers were in short supply on the island, so we often went to burial grounds."

I thought of the last Bela Lugosi film I had watched with Glenn, an early one set on Haiti, *White Zombie*. I gulped. "Were there any zombies?"

Carl looked at me like I'd lost my mind. "No," he answered.

Thank goodness! I don't know if I could handle ghost pirates *and* zombies in the same adventure.

"Go on," I urged.

"Graves in burial grounds, at least on Haiti, had some semblance of order. Graves were spaced evenly apart. And there were always personal items, no matter how trite, buried with them."

"And down there?" I asked, pointing to the pit.

"Chaos. Skeletons stacked on top of others every which way. Nothing there except the bones. I heard the State Archeologist wondering why there were no clothing remnants. And the skulls—"

A low rumble began at the other end of the parking lot, erupting into a scream once the sound waves hit. "CARL!"

Carl's Marty Feldman eyes bugged out. The sound had come from none other than Cincinnaticus Pearson, MD, his massive frame looming, even at sixty yards.

"It's okay, Carl. Let me handle this—" By the time I turned back to Carl, he was gone. He had the funniest running gait I had ever seen. As I watched him beat a path toward a side hospital door (the side opposite his preceptor/tormentor), it reminded me of a cross between an orangutan and a hippopotamus.

I boldly walked up to Cincinnaticus Pearson, MD, displaying my pearly whites. "Dr. P, how's it hanging?"

"Where's that resident of mine?" he screamed.

"Now Dr. P, if you want Carl to turn on, tune in and *not* drop out, you are going to have to tone it down a bit."

He frowned, as if noticing me for the first time. "What on earth are you talking about?" His countenance softened as he recognized me. "You're that guy. Are you going to help with the computers?"

"It will be my pleasure to serve," I said, clicking my heels together. "Daniel O'Dwyer, late of Environmental Services and newly hired Informatics Pharmacist, at your service."

"Bertha, my beloved," I said to Scott's secretary as I entered the Human Resources' office. She gave me a blank stare, which could only mean she loathed me. I put the back of my hand to my forehead, theatrically, acting like she had broken my heart a' la Rudolf Valentino in a classic, silent love scene. I mouthed the words, "Don't do this to us, Bertha. Don't push me away," pretending they were on title cards between scenes.

"How's Ebenezer?" I asked out loud, walking over to the aquarium on the bookshelf. I didn't spy the peacock mantis shrimp until it shot out of its hidey-hole and—*bam!* Ebenezer struck the glass right where I was peering in. I jumped back.

"I don't think Ebenezer likes me," I said.

"It may be a deadly sea creature," Bertha stated flatly. "But it can't be all bad then."

Scott entered the front door, stopping when he saw me. "Daniel! Oh, Daniel. I'm so glad to see you. You're the bomb dot com!" he exclaimed, straight-faced.

I exchanged a glance with Bertha; she gave me a shrug. "Scott," I said. "Let me give you a small piece of advice."

"Sure," he said, smiling.

"Don't ever say that again."

"What?"

"That bomb thing."

He looked hurt. "I'm just trying to be hip, to stay in tune with the times. I want to be able to communicate with the employees, speak their language."

I looked at him, pretending to mull it over. "I'm afraid I'm going to have to go with Nancy Reagan's famous drug slogan on this one and 'Just Say No'—don't ever say that again."

Before he could say something else "hip", I motioned toward the aquarium. "Ebenezer is particularly violent today." The multi-colored mantis shrimp disappeared back into its crevice.

Scott walked to the tank. "He must be hungry."

"What does he, er...it eat?"

"Oh, live fish, worms, crabs, shrimp—"

I glanced at Bertha. "Humorless secretaries," I offered.

"Unfunny pharmacists," she shot back.

I had my face near the front of the aquarium when Ebenezer shot forward—*bam!* I nearly leaped into Scott's arms.

"Um, Scott. That looks like a crack in your tank."

"Where?"

I pointed. "Right there, where Ebenezer just hit."

He moved closer. "Nonsense. That's just algae."

"In the words of Mark Twain," I said. "Denial ain't just a river in Egypt."

Scott moved his face closer to the glass. The peacock mantis shrimp swam lazily along, its rear legs propelling it through the water. "Beautiful. Just beautiful," he gushed.

"So was Lizzie Borden." I clapped him on the shoulder. "Let's do this, big guy. I wanna be employed."

He led me into his office where he presented me with a new employee badge. "We used your housekeeping picture," he explained.

"Daniel O'Dwyer, Information Services," I read. Thinking of TV cops, I flipped out my badge as I said my name. "Daniel O'Dwyer—Boiling Grove Community Hospital—Information Services. Hold it right there!" I turned and pointed my cocked finger-gun at the photograph of the hospital board of directors. "Information Services. O'Dwyer...Daniel O'Dwyer." I looked closely at my photograph on the badge and grimaced. "I've seen better mug shots. Worse than Nick Nolte's, and that's pretty bad."

Scott had sat down at his desk. "I'm sorry. Nick who?" When I didn't answer, he banged some keys on his computer. "Now, we just need a few tidbits of information and it's off to your new department. Has anything changed since your last employment here?"

"Well..." I said, thinking. "I started shaving with three blades instead of two, my mom got a Jitterbug and I have been double-yodeled by an Amazon hardhat woman."

God love Scott. He doesn't have much of a sense of humor, but he gave me a small smile and a faraway look.

"Back on Hawaii again?" I asked him. "In your giant grass skirt, sipping a Mai Tai?"

The smile widened. "If only," he said.

"Do you still have your coconut bra?" I asked. It was a little gift I had given him at Christmastime after my housekeeping gig.

He pointed to the back of his office door, where the coconut bra hung over a hook.

"In case of emergencies?" I asked.

He smiled and nodded. "I've kind of missed you around here, Daniel. It's been boring."

Well, I'll be! That's the nicest thing any human resources representative has ever said to me. I pretended to wipe a tear from my eye. "You're all right, Scott. I don't care what Mr. Ramrod says."

With that he sat bolt upright in his chair (yes, ramrod straight). Ralph Ramrod was the CEO. I'd never met him, but I had been bored to tears by the videos he made for employees, discussing everything from lunch punches to the Ebola virus. ("The Ebola virus is, um, some bad bacteria, um, sorry, not bacteria but a virus that can be deadly. It is best to avoid it if at all possible.")

"I'm joking, Scott."

"I knew that," he said, wiping the sweat from his brow. "Did you say double-yodeled by an Amazon hardhat woman?"

"Yes. Sparkle. And before you ask, she is *not* a pole dancer."

He looked back at his computer screen. "No, no, no. I mean has any of your information changed. Address, phone number, emergency contact?" Frowning, he turned back to me. "Her name is really Sparkle?"

"None of my information has changed and Sparkle was her Name-O."

"Okay, very well," he said, continuing to scan the computer screen. "It looks like everything is in order. Wait a minute—"

"What?" I asked. "What did you find? Please tell me I'm 4-F and send me home. I've got flat feet, a plugged puncta and, due to loud rock n' roll music according to my mother, I can't hear well out of my left ear."

Scott looked up, frowning. "We don't have a mobile phone number for you."

"What?" I said loudly, cupping my left ear. "That's my trick ear, Scott. What'd you say?"

"We need your cell phone number," he shouted.

"I kicked the habit," I answered.

"What do you mean?"

I shrugged. "I don't have one any more. In fact, I haven't had one since I've lived on the island. I realize it makes me very un-hip."

"Oh my, my, my." He seemed to being fretting.

"It's okay, Scott. It's a personal choice."

"No, you don't understand. The members of your team need to be able to contact you at a moment's notice. Especially Dr. Pearson."

"WHAT?"

"We're heading into the home stretch. There isn't much time to get everything built, tested and the bugs worked out."

"Dr. who?"

"Daniel, there are times when I don't know whether to take you serious or not. Are you referring to the British science fiction show in a humorous way?"

"No!" I cried. "You said Dr. Pearson. What in the world does he have to do with the new computer build?"

"He's the physician in charge of testing."

I slapped my hand to my forehead. "What idiot..." I stopped when I saw the hurt look on Scott's face. I took a deep breath. "Isn't there a younger, more computer savvy physician on the team as well?" I asked hopefully.

Scott wasn't listening to my whining. He was desperately searching in his top desk drawer, throwing out boxes of pens, huggies, pocket umbrellas, drink coasters and badge holders, all emblazoned with the BGCH logo.

'No thanks, Scott. I don't need any more BGCH swag," I said.

Ignoring me, he opened the bottom drawer and continued searching.

"Eureka," he cried, pulling out a small black, plastic square.

"Oh no," I said, backing away. I hadn't seen one of those since my days in West Virginia and there was no way in hell I was wearing one again.

"Now, I just have to find the number," Scott said.

"Nuh-uh, no way, no how," I stated flatly.

I hadn't seen Scott look that serious since the drug ring was running rampant in the hospital. "I'm sorry," he said. "It's a condition of the job. They must be able to reach you and without a cell phone..."

I thought of telling him to throw it out the window, to drop it in the aquarium and let the peacock mantis shrimp pulverize it; tell him to stick it between pages seventeen and eighteen of the Human Resources Handbook where the radiance of the sun has lost its luster.

Jaclyn's face floated before me: "*You are rudderless; you are infantile. You are rudderless, you are infantile.*"

"Fine!" I shouted. "Give me the beeper!"

Elbow on the table, left index finger on my forehead, I looked through the V's of my remaining fingers, spying a letter opener on a nearby desk. Could I reach it? I imagined lunging for it and ramming it in my right eye, putting me out of my misery.

The representative from the computer company in the front of the room described, in rich detail, the genesis of the company with the aid of three PowerPoint slides. It seems founder, Frederick Soit was ahead of his time, a true entrepreneur, a savant, a saint. I studied his picture on the slide, his large, crooked eyes and his goofy smile. Boy, it's a big old goofy world.

Goofy. My mind wandered; did Jaclyn find me goofy as well as infantile? Was the cartoon character Goofy ever involved with a woman or was he too smart? I remember Goofy loved his car, Dolores ("I'm a-gonna wash Dolores. She's a-gonna look ga-lorious.") but I don't remember a female Goof. But he did have a son Max later in his celluloid life so he must have copulated, um, conjugated...er, been amorously animated with a drawing of the opposite sex. (Perhaps they only did it once; Goofy's "Yaaaaaaa-hoo-

hoo-hoo-hooey!" would wake the whole neighborhood.)

The representative must have said something funny because the woman next to me laughed. No, wait. She's checking her phone under the table and watching a video of a bulldog in a tutu surfing. The things I miss out on.

Just my luck that my first day, check that, my first two hours were spent in a high-level meeting with a representative from the new computer system vendor, Medi-Soit. I hadn't even had the chance to meet any of the other "IT Team" members before the meeting started.

The representative had moved on to the history of Medi-Soit software. Why we cared about the earlier versions, I had no earthly idea. This was excruciating. I couldn't roll my eyes back in my head, however, and pretend to lose consciousness because I was the "new guy"; everyone was staring at me.

I looked at the computer in front of me. We were in the testing lab but apparently, we would be doing no testing today. Why did Scott say there wasn't much time left, the project was in the home stretch? Seemed like it was just getting underway. Computer systems in hospitals are complex and tied together with intricate interfaces; changeovers in the medical world usually take at least nine months to a year of extensive work to complete.

I sighed and started pushing the computer mouse around the table in front of me. As the representative droned on about the advantages of Medi-Soit over the competition, I wondered how someone had come up with the name "mouse" for this particular hardware. I guess it kind of looks like a mouse. I moved it around the tabletop, squeaking a little. A barcode scanner, in a base sat on the left side of the computer screen. I removed the scanner and as I started "chasing" the mouse with it, the mouse became Jerry and the scanner Tom. "You will never catch me, pussy gato," I said as I ran the mouse Jerry over the top of the computer screen. Scanner Jerry tried to climb the screen, but of course fell off and onto his flat head. "Oomph!"

I stopped because the representative's monotone had ceased. Everyone was looking at me (including the team members who had been checking their phones beneath the table).

"Hi, my name's Daniel," I said. "I'm new."

The representative cleared his throat. "I see. And what is your background, Daniel?"

"Pharmacist and then housekeeping." There were snickers around the room as the representative was momentarily silenced.

"Well...um, that ought to come in handy with this system. Did you have a question, Daniel?"

I started to ask him if he thought Tom and Jerry were friends or enemies, a burning question that had plagued me throughout my life. Instead I asked, "What is the timeline for implementation? Human

Resources told me we were in the home stretch when they hired me."

"As a matter of fact," the representative replied self-importantly. "That is my next topic." He clicked to the next PowerPoint slide.

I gasped. My eyes had immediately gone to the end of the graphic line. Three months!

"Is there a problem?" The man was clearly getting annoyed with the sounds escaping my person.

I looked around the room, hoping another member of my team would speak up. All were silent, watching me. Rah-rah team.

"First, the complete timeline is for a five-month period, which seems short in my experience—"

"Your experience in housekeeping," the man commented snidely.

I smiled at him. "Actually, that was some of the hardest work I've ever done. My hat's off to that department. Underpaid and underappreciated. But my computer experience in a hospital was in pharmacy. I was involved with the set-up of two systems."

I looked back at the timeline. "And according to your timeline, we are already two months into the project."

"Yes. We are on schedule." He beamed proudly, as if he were about to deliver a bouncing baby boy or girl.

"With three months to go, we should be testing the crap out of the system," I blurted. "Working out the bugs!"

"We are on schedule," he repeated firmly. "In fact, we are right here," he said, using a pointer to indicate a place on the timeline labeled "Change Beaters".

I glanced helplessly at a man across the aisle from me. He shrugged, displayed the inside of his wrist and pulled an imaginary razor blade across it.

Before the representative changed to the next PowerPoint slide, I looked to the end of the timeline quickly. Testing was only marked one month out from go-live. Incredible!

A huge yellow food carton with a red cap jumped out on the next slide. It looked like an Egg Beaters' carton I had seen in the refrigerated section at Food Lion. Except this one had a silly face drawn on it. The carton was labeled "Change Beaters" in red lettering.

"The phase we are about to enter is the *fun* phase!" the representative exclaimed.

I thought back to the two computer system implementations I had survived. I recalled the "fear of the unknown" phase, the "hard work and long hours" phase, and finally the "screaming expletive" phase. Nope, don't remember any fun phase.

The representative changed to the next slide; on it were several frowning hospital employees. "Healthcare workers, in general, do not like change," he said mechanically.

"Especially nurses!" one woman with R.N. on her badge shouted. Laughter followed.

"So, anything we can do to allay that fear," the representative continued, louder. "The better chance there is of success."

"I volunteer to be a Change Beater," the man with the imaginary slit wrists called out. "Do I get a bat? A paddle? Or maybe a blackjack?"

The room was coming alive. Finally, the attention had been diverted away from me.

A grim looking, older woman stood in the front of the room and glared. She snapped her fingers and pointed at each side of the room. The room became immediately quiet.

"Thank you, Ms. Pickles," the representative said. Pickles? I didn't have to wonder if she was of the sweet variety or one of those garlicky, nasty Kosher dills with bumps and warts.

The representative changed to the next slide which showed the same workers from the previous slide, except they were smiling, bass drums strapped to their body and holding large, felt bass drum mallets. The bold words on the screen proclaimed, "Change Beaters (beating the drum for change)".

Ms. Pickles clapped exuberantly. A smattering of weak applause followed from a few other employees (obviously not wanting to get on the bad side of Pickles).

"Thank you!" the representative cawed. "I was on the focus group that developed the program. We think it's paramount to have change discussions in every department. For that reason, we will ask for each department in the hospital to provide one employee to be a Change Beater. And..."

He moved across the room to a table with two large cardboard boxes on top, and sticking his hand in one, he pulled out a small cellophane package. Removing the wrapper, he held up the small, toy bass drum proudly. "Medi-Soit" was printed on the head of the drum. "Each Change Beater will get their own drum to beat."

Hmm. Talk about marching to the beat of a different drummer.

Ms. Pickles took the stage. "We'll also have weekly meetings with posters and handouts for the Change Beater to take back and educate his or her department."

"This will be great," the representative added, enthusiastically.

Scanning the disgruntled faces of my team, I slowly raised my hand.

"Yes, Daniel," the representative said.

"I'm going out on a limb here. But shouldn't we use the manpower and the time for testing instead?"

Ms. Pickles huffed and pulled a paper out of her pocket. She unfolded it

roughly and scanned it with her finger, stopping near the bottom. "Mr.—
O'Dwyer. I would like to see you in my office at the end of the meeting."

I felt like I was back in elementary school again, when the group went,
"Ooooooooooo."

Jaclyn looked exhausted, but still managed to smile. "That didn't take long,"
she said. I had just finished telling her about being called into the Pickle
"jar" and being put in my place.

"I guess by now you know she runs the Information Services
department with an iron fist," Jaclyn said. "You should try to avoid her."

I gave her a thumbs up. Reminded of an old Arlo Guthrie folk song I
heard on Deep Tracks last week, I sang (without thinking), "I don't want a
pickle, just want to ride on my motorsickle."

I waited for Jaclyn to sigh; when she didn't, I was ecstatic. It was
lunchtime and we were moving some food-like substances around on our
plates in the hospital cafeteria.

"I *am* happy you took the job, Daniel. I think it will be good for you."

I winced. "Good for us?"

She smiled wanly. "I think I just need to get away from the hospital for a
while."

"I can certainly identify with that," I said, realizing it might be a stupid
thing to say on my first day back.

"I leave for the conference day after tomorrow. It's in Boca Raton near
where my sister lives, so I'm going to spend some time with her afterward."
She spooned some green goop into her mouth. "It should be good
therapy."

I had orange goop on my plate. I'm sure it appeared somewhere on the
food pyramid (probably the basement).

"So, how long are you going to be gone?"

"I'm not sure. The conference is five days and I've never combined
vacation time with a conference. Regardless, it will be the longest time I've
been away from the hospital since I started."

I put my hand on top of hers. "You have a great time. I'll hold down the
fort while you're gone and I promise you the walls will still be standing
when you return."

She placed her other hand on top of mine, sending a small jolt to my
heart. "It may be okay. I just don't know." She followed this with a long
sigh.

What she said next rattled me.

"Life is not a Hallmark movie."

10 - LITTLE WILLIE, WILLIE WON'T GO HOME

I nodded my understanding, inwardly thinking, *What the hell is a Hallmark movie?* The only Hallmark I knew made Christmas ornaments. Was it a movie made with talking Christmas ornaments? Like those Lego movies they were making now?

Jaclyn removed her hands from mine and pointed at me. "But I better not hear about you catting around town while I'm gone!"

I raised my hand in pledge, just as a shadow fell over the table.

"Hey there, Eye Candy!"

Sparkle stood over us, wearing tight jeans and an even tighter top. It was a testament to the strength of the fabric, elastic and Lycra that we didn't have a sparkly explosion.

"How's it hanging, Eye Candy?" Sparkle didn't try to hide her enthusiasm and her voice carried throughout the cafeteria. Heads turned to look and smirk at the so-called "eye candy".

Jaclyn's mouth hung open as the uncomfortable silence surrounded us. Sparkle grinned; Jaclyn glared. I could think of several places I would rather be (including being sucked into a black hole 32 million light-years from Earth).

I coughed. "Jaclyn, this is Sparkle. She's the foreman on the construction team that's working in the parking lot. Sparkle, this is Jaclyn." Uncomfortable silence to the nth power. "Um, did you hear about the skeletons?"

Jaclyn, ignoring my last question, scanned Sparkle head to toe, saying, "That's a new kind of work uniform."

Sparkle laughed loudly. "We got another job going on, but with this one closed down temporarily, I'm off today." She held out her forearm where a

Band-Aid held down a cotton ball. "Decided to get my sports physical and lab work out of the way today. We gotta have one every year."

"You have to have a sports physical to work construction?" I asked, somewhat perplexed.

"Lord no," Sparkle answered, laughing loudly again. "Don't you think he's just the cutest little thing?" She directed her question to Jaclyn, but did not wait for an answer as she quickly pivoted to face me. "But I have to have a sports physical for the Roller Girls." Sparkle struck a pose, knees bent, arms squeezed to her sides.

Jaclyn mouthed the words "Roller Girls" to me with raised eyebrows.

"What's Roller Girls?" I asked.

Sparkle bent down to table level and flexed her arm, displaying a huge bicep. Suddenly she extended her arm out and forward, in a clothesline maneuver. "The Cape Fear Roller Girls! Roller derby—at its finest."

"Hey!" came a yell from across the cafeteria. A man stood and pointed toward us. "It *is* her!"

"Told ya so! Told ya so!" added a woman's voice. Four people from different sections started making their way to our table, bumping others and knocking chairs out of the way. All four wore employee badges. A door slammed, a mop dropped and we were surrounded by women in hairnets as well. All appeared star-struck.

"I'm your biggest fan!"

"Marry me, Sparkle!"

"Look, I have your number tattooed on my hand!"

Sparkle's comment from the pit suddenly made more sense. Hadn't she said something about a two-minute jam?

As cell phones took videos and pictures, Sparkle smiled and greeted each person like a long-lost friend. Her fans were excited. It was obvious she was a smash hit. They were babbling roller derby terms, comparing hand sizes, bicep sizes; one guy asked her to shove him. The crowd kept growing, although I had my suspicions some people had no clue who she was, instead drawn to the idea of a celebrity.

"You are the best fans ever! Cape Fear Roller Girls absolutely *love* you guys! Tell you what, head on outside by the picnic tables and I'll be there in a few minutes. We will talk and take pictures as long as you want."

When the crowd exited the cafeteria, Sparkle smiled and sighed. She turned and studied Jaclyn. "You want to try out? We need another redhead since Au-Burn Yo Ass left."

"Au-Burn Yo Ass?" Jaclyn asked, slowly.

"Sure, we all got roller derby names we go by. It's kind of like our secret life," Sparkle said.

"Did Au-Burn Yo Ass move away?" I asked.

"Not exactly," Sparkle answered. "She'll be back. Just not for three to five years. It seems her roller derby name was more than a nickname, kind of like a way of life. The Fire Marshal found her lighter at the scene."

Jaclyn and I nodded awkwardly. Sparkle stood over us, motionless, so I felt the need to ask, "Was she a blocker or a jammer?"

"A jammer? Oh hell no. Au-Burn Yo Ass was a middle of the pack blocker. She could throw a hell of a C-block." She flexed again. "I'm the jammer, Eye Candy!"

"What's your roller derby name? Sparkle Leigh?" I couldn't help asking. Jaclyn shot me a dirty look.

Sparkle smirked. "You mean go by my real name?" She turned and pulled the back of her shirt up, revealing a tattoo, right between the dimples above her buttocks, of a roller skate with a name over it. "Spar-Kill!" she shouted (emphasis on the second syllable). You could hear flatware and glassware hit the floor all around the cafeteria.

It is my considered opinion that the personalities of cats mirror the personalities of humans more than any other creature on earth. Some cats think they're badass and don't want to be touched (Fairbanks was laying by the electronic eye to the cable box, daring me to make him move), some cats think they're Queen Nefertiti (Pickford was stretched out on the top of the couch, lounging like she was floating down the Nile), some cats are effeminate named bullies ("Hello *Francis*...") and some cats, I thought while looking at my other houseguest, are just plain loco, bat-shit crazy.

"Willie," I said, thumbing through the Brunswick County phonebook. "We've got to find you a Catholic priest. Preferably a nautical one."

Willie didn't take the hint. He was seated on his stainless-steel stool, carefully spreading organic peanut butter (from my kitchen cabinet) on saltines (also mine) and monopolizing *my* television set. At least the Butte Creek Organic Pale Ale in his hand wasn't something I had purchased (unless it was available on Amazon—note to self: check my purchase history). He had just flipped from the hockey game I was watching and started surfing. The jump from channel to channel was mesmerizing (and a little nauseating). Two seconds and the visions were gone. It was a little like watching a roulette wheel.

"Round and round she goes. Where Willie stops, nobody knows."

Willie smiled, stopping on a channel I didn't know existed with a show I couldn't imagine anyone watching, let alone producing—HGTV's "Tiny House Hunters". I glared at him but he wasn't about to change the channel or budge from his stool (or my house).

The show hadn't started, so I had high hopes it was some kind of science fiction series about microscopic houses that travel through time and space, perhaps with evil aliens trapped inside, and the rough, adventurous bounty hunters paid to capture them. I should have known better.

Fade to quick transitions of pictures from one small house to another. Female voiceover: "Across the nation, people are going small—really small. Buying tiny houses. Some just a microscopic one hundred square feet. This tiny trend is picking up big…"

OMG! WTF! (In the vernacular of the times.)

"Allen S., from Austin, waited until his thirties to get married." (A blonde, pale, almost translucent man appeared on the screen, smiling mischievously.) "For years he was a single college graduate, bouncing around the eastern United States from condo to condo…West Virginia, Virginia, North Carolina. Until he met Gigi—" (A pretty, olive skinned woman appeared next to the would-be albino.) "He went from five-day skiing trips and flying to Vegas on a whim…to a wife, three kids, two dogs, a cat and a mother-in-law."

Allen and Gigi appeared on screen looking at a bathroom that wasn't much bigger than an outhouse. The man looked strangely excited; his wife horrified.

"Allen and Gigi had a child of their own, but now she's off to college. With all four kids out of the house…"

Gigi looks at Allen and says, "Where are we going to put everything?"

Allen turns to the camera, "I'm a minimalist."

Gigi looks at Allen as if he is less of a minimalist and more of a loon. Looking him in the face and then gazing downward, it's as if she has a strong desire to make a minimalist joke.

"Do you think they'll buy the tiny house?" Willie asked breathlessly.

I watched Gigi scowl as she went into the kitchen, or rather pantry with small sink and even smaller cooktop.

"Odds are more in the favor of a tongue lashing for Allen S.," I said.

Female voiceover: "Will Allen S. and Gigi find an empty nest that's big enough? Will they be able to find a tiny home that has it all?"

A Texas tourism commercial came on: "Everything's bigger and better in Texas!" (Not if Allen S. from Austin has his way.)

"What is HGTV?" I asked Willie. It was on an upper channel I never knew existed.

"Home and Garden Television."

"And you've watched this show before?"

"Sure. Reminds me of the *Silent Cow*."

I glanced over at him. "Speaking of the *Silent Cow*…"

He clammed up, turning away. I could see getting him out of my house was going to be harder than convincing a Jehovah's witness to accept blood products in a trauma situation.

Blood? "Willie," I said, remembering. "Tell me about your lab results from the hospital?"

He took a drink of Butte Creek Organic Pale Ale and looked at me sourly. "S'nothing."

"S'nothing? S'nothing? What are you, fifteen years old?" If Willie was saying "s'nothing", then it must be something. I thought of all the ways I could trick him, coax him into telling me. Bribe him. In the end, I settled for intense empathy. "Damn it, Willie!" I yelled. "I'm your friend. If you can't tell me, who can you tell?"

Willie pulled himself off his stool and began to aimlessly walk around the room. He stopped in front of the art on the walls, leveling each frame and checking for dust (okay, you got me—they aren't "art" per se, but Bela Lugosi movie posters). He turned and studied me, his eyes tearing. "Friend?" he almost whispered. "Sometimes I think you just tolerate me."

"Ha!" I laughed, but couldn't shake the mental picture of a hammer hitting a nail on the head. "C'mon, I'm letting you stay in my house. Don't you think that goes beyond drinking buddies?"

Willie looked at me gratefully before shrugging his shoulders and returning to his stool. "It's nothing grave. My white blood cells are up and they wanted to draw more blood, run more tests. I could not allow it. The longer I stayed in the hospital, the greater the risk of developing a nosocomial infection from all the unsafe practices. Odds were I wouldn't make it out alive. Understand?"

Increased white blood cells could mean Willie's body was trying to fight off an infection or there could be a more serious underlying disease. Or it could simply be due to stress—the stress of being hospitalized plus GPS (ghost pirate syndrome).

"Once they knew I was leaving AMA, they tried to talk me into taking an antibiotic," Willie continued. "I refused but they still stuck a prescription in with my discharge papers."

"Maybe you should take it," I offered, instantly regretting it.

He looked at me like I had lost my mind. "You, of all people! Antibiotic use is rampant; got a runny nose, here's some ampicillin. A cough, have some erythromycin. Meanwhile, resistance to antibiotics is building up, creating super-bugs!"

Willie jumped to his feet and nearly squashed Pickford, who had picked an inopportune time to come down from the top of the couch.

"Super-bugs! *Super-bugs*, Daniel! Do you know what I see in my nightmares?"

"Ghost pirates infected with super-bugs?"

Willie groaned as "Tiny House Hunters" returned. A sudden thought came to me. "Willie, what's a Hallmark movie?"

Glad that I had changed the subject, Willie said, "There's a Hallmark channel somewhere near HGTV. They show hokey, romantic movies. You know, chick flicks with added estrogen. I think they are mostly made specifically for the channel. I've caught a few scenes from some Christmas movies."

I nodded, resisting the urge to change the channel to check it out. Was the key to a successful relationship with Jaclyn hidden somewhere in a Hallmark movie?

The last of the daylight winked out behind the kitchen blinds as I made a decision. "Willie, my man. It's time we get you back aboard the *Silent Cow*."

It's funny how, with the passage of time, the human mind can rationalize certain events. By now, I believed what had happened on the *Silent Cow* could be explained away by overactive imaginations, circumstance, perhaps an undigested bit of beef. I was convinced the only spirit to invade the landlocked houseboat was that of a silent screen actress in the form of my cat, Pickford.

But as we made our way down the dark path through the oaks and pines, shining my old, winking flashlight in front of us, we could hear a deep rumbling ahead. Willie turned to run; I grabbed him roughly by the wrist. I positioned myself behind him, blocking him on the narrow path, and pushed him along.

When the *Silent Cow* came into view, the rumbling ceased and I felt a little better. Nothing more than a generator or perhaps Willie's refrigerator on the fritz. A bright light suddenly shined through the porthole of Willie's bedroom.

"Willie," I whispered. "I think there's someone on the *Silent Cow*. Is there anything of value on the boat?"

Willie's eyes grew wide. "Ian!"

Of course. I had forgotten about the autographed photo of Ian Anderson. Any burglar with an ounce of credibility wouldn't pass up the chance to break in a houseboat in the middle of a secluded, wooded lot to steal a picture of the Jethro Tull flutist.

Shining the flashlight (*wink, wink*) back toward the path, I searched for a weapon. I spotted something blue; reaching down, I picked it up by the handle.

"Willie," I growled, swishing the racquetball racket to and fro to shake off the webs. "Why is my racket here?"

"You took your golf clubs," he said simply. "The spiders have been unusually active this year."

"Here, you take this," I said, plunking the racket roughly into his gut. I reached down and picked up a thick tree limb about three feet long that would have made Sheriff Buford Pusser proud. I turned, walking tall, and led the way toward the cabin door.

The first thing I noticed, when the door creaked open, was the temperature. On Oak Island, temperatures rarely fell below freezing and yet the interior of the *Silent Cow* felt like a deep freeze. I let out a puff of air which immediately condensed to a vapor.

I pulled Willie into the cabin; he shivered and brandished his racket, turning in all directions with wild eyes. I patted the top of the tree limb on my upturned left palm, menacingly.

A deep, eerie moan came from the direction of the bedroom. Willie turned to run and I grabbed him again, pushing him toward the sound. Damn it! This was his house(boat) and we weren't leaving until we took it back. Intruders beware! I slapped the branch in my hand; Willie whimpered.

Standing in the doorway to his bedroom, our breaths coming fast and heavy in the frosty air, we steeled ourselves for battle. I tilted my head toward the inside, urging Willie onward. He shook his head, the racket trembling in his hand. Very well; I burst through the door pulling Willie the Wimp after me.

The light in the room flashed, blinding us momentarily. I tried to blink the spots away but before I could see clearly, the light began flashing quickly, like a strobe light, reminding me of my disco days at the Galaxy 2000 ("The roof, the roof, the roof is on fire. We don't need no water, let the...")

It was impossible to see clearly, with the flashing light and the puffs of dense breath from our rapid-fire breathing, but I thought I could make out a shape on Willie's bed.

"Willie, someone's on your bed," I whispered. The motionless form looked strangely feminine.

Willie grunted. "Is it Ginger?" I asked, knowing the answer. Ginger, the bartender at the Oar House Lounge was full figured; the form on the bed was shaped like an hour glass.

Willie's answer was a shrill scream. His bed had started shaking—side to side followed by end to end. Violently shaking. I wasn't sure how the woman—if it was a woman—could possibly hold on. Just as suddenly it stopped. The temperature of the room seemed to grow colder. The light flashed bright again, blinding us. When I was able to focus, I screamed. In the flashing strobe, the figure on the bed levitated!

I had to support Willie as he fell over into me. For an instant, I saw the face of the floating form; it was definitely feminine, the mouth in a large "O" of surprise. She was a good three feet off the bed now, a strange fluidity to her limbs. We were involuntarily backing out of the room, when her head turned in our direction. A deep, inhuman voice (seemingly infused with raw eggs, nicotine, and whiskey) bellowed a command. With a loud, synovial *pop*, the head starting spinning!

Not waiting for Willie, I jumped from the deck of the *Silent Cow* and made a new path back to my house. The flashlight had winked out and we both ran blindly through the woods. Back in our spots in my great room, we were too shaky to brush the leaves and debris from our clothes. We sat through another whole episode of "Tiny House Hunters", staring at the screen blindly and still panting heavily. When our breathing finally slowed, a show called "Flip or Flop" was about to start. I could only guess it wasn't about flip flops, sandals or presidential policies. I didn't pay too much attention to the screen, trying instead to get my heart rate under control.

When Willie finally spoke, I jumped. "Your mother sells rocks and shells."

"What?"

"Your mother sells rocks and shells," Willie repeated.

I looked at him, amazed, shaking my head slightly. "I don't think that's what the floating woman on your bed said."

"I guess by the seashore," Willie added.

I decided to let Willie think that was what the demonic voice had shouted at us. "Willie, have you been watching any horror movies lately?"

"Not really. There was a marathon a few weeks ago, but I slept through most of it."

"Do you remember any of the movies?" I asked.

"Umm, just that one with Linda Blair."

"I see. By any chance, was that after you noticed the presence of the ghost pirates?"

Willie stood and walked over to the refrigerator to fetch another organic beer. "After, I think."

Boy, those ghost pirates were really messing with Willie, recreating a scene from "The Exorcist" with—

"Oh my God! The girl! We need to call the police—or a priest—or somebody!" I cried. I jumped up bravely. "We must go back and save her!"

Willie blushed and stayed seated.

"Do you know her? Have you ever seen her before?" I asked.

"Pam," Willie said.

"We must go save Pam, then! I don't have any holy water, but I have half a bottle of Pellegrino sparkling water in the refrigerator that Jaclyn left."

"Polythene Pam," Willie added.

I stopped in my tracks. "What is she, a hooker?"

"She's a doll."

Between the strobe, the blinding light and the heavy air, I hadn't gotten a good look at "Pam". I guess she may have been good looking, but I didn't see what that had to do with the situation at hand.

"Since Ginger, I've kept Pam under the bed, since I don't need her anymore," Willie explained.

"You sicko!" I started to say more, but suddenly my grandfather, Finnian spoke to me from the grave. He used to tell me, "Everyone has the right to be stupid, but you are abusing the privilege." *Polythene* Pam; kept under the bed; a doll; the big "O" look of surprise on her face…

I slumped back down on the couch. "You sicko," I repeated, without much gumption.

"What I don't understand," Willie said. "Was I had her *deflated* and under the bed. How did they blow—"

The phone rang loudly once, then stopped.

"Must have been my mom, butt-dialing me again with her Jitterbug ," I said.

"Oh yeah," Willie said. "I forgot. Someone called while you were at work."

I waited. He took another drink of his Butte Creek Organic Pale Ale and resumed watching Home and Garden Television.

"Well?" I cried.

"Freeway somebody."

Willie and his "photographic" memory strikes again. Freeway? Neutre— the veterinarian?

"Freeway?" I prompted.

He nodded. "No wait. Neutron. A Doctor Neutron."

11 - ROBOT CHICKEN BURRITO SPRINKLED WITH POWDERED FENTANYL

Pharmacist's log: Boiling Grove Community Hospital. Day two. Lackluster, the standard.

What the hell am I doing here!

Feeling like a mouse in a trap, I tried to think of something other than the computer system. Impossible with all the monitors and keyboards glaring at me, taunting me. Somebody beat the "Change" drum loudly—iceberg ahead!

Earlier I had spent ten minutes in the bathroom stall outside the computer lab, on the verge of hyperventilating, wanting to scream; all that would come out was a little squeak.

Pharmacist's log: Logic rules other hospital departments. When I worked in Housekeeping, everything was logical. The schedule, job duties, equipment, supplies, even the breaks and lunches. The only thing logical about working in Information Services on a new computer build is…wait, I'll think of something. (I don't know—ask me tomorrow.)

"How was your morning?" Jaclyn asked, picking out a table in the cafeteria for lunch.

"Illogical."

"Indeed, Mr. Spock."

Pharmacist's log: Final entry. Danger—rant building. Arg!

My tirade spewed forth. "So, we've been told (over and over), Medi-Soit is a major player in hospital information systems. But you could sure fool me!" My tone was forceful, half-shouting, sounding like Perry Mason in front of the jury having a nervous breakdown. "I've spent the morning chomping at the bit to get started testing the pharmacy build. Guess what?"

I didn't give Jaclyn time to answer. "There is no pharmacy build!" I wailed, throwing my arms in the air. "Can you believe it?"

Jaclyn opened her mouth to ask a question but I cut her off. "There's a test system that includes pharmacy, and the company copied the test data to the production system two months ago. The I.S. employees, including a pharmacist who was on the team then, started building and testing the system. The pharmacist built order sentences and order sets with medications. And after four weeks—" I smashed my fist on the table, startling Jaclyn and causing a passerby to spill coffee on her scrubs. "The production system crashed!"

Jaclyn stared at me curiously; I was wild-eyed and had a bit of spittle running down my chin. "Everything was lost! All the work! A month ago!"

"Isn't there only three months left until go-live?" Jaclyn asked incredulously.

"Yes!" I yelled. When the occupants of the next table turned to stare, I lowered my voice. "And Administration won't push back the date. They believe the rosy piece of fiction handed them by Medi-Soit in the form of weekly updates."

"Wow," Jaclyn said unenthusiastically. "Just—wow."

"I talked to most of the I.S. employees this morning, since there wasn't anything else to do. Radiology, lab, nursing, respiratory therapy—"

"Pickles won't like that," Jaclyn said, stating the obvious.

"Don't worry. I was very, very careful. Anyway, they all said the same thing. All the work they had done, everything, was lost and they can't work on anything new until the production system is fixed. It's a cluster."

Jaclyn chewed pensively on a piece of meat that looked like a cross between beef and shoe leather. "At least you've got another pharmacist there who already has experience with the system." She picked a bit of gristle from between her teeth and threw it on her plate disgustedly.

"Had. *Had.* She said to hell with it after the crash. Someone told me she took a signing bonus to go work at Walgreens."

A large shadow fell over the table, causing me to have a yodeling flashback. That's all I needed now, a Sparkle reappearance. I looked up quickly, surprised and delighted to see a nervous Carl standing there, wringing his hands.

"Carl, my man! How's it going in the realm of Cincinnaticus?"

Carl looked at Jaclyn shyly. "Sorry to interrupt," he muttered.

Jaclyn's smile reassured Carl and he turned to me.

"Pull up a chair, Carl," I offered. "We can chew the fat, or the cartilage or tendon, depending on what you got there to eat." I pointed at his tray.

He shifted on his massive feet, looking down to the floor. "No, no. Just need to talk to you later. Important." His last word was so low, we had to lean forward to hear it.

"Sure thing. You know where the I.S. offices are?"

He nodded.

"Come down anytime. I'll be there twiddling my thumbs. When I get tired of that, I'm going to sit on my hands."

We watched him walk to the back of the cafeteria and sit at the farthest table, facing the wall.

"Poor kid," Jaclyn said empathetically. "He doesn't stand a chance with Dr. Frankenstein as his preceptor. His last student actually ran out of here crying and didn't come back. The last time I saw her, she was working the drive-thru at Taco Bell."

I let that sink in. "From diagnosing Bell's Palsy to preparing Nacho Bellgrandes. Sad—sad to let one man ruin a kid's dream." I glanced back at Carl. "Someone ought to have the cojones to approach said doctor and point out the error of his ways."

Jaclyn was frowning at me. "I thought Dr. Pearson was the one who got you the computer job?"

"Yes. I got the job by command of King Doctor."

Jaclyn gave me a stern look. "Please don't do anything you're going to regret."

It was my turn to frown at her. The trait I admired most about Jaclyn was she never, ever, lectured me. And there it was. She didn't say it with a smile on her face. She meant every word. Another ominous relationship sign? Was this a scene straight out of a Hallmark movie?

"Yes ma'am," I gulped. "When does your flight leave?"

"This evening, 5:10 from ILM."

"The conference lasts five days?"

I noticed a slight grimace when she answered. "I've been meaning to talk to you about that. I mentioned my sister before; I am going to stay an extra five days with her in Boca Raton. I'll be gone ten days."

Realizing I was holding my breath, I let it out slowly. "Good for you," I said, feigning excitement. "You didn't have a vacation last year and I know you need to get away from…everything."

A single tear escaped her eye and she quickly wiped it away. "Yes, I do," she said softly.

"And it will do you good to go a little crazy with your sis," I added.

"Yes, it will."

"Can I take you to the airport?" I offered.

She smiled sadly. "We are leaving at three. You can't leave early. Pickles wouldn't like it."

"Oh yeah," I said, looking down at my name badge. "I forgot I had a job. Now if there was only some work to do."

"And I meant what I told you," she said. "I better not hear about you being seen around town with other women, *Eye Candy*."

"Jim! You ole son of a gun."

James Dieter, a small, wiry man, was my old housekeeping boss. He grinned wryly at me as he stuck his head over the partition in my work cubicle.

"How'd you get that tall?" I asked him. "Are you standing on Ora back there?" Ora Dinwiddy had been an Environmental Services' colleague with a colorful, limited vocabulary.

In a perfect imitation of Ora, Jim said, "Booooo-shit!"

His head disappeared and he jumped around the corner. I stood and he grabbed my hand, pumped it and punched me on the shoulder (reminding me of an old pain, "mop shoulder"). "Damn, Daniel. It's good to see you. Housekeeping sure has been boring without you. Nobody's been sent to the ER and there's been no attempted murders with syringes full of drugs." He punched my shoulder again. "Just—damn—boring."

"I'm glad I was so entertaining."

Jim scanned the offices with a skeptical eye. "You like it here, Mr. Hoity-Toity?"

I laughed. "As with anything in life, there are advantages and disadvantages. Advantage: it's not quite as odoriferous as my last job. Disadvantage: nobody knows what the hell they are doing."

"Not surprised. Not surprised." He lifted a barcode scanner from its cradle near my computer and aimed it at me. "I could use one of these to keep track of my employees. Turnover's so bad, I can't keep track of the names of all my new employees. Slap a barcode on their ass and..." He paused to press the button, sending a red light my way. "I could identify each and every one when they walked by."

I laughed. "I *have* missed you, Jim. Would you like to be in charge of Information Services, too?"

He dropped his head and his voice. "You'd better be careful, Daniel. The great Pickles won't like you talking like that."

"I was joking. You wouldn't want to be in charge of this fiasco, believe me."

"You couldn't pay me enough," he mumbled. "Anyway, I got to get back to work. I can't lollygag around all day like you." Starting to leave, he turned back and handed me the scanner. "Your magic wand, computer guru."

"Not me," I said. "Only thing I'm an expert on is Fat Tire."

He disappeared and just as quickly reappeared. "Oh, I forgot. There's some dark, gangly kid in a lab coat hanging around in the hall. He asked about you."

Carl was lingering near the back wall of the hallway, looking like a lost, abused puppy. Even though his complexion was dark, I could make out some creeping scarlet.

"You okay, Carl?"

He looked up at me and almost smiled. "I guess. Dr. Pearson just gave me a tongue-lashing in front of the other doctors. I wanted to run away. I guess I cried a little."

My pulse quickened, my heart breaking for my young, naïve friend. My first impulse was to hunt Cincinnaticus Pearson, MD down and give him a taste of his own medicine.

Please don't do anything you're going to regret. Jaclyn's lecture came crashing down on my head, stopping me in my tracks. An appalling thought crossed my mind, perhaps I needed to be lectured.

I put my arm around Carl. "Step into my office, Carl. We'll figure something out." I led him to my stupendous, useable, info-pharmaceutical cubicle.

I guided Carl to my chair. "How does it make you feel when Dr. P reams you?"

His chin dropped to his chest. He whispered a word I couldn't hear.

"I'm sorry. I couldn't make that out."

"Loser. Like a loser," he sniffed.

"Okay." I paused to think. "We've got to turn that around. He yells at *all* his students and I personally believe it's just habit on his part. It's all in how the students respond to being berated."

He frowned at me. I had to think of a way to get through to him.

"Do you want to be a doctor?" I asked.

Carl meekly nodded, not instilling much confidence in his answer.

I moved closer, shouting like an a-hole army sergeant, "I said, do you want to be a doctor?"

"Yes, sir," Carl responded, with a tad of enthusiasm.

"Okay. At this point in your career it's all about survive and advance. So, we must come up with a way to deal with the volcanic Dr. P."

Carl perked up. "Can you make him disappear?"

My eyes widened. "Sure. I'll just call some of my Mafioso friends and get him whacked. NO! I can't make him disappear. You, my friend, are going to have to learn how to deal with him."

Carl shook his head sadly.

I thought some more. "What makes you happy, Carl? What makes you laugh?"

"*Robot Chicken*," he responded immediately.

Robot Chicken? What's Robot Chicken, something on the dinner menu at *Westworld?* Finally, I had to admit I didn't know what he meant.

"It's a television show on Adult Swim on Cartoon Network," he said excitedly.

"Okay," I said. "When Dr. P is yelling at you, I want you to think happy, funny thoughts. I want you to pretend he's Robot Chicken."

"Well," Carl said, wincing. "Robot Chicken is really not a character. It's a show, a comedy show with sketches using old toys and stop animation. I mean, a Robot Chicken appears in the opening titles, but he's not really a character in the show."

"Hmm. Do you have a favorite episode? One that makes you laugh all the way through?"

Carl paused to think and soon began laughing.

"That's the one!" I cried. "Whenever Dr. Pearson is yelling at you, I want you to pretend he's acting out that episode of *Robot Chicken*, all the way from start to finish."

"I don't know," Carl said, shrinking back in the chair.

"You can do it! I tell you what, we'll go out in the parking lot later and practice. I'll puff up like Dr. P and yell at you; you can pretend I'm that episode of—"

"The parking lot!" Carl exclaimed. "That was the important thing I wanted to discuss with you!"

Carl jumped up and started pacing. I'd never seen him quite so agitated.

"The Medical Examiner closed the investigation. Claims the ten skeletons were Indian children burials!"

Ten Little Indians, I thought, remembering the Agatha Christie mystery.

"Like I told you before," Carl continued. "There's no way that was an Indian burial site. I agree they were skeletons of children, based on the size, but thrown in all together like that? No way! That was a mass grave!"

"But Carl, why would the Medical Examiner lie about it?"

Carl paced faster. "I don't know. I don't know! I'm not an expert, of course, but I don't think those skulls had the characteristics of the American Indian. And two skulls I saw at a fairly close range; they had something wrong with the eye sockets."

"What?"

Carl stopped and shrugged. "I'm not totally sure, but they didn't look right. I wish I could have examined them."

"Carl," I said, putting my arm around him. He looked up at me expectantly, a slight look of fear on his face, like I was going to verbally beat him to a pulp like a certain giant doctor. "Carl..." I gave him a smile. "I believe you."

His face glowed.

"Now," I said. "Let's go out to the parking lot so I can yell and curse at you."

The view from the front windows of Duffer's Pub and Grille atop the Oak Island golf course clubhouse was magnificent; Atlantic Ocean as far as the eye could see through the palms and live oaks (as opposed to The Dead Oaks, a band from my high school days—I played mean maracas). Due west, to my extreme right, the setting sun colored the breaking ocean waves a stunning pink. Dr. Valeree Neutre looked particularly stunning as well, dressed in a bright pink sleeveless Polo and white skirt, her strawberry blonde hair windblown. She had just finished a round of golf and had bid her auburn-haired playing partner adieu.

After a long, stress-relieving post-work run, I had taken a shower and met her at the agreed upon time and place. She had asked me something, I think. I wasn't sure because I was swimming in those incredible blue eyes.

"Uh, what? I'm sorry, I missed what you said," I stammered.

She smiled and even though I was sitting, I went weak in the knees. "Are you an author?" she asked.

"An author?"

She pointed to my drink, a mixture of Gosling's Black Seal Rum and Gosling's Ginger Beer called "Dark & Stormy".

I nodded my understanding. "If I wrote a book, it would be, 'It was a dark and stormy night. Jesus wept. The End'." She laughed. "The truth is I like rum," I added.

She laughed again. "You never know until you try. You might be the next great American writer."

It was my turn to laugh. "An apothecary author. That's a good one. Banish the thought. What would a hospital pharmacist write about anyway, drug diversion and hospitals? Nobody would want to read that drivel."

Amidst more small talk (most revolving around golf; more specifically the alligator on hole #4 who stole my golf ball), the waitress delivered our meals. On my plate were two delicious looking fish tacos; on her plate was a seafood burrito from the starter's menu which looked like it could feed a family of four.

"I had a pack of Lance's cheese and peanut butter crackers for lunch," Dr. Neutre said sheepishly.

"While golf is dangerous," I said, thinking of my golf ball beside the tail of that infernal alligator (including a brief glimpse of Edgar Allan Crow, my pack of sunflower seeds in his beak). "It can also leave you ravenous. It looks delicious."

"It is," she said, eagerly cutting into it. "It's always my reward for charging around eighteen holes after a half day of work on Thursdays."

She came up for air halfway through the seafood burrito, grabbing her glass of Sweet Josie Brown Ale.

"How is Fairbanks?" she asked, gently dabbing the foam from her upper lip.

"I kept him in the house as long as I could, until he raised a single claw and threatened to eviscerate me. I let him out and made him promise to play nice with Francis. He was mostly healed." I picked up my second fish taco. "Thank you for asking, Dr.—"

"Valeree," she said, pointing her fork at me.

"Valeree," I said, smiling. "Now, what can I do for you?"

Slightly embarrassed, it didn't take long for her to work up the resolve to confide in me. "We use fentanyl in the practice, mostly for anesthesia in surgeries, sometime for pain in trauma cases."

I nodded. Fentanyl, an opiate narcotic, is a Schedule II controlled substance due to its high potential for abuse. While fentanyl had been in the news lately (numbskulls on the street cutting heroin with powdered fentanyl, causing multiple overdoses), hospitals and veterinarian clinics purchased it in the injectable form made by pharmaceutical manufacturers.

"So, do you use paper DEA-222 forms or the electronic controlled substance ordering system?" I asked, to get her to continue.

"Paper," she answered. I wasn't surprised; hospital and retail pharmacies converted to the electronic system several years ago since it was much easier for ordering large volumes of narcotics. It basically was an electronic signature on an electronic 222 form. But for smaller practices, including veterinarian clinics that didn't order on a regular basis, a paper form would be sufficient.

Dr. Valaree Neutre dropped her head and spooned a large portion of seafood burrito into her mouth.

Spearing the innards on my plate that had spilled out of the fish taco, I nibbled on them pensively. "I'm certainly not here to judge. You aren't the first benevolent practitioner who's been taken advantage of, and you certainly won't be the last. But you need to confide in me if you want me to help."

She patted her mouth with a napkin. "I just feel so ashamed. Someone has been stealing fentanyl right under my nose. I feel so stupid."

"Ah, let me tell you about the three stages of being the victim of drug diversion bamboozlement. First stage—" I opened my eyes wide, forming my mouth in a large "O". "Surprise, astonishment. Shock."

She nodded her head.

"Second stage: Guilt, a sinking feeling in your gut." I changed my voice to a higher pitch. "If I turn in (fill in the blank), their life will be ruined. What will happen to their spouse, their kids?"

Suddenly her countenance changed. "Oh, I'm over feeling guilty. Mostly now, it makes me mad," she said vehemently.

I held out my arms. "Behold! Stage three."

I watched her crumple up her napkin into a fist and slowly release it. "Keep this in mind—it is not your fault," I said. "Sure, there may be some processes involving controlled drugs you need to tighten up, but *you* did not steal the drugs. For whatever reason, addiction, money…somebody stole those drugs from your practice—from you—from your pocket."

She put down her napkin. Her fantastic blue eyes glistening, she smiled, reached over and put her hand on top of mine. "Thank you, Daniel."

From the corner of my eye, I noticed someone had stopped beside the table. I looked over and recognized the face, but had to think hard to remember the name—Adrienne. One of Jaclyn's golf partners. I had played with her and Jaclyn a couple of times. She glanced from Valaree to me, a sly smile forming.

Oh crap.

12 - EGRETS? NO EGRETS

Friday evening, alone with Jaclyn on my couch. We share a private meal of grilled red snapper, grilled plantains with a butter glaze and two glasses of Pinot Grigio. The food and drink, however, are merely a distraction. I crave more. Running my fingers through her soft hair, I can no longer hold back. The pent-up thoughts and desires of the day—hell, all week—are more than I can stand. I pull her head back. Her red, sensual lips beckon, causing my heart to flutter. She moans softly. I bring my face close to hers and whisper, "I want you Jaclyn. In every way…"

I opened my eyes. Friday evening and the reality of the situation came crashing down—I was sitting in the hospital parking lot in my Cube with my lips pursed, about to kiss the steering wheel (not even a soft, cushy leather steering wheel, but a cold, hard plastic one.)

I shoved my Toots & the Maytals CD into the console and started the Cube's voracious engine. Still in park, I stomped on the accelerator in frustration; the interior shook as the engine burped, sending a large plume of black smoke out the exhaust pipe. Seems I would not be racing Danica Patrick anytime soon.

I pounded on the steering wheel, no longer feeling amorous towards it. My first frustrating week of work was over and I didn't feel like I had accomplished a damn thing. Everyone else in the I.S. department was equally disheartened, but it seemed they had grown numb to the situation. And Jaclyn was two states away. And Willie was still in my house, probably on the couch where I had just imagined a reclining Jaclyn.

Ain't no way I was going home.

I pulled the Cube out of the parking lot and onto Highway 17 just as the Toots & the Maytals' song "Pressure Drop" started.

"Pressure going to drop on me, indeed," I said, knowing the lyrics were written about the dropping barometric pressure, but also had the double meaning of a storm coming for you. "Not if I can help it!" I cried, as I headed for the island and one of my favorite watering holes.

I walked past the food truck in the parking lot and through the door of No Egrets just in time to catch an old country 45 record by Hank Thompson "On Tap, In the Can, Or in the Bottle" playing on the Wurlitzer. The smell of nachos, hamburgers, onion rings, filled the air almost as much as Hank did. I took another deep sniff—was that sausages? Brats? Weiner schnitzel? I felt the tension melt from my shoulders.

"Daniel!" Glenn cried from behind the bar. "Get over here, you long-lost son of West Virginia!" Glenn, the owner with his wife Glenda, was behind the bar, jumping from customer to customer lined along the brass rail and bar.

"Hey Glenn, when did you get food?" I asked, eying a sausage and kraut dish nearby.

Glenn pointed out the front door. "It's the Sonora sisters' new venture, a food truck. They call it 'Flocking Good Food'. Pretty good menu; everyone seems to like it." He stopped to grab a huge bagel lathered with pink cream cheese and took a quick bite. "Even have 'Flocking Bagels'."

With all the bar seats occupied, I turned to look for a place to land. A few more tables had been crammed into the quaint bar; most of the seating had been claimed by two or more people. A table in the middle of the room had seven large men surrounding it. Off duty firefighters from the station next door—boisterous but somehow well behaved.

"Hey, it's Daniel!" one shouted.

They gave a group cheer as I waved and pointed in their direction. I felt comfortable in No Egrets, part of the gang. But as I scanned the other tables, I noticed plenty of new faces, young professionals, retirees and a mix of undefined. Matilda had been right; No Egrets had gotten busier since the anniversary party. ("Too uppity", as Matilda had proclaimed.) Matilda erupted with a loud belch from the end of the bar; it certainly hadn't stopped her from occupying her usual barstool. Being Friday, she was chugging a Long Island Ice Tea.

"Madame Matilda!" I yelled with glee, making my way down the bar to her stool. I stopped beside her; she looked up at me groggily. "The *Silent Cow's* still haunted. Do you have a Plan B?" I asked.

"Wha?" The old woman leaned forward so she could hear the white boy over "Play That Funky Music" which had just fired up on the Wurlitzer.

"You know, the ghost pirates?" I yelled.

She looked at me as if I had lost my mind and me no speaka da English.

"You were wearing a veil and drinking a Rose Kennedy Cocktail," I shouted.

"Sunday," she mumbled, which didn't mean she remembered being on the *Silent Cow*, because she always drank Rose Kennedy Cocktails on Sundays. But then she added, "Two Sundays ago, little squirrely guy on a houseboat. He never paid me." She nearly screamed the last sentence.

From the barstool beside Matilda, Richard Crabgrass turned and let out a gasp. An aspiring actor who tried out for parts in all productions at Wilmington's EUE/Screen Gems Studios, Richard was dressed in a bright pink shirt with puffy sleeves and white pants. "Matilda. I'm shocked!" he exclaimed, overacting (especially in the facial region). "And Daniel, how could you? How could you pimp out this poor old woman like that?"

Matilda and Richard often locked horns, so I decided to play along. "Just a way for me to make extra money. Why, on a good night, Matilda can bring in seven or eight large."

Richard laughed so hard I thought he was going to fall off his stool. "Seven or eight large *belches*, maybe," he said, between guffaws.

I awaited Matilda's comeback breathlessly, but she just sat there staring straight ahead. Slowly, she reached over the bar and grabbed a folded paper bag from the shelf below. Throwing it on the bar in front of Richard, she picked up her glass and took a slug of Long Island Ice Tea.

Richard looked at me and I shrugged. He addressed Matilda: "What's the bag for?"

She turned. "Do us all a favor, crawl in there and try to act your way out—you melodramatic hambone."

It didn't happen very often, but Richard was struck speechless. His mouth was stuck in the "open" position, his eyes unblinking.

Matilda reached over and opened the paper bag, placing it in the actor's free hand. "We could all use a year or two of silence. Starting…now!" And then the old woman did something she didn't do very often—she smiled. But it wasn't a friendly smile, more like the smile of a creepy clown or the Grinch. I can't speak for the rest of those close by, but it made the hair on the back of my neck stand up.

Glenda, who had just delivered drinks to a table, was sliding behind the crowd on her way back to the bar, when she heard the last act. She stopped, snapped her fingers and waggled an index finger in Matilda's direction. "Ma-*tilda!*"

"He started it," Matilda said sulkily, pointing at a still frozen Richard. He had closed his mouth but his eyes were still freakishly wide. How long could he go without blinking?

Glenda looked to me for confirmation. I nodded since Richard had thrown the first barb. She shook her head slowly, not apologizing to

Matilda, no doubt because ninety-five percent of the time Matilda was the instigator in her verbal sparring matches with the actor.

"Doesn't matter," Matilda said to me, ignoring Glenda. "I've hung up my crystal ball. No longer into the spirits—" The old lady paused to take another long drink from her Long Island Ice Tea. "I'm going to have a new job."

"Oh yeah." (Not able to help myself) I asked, "What's that?"

"Uber driver."

Matilda had made her announcement in a louder than usual voice, just as Tammy Wynette sang the first chorus of "Stand by Your Man". It had become a big sing-along at No Egrets, probably stemming from *The Blues Brothers* movie scene.

Matilda turned back to the bar. I looked at Glenda; she looked at me blankly. Richard was too stunned to laugh.

On her barstool, Matilda rotated back to us after another long pull from her glass. "Went to the library to fill out the application on-line," she said. "On a side note, those librarians are bitchier than you, Glenda." The old woman smirked (which was much less creepy than her smile). "So that's right, good people of Oak Island. In a few weeks, I'll be driving touristas all over the island, making mucho moulah."

Besides the fact that Matilda had mushed both French and Spanish into her last sentence, there were many other things wrong with this picture—about three to be exact (no wait, four). Matilda's age was unknown, but current guesses had her around seventy, at least. Nobody was sure she actually had a driver's license. That didn't matter, because Matilda didn't own a car. She drove a vintage Vespa around the island, scattering pieces of metal behind her like a 1960s sedan in a Demolition Derby at the county fair. And finally, Matilda was usually soused from the time No Egrets opened until they closed. I shuddered, thinking about *The Andy Griffith Show* episode where Otis buys a car.

As Matilda banged her empty glass for a refill, Glenda pulled me a little way down the bar. She rolled her eyes at the old woman, then dismissed her. "Good to see you, Daniel," Glenda said. "Haven't seen you around much lately."

"I've rejoined the working world for the third time."

Glenda's smile lit up her face. "Good for you!"

I couldn't help a slight grimace. "Yeah, so far, the third time has *not* been the charm."

Glenda's attention was drawn to a table where a customer waved at her. "Business is booming," I noted.

"Yes," she said, turning to leave. "It's a blessing—and sometimes a curse."

Glenda left as her husband, Glenn, brought me a nice, frothy mug of

Fat Tire from the tap (not the can, not the bottle), just as the Wurlitzer changed to disco, playing the song "That's the Way I Like It" by KC and the Sunshine Band.

"Uh-huh, uh-huh," I sang along with the song as I tipped the mug.

"Hey Daniel," someone called. With mug raised, I couldn't see who it was with my left eye (could only see a river of dark, brown liquid), so I closed it and focused my right eye down the bar.

Officer Hans Rodriguez was motioning me from a barstool.

"Hands," I said as I approached him, using his more familiar nickname. "Have you been tracking any more alligators on the beach, Officer Rodriguez?"

"Nary a one," he answered, as he stuck out his hand for me to shake. "The big case I broke this week involved 'Numbskull A' breaking into a 1987 Yamaha boat and stealing a Yamaha 15 HP two-stroke motor, a red metal gas container and a boat battery worth $1160. 'Numbskull B', father of 'Numbskull A', then stashed the booty in his home until 'Numbskull A' sold the motor to 'Numbskull C', who knew the motor was stolen and sold it to someone else. 'Numbskulls A, B and C' are now in the Brunswick County Detention Facility where I'm no doubt they will live happily ever after." He took a drink of his beer. "No doubt some lawyer will get them off, though. Don't get me started on that," he said morosely. "And I'm off tonight and the weekend, so please don't call me officer."

"Will do. What's up?"

Hands turned all the way around on the stool to face me. "Did I hear you say you were working again?"

"Afraid so."

"Are you back at the hospital?"

"Afraid so."

"Good," he said, motioning me closer. "Listen," he said, dropping his voice. "Can you do me a favor?"

"Sure, anything." (Who am I to refuse a favor to a friend, especially a cop-friend?)

Hands looked around the bar; spying an empty table, he gestured toward it. We walked over with our drinks and sat down.

"My nephew," Hands said. "He's at the hospital." He paused, apparently searching for words.

"A patient?" I asked, trying to help him along.

"What? Oh no," he answered. "He's in medical school. He's…" Hands gestured with his hands skyward, then splayed his fingers and contorted his face, searching for words again.

I looked at Hans Rodriguez carefully, his dark complexion, his mannerisms. And then it came to me. His nephew!

"No, don't tell me," I said. "Let me guess. Is he taller than Kobe Bryant but shorter than Shaq?"

Hands frowned but nodded.

"Speaking of Shaq, is your nephew's shoe size smaller than Shaq's but bigger than Lebron's?"

"Umm, I guess. He's got big feet."

"Does his eyes go like this when he gets excited?" I made circles with my hands, placed them over my eyes, then made my fingers explode outward. "Answer 'neep' for no or 'ack' for yes."

Hands laughed. "You've met Carlos!"

"Carl," I corrected.

"Oh yeah. I forgot, he wants to go by the name Oma calls him."

When he saw my look of confusion, he explained, "His grandmother. Mutti to my brother and me. Our mother is very German. She refuses to call her grandson Carlos and has always called him Carl."

"That explains a lot," I said. "Except his white coat has 'Carlos' embroidered on it."

"His birth name. I guess with all the stupidity going on in the world today, he doesn't want to associate with the Latino community. Afraid he will be deported behind a ridiculous, imaginary fifty-foot wall. Who knows how kids see the future these days? All I know is, it's a good thing mi papi es muerto. It would kill him if he knew what was going on, I mean, if he wasn't already dead."

I tried to keep up, while Hands bounced back and forth between his German and Mexican heritage.

"I'm really glad you've already met him," Hands continued. "Carlos is...brilliant, but he's socially backward. That's why he ended up going to Haiti for medical school. His grades and test scores were off the charts, but he just couldn't get past the interviews here in the states. We figured a language barrier might just be in his favor, and we were right. He graduated in the top fifteen of his class. I guess the Haitians thought 'neep' and 'ack' were American slang for something."

"Where did that particular, um, coping mechanism come from?" I asked, referring to "neep" and "ack".

"I don't know," Hands answered. "They aren't derived from German or Spanish, that's for sure. It's just something he started doing when he was young, whenever he would get into a situation that made him nervous."

"Yeah, that's when I noticed it."

"So, how did you meet Carlos?" Hands asked.

"We just kind of ran into each other." (Cue the snare drum and cymbal again, *Ba-dum-tish!*)

Hands took a drink of his beer. He paused to study the outside of his glass, watching the condensation race to the bottom. When he turned back to me, he was deadly serious. "We are all so worried about him. He needs to complete his residency here in the states so he can get licensed. Being a doctor has always been his dream. I don't know what he would do if he fails."

I searched my friend's face, seeing nothing but concern and worry. "I don't say this lightly, but has he ever been on medication?"

"Medication, psychotherapy, even hypnotism. We've tried everything we could find," Hands said. "The medication made him slow and sleepy. Turned a brilliant mind stupid."

I nodded. "I understand. As a pharmacist, I can't tell you how many times I've seen the next 'wonder drug' come along. All is well until it flops, making way for the next 'wonder drug'. Some do too much. I used to have this little one-panel comic in my pharmacy—framed. It showed a young Shakespeare on his momma's lap at the doctor's office. Little Shakespeare had a quill in his hand and was writing a mile a minute on a piece of paper. The doctor said, 'Don't worry Mrs. Shakespeare, we'll give young William Ritalin so he can be just like all the other little boys'."

Hands nodded his understanding, almost smiling. "I don't have kids, but our family has always been close. We all have a vested interested in Carlos—Carl, and want him to succeed." He looked at me, hopeful. "The doctor he's with, is he nice? Is he helping Carlos?"

I swallowed hard. Gulped really. Couldn't slide that by a good cop. Hands groaned. "Dios mío! No!" he exclaimed. "Is it that bad?"

"Dr. Pearson is…" I searched for diplomatic words but there were none to be found. "Well, in truth, kind of loud and mean."

Hands groaned again. "You couldn't lie to me? You couldn't say something to make me feel better?"

"You know I don't have a poker face. Besides, lying to a friend is not in my DNA. And lying to a cop is just plain stupid. But look," I said cheerfully. "I am in the equation. Turns out, I'm helping Dr. Pearson on a computer project. A little bug in his ear here, a little shove there. It will be okay for Carl."

Hands looked less than convinced as he slowly twirled his beer glass.

"I am also working with Carl on coping mechanisms," I said. "Molding him a little."

He looked at me. "So, you're trying to be Professor Henry Higgins?"

I was surprised by his sudden reference to a movie classic, wondering if *My Fair Lady* had been watched often in the Rodriguez household. I pictured Rex Harrison's character trying to teach Carl (dressed in Audrey Hepburn's cockney rags) to say "The rain in Spain stays mainly in the plain." ("The 'ack' in Spain stays mainly in the 'neep'.")

"Well, no," I answered slowly. "Not so much like that. More like Emily Post. Teaching manners, etiquette."

"Emily Post? You?" Hands smiled a little. "I think I better write to

'Dear Abby' as well. With Carlos, we're going to need all the help we can get."

He reached across the table to shake my hand again. "Anything you can do, Daniel, I will be forever grateful. And if you can get us through this, my family would probably adopt you."

I laughed. "I could use a good home-cooked meal."

Hands finally smiled broadly. "Holidays, you would not believe!" He raised his hands in the air. "Schnitzel and sauerbraten on one side of the table, enchiladas and pozole on the other. The kids in the family, they don't know any different."

"Mmm" escaped my lips, my mouth watering. "Just for holidays?"

Hands laughed. "And when Carlos gets licensed." He took a drink of his beer and I followed suit. "That would be a huge weight off our shoulders. Later, we could figure out how to get him to interact with his patients."

I wiped Fat Tire foam from my lips. "There are all kinds of different specialties out there. He wouldn't necessarily have to see patients."

"What do you mean?"

I thought of Carl's obsession with the skeletons. "He could be a radiologist or pathologist."

"Really?" Hands perked up, looking a bit optimistic.

"Sure. It would take additional training."

"Sounds great! Do you think Carlos is interested in something like that?"

"I can almost guarantee it. Did you hear about the skeletons found under the hospital parking lot?"

Hands nodded. "What kind of policeman would I be if I didn't know about that?"

We paused as Glenda passed by to see if we needed refills. "Carl was fascinated by the skeletons," I continued after we nodded to Glenda. "Particularly the skulls. He got to see them up close and became a whole different person when talking about them, mature and confidant."

"Really?" Hands paused to shake his head in wonder. "Why is he so interested in an ancient Native American burial ground?"

"He doesn't think the remains are Native American."

"What?" Hands cried. A green-haired girl from the next table turned to look at him. She had a light green tint to her skin, green fingernails and a green nose ring. Hands gave her a sharp look and she turned away.

"Good lord," he mumbled. "What was that?"

"I think Hulk and Swamp Thing cross-pollinated and had a child," I offered.

Glenda returned with our drinks, placing new coasters down first. "How's Glenn doing?" I asked her. "He hasn't called to go running recently." Glenn had been a regular running partner until six months ago.

"Hah!" she laughed. "I've been after him to call you but he always says he's too tired since the bar got busy. I just pat his expanding gut and say, 'I understand, dear" and he snarls at me."

It was my turn to laugh. "Oh, the things I miss being a wretched bachelor," I said.

Glenda walked away, still laughing. Hands was smiling and watching her, but when she left, he turned back to me. In a policeman's low so-other-people-can't-hear voice, he asked, "What do you mean Carlos doesn't think the remains are Native American? That's what it said in the newspaper. The Medical Examiner released his findings. I don't understand."

"He says the skulls don't have the characteristics of the American Indian. He also mentioned something wrong with the eye sockets."

Hands sat staring pensively at his beer, not responding. I felt compelled to continue. "Carl doesn't believe the Medical Examiner, I know it's crazy—"

"I believe Carlos," Hands stated matter-of-factly.

I had to ask the same question I had posed to his nephew: "But why would the Medical Examiner lie?"

"No idea," Hands answered. "He's fairly new and I've never met him. All I know is, when Carlos is truly interested in something and becomes fixated on it, I've never known him to be wrong. He's almost mystical that way."

"And that, my friend," I said. "Is why he would make a great pathologist or any kind of forensic physician, including Medical Examiner."

Hands was nodding slowly, clearly thinking.

"And then he could carry a badge like his uncle," I added.

"Huh?" Hands said, emerging from deep thought. "Badge? I don't think MEs carry a badge."

"They don't? They do on *CSI* or *Bones* or one of those shows I've seen."

"Don't believe everything you see on TV," Hands said. "Real investigative work is twenty percent investigation, twenty percent waiting and fifty percent paperwork."

"What's the other ten percent, donuts?"

"Ha-ha," he deadpanned, pointing to his beer. "Relaxation techniques."

From my peripheral vision, I saw a huge man coming up behind me. When he slapped me on the back, I nearly expelled a lung onto the table.

"Daniel! How's your cat?"

I turned to face Bobby, craning my neck to look up to his head. "Hey Bobby. Fairbanks has been patched up and is back on the prowl. How's Tito?" I asked, referring to the turtle and not the Jackson.

Bobby laughed and pointed his index finger at me. Slowly he pulled the finger back in and extended his thumb up. "Tito is back on the prowl, too."

"My advice would be for Tito to avoid Ms. Michael at all costs, then," I said. Bobby laughed and slapped me on the back again, nearly detaching the other lung. "See you guys around," Bobby said, walking off in the direction of his barstool.

Hands and I drank in silence for a while, stealing glances at the college women's softball game on the television on the far wall.

"I've got to tell you, Hands," I finally said. "I am curious about those skeletons, too. How did they end up there? Who do they belong to? What happened to those children?"

Hands nodded. "Once you get a taste of being a P.I., you just can't stop, can you?"

"I was never a private investigator. Rx-Dick, maybe."

We both glanced to the TV where a big, burly pitcher whipped an underhand throw to the inside corner of the plate, catching the batter looking for the third strike.

"What's the history of that area?" I asked. "You know, before they built the hospital."

"I don't know. The hospital moved there from another location, but I'm not sure when. I didn't grow up in this area, so I'm not the one to ask."

"Any idea who would know?"

Hands twisted his mouth to the side. "Not sure. I can ask around. Maybe some old-timer who's been here a while."

I thought of my Rummikub partners at the Oak Island Recreation Center. "I may know some seasoned folk who could help." I tried to remember what time they played on Saturdays, early or in the afternoon? I could just swing by early—and then Fairbanks, Tito (and even Fifi the foo-foo dog) invaded my thoughts; I had promised Dr. Valaree Neutre I would come in right after they opened at eight tomorrow. I had almost forgotten I had something on my calendar, so to speak.

Rx-Dick—undercover, underwhelming, underachiever. Dr. Neutre asked me how I was going to play it, especially since some of the employees she suspected of the theft would be working. I had winked at her and told her I had it all planned out, which was half true and half fibbery. I knew what I had to look for, but no idea how I was going to pull it off. I looked at Hands, thinking of asking him for his input, but he was happily watching women's softball and tossing beer nuts into his mouth. He was off-duty and I certainly didn't want to piss him off talking shop. I'd have to wait until another time when he was wearing his badge...his badge!

"Hands, I promise to look after Carl, but I need a favor," I said. "Do you have an extra badge holder or wallet I can borrow?"

13 - HELLO KITTY, GOODBYE OLD YELLER

I still didn't have a solid plan as I approached Neutre Veterinary Clinic Saturday morning. But I had loaded my pockets with a few props, so I had options. I would do what I do best, just waltz in and wing it. I parked the Cube down the street, walking the remainder of the way to the clinic because I didn't want the world's squarest car to blow any kind of cover I might come up with.

I glanced at the LED sign in the front window as I approached: *Fifty Shades of Spay* had been replaced with *Dog Spay Afternoon (discounts after 1 p.m.)*. Begrudgingly, I had struggled into dress shoes (too snug), dress pants (too tight), a shirt and a tie (too restrictive), thinking I was probably breaking the Oak Island dress code law (punishable by fourteen days solitary confinement on the beach in swimwear and flip flops). I adjusted my tie (initially I had put on my Pokey and Gumby tie, but changed the last minute to my Jerry Garcia multi-colored abstract tie), put on an old pair of Ray-Ban sunglasses I had found in a drawer and strutted through the front door like I was someone important.

The receptionist! I hadn't thought about her; the same woman who had flirted with Fairbanks looked up at me from the desk. I struck a Men in Black pose. Turning to the side, I struck a Matrix pose.

"The Brunswick County Sperm Bank is down the block," she said dryly.

My cover blown, I put a finger to my lips. "Shh. I'm on a mission," I said.

"From God," she replied.

"No!" I said roughly, wishing I had thought of that retort. "From a doctor of veterinary medicine. I'm working undercover for your boss."

"So—you're a secret *agent*." She said the last word rather loudly, and from the corner of my eye I saw another employee sticking his head through the inner door. His eyes got big and he ducked back inside.

Pursing her lips, the receptionist's eyes drifted up and down my wardrobe. "You look more like a Deadhead lawyer."

I smiled and twirled my tie. "You must be familiar with the Jerry Garcia tie collection."

She nodded.

"Ain't no time to hate, barely time to wait," I sang. She frowned. "When life looks like easy street, there is danger at your door," I continued singing. She shook her head. "Every silver lining's got a touch of grey?" I asked in a normal voice. Head shake. "What a long strange trip it's been?"

"I don't know any Grateful Dead songs," she countered. "I buy the ties for my husband and he gets a lot of compliments on them."

Dr. Valaree Neutre entered the room, white lab coat flowing and blue eyes blazing. She walked over to me, hand extended. "Mr. O'—"

"Fenty," I interrupted quickly, winking at her. "O'Fenty." (Don't tell me I can't think on my feet.)

She smiled nervously. "Of course. Thank you for taking the time to visit our office today."

I shook her hand professionally. "You are quite welcome—am I to assume you are Dr. Neutre?"

She quickly regained her composure. "Yes. I'm sorry. I'm Valaree Neutre. This," she said, nodding toward the receptionist. "Is Cassidy Weir."

"Really?" I asked, shaking the receptionist's hand. "Are you related to any members of the Grateful Dead?"

Cassidy smirked at me, shaking her head yet again, clearly clueless as to why I had asked. To have a first name of a Grateful Dead song and the last name of "the other one" in the Dead seemed like more than coincidence. And she didn't know any of the songs. Bet her mom and dad were Deadheads.

"Let me take you back to the rooms," Dr. Neutre said, taking me by the hand. As we walked toward the door, she whispered, "How are you going to play this?"

"Leave it to me," I whispered, without a clue. I had watched Humphrey Bogart as Private Investigator Philip Marlowe in *The Big Sleep* before going to bed last night and I really enjoyed the part where he entered the book shop, pretending to be a nerd or whatever they called it back then. Geek? Dork? Square? I thought I might play it like Bogie.

The first thing I noticed at the end of the hallway was the head of the earlier employee poking around a corner. He quickly disappeared when he saw me. I could tell Dr. Neutre saw him as well because she grabbed me by the elbow and hustled me into that room.

There were two employees in the room, a man and a woman, both in tan scrubs. They stood at attention when we entered, a little apprehensive, a little fearful.

"This is Brad Jervins and Angela Kiernan. They are my vet assistants. This is—" Dr. Neutre hesitated, trying to remember my fake name.

"O'Fenty," I said in a nasally voice.

"Oh yes, O'Fenty. He's going to—"

Cassidy Weir ran into the room, out of breath. "Mrs. Rowasa—is out front. Fifi has had— a complete mental breakdown. She wants you—right away."

"Crap," Dr. Neutre muttered softly so only I could hear.

"It's okay," I said nasally. "You take care of Fifi. I will look around. I'm sure your fine employees here will help me."

I watched Dr. Neutre back out the door, followed by the sound of her heels clicking down the hallway. I turned back in time to hear Brad whisper to Angela, "DEA agent."

That was all I needed to hear to change my approach, from nerdy Bogie to in-your-face, crazy Bogie from *Treasure of the Sierra Madre*. I started to say, "Badges? We don't need no stinkin' badges!" when I remembered one of the props in my pocket.

I pulled the badge wallet Hands had loaned me out of my pocket and flipped it open. Unfortunately, I pulled out a red foam clown nose with it, which floated to the floor. I'm not sure why I brought the nose, other than I found it in a drawer and stuck it in my pocket, I guess so I'd be ready to go all psycho clown on somebody at a moment's notice.

As I bent to pick up the clown nose, I realized the badge wallet was still open. I quickly flipped it closed, hoping they didn't notice my badge was a replica of Barney Fife's badge, with "Deputy Mayberry" in black letters on it. Annie, God rest her soul, had bought it for me when we dressed up for Halloween as Barney and Thelma Lou. I trembled at the thought, remembering going home after the party and the un-Thelma Lou-like things she had done to me in bed.

The employees cowering before me, I decided to play it strong and silent. I gave them my best Clint Eastwood as Dirty Harry Callahan eye squint. I held it for a full minute, but when I didn't get a reaction I realized I was still wearing the Ray-Bans. I removed the sunglasses slowly, unleashing the full effect of my squint on the unsuspecting saps (to use a word from Bogie movies). No reaction. I carefully folded my Ray-Bans, placing them in the pocket of my dress shirt. I took a step toward the man and woman, backing them against the wall.

"Tell me about ordering and dispensing controlled substances," I said in a low, whispery voice. Brad frowned while Angela actually jumped.

"What?" I growled to Brad.

"Your voice changed," Brad said tentatively. "And why did you have a clown nose in your pocket?"

"Why do you think?" I growled, maintaining a stoic face as I struggled to think of an answer.

"Walgreen's Red Nose Day," Angela offered in a trembling voice.

Walgreen's Red Nose Day? Maybe that was how I ended up with the clown nose, I honestly couldn't remember. I could sense Brad watching as my face softened, thinking about the benevolent drive to end child poverty.

"Negative!" I barked. "Clown nose out," I said, pulling it out of my pocket. "I'm here for a fun time. Clown nose in—" I paused to replace it in my pocket. "All business—no joking around."

I gave them a stern look, hoping they would buy my lame answer. Brad, a dark, strapping twenty-something, continued to frown while Angela, rotund and perspiring heavily, seemed to buy it hook line and sinker.

"Can I see your badge again?" Brad asked, still frowning.

I grabbed a pen from my front pocket (careful not to dislodge the red foam nose) and a small writing pad from my back pocket. I slammed the pad onto the countertop. *Whap!*

"No! You cannot see my badge again!" I yelled. Leaning forward, I glared at his nametag. "Brad Jervins. Middle name and employee number?" I asked, planning to write it down in the notebook. Angela was staring at the notebook—on the pink cover was Hello Kitty. Damn! The Cube had been Annie's and I had retrieved the notebook from the back of the glove compartment. I guess I never cleaned it out after she died.

I flipped the notebook open. "Full name?"

"Bradley Navin Jervins."

Navin? Before I could ask if he was the adopted white child of poor African American sharecroppers in Mississippi, he said, "Hey! Wait a minute. Where's your jacket? In all the TV shows, the DEA agents are wearing black jackets with 'DEA' in bold, white letters."

"Jacket's in the car," I said gruffly, careful to keep it generic. In truth, my jacket *was* in the car—the windbreaker Fairbanks had shredded. "And this ain't no TV show."

I carefully wrote down his full name in my Hello Kitty notebook. "Now, I'm not going to ask this again. Tell me about controlled substance ordering and dispensing."

Angela Kiernan spoke up (I made a show of looking at her name badge and writing down her name). Her voice was low and tremulous. "We can't order the fentanyl. Only Dr. Neutre can order it."

"Aha! Fentanyl!" fake DEA Agent O'Fenty cried, flapping Hello Kitty. "What other schedule II narcotics do you use here at the clinic?"

"None," she said so low I could barely hear.

"Okay. So, youse guys fill out the DEA-222 form and order the fentanyl," I said, trying to bait a little trap. Either a paper 222 form or an electronic version is required for ordering Schedule II controlled substances and there's no other (legal) way you can get them.

"No!" they cried together. Brad spoke next. "It's the doctor's DEA number and forms. Only she can sign them."

"These forms are paper?" I asked, getting confirmation from Angela's nod. "And who places the order with the drug wholesaler?"

"Well, any of us can," Angela replied.

"Hmm. I see. And you mail the DEA form with the order to the wholesaler?"

They both nodded. "Can I see the forms?" I asked, taking a chance. When Brad removed a key from an unsecured drawer and unlocked a cabinet in the room, I had the first prickling sensation of discovery. Brad opened the cabinet and my eyes grew wide.

The DEA-222 forms were right beside sixteen cartons of fentanyl vials; at first glance they seemed to be five milliliter vials. A couple extra vials were beside the cartons, so it looked like the clinic had four hundred and two vials in stock. I suppressed a gasp; a MASH unit on the front lines wouldn't stock that much fentanyl.

"Here's the forms, sir." I jumped when Angela poked the forms into my hand. Looking down, I noticed the beautiful, looping, flowing signature of Valaree Neutre adorning the otherwise blank form on top. I shuffled the forms and saw the first five forms were pre-signed.

"When you fill out the top part of the forms with the drug name, what do you do next?" I asked.

Angela took the bait and started to run with it. "You send the top copy of the form to the drug wholesaler with the order. You have to be really careful filling out the top part of the form, because if you make a mistake and cross anything out, the drug wholesaler will send it back to you."

Brad hissed at her. Quickly I asked her, "So, you've made mistakes filling out the DEA-222 form before."

Angela nodded. Her next words were cut off when Brad discreetly kicked her in the shin. She grimaced, keeping her mouth shut afterward.

My next question, "Where's the detailed ordering, receiving and dispensing records?" was cut off by a yip, a squeal and a shout. The sound of tiny toenails on linoleum grew louder until a small dog tried to put on the brakes in front of the door in the hallway, skidding past in a twirl. A few seconds of silence was followed by an explosion of fur into the room. Fifi furiously ran around the room, barking, growling and slobbering. We were too stunned to react and could do nothing but watch the spectacular canine meltdown. Fifi actually bumped into our legs but didn't seem to notice. *Yip! Yap! Grrrr! (slobber-slobber)*

Dr. Neutre ran around the corner and into the room, huffing and puffing. She pointed at the blur of a dog running laps around the room and tried to speak. My old nemesis, Mrs. Rowasa came up from behind and pushed the doctor out of the way. She put the back of her hand to her forehead.

"Oh, Fifi! My Fifi! Somebody *do* something!"

Always willing to lend a helping hand, I looked around for a net, lasso, or tranquilizer gun. Nada.

Dr. Neutre found her voice. "For heaven's sake!" she shouted to her employees. "Corral that mutt!"

Mrs. Rowasa looked at the doctor in disbelief, as if she had just called Fifi something blasphemous.

Brad and Angela dropped to the floor, waited until Fifi ran between them, then closed in on the frantic pooch. Scooping the dog off the floor, Brad cried out. "Damn dog bit me!" He drew his hand back; I grabbed the hand before it could start its forward motion toward the dog. I didn't particularly like Fifi, but I was finding I liked Brad a lot less.

Mrs. Rowasa let out a gasp and fainted. Dr. Neutre swooped in and deftly caught her mid-air, no doubt saving broken bones (and a lawsuit). I helped Valaree carry the woman to a lounge in the back of the office where we carefully laid her on a couch. The older woman smelled of elderberries.

Valaree left the room for a minute, returning with an ammonia inhalant. She paused before breaking it under the old woman's nose. "How was it going back there? Why do they think you're a DEA agent?"

I shrugged. "Dunno, but I just ran with it. I never told them anything about me other than my fake name."

"What do you think?" she asked, still poised with the unbroken ammonia ampule.

"I think you better wake up this fine lady," I said (in case she was playing possum and could hear me). "I need to look at some paperwork and then I'll give you a full report later."

The doctor broke the ammonia ampule and the old lady sputtered to life.

I thought about the veterinary clinic notebook as I drove toward the Oak Island Recreation Center. The pages should have contained the fentanyl receiving and dispensing records, but they were an illegible mess. About the only thing the notebook had going for it was the glossy color photo of Old Yeller on the cover (the Disney Old Yeller, the dog poised and ready to protect the family, well before the tragic [spoiler alert!] rabid goodbye). I had been left alone to examine and review the fentanyl stock and all the records since it was all hands-on deck after foo-foo Fifi went cuckoo. When I left, the waiting room was filling up and I told Valaree I would write up my findings and give her a full report later. (One thing that had to go was

Old Yeller the notebook—it needed to bite the dust just like [spoiler alert!] the real Old Yeller.)

I walked through the door of the rec center and it was as if I had never left. Everything, and I mean *everything*, was in the same spot. Ray, Irene and Jean were sitting at the same Rummikub table in the same chairs. I looked at them closely, trying to remember what they were wearing last time. Not sure, but it's possible they were wearing the same clothes. Excitedly, they motioned me over. The fourth chair was empty—again.

"Where's Alvin?" I asked, referring to their missing partner.

"Oh," Irene said. "His blood sugar was dropping so he went to the vending machine."

"Uh-huh." I glanced at all their faces to gauge the reaction to my next statement. "You know, I'm beginning to think Alvin doesn't really exist."

Ray looked bemused, Irene smiled wryly. "Pish-posh," Jean said. "Alvin is one of our oldest and dearest friends. He just has a lot of health problems and he doesn't like to sit still for long."

Ray was nosing the facedown tiles in the middle of the table with one finger. Suddenly he put a hand to his chest, feigning a heart attack. "Come on! I don't have much time left. Let's play the game."

Irene picked up a wrapped cough drop from the table and threw it at Ray. It bounced off his chest and landed with a *sploosh* in the coffee cup in front of him. "That's not funny, Ray!" she cried.

"Geesh," he said sheepishly. "Sorry. I guess it's *not* funny anymore. Used to be. Used to get a whole room going. And then—what was his name? — he ruined it. You remember him, the guy who died because he wouldn't let the ambulance attendants take him until the game was over. James? Jimmy? Jake? Well, he did leave before the game was over, even though he was still sitting at the table. His heart, his liver, his lungs—his internal organs couldn't wait until the game was over. Splatted right down in the middle of the table. And you know what?" Ray looked right at me. "The guy was cheating! Had tiles up his sleeves, in his pockets and under his damn toupee!"

He picked up fourteen tiles from the pile in the center of the table and placed them on his plastic "bleachers". "Besides," he added. "When I go, I want to get hit by a bus."

"Number one," Jean said, displaying her freshly polished, bright orange fingernails before holding up her index finger. "You never, ever speak ill of the dead. Never. That's sacrilegious."

"Bullshit," Ray interjected. "Bastard was cheating."

Jean crossed herself like a good Catholic girl. "Number two..." She paused, causing everyone at the table to look up. "Wait? What were we talking about? Oh yes, number one was don't speak ill of the dead. Number two, you don't *know* he was cheating. Could have been some sort of good luck thing."

"How does stuffing tiles under your toupee bring good luck?" Ray demanded. "They weren't there to grow hair! James—Jimmy—Jake, he was CHEATING!"

There was a room-wide groan. Obviously, this argument was not a new one.

"Number three, I can tell you now, without fail, *Raymond*, you will *not* die by getting run over by a bus. No bus."

Ray waited for Jean to explain but she was quiet as she picked up her fourteen tiles. Finally, he could stand it no longer. "Okay, how do you know it won't be a bus. I could walk out of here right now and get hit by a bus!"

Jean smirked. "You cannot walk out of here and get hit by a bus. No commuter buses run on Oak Island, old man. You will most likely die from getting hit by a gold Chevy Malibu."

"Chevy Malibu? What are you, some kind of fortune teller?" Ray yelled.

"*My Chevy Malibu, you old fart!* If you don't shut your trap and play the game!"

There were cheers and jeers all around the room.

"If you're set on a bus, Ray, I've got a cousin that drives a bus in Los Angeles," I said, wanting to join in the conversation. "I can hook you up."

All three heads turned to stare at me. "Goodness, Daniel," exclaimed Irene. "We can joke about it, but you can't. It just comes off as morbid when you say it."

"Sorry."

Irene also picked up her fourteen tiles so I did the same. "I thought we had to pick up one tile to see who goes first?" I asked.

"In the interest of time, we are going to let you go first," Jean said. "We know you are in a hurry."

I laughed, scanning and rearranging my tiles. "What makes you think I'm in a hurry? I'm on island time."

"Nonsense," Irene said. "Young people are always in a hurry. And you have that look in your eye. You need to be someplace. But you needed to come here first, for some reason."

"I bet it's money," Ray said. "Jean, get your purse. The boy needs cash." Then Ray gave me a weak punch to the shoulder. "Liquor? Hooker? What's on the agenda for us tonight?"

Irene's eyes narrowed. "It may not be Jean driving the Chevy Malibu. Quit embarrassing the boy! He just wanted to come by for advice. Right, Daniel?"

As usual, my aged sages hit the nail on the head. I *was* in a bit of a hurry. Now that I was working through the week, the weekends seemed shorter. There was never enough time to get everything done. When you are unemployed, weekends seemed seven days long. My new job had shot my island lifestyle right in the bum.

I was delighted to see I had 9, 10 and 11-point tiles of different colors and I could actually start the game instead of pass. I laid them down proudly.

Ray laughed. "Look at Daniel! I think he's been playing Rummikub with others behind our backs."

"I would never cheat on you guys. You're my one and onlies," I said, with a touch of seriousness.

The game progressed in silence for several rounds. Finally, Ray gave me a Dick Van Dyke look, not the befuddled Rob Petrie kind but more the inquisitiveness of Dr. Mark Sloan from *Diagnosis Murder*.

"So...what do you need from us?"

I started to protest, to claim I had only come for their company, but they would see through me like a pair of fishnet stockings.

"You know," said Ray. "I had my son show me an episode of *The X-Files* with The Lone Gunmen. While they did help those two FBI agents solve mysterious cases, there are a couple of big differences. First, those are three ugly guys; we're much prettier."

I laughed. "True dat," I said. Everyone at the table frowned at me as if I had spoken Chinese.

"Second, they cheat," Ray continued. "Just like James, Jimmy, Jake or whatever his name was."

Hmm. I had never thought of The Lone Gunmen as cheaters. I guess they did hack into some computer mainframes, but the information usually helped Mulder and Scully. "How so?" I asked.

"They use computers—" Ray pointed to his noggin, then directed a finger toward Irene's head then Jean's. "These are our computers."

"Well," I said. "I can't argue with that." It was my turn and I was able to add a tile to an existing run on the table.

Jean said, "The Lone Gunmen? That's a silly name. You can call us...the Happy Rummikubers."

I couldn't help but chuckle. "Perfect. That's perfect."

Irene laid a hand on mine. "I feel there is something you want to ask us?"

"Okay, you got me," I said. "I *did* come here because I missed your company, but I also wanted to pick your brains."

Ray smiled and stuck his dentures out of his mouth at me.

"Get those back in your mouth, or you won't need them anymore!" Jean cried, shaking a fist at Ray. "You'll need a feeding tube instead!" Jean closed her eyes and took a deep breath, calming herself. "Go ahead, Daniel."

"Were any of you living here when the hospital moved to its new location?"

Irene shook her head but the other two nodded. "The hospital moved in

1978," Jean said.

"Really? I was thinking '79 or '80," Ray said thoughtfully.

"No, '78. I remember because it was right around the time of the cult in Jonestown when Jim Jones gave those poor souls the Kool-Aid," Jean answered.

"Hmm," Ray responded. "I could have sworn it was around the time USC won the Rose Bowl. Pretty sure it was '79."

I could see this wasn't going to be easy.

"How can you remember who won a football game almost forty years ago?" Jean asked, astonished.

"My memory is like a steel trap!" Ray cried.

"Steel trap?" Irene laughed. "You can't even remember what you had for breakfast yesterday."

"Yes I can!" Ray frowned and dropped his head, before looking up and shouting, "Fruit and yogurt!"

"Bull-poop," called Irene. "You had a loaded biscuit at the Old Bridge Diner. And you ate every bit of that huge mound of food."

Happy Rummikubers? I might have to change their name to the Snippy Rummikubers.

"Oh yeah," Ray said. "It was yummy. What I was going to say was I moved from Jersey to the area right around that time. Ah…Jersey. I could sure go for a Trenton tomato pie." Ray had a dreamy look on his face as his eyes seemed to roll back in his head.

"I don't think you moved to the island until 1980, Ray," Jean said.

"You're right!" Ray cried. "I moved right after the Phillies won the World Series. Steve Carlton: best damn pitcher—ever. And Schmidty—wow!"

Irene shook her head in exasperation, turning to me. "Why are you asking about the hospital location?"

I couldn't keep the disappointment from my face. "I was hoping one of you knew what was located there before the hospital. They were doing some construction, tearing up the parking lot, and found skeletons."

"Ooh," Jean and Ray exclaimed in unison.

Irene snapped her fingers. "I heard about that in line at Lowes Foods. But the woman who was talking about it was drinking a glass of wine while shopping. I thought she was loopy. The things they let people do in public places these days."

The last time I shopped at Lowes Foods, I wheeled around drinking a craft beer (they even have cup holders on the shopping carts), so I acted like I didn't hear that last part. "It's true," I said. "Several skeletons. Of children."

The two women, obviously mothers themselves, reacted normally, with extreme sadness. Ray, on the other hand, was angry. "Sonofabitch!" he cried.

"Wait," Jean interjected. "Was it a cemetery or something? Burns me up when companies can move cemeteries or build on them."

I could only answer with the truth. "Dunno."

Silently, we played the game, going around the table twice, laying down tiles.

"Are there any local historians, maybe somebody at the library who would know?" I asked.

They looked at each other, then back at me, saying at the same time, "Driftwood."

I waited a few seconds, and when no other information was forthcoming, I asked, "You mean a magical, mystical piece of floating wood is going to tell me the history of this area?"

"Well," Ray answered. "He might be a little mystical if he's doing some magic mushrooms."

"Explain," I begged.

"Driftwood is a...well, he's a man who knows all about the area. He can tell you anything—if he feels like it," Jean said.

"Okay, now we are cooking with gas," I said, using a phrase I figured they would understand. "Where does this Driftwood live? I've got some time today and tomorrow."

They looked at each other, shrugging. "That's the problem," Irene offered. "Nobody really knows. He just shows up."

"He has to live somewhere. I'll ask the police," I said.

"I don't think they know how to find him," Ray said. "One time he was wanted for questioning when he witnessed a deadly weekend fight on the beach, and they had to wait until daybreak on Tuesday."

I was poised with a tile (instead of posed with a towel, like a 1970s Joe Namath commercial), stopping to stare at the three. "You mean to tell me the only time you can find Driftwood is on Tuesdays before the sun comes up?"

Ray shrugged; Irene and Jean nodded.

"Any particular area of the beach?" I asked.

"No," Ray answered. "Could be anywhere from Caswell Beach to The Point."

"Great," I said, looking at them disgustedly. "So, I just need to find this Driftwood somewhere along fourteen miles of beach, give or take. What does he look like?"

They all hemmed and hawed around for a minute, until Jean spoke. "I guess he looks like a hippie-beatnik-Vietnam vet-bohemian-avant-garde kind of guy."

My puzzled expression caused Ray to say, "Yeah, a real freak."

"Oh good," I said sarcastically. "That should make him stand out from all the squares on Oak Island."

"Really, you can't miss him," Irene said. "He doesn't wear a shirt, just an old army jacket with a large peace sign on the back."

"And sometimes he doesn't wear any pants," Jean added, blushing.

"Awesome. Can't wait," I said dryly.

Ray laid down a tile; he only had one left. "Chances are he won't talk to you, though."

"Why's that?"

"He's kind of squirrelly that way."

"Isn't there some kind of password I can use? He knows you guys, right?"

Ignoring me, Ray got up and walked between the ladies' chairs. They huddled together, talking in hushed tones.

"Tell him—Ken Kesey's Merry Band of Pranksters sent you," Ray finally said, standing up straight.

I frowned. "You mean Ken Kesey, the author of *One Flew Over the Cuckoo's Nest?*"

"That's the one," Irene answered. "If you say what Ray told you, Driftwood just might talk to you."

"Ken Kesey's Merry Band of Pranksters," I repeated.

"*Sent you,*" Jean emphasized.

I looked at my three friends, my Happy Rummikubers, as Ray took his seat and play resumed. I thought about Ken Kesey and *One Flew Over the Cuckoo's Nest.* I thought about Jack Nicholson as Randle Patrick McMurphy in the movie, thinking I might use one of his lines on my colleagues this coming week at work, "Which one of you nuts has got any guts?" (It's about time someone stood up to the Mighty Pickles.)

Ray laid down his last tile. "*Rummikub*, you bunch of losers!"

14 - POLLIWOG A CRACKER?

Saturday night. The big date night. A big song night: "Another Saturday Night", "Saturday Night's Alright for Fighting", "Saturday Night at the Movies", and even "Saturday Night Special". In my teen years, I spent Saturday nights hanging out at Pizza Hut, bumming pizza and filling up plate after plate from the all-you-can-eat salad bar (local legend Rum Dum once picked up the entire metal bowl of salad from the middle and began piling on the toppings—when confronted by an employee, he said, "I paid for all-you-can-eat salad and I'm going to eat it all!"). My first kiss on a Saturday night, after sitting through that universal "date movie", a *Halloween* sequel (nothing like lunatic Michael Myers to put you in a romantic mood). The first time my mom grounded me was for Saturday night shenanigans— extremely late night shenanigans—almost "time to get ready for church Sunday morning" shenanigans.

But of all the things I've done on Saturday nights, this one is the most disturbing—sitting at home with someone named Willie and watching Hallmark movies.

On the drive home, I had still been thinking of Old Yeller, so I stopped and bought a six-pack of Old Leghumper, an American Porter brewed by Thirsty Dog Brewing Company. I popped the first bottle, retrieved a California Blonde organic beer from Eel River Brewing for Willie and turned on the television. Willie grabbed the beer and the remote out of my hand, flipping the channels until he ended up on Animal Planet. We watched the last half hour of a most curious program about polliwogs. I think the name of the episode was "Tantalizing Tadpoles". Try as I might, my interest was not piqued by polliwogs.

"Want a cracker?" I asked Willie. "I bought some Cheez-Its."

Willie made a face. "No, but there are some organic Einkorn crackers in the cabinet, grab those. They are sourdough, made in Italy by artisan bakers."

"Sounds expensive. Where'd you get them?"

Willie shrugged. (I reminded myself again to check my Amazon account.)

"Does Pizza Hut deliver this far on the island?" I asked hopefully, thinking of my youth.

"Nope."

I made a disgusted face similar to the ones I made in my youth when my parents told me I couldn't go to Pizza Hut on a particular weekend. Suddenly, a thought occurred to me. "What, um, channel did you say Hallmark was on?" I asked, feeling slightly stupid.

Willie hit the guide button and searched until he found it. "You want it on?"

"I guess." I took the time to explain to him what Jaclyn had told me, *Life is not a Hallmark movie.*

"What do you think it means?" I asked.

"Not a clue," he said, pushing the Select button and changing to the Hallmark Channel. "Let's see if we can figure it out."

The first Hallmark movie was set in the summer. A career woman was engaged to a good-looking, humorless lawyer and life was good (if not frantic) until her father hired a good-looking, stranded traveler as a handy man. Sparks flew. The second movie was set in December (a Christmas movie—now?) about a television reporter who returned home to do a story on a long-running Christmas tradition in her town. Even though she recently became engaged to the good-looking, ass of a sportscaster in New York, it seemed she had lost her Christmas spirit. Until her mother set her up with an old flame, who was of course good-looking and fun. Sparks flew.

As the credits of the second movie rolled, accompanied by "Jingle Bell Rock", I turned to Willie. "You got it figured out yet?"

He shook his head, appearing to be in a trance. "No, but it's like I can't look away. Is there another movie coming on?"

"I think so," I answered, simultaneously hoping there was another, yet praying there wasn't. "*Summer Love*, I think is coming on, but I swear the scenes they showed had snow and Christmas decorations." I was feeling as woozy as Willie and it had nothing to do with Old Leghumper.

Willie's eyes appeared dilated as he said, stringing his words together, "Maybe they fall in love in summer but find a time machine and get transported back to a Christmas when they first met."

Giving him a look, I started to tell him that was ridiculous, but decided, on second thought, I didn't want to rule it out for a Hallmark movie. I had only seen two to this point and while there had been an absence of science fiction in those, the plots of others may run to the fantastic and otherworldly (I prayed). (Maybe a career woman was engaged to a good-looking, droll bank executive and all was right with the world until her astronaut brother returned from Mars with a weird-yet-still-good-looking alien. Sparks flew.)

Willie had his feet propped on the footrest of his stainless-steel stool, and I couldn't help notice his giant "Mickey Mouse Yellow Shoes" slippers. He looked right at home and suddenly the anger swelled. "Willie, I don't want to harp, but have you been out to the *Silent Cow* recently?"

"Don't want to harp?" he answered with a growl. "You harp more that Harpo Marx ever dreamed of harping!" His eyes darted in the direction of the back of the house and his boat; I could see his anxiety building.

"Come on," I said, rising. "Let's check it out."

"But the next movie," he whined.

"Doesn't start for ten minutes. We won't miss it."

Reluctantly, Willie stood and I guided him out to my back deck. Normally, in the twilight and through the heavy foliage, Willie's houseboat cannot be seen from my back deck. The *Silent Cow* gleamed like an oblong, demented jack o' lantern, shafts of ethereal light shooting out its windows. We gasped as the light seemed to shift and blink, rotating through the interior of the houseboat like the beacon atop the Oak Island Lighthouse. When we heard a piercing wail, we scrambled back inside the house.

With our backs against the inside of the door, we paused, breathing heavily. "Willie—so help me God, if the Air Force, CIA or Mulder and Scully show up at my door…"

"What do you want me to do?" he cried.

"I don't know," I said, dropping my voice. "I don't know what's going on, let alone how to stop it. But you have to break up that ghost party somehow."

"I know…I know."

I walked to the refrigerator, grabbing a California Blonde and an Old Leghumper. "Think back to when it first started," I said. "Did you find something on the boat or disturb something that could have conjured up the ghost pirates?"

"I don't know," Willie said. "My mind is so muddled."

"Willie!" I cried, grabbing him by the shoulders and shaking him (and the California Blonde and Old Leghumper). "It's your home! Get mad at them damn ghosts!"

He straightened. A look of resolve crossed his face. Willie slammed a fist into an open palm.

"Now we're talking," I said, egging him on.

"I want my houseboat back!"

"Damn right!" I cried. "The *Silent Cow* will roar—I mean moo—again!"

Willie was pacing now, looking more like the Willie of old. When he stopped in front of the television, I thought he had hatched a plan. The opening rifts of a sappy song filled the room.

"You've figured it out!" I cried. "What are we going to do?"

"I'll figure it out later," he said, staring at the screen. "After this next Hallmark movie."

On Sunday, I punished myself with exercise. After attending the nine-thirty contemporary service at Ocean View United Methodist with Glenn and Glenda, Glenn and I ran a leisurely three-mile course. After leaving Glenn, I ran ten more miles at a faster pace. Being a working man again, my exercise routine had suffered and I seemed determined to make it all up in one day. I had plenty of time to think while I ran. I had a vague memory of calling Jaclyn after the fifth Hallmark movie—she hadn't answered her phone and I left some kind of cryptic message about I was glad she was a career woman and I didn't want her hooking up with the handyman and I hoped she hadn't lost her Christmas spirit. I think I even called back a second time and left another message blaming the first message on polliwogs and Old Leghumper. Guilt, even the irrational kind related to *thinking* you have done something but don't know what, can make a man do strange things. I had even called my mom to ask her about the Hallmark movie/life riddle, but she had problems with her Jitterbug ("What? I can't hear you, Danny. Life is not a what? What's a ballpark movie?").

After the run, I rode another two miles on my bike, trying to rid myself of the Hallmark hangover. I was going to have to watch manly movies the rest of the day to balance it out, like *Cool Hand Luke* and *Scarface*.

Monday morning descended upon me like that one wacky aunt with bunions and cigarette halitosis who would show up and hug too long at Christmastime (*she* had the spirit), always with the promise of Legos but bearing gifts of underwear and suspenders instead.

The day started when I stepped on Pickford while trying to feed her. The sounds that came out of her were horrific, and very unladylike. I imagine the only thing worse than being blasphemed by a calico cat would be facing an insult-hurling Siamese.

Pickford had just settled down when Willie emerged from the bedroom; before he could fall over the cat, he suddenly doubled over, holding his right side. I offered to call 9-1-1, drive him to the emergency room, ibuprofen... "I know where I can get some easy fentanyl," I told him. He declined them all, claiming the pain had passed.

Closing the door to the Cube, I was uneasy about leaving Willie. He didn't look well this morning. I gazed at my face in the rear-view mirror—ugh. Don't look so good myself. Must be a good case of going-to-work-itis. Reluctantly, I backed out of the driveway—*thunk!* No way! *Thunk!* I rolled down the Cube's window, stuck out my arm and shook my fist at the diabolical, pine cone bombing squirrel.

When I exited the Cube, I realized I didn't remember much of the drive to the hospital. Walking across the hospital parking lot, I heard the unmistakable roar of heavy equipment and veered toward the sound, still in a trance. At the edge of the pit, I could see the workers swarming below. I turned to go and walked right into a giant bosom. Although muffled, I heard the distinct sounds of a long yodel.

I pulled back, gasping for air. "Isn't it a little too early for yodeling?" I asked.

Sparkle laughed loudly. "It's never too early for yodeling." A low pitch began in her chest, followed by a quick change to falsetto. The rapid changes of pitch she displayed were amazing. The same worker walked by. "Damn. You been double-yodeled twice and are still alive to tell the tale."

"That's incredible!" I exclaimed when she had finished her vocal acrobatics. I had never considered the skill and technique involved in yodeling. "Where did you learn to do that? To have that kind of control?"

"My grandfather. He was determined to learn after he heard Jimmie Rodgers. And me, well, I was next in line. Can't say I was excited at first. Gramps just knew it was a dying art and somebody had to carry it on."

"Jimmie Rodgers," I said, trying to remember.

"The Singing Brakeman, famous in the 30s I think."

"Oh yeah!" I snapped my fingers. "Blue Yodel songs."

She reared back her head and sang:

"She got eyes like diamonds and her teeth shine just the same
She got sweet ruby lips, and hair like a horse's mane
Oh-di-lay-ee-ay, di-lay-dee-oh, de-lay-ee."

I laughed and clapped. "That was great! They don't write 'em like that anymore."

"Damn right," Sparkle answered, just as an empty soda can came flying up at us out of the pit.

"There's a reason!" came a voice from the pit, as the empty can landed at my feet.

"Asshole!" Sparkle shouted to no one in particular. "Get your butts back to work!"

Sparkle turned back to me, more amused than mad. "Gramps won some yodeling contests singing that song."

Yodeling contests? I had never thought of contests, but it didn't surprise me in the era of county fairs and live radio shows. "Too bad there aren't any contests now," I said. "You'd be a shoo-in."

"Gramps was right, a dying art." Sparkle looked sad. "I have won a few yodeling contests on the internet where you send in a video. But no one is impressed except for other yodelers and really old men. They like the throat control."

I thought it best to act like I didn't hear that last part.

"I tried yodeling at the National Hollerin' Contest in Spivey's Corner, North Carolina; they were impressed, but I didn't win. Hollerin' is a little different than yodeling."

I tried to picture the farm folks of Spivey's Corner (population 448) and their reaction to an Amazon woman yodeler.

Sparkle brightened suddenly, slapping me on the back. "But I'm sure glad to see you, Eye Candy. And I'm sure glad to be back to work. They just cleared the job to resume late Saturday."

I glanced into the pit and saw my tussle buddy, Tank. He saw me and scowled. "No more skeletons in the closet, so to speak," I said.

I was surprised to see Sparkle shiver. "I hope not."

I left Sparkle and entered the hospital, dreading another week of hurry-up-and-implement-a-nonexistent-computer system. Amazing how one's mood can turn foul just by walking through a set of doors. I got on the elevator as a group of residents stumbled off, laughing so hard they were almost crying. As the elevator doors closed on the scene, I heard one of them say, "That was like the funniest thing—ever!"

The elevator opened and I stepped out on my floor, turning in the direction of the Information Services office. From behind I heard a masculine bellow. No, it was more like a roar, a holy hollerin'. Folks at Spivey's Corner would definitely crown this guy king. More rumbling and grumbling from behind, and I had no doubt to whom the voice belonged.

"Where is that freakin', frackin' office!" Cincinnaticus Pearson, MD, roared. His massive frame bounced from one office door to the next. The hallway, usually bustling with employees, was strangely vacant. He hadn't spotted me yet and I could easily have ducked into the I.S. office, but that would have been a little cowardly. What's the worst that could happen if I showed myself? With a little luck, maybe he would fire me.

"Dr. P," I called cheerily. "What's shakin'? How's it hangin'?"

"What?" he cried, whipping around to face me. In that instant, I realized how David must have felt when Goliath squared up to him.

"You know," I continued. "How's the world treating you? How's it spinning?"

"What?" he yelled.

I made a circular motion with my finger. "You know, like a centrifuge."

Dr. Pearson used all the available hallway space as he thundered toward me. "I am *not* looking for the Lab," he angrily replied. "I am looking for—" He stopped and studied me. After a few seconds he seemed to recognize me. "Oh…it's you."

"The one and only. What are you looking for, Doc?"

His face grew beet-red again. "I'm looking for the office of that tall, goony Human Resources guy! I want that kid fired!"

I wondered what poor kid ran afoul of the mighty Cincinnaticus Pearson, MD. I wasn't about to tell him Scott's office was up one floor, almost immediately above us, and the stairs were directly behind him.

"What did he or she do? Get under your feet?"

"No! He deliberately laughed in my face!"

I caught myself before I could laugh. Some kid would have to have a lot of backbone to deliberately laugh—uh-oh. Suddenly I had a sinking feeling.

"Some…kid, laughed in your face," I said, repeating and not phrasing it as a question.

"That's right!" He pointed a sausage-sized finger at my head. "During rounds! In front of a patient!"

I didn't think it humanly possible, but his face turned a brighter red, about the color of the exhaust of a NASA rocket taking off, Apollo 13 maybe.

"What did this kid look like? Was he a patient's child?" I asked hopefully, my throat tightening.

"What? No! He's one of my residents! Or at least he was when the day started!"

I had to find out for sure. "Oh, was it that blond-haired surfer looking resident, the one from Southern California? I've heard he's a little disrespect—"

"What? No!" (So loud, I imagined his voice setting off car alarms in the parking lot.) "That tall, dark, goofy kid with the big feet!"

Crap! An involuntary "Neep" escaped my lips.

"That's him!" Dr. Pearson cried.

Now you've gone and done it, smart guy. *Whenever Dr. Pearson is yelling at you, I want you to pretend he's acting out that episode of Robot Chicken, all the way from start to finish.* Good advice there, Dear Abby. I had to think of a way to calm Dr. Pearson down, so I could figure this out. I could not let Carl's medical career end on advice I gave him. I couldn't let him, or Hands, down.

"You know, Dr. P," I said, putting my arm around his back (I couldn't reach his shoulders). "You know that nurse on 2 West? I heard she's been asking about you, you giant sawbones stud."

It was as if his countenance changed from night to day; the red changed from ire to blush. "Really? Really," he said in two different tones. He then cocked his head to one side as if bracing himself. "Who is it?"

I'd certainly boxed myself into a corner. I thought of my time on that unit as a housekeeper and blurted out the only nurse's name I could remember. "Dixie McCall, R.N."

"Dixie," Dr. Pearson said dreamily. I couldn't help wonder if he was thinking of the same Dixie McCall, R.N. I was thinking of—a little fireball of a nurse in an old fashioned white nursing hat who may have come to the New World on the Mayflower.

"Dixie," Dr. Pearson repeated, a faraway look in his eye.

"I tell you what, Dr. P, you let me talk to Carl about…his behavior and—"

"Carl!" Dr. Pearson growled. His misty expression had changed to thunderstorm. "Where is that office? I want him fired!"

"Did he hurt a patient?" I asked.

"What? No! In fact, he had all the right answers for a change."

"So, his biggest transgression was…?"

"Laughing—in my face!"

I put my arm around his back again and led him down the hall to the BGCH employee display, which exhibited pictures of employees under each five-year anniversary date. I was taking a big chance. What if he was confused and thought Dixie was some young, hot nurse? I pointed to Dixie McCall, R.N.'s picture, the only one under the "50 Year" column.

"Dix-*ie*," Dr. Pearson said, his tense shoulders relaxing. Bingo! Old and lukewarm was apparently just what the doctor ordered.

"You should ask her out," I said.

A look of horror crossed his face. "I c-c-couldn't—I c-c-can't," he stammered.

"I'll make you a deal," I said, reaching out my hand for a shake. "Let me talk to Carl and get him straightened out—"

"No—more—*laughing*," he said, with steel in his voice. He gripped my hand and there was steel there, too. Adding a big squeeze before he released my hand, I imagined hearing bones snap.

"No more laughing," I agreed. "If you give Carl a second chance…" I thumped my finger on Dixie's picture. "I'll get you a date with this cute, young thang."

When I finally walked into the office, all my Information Services cellmates were already wasting their time in their cubicles (the "walls" of the cubicle were low to facilitate teamwork). They all turned to watch me walk to my desk. I smiled and tipped an imaginary hat to each and every one.

I booted up my computer and waited, wondering what excuses Medi-Soit would come up with this week as to why the production system still wasn't live. Less than three months to go!

The first thing I noticed when my computer screen appeared was the color change. It was redder than normal; the picture of Tom and Jerry I had installed as wallpaper now made it look like the mouse and cat had come down with terrible rashes. Perhaps Jerry had developed an allergy to cheese and Tom had become allergic to mouse dander. Someone must have bumped the contrast or brightness button on the side of the screen. I reached around the monitor, trying to find the buttons. There didn't seem to be any buttons, so I figured the best way to fix the screen was to go to the Control Panel. I placed my hand on the mouse and moved the pointer over the Control Panel icon (which happened to be right near Tom's privates, prompting a thought about that particular area being a Control Panel for too many males). But when I left-clicked on the icon, nothing happened. The mouse didn't feel right. I tried left-clicking four more times, finally picking up the mouse and examining its underbelly. I blew on the bottom, trying to dislodge any dust that may have gathered. Putting the mouse back down, I left-clicked again. Nothing. I decided to try to right-click, and low and behold, it worked. The window that opened, however, was not the Control Panel. Oh, it was about *control* all right, but not control of the computer. An S&M page appeared with a scary, beautiful woman in black leather, wearing a black mask and sporting a black whip. I heard a snicker behind me as the woman on the screen spoke. The volume on my computer had been turned all the way up, and the woman said (in a German accent), "You have been vewy, vewy bad and must be punished, Dani-el." She cracked the whip menacingly at the same time someone behind me cracked up. I turned to see my IT Team members gathered in a semi-circle behind me. They all burst into laughter.

"That's a good one, guys," I said, smiling. I turned and applauded them.

"I am Derica," the voice boomed from the computer speakers behind me. "Your dominatrix!" I turned back to the screen. "If you want to please me, you will do exactly as I say." I was staring at the screen, almost in a trance, when Derica snapped the whip—*crack!* I jumped a few inches in my chair. A close-up of her face filled the screen. "You are my *slave!*" Derica cried (and I believed her).

The laughter behind me intensified, then stopped all at once. I turned; my co-workers had broken away faster than businesses moving away from mainframes. I stood, confused, until Ms. Pickles screamed in my ear, "O'Dwyer!"

"Yes, ma'am," I said sheepishly, turning to face her.

"Didn't we have a talk about following the rules! Didn't we? Do you think this is funny?"

"No, ma'am. Not funny," I said.

"Down on the floor, slave!" Derica's voice boomed. "I want you to lick my boots!"

My cubical neighbor, Stanley, appeared and quickly ran to my computer, muting the sound.

"Explain that!" Ms. Pickles had roared so loud, I couldn't stop the mental image of her in black leather with a whip. Unfortunately, some things just can't be unseen.

I saw several frightened pairs of eyes peering over low cubicle walls. "I…um, just…" Stanley was still standing nearby and he looked terrified.

I took a deep breath. "I'm real sorry, Ms. Pickles. It was just a joke."

Ms. Pickles puffed up (from a gherkin to the size of one of those you would see floating in large jars at general stores) and did something only my fourth-grade teacher and Jaclyn had ever done to me—she grabbed me by the ear.

"Come on," she said, painfully stretching the skin and cartilage of my left ear and leading me out of the room. "We are going to Human Resources."

The next thing I knew, I was standing between two of my favorite women in Scott's office, Ms. Pickles and Bertha, Scott's secretary.

"Hello, Moneypenny," I said to Bertha, in a poor imitation of James Bond.

Bertha looked at me with a combination of disdain and amusement. "Knew it would only be a matter of time until you were brought to the principal's office. Hello Edwina."

Edwina? I should have guessed. Edwina Pickles nodded to Bertha.

Feeling their uncomfortable stares and lack of love, I walked over to the aquarium tank on the shelf. "How's Ebenezer?" I asked. It was as if the peacock mantis shrimp could hear me. It shot out of its underwater cave and charged at me, striking the glass and sloshing water out the top. *Bam!* Lack of love all around for Daniel O'Dwyer.

Bertha pressed the intercom button. "Mr. Unites, Edwina Pickles is here to see you. She's brought in a bad seed."

"Hey!" I cried. "Only my mother and J. Edgar Hoover are allowed to call me that."

I was still examining the peacock mantis shrimp when Scott opened his door. The beautiful creature shot back into its crevice when Scott approached. "I think Ebenezer has anger issues," I said. I ran my finger along the front of the aquarium glass, feeling a definite bump. "Scott, I'm telling you this glass is cracked and it's a little bigger than the last time I was here."

He stuck his nose to the glass. "Nonsense. That's algae."

"Enough chit-chat," Edwina Pickles said forcibly. "Mr. Unites, I want to talk to you about Mr. O'Dwyer."

Scott sighed and slumped noticeably. "Very well," he said. Bertha smiled as I was led into the commandant's office.

Scott retreated behind his desk and sat down, with a look on his face like his dog had died (or his peacock mantis shrimp). "What seems to be the problem," he said professionally. (A statement he had no doubt uttered hundreds, maybe thousands, of times.)

Edwina Pickles pointed a trembling finger at me. "He had porn on his computer."

Scott's head dipped and his giraffe neck pirouetted to look at me. "Is this true?"

"Technically," I answered. "It wasn't porn. It was S&M."

Scott put a hand to his chin and gripped it. He studied me; he studied Ms. Pickles. I had to hand it to him, his gaze was effective. I was almost ready to rat out my fellow employees. Daniel da Rat. I didn't like the sound of that. Daniel da Snitch. Daniel da Mouth. Daniel da Stool Pigeon. Nope, none of them sounded good.

"And why did you have S&M on your computer?" he finally asked. "A clear violation of the Employee Handbook."

I started to say, *"Because my girlfriend's out of town and took the whips and chains with her"*, but thought better of it. "Because…it was a joke. I realize now it was wrong, and I'm sorry." I turned to the peeved Pickles. "I'm sorry, Ms. Pickles."

"Not good enough!" Edwina Pickles barked. "You should have been working! Instead, you were disrupting all the employees."

Something was bubbling to the surface and I tried to hold it back.

"Ever since you started," she continued. "You've done nothing but distract the employees! And you haven't done any work at all!"

Mount Krakatoa exploded and lava began flowing from my mouth. "There *is* no work to do! With less than three months until go-live, there is no production system and the test system is crap! There are only a few drugs in the test system instead of the thousands that will be in production. It will take several months to build drug sets for each drug and then group them into order sets. And that's just on the pharmacy side."

Edwina Pickles crossed her arms in a huff. "If Medi-Soit says we are on schedule, then we are *on schedule*."

I couldn't help myself. "No! No, we are not on any kind of schedule." I leaned toward her, the corner of Scott's desk separating us. "What that company is selling you is a big load of contradiction; it is inconsistent with reality and illogical."

She frowned. "I don't understand."

I tried to think of a real-life example, but came up empty. Scott's face had a strange glow and I could almost see his HR mind working, trying to come up with a simple answer to a complex employee problem by way of psychology.

"It's a paradox," Scott finally said. "Like the first lady choosing an anti-cyberbullying campaign while the president continues to tweet vitriolic statements about people."

I looked at Scott like he was crazy. Bringing up the president these days was not a good way to calm and unite people toward a common goal. Loathe him or love him, strange feelings are aroused by politics. But I was astonished when a slow, sardonic smile spread on Edwina Pickle's face. Scott grinned and mouthed the words "Hillary supporter" to me.

"Look, Ms. Pickles," I said in a calm tone. "I want nothing more than to get the new computer system set up so physicians and hospital employees have a smooth transition ordering drugs at go-live. Based on prior experience with two other systems, I feel there is not enough time left."

"What would you have Edwina do?" Scott asked.

"Talk to her other employees. See what they think."

She looked from me to Scott. "Edwina, I think that's good advice," Scott prompted.

"Very well," she said, businesslike. "But if *he* goofs off again, he will be disciplined." (Unfortunately, the image of Edwina Pickles in black leather with a whip returned to my mind with a vengeance.)

I stopped by a man standing in front of the large glass window and peered into the room with him.

"You picking one out?" I asked.

He pointed to the end of the nearest row and gave me a goofy smile.

"Excellent choice. Congratulations. She is beautiful," I told him as I walked past and entered the newborn nursery. Scott had sent me on a quick errand to deliver breastfeeding pamphlets which had been sent to Human Resources by mistake. I glanced down at the front of the top pamphlet: "Breastfeeding and Your Baby: Eat Local".

I opened the door slowly, stepped inside and made sure the door didn't slam behind me. The inside of the nursery was serene, sleeping babies in their plastic bassinets and three nurses cradling babies. Classical music played softly. I listened to the beautiful piano piece, identifying it as "Goldberg Variations" by Johann Sebastian Bach. Ah, Bach. No wonder the babies were sleeping soundly. I tiptoed over to the nearest nurse and held up the pamphlets for her to see. She pointed to a countertop so I walked over and placed the breastfeeding pamphlets next to other educational material. On the way out, I stopped at the door to appreciate the tranquility one last time. Perhaps they ought to pipe Bach into the Information Services office.

A shrill alarm sounded and I jumped back, knocking over a pyramid of infant formula cans. The cans clattered to the floor. The alarm was followed by what sounded like loud, tinny heavy metal music. Was that AC/DC's "Highway to Hell"? I tried to pick up the cans but fumbled a few. When I turned back, the nurses were glaring at me and most of the newborns had wide eyes. The shrill alarm sounded again. It seemed real close. The heavy metal music followed; definitely "Highway to Hell". All the babies started wailing along with the lads from down under. Not even Bach could save this scene.

The nurses were still glaring at me, while they tried to calm the babies in their arms. What did I do? It must be one of their cell phones with an aggravating ring tone. It certainly wasn't *my* phone.

The irritating alarm sounded for the third time, blaring closer than ever. One of the nurses, running around the bassinets, pointed at my midsection and yelled, "Get out of here!"

I looked down in the direction of her pointing finger just as AC/DC blasted again. I found myself staring at the beeper attached to my belt. "Highway to Hell" screamed up at me from my midriff. The beeper Scott had given me! I had forgotten all about it. Who in the world would be paging me?

I glanced in the direction of the department phone on the countertop by the breastfeeding pamphlets. "Can I use your phone to answer my page?" I asked loudly, overtop the crying babies.

"Get out!" the nurses cried in unison.

15 - SHOWGIRLS AND SEAGULLS

I yawned long and loud, scaring a few seagulls nearby. I had been to the beach "after dark" but never "before light". The big difference I could see (as I squinted into the darkness) was the complete absence of life in the hour before sunrise, besides seabirds. Nighttime, there would be dog walkers, a few swimmers, partyers and sporadic groping teenagers entwined on towels back near the dunes.

I hadn't been awake at this time since I worked the midnight shift in housekeeping at the hospital. On my "fun scale" of 1 to 10, working midnights had rated somewhere between bunionectomy (1.5) and the last part of *The Today Show* with Hoda and Kathie Lee (0.15). I took a deep breath, trying to be chipper, attempting to be optimistic—oh hell, I am not, nor ever will be, a morning person.

It was Tuesday and I was in search of Driftwood, a man I had never met (or even seen in a picture). I remembered what my Happy Rummikubers had said, he'd be wearing an old army jacket with a large peace sign on the back (and may, or may not, be wearing pants). And he may, or may not, talk to me even if I do find him. Which can all be translated into *What the hell am I doing here?* or in the words of Forrest Gump, "Stupid is as stupid does".

I took off jogging. At least this day would include exercise, which would probably be offset by the four or five Dr. Peppers and iced teas to keep me awake at work. ("O'Dwyer," Pickles would thunder. "You are spending all your time in the bathroom! You should be working!") I had started at The Point and was determined to search the entire island coastline. For what purpose? To find a man who might have some historical information about the land where the hospital was built? To maybe shed some light on the bodies that were buried there? *If* he decides to speak to me. It was beginning to feel like searching for a white cat in a snowstorm.

I jogged onward, scanning the darkness for life. All of this based on a hunch by Carl. I couldn't help grinning. Carl had found out about my beeper and sent me a text message on it. I didn't know you could send text messages to beepers and was quite surprised, standing outside the newborn nursery, when I finally figured out which button to push and the words appeared. "Great day. In your office waiting. Carl" was displayed on the tiny pager screen.

Carl was still there, waiting patiently at my desk, when I arrived back at the Information Services' office. Jumping up when he saw me, he was more excited that a roomful of screaming babies.

"I did just like you told me," Carl said. "On rounds, when Dr. Pearson started yelling at me and asking questions, I imagined my favorite episode of *Robot Chicken*! It was epic!"

Carl had no idea how "epic" the scene had actually become. Epic on the scale of Pearl Harbor or Hiroshima, if Dr. P had found Scott's office before I found the good doctor. Epically funny to the other residents.

"Carl, you didn't laugh in his—"

"And Dr. Pearson asked *me* to diagnose Mrs. Robson and when I ticked off all the symptoms and came up with neurocysticercosis, he nearly lost it. You should have seen the look on his face."

"About the look on his face, Carl. Was he mad?" I asked.

"Yeah, but he's always mad. But there was a sense of wonder there, also. You see, he gets me so flustered, I usually don't come up with an answer or I come up with a wrong one."

And then he had smiled and slapped me on the back, an obvious attempt to thank me in a masculine, socially acceptable kind of way. It was so awkward it was sweet.

"But I came up with the correct diagnosis today," Carl continued, a look of triumph on his face. "It was the greatest day of my life."

Carl beamed at me and I couldn't help but marvel at the complete lack of "ack" and "neep". How could I tamper his enthusiasm for imagining Dr. P as Robot Chicken, yet still help him maintain his confidence?

"That is great, Carl," I said, slapping him on the back. "Now, we just need to figure out a way to dial it down a bit."

"What do you mean?"

"Well, it seems to work, but you can't laugh out loud. You might upset…um, the patient."

"The patient?"

"Yes. I don't think it's good to laugh with one breath and in the next one say neurocysticercosis."

His face became a mask of horror. "Oh my God! I didn't think of that!"

I put my arm around him. "It's okay in this situation. You probably saved Mrs. Robson's life."

He looked at me, hopeful. "You think so?"

I nodded.

"But what can I do?" he asked.

I thought for a minute. "What is your least funny episode of *Robot Chicken*?"

"That's easy," Carl answered. "The 'Kramer Vs. Showgirls' episode. I don't think it made me laugh at all; maybe I smiled once or twice."

"That's it!" I cried. "The next time, imagine that episode when Dr. Pearson is yelling at you. It's okay if you smile a little. An occasional smile exudes confidence."

I remember when Carl left my office, he was walking particularly tall and straight.

A shape in the distance caused me to slow my pace. I stopped in the sand, trying to make it out. It could be a man. I walked briskly in that direction, but when I got there, the beach was deserted. I resumed running, and soon I could see the Ocean Crest Pier ahead. Again, the shape of a man appeared to be standing by one of the wooden pilings. I sprinted under the pier and stopped. No one. This was like some inverted game of "Where's Waldo?"

"Where's Driftwood?" I cried.

From the corner of my eye I thought I saw a form down by the piling in the water. Sprinting there, my only reward was wet shoes from a crashing wave. This was maddening!

As I walked dejectedly back under the pier to dry sand, I heard a slight scraping sound above me, kind of like fingernails on wood. He must be on top of the pier! I started to run to the stairs but changed my mind. If it *was* Driftwood, he would just disappear if I kept running in all directions like a dog chasing seagulls. I decided to do what I do best.

"Mr. Driftwood, sir, if you're here, I just need to ask you a few questions," I called loudly. I waited a minute to see if there was an answer, and then realized how stupid that sounded—like I was a cop. "A few questions about the history of the area, that's all," I added hastily. "I was told you were kind of an expert on Oak Island and the places around it."

Silence.

"I met some friends of yours and they told me to tell you—" *Crap!* What was it they told me to tell him? I thought of Ray. Something from *The Dick Van Dyke Show*? Maybe dialogue from that crazy episode about the aliens and the walnuts? ("I lost my sense of humor and my thumbs!") No, that wasn't it. What was it?

I heard another soft scraping noise from above. Looking up, I couldn't see anything. Wait a minute! I had a penlight on my keyring. I pulled it from my pocket and aimed it straight up. *What the hell?*

The small shaft of light illuminated something...living. Something stuck on the underbelly of the wooden pier. As I moved the penlight, I could make out two peering eyes (from the pier, no less). I blinked once...twice. It was hard to focus in the feeble beam of light. The shape became a dark manta ray. It looked almost bat-like. Perhaps it *was* a giant bat. My thoughts immediately strayed to Bela Lugosi and I covered my neck with my hands.

With the penlight pinned to my neck and pointing toward the sand, I couldn't see the shape above. Before I could run, something large dropped from above and landed right in front of me. I screamed high and loud, like Janet Leigh in the shower scene of *Psycho*. The dark shape in front of me did not move.

"What are you? What do you want?" I cried.

Before I heard the sound, I smelled a foul stench. The voice was somehow gravelly, raspy and scratchy at the same time.

"Who put the *ram* in the rama-lama-ding-dong?"

I relaxed slightly, letting my hands fall from my throat. I'd never heard Bela Lugosi say a line like that before. I shined the penlight in his face, revealing a gray beard and red eyes. It had to be Driftwood. Had he given me some kind of riddle, some kind of test I had to pass?

He spoke again—no, it was more like growled. "Who put the *bomp* in the bomp-shooby-dooby-bomp?"

Suddenly I remembered what Ray had told me and nearly shouted it in his face. "Ken Kesey's Merry Band of Pranksters!"

I still had the penlight directed at his face. I could see his features scrunch, then release, as if he was thinking, trying to remember. Suddenly he smiled and his eyes seemed to fog over. "Coolest...bus...ever," he said, pausing between each word and inhaling, as if he was taking a toke. "Further," he added cryptically.

I had looked up Ken Kesey's Merry Band of Pranksters after the Rummikub match and knew Ken and his friends had used the money he made on his book, *One Flew Over the Cuckoo's Nest,* to buy an old school bus which they painted in psychedelic colors and drove around the United States in the 60s. The bus was fueled with gasoline; the trip with LSD. Many new Pranksters were "enlightened" along the way, including the Hells Angels, Jefferson Airplane and the Grateful Dead. I had every intention of going back to ask my Happy Rummikubers if they were once Merry Pranksters.

A string of words emerged from Driftwood, but I could only make out a few phrases: "Nothing lasts...Stark Naked...Sometimes Missing...Never Trust a Prankster." He paused to sing a jingle: "Better living through chemistry—that's the promise of Dupont."

He twirled around twice and said, "Acid Test," mystically. His body started to jerk and sway, as if reliving those days listening to the Dead, dropping acid and hallucinating. The first rays of the sun appeared over the ocean, backlighting the weird, flashback dance. Lucy in the Sky with Diamonds, indeed.

"Turn on, tune in, drop out," I said, watching him sway. "Timothy Leary and all that," I added.

He stopped dancing and turned to me, eying me suspiciously. He moved so close to inspect my face that I thought I was going to faint from the overripe, rancid smell of body odor, fish and halitosis. He did not speak, but I heard distinctly (in my head), "Man, I dropped acid with Timothy Leary. I knew Timothy Leary. Timothy Leary was a friend of mine. *Man, you're no Timothy Leary.*"

I stepped back, swaying a little myself, shaking my head. Is there such a thing as secondhand acid flashback?

"Driftwood," I said, shaking my head to clear it. "The Merry Pranksters sent me." I decided to get right to the heart of the matter. "I need to know what was on the property before the hospital was built. They said you could help. What was there before 1978?"

The sun peeked over the horizon so I could make out Driftwood's dirty gray beard, his red, beady eyes above, staring at me with a puzzled expression.

"The hospital's over on Highway 17." I paused, trying to think of landmarks nearby that may have been there in 1978. "There's an old white country church with a red door on the road in to the hospital." I remembered walking to the back of the property one time, back through the trees a little way. "There's some kind of barn near it, too. It's falling down now, but it has a white silo beside it."

Driftwood's eyes flashed, he put his hands to the side of his head and squeezed. "No!" he shouted. He looked to the sky in horror, like the Luftwaffe had suddenly appeared, ready to bomb us from existence. I recalled either Irene or Jean telling me Driftwood had been in a different war, Vietnam. If he was having a flashback to the war, there was no way I could comprehend his horror.

Driftwood turned and walked to the ocean; in the crimson sunrise, I was extremely happy to see he was wearing pants. The red peace sign on the back of his army jacket moved away from me while I tried to think of a way to get him to talk.

I ran down behind him, slowing before I got there, so as not to spook him. "Driftwood, I used to be…I am a pharmacist. If you are suffering from PTSD, I recently read an article about using doxycycline, a common antibiotic, to treat the anxiety and stress from the war."

He picked up his pace; I thought he was trying to get away from me when he stopped, bent down and reached for a piece of wood in the surf.

"That's a good one," I said, trying to make conversation.

Driftwood grunted. "Not for P.W. Adams."

I had heard of P.W. Adams, an artist who lived on the island. Famous in North Carolina, demand for his driftwood sculptures was starting to spread to other states and even other countries.

"Needs more wood than I can provide," Driftwood grumbled. "Heard he's been getting it off eBay; the last batch came from Hawaii."

It felt like I was finally having a real conversation with Driftwood and I got excited (a.k.a. I said something stupid). There was a dirty patch, featuring an eagle, on the sleeve of his army jacket with the words "Door Gunner" above it. I pointed to the patch. "Thank you for your—" I paused because of the intense look of anger crossing Driftwood's face. Some veterans despised being thanked for their service, so I quickly corrected. "Thank you for your talking with me. It's very important to find out what was on the hospital grounds."

He continued walking and I could barely make out, "Why?" over the roar of the surf.

"Construction workers were tearing up a parking lot for an expansion, and found skeletons."

Driftwood stopped. I stayed behind him. "They were children. The Medical Examiner declared them to be Native American, but I have a friend who thinks differently."

Driftwood turned to the ocean and sat down cross-legged on the wet sand. A wave crashed over his bare feet, soaking his pants. He said something I couldn't make out, so I sat down beside him in the same fashion.

The pain I witnessed in Driftwood's face shocked me. He seemed to be reliving some past event, and for some reason I didn't think it was the war. I didn't move a muscle. I had no idea how to comfort a stranger, a loner, a recluse.

The only sound was the ocean as the tide started rolling in with stronger waves. The seagulls had gathered near the pier, as the first fishermen started dropping lines. I took in a deep breath of salt air, the panacea for all life's ills (pana-*sea*-a). It did wonders for me, but to look at Driftwood, it did nothing to clear the clouds, the cobwebs or the pain.

"O-wen!" he wailed, the force coming from his gut as he nearly doubled over to get the power to yell. The muscles in his neck strained. Veins were visible in his head, his neck, his clenched fists. "Owen!" he cried again, the sound dying in the crashing waves. And then he yelled something that made my blood run cold: "The Silo!" I looked close at Driftwood's face, surprised to see tears streaming down.

It didn't seem the time to ask questions, so we sat there in silence for what seemed like ten minutes, the waves breaking, soaking my running shoes, the seat of my shorts.

"Owen," Driftwood said finally. "My cousin. He was just a couple years older, but he was my hero. Hell, weren't no other males in my life." He laughed bitterly. "Owen was somethin'. He could run faster than the dogs and climb higher than the cats."

The lines in his face eased some. "Me and Owen. We never got into no trouble, at least not on purpose. Just boys, livin' on the poor side of town, always looking for somethin' to do."

He looked back to the waves; I had to lean in to hear his next words. "Well, one night, Owen 'borrowed' a car so we could go to town. Done it before and nobody ever cared. Always returned it by morning's light. This time the old bastard called the cops. Two poor boys in a nice Buick—in the early 60s in the south. You can guess how that ended. Me thirteen and Owen fifteen. Two young for jail, they sent us to what they called a boys' school." He paused, frowning. "Foulmire School for Boys. S'posed to reform troubled youth. Bullshit. More like a torture chamber."

His voice sounded hoarse; he coughed and tried to clear his throat. I imagined he hadn't talked this much in years.

"They fed us slop, took leather straps to us. All that was needed for me. But Owen, that boy was a rebel. Always. Didn't like being caged up; paced like an animal in the zoo. Always looking for an unlocked door. Always talking 'bout escapin' at night in the bunkhouse. I told him they ain't gonna like it if you run away. Told him they would hunt him down. And that's what happened. That's what happened to Owen.

"The first time he got loose—they beat him. Beat him bad. And he only got as far away as the barn. Hell, was he a runaway when he was still on the property? And they did it on purpose. They left that door open, knowing he would run. But Owen wouldn't see it that way. Thought he was smarter than the bastard guards. So, after he healed up some…

"Tried to get me to go with him. But I was just a young, scared kid. Looked right at me before he went through the open window of the bunkhouse, said he would come back for me." Driftwood paused, lost in the memories of his cousin. "Never saw Owen again. Without him, I was lost. A nobody. Just another piece of white trash to be kicked around.

"The one thing that kept me going was thinking Owen had made it, was somewhere on the outside. Thinking he would keep his promise and come back for me. Nobody ever talked about him, the guards, the so-called teachers. Never said they got him. It was like he got away clean as a whistle. Then one night, one terrible, godawful night…" A sob escaped Driftwood. He took a minute to regain his composure. "This kid, 'bout as old as Owen, sidles up to me one night after lights out. And he says, barely above a whisper, 'Owen's brother?' I say, 'No, cousin.' Talkin' was dangerous after lights out, so the kid just looks at me and shakes his head." Driftwood sobbed again. I started to move toward him but he held up his hand to stop. "The kid just shook his head. Then he said 'Silo' and crawled off."

Driftwood smacked his open palm on the wet sand. "The Silo! We'd all heard such bad things about The Silo, it had taken on a life of its own. Rumor was a man with dark goggles performed experiments on unruly boys in The Silo and the boys, they was either made feeble-minded or never seen again. Mantis. All us boys called him Mantis. Never saw him, but he scared the hell out of me. He was the bogeyman.

"After two years I got out," Driftwood said, wiping the tears from his face with the sleeve of his grimy army jacket. "My family had been evicted and had to move. I never found 'em. The darkies nearby, our friends, told me they never saw Owen return."

He stood and, noticing his wet pants for the first time, turned and walked toward the pier. I jumped up and followed him to a spot under the pier where the dry sand met the wet. He looked down at his wet pants again, and before I realized what he was doing, he had whipped off his pants and hung them on a pier beam to dry. Well, that explains that, I thought. I felt my own wet shorts, opting to stay clothed. Two men under the pier with their pants off? That was how rumors got started.

Driftwood plopped down bare-butt onto the sand.

"I hitchhiked to California right after that. The Merry Band of Pranksters picked me up one night. Took as many drugs as I could to forget, which worked until I got drafted. After 'Nam," he said, tapping the front of his head with two fingers. "There's bookoo bad up here I can't erase, no matter how hard I try."

Driftwood closed his eyes tight and bowed his head. "I see dead gooks. Forgot about Owen." He laid back in the sand just as a large wave crested and crashed the beach, covering him in foam. When the water receded, he said in anguish, "Now I see dead gooks and dead Owen."

I made it to the hospital on time, even managing to stop at the Flying Pig for a much-needed Green Swamp Latte. My usual routine involved entering my cubicle, twiddling my thumbs and wondering what the hell I was going to do for the next eight hours. Today, my co-worker Stanley immediately appeared, thanking me for not getting him into trouble for the little computer prank ("Merry Prankster," I called him, smiling, while I slapped him jovially on the back.) He also told me Ms. Pickles had been calling each employee into her office to have a frank discussion about the timeline of the new computer system. Her new attitude had the whole office "flummoxed" (his word, not mine). Oh, and I had two phone messages and someone waiting for me at my desk.

I rounded my cubicle corner; Carl jumped up from my chair when he saw me.

"It worked, it worked, it worked!" he cried. His eyes were bugging out he was so excited. "We had rounds and Dr. Pearson asked me for a diagnosis and I imagined him in the 'Kramer Vs. Showgirls' episode and I didn't laugh in his face, I just smiled and I told him my diagnosis and..." He paused to gulp down some air. "He smiled at me and told me 'Good job'." Carl nearly swooned when he repeated what Dr. Pearson had said and I had to move in to stabilize him.

"Hey Carl, that's great!" I exclaimed. "Just like Mary Tyler Moore, you're gonna make it after all."

"Mary who?" Carl asked, momentarily "flummoxed". "The girl who flunked out last year? She's back?"

"Never mind, Carl."

After Carl left, I called the number written on the first phone message page. It was Cincinnaticus Pearson, MD and he wanted to know what day I had arranged for his date with Dixie McCall, R.N. Apparently, it was going to take a little bribery for Carl to make it after all. I assured the good doctor I was working on it. Dixie worked nights and I would have to catch her then. "Can you talk with her tonight?" he asked, to which I reluctantly agreed.

After hanging up, I realized I had forgotten to tell Carl what I had learned from Driftwood. I glanced down at the next phone message and my jaw dropped, my heart leapt. Jaclyn had called! The message scribbled on the paper said she would be busy all day and would call back if she had a chance. I couldn't wait, so I dialed her number. After six rings, it went to her voice mail. I decided *not* to leave a message after my last few stellar attempts (which I still blame on Hallmark and Old Leghumper).

The last message was from Valaree Neutre. I called the number expecting it to be her office, but when she personally answered in a hushed voice, I realized it was her cell phone.

"Angela didn't show up for work today or call in," Dr. Neutre whispered. "I don't think she's coming back. But Brad is here. I haven't made any changes to the fentanyl cabinet and if he's the one stealing the drugs, I don't want to lose any more. When can you come back and tell me what I need to do?"

"I'll come in right after work," I promised.

I sat back and sighed. It was going to be a long, long day. I could feel the pressure building from too many commitments. Absentmindedly, I began spinning in my office chair. It made me feel better, if a bit woozy. Until Edwina Pickles roughly grabbed the back of the chair and jerked me to stop.

16 - YAK AND BULL

I opened my eyes and for just a brief moment, I thought I was in the "Land of the Giants". A huge keyboard spread in front of me. The spaces between keys were massive canyons and I was flying through them. But then reality returned—I had drifted off again at my desk. The last time my head had hit the desk, this time I landed squarely in the middle of the home keys.

Raising my head, I nearly knocked over my can of Red Bull—my first ever can of Red Bull. As a pharmacist, I knew there were a lot of interactions with medications (as well as heart muscle), but this was an emergency. It smelled like cranberries but tasted like Robitussin with Codeine. *Blech!* During one of my six trips to the bathroom (one for each Dr. Pepper, Sweet Tea and Red Bull), I missed Jaclyn's return call. The Red Bull must have gone to my head because I started thinking if I had a cell phone, it would be easier and I might not miss her calls. What the heck? (I should check the can; another side effect of Red Bull must be delusional thoughts.)

After work, I got behind the wheel of the Cube and headed for the island. Pulling into the veterinary clinic's parking lot, I realized I didn't remember much of the drive (another Red Bull side effect?) The clinic was just closing when I walked through the door. The receptionist, Cassidy Weir met me at the door and led me back to Dr. Neutre's office. I resisted the urge to ask if her parents were Merry Pranksters and she was conceived during an Acid Test while Jerry Garcia wailed away at his guitar. She was much too young for that to be the case; most likely she was conceived after Brent Mydland joined the band on keyboard in the 80s.

I stood in the hallway while Cassidy stuck her head through the door and told Dr. Neutre I had arrived. Brad Jervins emerged out of a back room, glared at me and walked out the back door, slamming it harder than necessary. I didn't even have time to pull out my Deputy Mayberry badge and flash it at him.

"Daniel, come in," Valaree Neutre said. She got up, walked around me and looked into the hallway. "Did you see Brad?"

"Yes. He went out the back door. Loudly."

She walked back to her desk, sat on top of it and sighed. "He's been angry all day. I made him count the fentanyl with me first thing this morning. He acts like I am unjustly accusing him and he won't talk to me. I was going to explain the need to change our process, that missing controlled substances are a crime, but then—*I got mad.* Mad that *someone*, whether it's Brad or not, is putting me through this. I don't need this right now!"

Her face was a mixture of anger and anguish, her blue eyes flashing. I wanted to comfort her, reassure her. Instead, I yawned. A long, wide one.

She frowned at me. "I'm sorry, am I keeping you awake?"

"Sorry," I said through the end of the yawn. "I had to get up really early this morning. The Red Pepper and Dr. Bull are wearing off." When I realized what I had said, I weakly laughed it off. "May I sit down?"

She let me sit in her chair while she remained seated on top the desk. I pulled a folded piece of paper from my pocket and smoothed it out in front of me. "Okay, I have typed it all out for you."

She looked down at the paper and back at me. "Don't worry, I typed it on my lunch hour," I said. "I didn't get in any trouble at work; I've been Pickled enough."

She squinted her eyes as if I had been talking in code and she was trying to crack it. "Sometimes," Valaree Neutre said. "I don't have any idea what you are talking about."

I nodded my understanding. If I had a nickel for every time I had heard that during my lifetime…

I pointed to the first bullet point on the page. "The paper DEA forms you use to order the fentanyl—"

"Yes, I know," she interrupted, sounding a little insulted. "It's my DEA number. I am the only one who can sign the forms."

"O-kay," I said, taken a little aback by her attitude. "Let's talk about signing them since you brought it up." I ran my finger down the list and stopped midway. "I found five DEA-222 forms that were blank as far as the drug and amount to order, but not blank at the bottom, the signature line."

"Sometimes I am so rushed, I don't have time—to sign them," she said, slowing toward the end when she realized how lame it sounded.

"Who fills out the top part, with the drug and amount?"

"Um…Brad or Angela."

167

"Who receives the order when it arrives?"

"Brad or Angela," she said softly.

"I see."

Her shoulders slumped. "Please don't judge me. There's a lot to do around here and it's hard to manage everything."

I reached for her arm, with the intention of mollifying her, but since she was sitting above me on the desk, my hand slid off and onto her leg, just below her knee. She tensed, looking at my hand on her leg and I quickly pulled it away. Smooth move, Ex-Lax.

"Look," I said, trying to forget the smoothness of her leg. "I am not judging you. The same thing has happened at countless vet clinics, physician offices, retail pharmacies and hospital pharmacies across the country. It used to be easy to trust people, but with the drug epidemic raging out of control, the processes need tightened up to prevent drug diversion." I paused, before adding, "And signing the forms ahead of time is an open invitation to anyone who even thinks about stealing."

She slammed her fist down on her leg in the exact spot my hand had been. "Dammit! Why does one or two bad apples have to ruin it for everyone!"

"Or ten or twenty or one hundred or five thousand. Drug addiction is a disease but at some point, whether at the beginning or end, it's also a choice. Lying, cheating and stealing to get your fix—is that a symptom of the disease? Getting caught and blaming your actions on drug addiction—is that a symptom or a cop-out?" I shook my head sadly. "It is not for me to say; all I know is drug use, whether illicit or abuse of prescription medications, has changed society for the worse."

Valaree Neutre's look toward me held something I could not decipher. I guess getting on my soapbox surprised her. Nodding her head finally, she asked, "So, what do I need to do to fix this?"

"First, you can't pre-sign the DEA forms. You *must* see what is being ordered; in fact, you should be the one filling out the top part of the form with the drug and amount. *Then*, you sign the form."

I tapped my index finger on the paper. "Another problem is the person receiving the order when the drug arrives. It should never be the person who filled out the form. How easy would it be for one person, without a witness, to order the drug and divert part of the order when they received it? If only one person is involved, how easy would it be to cook the books?"

"I see what you're saying," she said, nodding as she looked from the list to me.

This time I thudded a finger down on the paper, to the third bullet point. "Which brings me to the books. Your book, the cute one with the Old Yeller cover, seems to be written in some sort of Russian code. I could not decipher it, and believe me I have been able to interpret horrible physician handwriting hieroglyphics during my pharmacy career."

"Brad and Angela," she said again, this time with a slight growl in her voice. "They enter the numbers in the book."

Finger thud to the next bullet point: "And since you mentioned counting the fentanyl this morning—how often do you count the inventory."

She got up, pacing around the room in a circle. It was easy to see she was struggling with something. Finally, she came clean. "The drugs get counted when I remember to do it." She paused at a bookcase. "Which isn't very often," she added quietly, obviously embarrassed.

I resisted the urge to shout, *OMG! WTF!* (mostly because I am not a prepubescent girl and would never shout that in a million years). The doctor had her cheeks puffed out and seemed to be holding her breath; I wondered if she was flashing back to a particular coping mechanism from childhood. (I tried holding my breath once on my dad, to get him to buy me the new Skeletor figure—He-Man himself couldn't have smacked the oxygen back into my lungs any faster.) Calmly, I said, "It needs to be a perpetual inventory, or at least as perpetual as you can make it manually. There needs to be a count in the morning when you arrive and a count before you leave. *Every day.* Any discrepancies need to be resolved before anyone leaves after closing."

She finally let out her breath, blowing it out slowly.

"And," I said, pausing to make sure she was looking at me. "It needs to be written in English—the inventory numbers—by you. And no one else."

"Okay."

"And if you are the one to place the order, then someone else—a second person—needs to officially receive the boxes of fentanyl—with you—when it is delivered. A witness." I paused to sing the chorus of "Can I Get a Witness", thinking about the large, amorous nurse Flo singing it during my housekeeping days at BGCH.

"The witness should sign the book, too," I said. "And it would be prudent if there was a witness to sign each time a fentanyl vial is removed. Preferably not Brangela, for each other."

I stopped talking to let my findings sink in. Apparently, she thought I was finished, because she started cleaning off her desk, like it was time to go home. And she wasn't putting things away gently either. She seemed to be a little steamed.

"Whoa, Nelly!" I said (in honor of sportscaster Keith Jackson who had just died). "Where do you think you're going?"

She gave me a quizzical look. "You mean there's more?"

I motioned her back to the desktop and she returned to a sitting position. "Now," I said. "Let's talk about that flimsy kitchen cabinet you keep the fentanyl in…"

She listened intently as I explained, at the very least, the fentanyl needed to be kept in a sturdy, double-locked area. A metal, mounted lock-box inside a locked wooden cabinet would be the minimum storage requirements. When she asked about other options, I explained the Apoth-Allot automated dispensing cabinets at the hospital, how they required logins, continuous inventory counts and how you could get any kind of report out of the computer. I had researched smaller ones for veterinarian clinics (on my lunch hour, of course) and found one with good reviews called Paws to Count. When I told her the hefty price tag, she winced.

"You will still need to watch people if you go the dispensing machine route," I told her. "People who are determined to steal will find a way to trick the system."

"You're kidding!" she cried.

I thought of my first employment at Boiling Grove Community Hospital. "Nope—build a better mousetrap," I said. "I've seen so much drug diversion out of those cabinets I could write a book."

She dropped her head down to her bosom, burrowing her face beneath her crossed arms. From underneath the mound of hair, I heard a muffled voice, "Then what's the answer?"

"The automated systems are still your best bet, but you have to monitor the reports for diversion—stealing."

She groaned, obviously thinking of the time investment on her part, when there was no extra time to be found.

"There's no way you can monitor Old Yeller," I added.

We had spent nearly an hour discussing the different issues, when we decided to call it a night. I left my print-out on the desk and she led me to the front door. Unlocking it, she walked with me into the parking lot.

"I do appreciate your help," Valaree Neutre said as we strolled through the parking lot. "I will feel much better when I get this mess cleaned up. I've been losing a lot of sleep."

I stopped when I saw the Cube. The front driver's side tire was flat.

"Crap!"

I bent down to look at the tire, noticing a slash in the sidewall. I glanced back at the rear tire. Flat. Seeing as the Cube did not appear to be tilted to the driver's side, I didn't feel very optimistic about the tires on the passenger side. I walked around. Sure enough, both slashed as well. A Cube without tires is…well, a large, metal dumpster.

I put my hand over my heart, raising my other hand to the heavens. "If you prick us, do we not bleed? If you poison us, do we not die? If you slash our tires, do they not go 'pfftttt'?"

"Shakespeare?" she asked.

"Actually, my grandfather Finnian O'Dwyer. He was a Shakespearian actor of sorts, but mostly a gopher on films during Hollywood's Golden Age."

Valaree leaned over and ran her finger along the slash in one of the tires. "You don't have any psycho ex-girlfriends around, do you?"

"Not yet. My money's on Brad. He must have seen me drive up."

"Damn! Come on, I'll drive you home."

The outside of Valaree's black Cadillac Escalade shined like diamonds; the inside smelled like a kennel.

"Sorry," she said when we got in. "My usual passengers run around from window to window, panting and slobbering."

"I'd like to oblige," I said. "But I'm just too tired."

During the drive to my house, she told me she loved the Golden Age of Hollywood and asked what movies my grandfather had worked on. My grandfather, Finnian had passed about five years ago and I tried to remember our conversations about his time with the studios. The only thing I could remember was the time he was sent to get Greta Garbo out of her dressing room and she had screamed, "I vant to be alone!"

"My mom tells me I'm a lot like Finnian," I said as she pulled into my driveway. Finnian was on my father's side. "She says we are like two peas in a pod."

Valaree stopped on the driveway under the tree; I hoped the diabolical squirrel bomber was asleep or out on a date. Dents in the roof of her Escalade might not go over too well. I yawned. Home. I had already decided I wasn't going back to the hospital tonight to talk to Dixie McCall, R.N. I would go to bed early and get up early in the morning so I could catch the nurse before she left her shift.

Valaree looked out the front windshield, admiring my home. "The Prescription Pad," she said, reading the sign. "Looks nice."

"Thanks."

"Except for the guy leaning over your deck rail throwing up."

By the time I ran up the stairs to my deck, Willie was leaning so far over the side I didn't think I would catch him in time. I grabbed him by the back of his t-shirt and pulled him back to safety.

"I haven't thrown up since ninth grade," he gurgled. "The last time I ate—SPAM!" His eyes bugged out, his stomach gurgled and he ran back to the railing and barfed.

"Try not to think of SPAM," I said, causing Willie to spew over the edge again.

After the deluge, I got him to sit down and tried to get him to lean back in the chair. He had his hand on his side, leaning forward and wouldn't budge. He didn't even change his position when Fairbanks strolled out from under the chair, tail raised high. Seeming to sense the situation, the cat deliberately whapped his tail across Willie's face.

"Your side?" I asked.

Willie nodded.

"I think you need to go back to the hospital," I said.

When Willie didn't protest, I knew the pain was bad. Valaree Neutre appeared at my side. "Did I hear somebody mention SPAM?" she asked.

Willie moaned, ran to the rail and yakked a third time.

Valaree backed out of my driveway, peeling out and heading off the island, toward the hospital. Willie threw a fit when we tried to call an ambulance, claiming they were carriers of disease instead of patients. So, instead of a ride in a nice antiseptic ambulance, Willie was in the back seat of a Cadillac Escalade, grimacing amidst the dog slobber and pet hair.

When Valaree squealed around a curve, Willie fell over onto a pile of dog chew toys, each omitting a different, high-pitched squeak.

"Willie!" I cried. "Why did you take off your seatbelt?"

"Hurts." (*Squeak, squeak.*)

I had to unbuckle my seat belt to reach around and try to get him back upright. The cacophony of squeaks was deafening. Willie grabbed my arm with a vice-like grip, his eyes squeezed shut.

"It's going to be alright, Willie. We'll be there soon," I said, as the stop light turned green and Valaree burned rubber. My arm was starting to throb, so I reached down into the floor by his feet and got a replacement. I used my other hand to pry my arm from his grip and swapped it with a large, gently used, rawhide chew bone. Thankfully, Willie still had his eyes shut as he put both hands on the pre-chewed bone and clutched it to his breast like it would ward off his suffering. One day, if Willie flashed back to this scene, suddenly becoming cognizant of his surroundings, he would have to spend a full twenty-four hours in his decontamination shower, scrubbing his hide raw. ("Keep them doggies rollin', Rawhide!")

Valaree sped into the hospital parking lot like a demented Danica Patrick, taking the curve on what seemed like two wheels and pulling one front tire over a concrete parking bumper outside the ER entrance, taking up three parking spaces. One on each side, we practically carried Willie into the waiting room.

Fifty minutes and fifty questions later, we found ourselves in my old ER exam room. As I looked at the walls, ceiling and blue laminate cabinets, phantom jellyfish prickles once again invaded my, um…prickle area. To add to the memory, Physician Assistant Jill Comer walked in, stopping short when she saw me standing by Willie's stretcher.

Jill looked down at the diaphoretic face of Willie. "Mr. Welch. My name is Jill and I am a PA. What seems to be the problem?"

Willie moaned.

"He's got pain in the lower right quadrant," I told her on his behalf.

Jill approached Willie, saying, "Mr. Welch, we may need to get a CT scan."

"No, no, no!" cried Willie. "No radiation!"

Jill pursed her lips and looked at me. I shrugged. She palpated the area and Willie screamed.

"I'm going to have a surgeon look at you then. Dr. Olfend is on call—"

"No, no, no!"

Jill took me over to one side. "Usually in this kind of situation, I give the patient a lollypop. What do you suggest?"

"Well, I don't think tapping his nose is going to do it this time." She gave me a strange look. "Never mind. Can you knock him out?"

"Not legally. Only if we are going to do a procedure. I can give him something for the pain."

"I don't know, then. Jaclyn is pretty good at talking him down. As for me, after the 'bloodletting', as he called it, he doesn't trust me anymore."

"I'm going to have to call in the surgeon. It's probably his appendix." She started to leave, stopped, and added, "Dr. Olfend is an excellent surgeon. But don't stand too close. He spits."

Willie was moaning behind me. Valaree had picked up a clean washcloth from the counter and was wetting it in the sink. I returned to Willie's side.

"Willie, it could be your appendix. If it is, it's going to have to come out."

Valaree placed the cool washcloth on Willie's forehead; he sighed and didn't answer me.

A small, hurricane of a nurse blew into the room holding a syringe.

"Nurse Nancy!" I cried.

"Daniel," she replied. "Been staying away from the jellyfish?"

"Trying. I seem to be a jelly-magnet, though. They dig me."

"As long as they don't sting you." Nancy moved to Willie's side. "Mr. Welch, my name is Nancy and I am a nurse. I have a pain shot for you."

As I watched the nurse administer the injection, I couldn't help being reminded of the injection I had been given after the jellyfish sting. The injection that started my undercover adventure. The pain medication that had been replaced with saline. I watched Willie's face and within minutes his facial features relaxed and he was able to lay flat on the stretcher. No saline coursing through Willie's veins, only pure pain medication.

As Nancy was leaving, Jill returned to the entryway on a cell phone, speaking loud enough so we could overhear her conversation. "...no, no sign of an Amazon roller girl in a hardhat. There's a blonde woman with him, though."

Uh-oh.

Jill put the phone to her chest. "I have Jaclyn on the phone," she announced. "She wants to talk to you."

I held out my hand and she deliberately walked past me and handed the phone to Willie.

Willie listened, occasionally muttering, "un-huh" and "okay". He handed the phone back to Jill and said, "If you think I need a CT scan, I will consent."

Nancy put the phone to her ear. "I'm here," she said. After a few seconds, she handed the phone to me.

"Hello Jaclyn," I said. "Thanks for talking to Willie." Before she could say anything, I hurriedly added, "I've been trying to call you."

"Yes," she said. "I had some garbled message about Walmart and plumbers."

I didn't correct her. That made more sense than Hallmark and Leghumper.

"Who are you there with?" she asked.

Gulp. "Dr. Valaree Neutre," I confessed. "She's a veterinarian and I've been helping her—"

"The same beautiful woman you had dinner with at Duffer's Pub?"

How do you answer a question like that? *Yes, but it was only a business meeting, dear.* Thankfully, Jaclyn spoke before I could stick my foot in my mouth. "I have eyes everywhere, Daniel. Remember that."

"Yes, ma'am," was all I could think of to say.

"I've got to go. The conference wrap-up is getting ready to start. Please call and let me know how Willie is doing. He will be in good hands with Dr. Olfend." *Beep.* She was gone.

I handed the phone back to Jill. "Thank you very much," I said with a touch of sarcasm.

"Anytime." She moved around to Willie. "Mr. Welch, Dr. Olfend is on the way. How is the pain?"

Willie looked up at her with glassy eyes. "Better."

"Good."

"Ghost pirates trying to kill me."

Jill glanced at me. "He seems to be hallucinating."

"You'd think so," I said. "But no."

She started to ask a question, thought better of it, turned and left the room. I moved closer to Willie.

"Did I get you in trouble somehow?" Valaree asked, from the head of the stretcher. "Was that your girlfriend on the phone?"

"I'm not sure anymore. It'll be okay, Valaree. Not your fault." I bent down to Willie. "You doing okay, mi amigo?"

Willie took his hand and patted my face. "I love you, man."

"Yes, yes," I said. "That's fine."

"Friend," Willie said, patting my face harder.

"Yes, Willie. You've got a friend in me and all that."

Fortunately, Dr. Olfend walked in, breaking up the love- and friend-fest before it got extra mushy. A short, blonde man, possibly in his sixties, he had an air of German superiority about him even before he opened his mouth.

"I um Klaus Olfend. May I examine your area of pain?"

What did Jill mean when she said he spits? I was standing right next to the doctor and didn't see anything of the sort.

Willie pointed to his side and the doctor said jokingly, "Ve know is not your thyroid then." The only problem was when he said the "th" of "thyroid" and "then", he sprayed Willie with spittle. Sufferin' succotash! I started trying to think of other medical terms to get the doctor to say— thallium, electroshock therapy, thalidomide baby—but none of them seemed to fit the situation.

Dr. Olfend began pressing on Willie's abdomen, starting on the left side, all the while saying, "Mmm hmm." When he got to the right side, Willie's scream was blood-curdling.

Jill returned to the room behind the doctor. "No radiology," Dr. Olfend said to Jill. "O.R. stat."

"What is it, doc?" I asked.

"Appendix," he said, confirming my amateur diagnosis from the start. But then he added, "Ruptured." Dr. Olfend was looking right at me when he shouted to Jill, "Call out the O.R. team. Tell thhhem to get O.R. thhhree ready!"

They wheeled Willie out while I was still at the sink, "toweling" off. (No need for a shower now.) I thanked Valaree profusely, told her to go home and walked her to the Escalade. After promising I would have a tow truck at her office in the morning to collect the Cube, I watched her drive away. I looked at the stars in the sky and yawned. It seemed like a week ago I had met Driftwood on the beach with the stars reflecting off the ocean. The adrenaline buzz from getting Willie to the hospital was wearing off; I was crashing like the surf after a storm. With great effort, I dragged my lead feet into the hospital, in search of another Red Bull.

17 - GITCHEY LEGUMEE

Which is creepier? A. Being in a darkened cafeteria by yourself in the wee hours of the morning. Or B. Being in a darkened cafeteria by yourself in the wee hours of the morning, hearing your own lonely footsteps on the tile floor with muffled footsteps behind you; when you turn, no one is there. Or C. Dennis Rodman.

The serving area of the hospital cafeteria was pitch-black; the only area illuminated, a few tables near the vending machines. Willie was still in surgery and although extremely worried, hunger pangs had moved me from the surgery waiting room to the cafeteria in search of food. I looked around wearily, my stomach gurgling. There was a huge banner on the wall: Try the Superfood of the Month—Legumes! There were tantalizing pictures of all the types. I was so freaking hungry I could easily devour an appetizer of dwarf peas, wash it down with lentil soup, cleanse my palate with wax beans, enjoy a main course of kidney and garbanzo beans and finish it off with adzuki bean ice cream. Yum-yum! Instead, I walked over to the vending machine, fed it two dollars and chose a nasty looking, prepackaged beef burrito. As I plopped it into the small microwave nearby, I was reminded of a college roommate who would go to 7-Eleven every Friday night for a burrito and a 40-ouncer of Stroh's (which he called an oxygen bottle). I took a large bite of the burrito and remembered why I had only joined him once for his weekly snack. I quickly washed it down with Red Bull.

I returned to the surgery waiting room just as a handsome, young doctor poked his head through the inner door.

"Welch?" he called.

"Yes."

"I'm Dr. Gitchey, surgical resident with Dr. Olfend. Mr. Welch is in recovery. He came through the surgery fine, although his appendix *was* ruptured."

"Oh, that's great," I said, letting out my breath. The news was such a relief it left me lightheaded and giddy.

"He will need to stay in the hospital a few days for IV antibiotics, to make sure he doesn't develop an infection."

"Oh, that's great," I said in an entirely different tone. "You make it sound so easy."

He frowned at me, apparently confused by my answer. I felt the need to explain. "Willie doesn't like hospitals much. Getting him to stay in the bed will be like giving a cat a bath and trying to get it to stay in the tub."

Dr. Gitchey smiled. "Oh. Well, I don't think he will feel much like running out the door for a couple days, anyway."

I couldn't help giving surgical resident Gitchey the once-over. Sandy blonde hair, perfect bleached teeth, a Kirk Douglas chin dimple, healthy tan (if there is such a thing). My God, he was "Surgery Resident Malibu Ken" making my boy, Carl look like "Medical Resident Herman Munster".

He reached out his hand and I shook it. "Thank you very much," I told him.

"You're welcome. I just assisted Dr. Olfend, though. He's a brilliant surgeon and I've learned so much. Do you have any questions before I leave?"

I wanted to ask him if there was danger of Dr. Olfend drowning himself when he had on a surgical mask and said something like, "Thumb forceps, Nurse Thaxton." (I pictured a man in a diving helmet with it slowly filling with water.) Instead I asked, "Resident, huh? Do you know Carl Rodriguez?"

"The Neepster!" he cried.

I nodded, pulling him toward the wall, out of earshot from the others in the waiting room. "I'm a friend of Carl's," I confided. "I wonder if I could ask you something?"

"Sure."

"How do you think he's doing in the resident program here? Just between us."

The young resident grimaced and looked at his feet while he shuffled them.

"That bad, huh?" I said.

"It's not that Neep...er, Carl isn't smart," he said. "It's just he has trouble expressing himself. And it sure didn't help his confidence when he was assigned to Dr. Pearson. I don't think the guy's self-esteem can go any lower at this point."

"Exactly!" I agreed. "That's what I'm trying to help him with, his confidence. You from around here, Dr. Gitchey?"

"Call me Brian. Yep, I'm from Lumberton, just down the road."

"What are your plans after you finish your residency, Brian?"

He gave a pained little smile (like it was something older people, especially his parents, kept asking him). "Not really sure yet. I want to stay in North Carolina and I'd love to stay around here."

"How about Boiling Grove?"

The smile lit up his face. "Man, I'd love to stay here, join a practice nearby."

I put my hand on my chin, giving him a serious look, pretending to inspect him. I turned and walked a short distance away, muttering, "Mm-hmm, mm-hmm."

I walked back to him. "I have a confession," I told him. "I'm actually an employee here, a lowly pharmacist in I.S., but I have friends in high places—Scott Unites, the Human Resources Director plus the inimitable Dr. Cincinnaticus Pearson. For what it's worth, I could put in a good word for you. If you've gotten good evaluations while you've been here, maybe they know of someone looking for a partner."

"You'd do that for me?"

It was my turn to smile (albeit mischievously). "Sure. In exchange for a little favor…"

As I walked to 2 West in search of Dixie McCall, R.N., I felt like Hawkeye on that episode of *M*A*S*H*, trading favors with just about everyone in camp in order to get new boots. Come to think of it, I don't think he ever got those boots.

I stopped at the stairway door before the nurses' station, mouth agape. There was a giant poster on the door. I'd like to say the first thing I noticed was the enormous yellow Medi-Soit logo at the bottom or the huge, black banner at the top proclaiming "Change Beaters" with the smaller banner below asking "The New Medi-Soit Computer System—Are You Ready for *The Change?*" But my eyes were drawn to the huge head of Curly Howard of Three Stooges fame, his eyes wide and his mouth twisted, with a speech bubble stating, "Soit-enly!"

I couldn't pull my eyes from Curly and all I could think was, *man, that sure explains a lot.* A corporation with Moe, Larry and Curly as executives, masquerading as a computer company selling medical systems. (**Moe:** "Hurry up, you knuckleheads! We only have two months to get this system set up and rolling!" **Larry:** "Rolling? Has it got wheels?" **Moe:** "Sure, let me show you." *Moe's arm goes round like a wheel until his fist lands on the top of Larry's head.* **Larry:** "Ow! What'd you do that for?" **Curly:** "Only two months? Let's sympathize our watches!" **Moe:** *Brandishing a small mallet.* "Sure!"

Larry: "When you hear the conk on the dome, it will be 3 o'clock.")

The last time I had been on 2 West I had been working the midnight shift in housekeeping. It had been the first time I had worked midnights and the first time I discovered my body did not respond well to sleep deprivation. After being awake sixteen hours today, my body was starting to relive those moments—stiff neck, achy joints, zombie mind. I trudged around the corner to the nurses' station wondering if I could find some corner to curl up and take a nap. Dixie McCall, R.N. was the furthest thing from my mind.

"Hey, I remember you," came a voice from the other side of the nurses' station. It was my buddy the unit clerk, the one who had played the joke on me. "You here looking for Nurse Stampede?" The nurses and nursing assistants behind the station turned to look at me.

Before answering, I looked to make sure Dixie was nowhere in sight. "Ha-ha. Yes. Dixie Stampede. A joke that will live in infamy."

"It certainly will around here," said one of the nurses. "We will always remember it."

I smiled. "Well, I hope when you are depressed, having a crappy day, you will think of me and be cheered. That is my one wish." They all laughed, but stopped abruptly. I could sense a strong presence behind me.

Dixie McCall, R.N. still wore her little white nurse's cap perched atop her white hair; her skin seemed dotted with a few extra wrinkles and age spots. She was barely tall enough to see over the raised counter of the nurses' station but that didn't stop her glare from scattering all the personnel behind it. She still had the sultry (but scary) look of a singer in a smoky jazz joint, belting out classics like "Cry Me a River", "I'm in the Mood for Love", and "Can't Help Lovin' Dat Man" (was that last one really a classic?) I started to open my mouth to make my pitch, hoping "Dat Man" would be Cincinnaticus Pearson, MD.

"I'm sorry, you should not be in this area. Visitation ended several hours—" she started, then stopped when she got a good look at me. "You!"

I gave her a weak smile and an even weaker finger wave.

"You're the one who called me Dixie Stampede!" It looked like her anger from that night was returning, and I hadn't even said a word. "I am *not* Dolly Parton's defunct horse show from Myrtle Beach and I do *not* think that's funny!"

There was muffled laughter and snorts from the nurses' station.

"Yes ma'am. I'm sorry. It was all a huge misunderstanding." I couldn't believe I had to grovel once again for a joke in which I was the butt.

Dixie McCall's face was red as a beet, red as a lobster, corpuscle red. I had to find a way to calm her.

"Nurse McCall, I saw your picture on the employee board.

Congratulations on your fifty years at the hospital. That is quite the accomplishment."

She sputtered, her eyes grew wide, the fury seemed to dribble out of her like urine through a catheter.

"Thank you," she said in a much lower voice.

"Nurse McCall, can I have a word with you in private. I am here on behalf of a friend."

She led me to the empty nurses' lounge, causing raised eyebrows on all the employees still watching us. Once inside, she turned, craning her neck to look up at me. I crouched a little so I could look her in the eye.

I decided to lay all the cards on the table. "Nurse McCall, are you single?"

The aged nurse may have been diminutive in size, but the roundhouse slap she applied to the side of my face knocked me off balance. Still crouching and falling backwards, I tried to straighten but my momentum took me back over a chair and I flipped, landing with a crash on my keister. As I sat there stunned, I could see a sliver of the bright hallway fluorescents under the door, several shadows moving through the light. I imagined the entire staff of 2 West outside the door, eavesdropping.

I decided to stay seated. "I think you misunderstood. I'm not the one interested."

"You have some nerve! First you make a joke about my name and then—" She stopped, blinking several times and with her small intake of breath, I was reminded she was indeed female instead of a demented Florence Nightingale zombie slapper. "Someone's...interested?"

It felt safe enough to stand, so I did—keeping the chair between us just in case. "Yes ma'am. A doctor."

"A doctor," she repeated dreamily. "Here? Who is he? What does he look like?" Her tone changed suddenly. "It *is* a man, right? I am not a lesbian."

"Yes, a man. And he is tall," I said. (*Like Frankenstein's monster*, I wanted to add.) "And he's...um, well-built." (*Like Elvis during his peanut butter and banana phase.*)

"Is he nice, well behaved?" she asked.

I nodded. (*Like a wild boar who just received a surprise enema.*)

"What's his name?" she asked breathlessly.

"Dr.—Pearson," I said, clamping my eyes shut, expecting the worst.

"Cincinnaticus," she said, still dreamily.

I opened my right eye, spying the rapturous look on her face. I opened my left eye wondering if I had ended up in another dimension. Perhaps I had traveled to a time where Cincinnaticus Pearson was suave, well-mannered, and not a giant butthole.

"So, is it okay if I tell him you're interested?" I asked.

She nodded demurely, perhaps her first demure act in a quarter of a century.

"Great!" I said, heading for the door. A sudden thought caused me to stop. I turned back. "You've been at *this* hospital fifty years?"

"Lord, no. This hospital was built in the 70s and they changed the name. Before that it was about thirty miles down highway 17 in that direction," she said, pointing. "They tore down the original building."

I moved toward her. "Do you remember what was at this site before the hospital was built?"

"Sure," she answered. "The Foulmire School for Boys."

"Do you know anything about the school?" I asked, holding my breath.

"Not really."

I let out my breath dejectedly.

"But I met one of the doctors that worked at the school on several occasions."

Sharp intake of breath. "Do you remember his name?"

She shot me a glare. "*Of course.* I have a mind like a steel trap. Dr. Mantellus."

Mantellus? I thought of Driftwood. *The boys called him Mantis.*

"You wouldn't happen to know if he is still alive, would you?"

Her eyes narrowed. "Why?"

"A friend of mine is trying to find out what happened to his cousin, a, um…patient of Dr. Mantellus who attended the reform school." Calling Driftwood's cousin, Owen a *patient* of the doctor was about as truthful as calling Driftwood my friend.

Dixie McCall studied me, crinkling her nose and unleashing a new horde of face wrinkles. "Dr. Pearson?" she asked.

"Will be contacting you soon." I remembered Dr. P's near panic attack at the thought of making a date with her. "Or maybe I will personally set up your date." I started humming "Matchmaker" from *Fiddler on the Roof.*

A huge smile erased the horde of wrinkles. Not sure if it was due to the possible romance with a doctor or she really liked that scene with Hodel and Chava.

She dropped her voice. "I shouldn't be telling you this, but the last time Dr. Mantellus was a patient on 2 West, he was discharged back to Mendle's Psychiatric Center." She made a quick face. "I'm sorry, Mendle's Mental Health and Convalescent Center as it is now called. It's over near Fort Fisher and Kure Beach."

"Thank you."

"That's been a while ago and he was pretty old and in bad shape then…"

I nearly jumped out of the bedside chair when I heard the sound of a food tray crashing to the floor. The last thing I expected to see on the floor of Willie's room was a Catholic Priest flailing about in turkey giblet remnants and jiggling Jell-O cubes.

I closed my eyes. After fussing around Willie, making sure he was going to be okay, I had collapsed into the chair and fallen immediately asleep. I must be dreaming. Or hallucinating. Could "Catholic priest doing the backstroke through giblets and gelatin" be another side effect of Red Bull?

Earlier, I had picked at Willie's tray, sampling the food (after he finished looking at it, making derogatory remarks about the kitchen staff and shoving the bedside table with an order to "get this out of my sight"). Turkey giblets along with instant mashed potatoes and Brussels sprouts seemed a strange post-op meal. And what happened to legumes—the Superfood of the Month? There was no way Willie would eat anything from the cafeteria anyway, so it was a moot point. I'd have to run out and get him some organic crap on my lunch hour.

The tinkling, rolling sound of glass across the floor and a sharp cry caused me to open one eye. Yep, it was a priest floundering in the food, his cassock soiled. He tried to get up by bracing his hand on the floor, but it slipped in what appeared to be gravy and he fell heavily on his shoulder and rolled to his back. I expected to hear a Hail Mary, but instead the sound of barely suppressed laughter reached my ear. I stood and walked over to stand directly over the priest.

"Need a hand?"

The priest was surprised to see me. After a few seconds, he resumed chuckling. "You have no idea. Are you an angel? Did God send you to help me out of my ridiculous predicament?"

"An angel of the Lord appeared to him standing at the right side." After I said it, I grimaced, looking to the ceiling, expecting a real angel of the Lord to smote me. There are times I should think before I speak.

He looked at me with wide eyes. "You are a strange angel."

I laughed. "I've been called a strange agent before but never a strange angel." I reached down my hand, he took it and I helped him to stand. His foot slipped only once in the mess as I helped him maneuver out of it.

"I am Father Spinelli," he said. "Thank you."

Father Spinelli looked to be late forties, early fifties, a bit overweight and out of shape for a priest. As he adjusted the thick, black plastic frame of his glasses on his nose, he smeared giblet gravy on his cheek. He had kind eyes and a clumsy grace about him.

"Are those turkey giblets?" he asked, looking down. "I'm afraid I made a mess."

I suppressed a sudden burp and tasted giblets. "Yes," I coughed. "I ate some of them earlier and they may just end up on the floor, too."

The priest looked aghast. "I'm sorry Mr. Galvin. Let's get you back to bed." He took my arm to lead me toward the hospital bed.

I planted my feet and stopped him from pulling me. "Whoa there, Father. I'm not Mr. Galvin. I'm Daniel O'Dwyer."

Father Spinelli looked to the hospital bed, spying a body under the covers. "I'm sorry." He appeared flustered, adjusting his glasses. "You are just visiting Mr. Galvin?"

I smiled. "You are having a bad night, Father. This is Willie Welch's room. And that," I said, pointing toward the bed. "Is Willie Welch."

"Oh my," he said. "Is Mr. Welch a practicing Catholic?"

I didn't know how to answer that question. The only things I had seen Willie practice were organic living and irritating the hell out of me.

"Chaplains don't usually get calls in the middle of the night unless it is for last rites. And I received a call that Mr. Galvin needed to see me urgently."

"Willie had emergency surgery and was just moved here a few hours ago. Maybe Mr. Galvin was in here before that."

"Oh dear. That doesn't sound good for Mr. Galvin. I need to find him one way or another." He turned to the door, but had another thought. "Your friend, Mr. Welch, is he going to be okay?"

I looked down at the drugged, serene face of my friend. "Yes. He had a ruptured appendix. As long as we can fight off the infection," I said, pointing to the intravenous piggyback bag of antibiotic dripping through the IV tubing. (And as long as they make restraints strong enough to keep him in bed after he awakens.)

I had another thought. "Father Spinelli, do you think maybe the Lord sent you in here for a reason?"

"Yes, that happens to me all the time. My life is devoted to His guidance and He has sent me off on some crazy tangents." He chuckled. "Some will tell you I am a bit, oh, scatter-brained and maybe, you know—out there." He laughed loudly this time. The Father pointed to the spilled tray and continued: "But the Lord, he also knows I'm a bit clumsy and I think He likes a good laugh every once in a while.

"Mr. O'Dire, would you like me to pray for Mr. Welch?"

Ignoring the mangling of my last name, I said, "Definitely. But Willie has another problem you may be able to help with." I looked him directly in the eye, to gauge his reaction. "Have you ever been involved with an exorcism of a—"

"Oh my, yes!"

Before I could get a word in, Father Spinelli proceeded to tell me the story of a possessed woman he was called in to help. At the time, he did not believe in possession; other possible cases he had seen before turned out to be extremely delusional people in need of therapy. But this one, he claimed, was real. He saw the woman, ninety pounds soaking wet, throw a two hundred-pound Lutheran deacon across the room. She spoke in multiple voices and languages, including Latin. And worst of all, he shivered when he told me this part, she knew things about his past that not many people knew. It all sounded right out of a Hollywood movie to me, but the way he told it made me believe.

His eyes were still lost in his experience when I said, "This is definitely possession of a *she*, just not a person."

"Oh?" he asked curiously.

"*Silent Cow.*"

He frowned, pulling back from me a little. He looked deep in thought. "You want me to exorcise a demon from…livestock?"

I laughed. "No, the *Silent Cow*—she's a boat." I gestured toward the hospital bed. "Willie's houseboat."

The priest laughed, long and loud. "You have no idea the visions that were flashing through my mind, all of us walking around a cow in a field, trying to banish a demon from the poor creature."

"Watch out for cow patties," I couldn't help adding.

Father Spinelli howled loud enough to wake the dead…er, demons; Willie however, loaded with propofol, midazolam and fentanyl from the surgery, slept on.

After he calmed, I told him a story: "The Haunting of the *Silent Cow*." The only parts I left out were Madame Matilda and her Ouija board, Pickford and the toothbrush and Polythene Pam (I didn't think the ghost pirates inflating a blow-up doll and levitating it would entice him to help Willie).

"I don't have any experience with the exorcism of places." Father Spinelli put a hand to his chin, thinking. "I may have some colleagues that would know what to do."

I thanked the priest, giving him my home and work phone numbers, telling him not to worry about cleaning up the spilled tray.

"But you may want to change your robe before finding Mr. Galvin," I said, pointing to the food stains on his cassock.

He looked down, shook his head and Father Spinelli, the clumsy priest, left the room laughing at himself.

After cleaning up the mess, I collapsed back into the beside chair, falling asleep instantly. Strange dreams of exorcism filled my head, but the weirdest one involved priests in a pasture, surrounding a cow. I became agitated when the once silent bovine started speaking Latin in multiple voices, saying things like "Remugis!", "Vitula eligans tacere ultra", and "Bovem de stercore", but woke up wild eyed, in a sweat when Matilda appeared on the back of the cow in nothing but a red polka dot bikini, singing an old dirty blues song, "If It Don't Fit (Don't Force It)".

No matter how hard I tried, I could not unsee that image. And I kept hearing the words to the dirty blues song. (*You don't seem to understand my position, I never let you put my works out of commission! If it don't fit, don't force* it.) There would be no more sleep for me. I stumbled out of Willie's room, trying to forget Matilda in a red polka dot bikini atop the not-so-silent cow, to search for more Red Bull.

18 - FRUIT CUP AND (DRUM) ROLL

I thought by this time, I would be cruising in first gear on my job, preparing to shift into second gear. I sat at my cubicle desk, stuck in park. With nothing else to do, I started a staring contest with my computer monitor. First one to blink loses. After two minutes, the computer monitor went to sleep.

Normally I would celebrate such a victory (screaming something like, "Take that Dell! I beat you, bitch!"), but I just sat there numbly, worried I was getting hooked on Red Bull.

The most exciting part of my day so far had been the hour I spent in the cafeteria right around the morning shift change for the nursing staff. All the talk had centered around the upcoming total solar eclipse.

"I went to five stores looking for eclipse glasses, and they are all sold out!"

"In my day, you just poked a hole in a shoebox or a paper plate." (Said by an older nurse who was subsequently ignored by the younger ones.)

"Where am I going to find eclipse glasses?"

"Will you really go blind if you look at it?"

"Yes, that's one of two things that will make you go blind."

"My kids are dumber than stumps. I told 'em they can't look at the eclipse without glasses but I'll probably have to keep 'em locked in the basement. They can look at the next one."

"The Department of Transportation signs on the highway say something like, 'Solar eclipse coming. Plan ahead.' What do they mean by plan ahead? What's going to happen?"

"I got some eclipse glasses at Eagles several weeks ago."

"Did they have ISO stamped on them somewhere?"

"What?"

"If they don't meet the ISO standards and have ISO stamped on them somewhere, you got took."

"Damn!"

"You know, if you have old welding glasses or goggles, some of them are safe to use." (Older nurse—ignored.)

"I'VE GOT TO FIND SOME ECLIPSE GLASSES!"

Truth be told, I had forgotten all about the total solar eclipse. When was it, next Monday? From the cafeteria talk I had sensed more fear than Y2K, more excitement than the Bicentennial of the United States, and more merchandising opportunities than a new Star Wars movie.

After the cafeteria, I had gone back to Willie's room to find him rousing from his stupor. He looked at me with bleary eyes and I wasn't sure he recognized me. He never tried to speak, just surveyed his surroundings, then closed his eyes without a word. Not one word, which was good news. The longer Willie stayed stoned, the easier it would be to keep him in the hospital. A quick word with his nurse and he assured me Willie was doing fine, with no evidence of infection.

Still early after leaving Willie's room, I decided to nose around a part of the hospital I had never been in, walking past office doors with names like "Quality", "Risk Management", "Ethics and Compliance". I was half searching for a locker room with a shower, half snooping. A rotund man exited a door marked "Financial Services" just as I rounded a corner. He looked at me suspiciously.

"Sir, you aren't wearing a hospital ID and you don't belong in this—"

"Okay, okay!" I half-growled, not liking the tone of his voice. I reached into my right pocket for my ID. Empty! His eyes grew wide and he started breathing heavily. What did he think I was reaching for, a weapon? My ID wasn't in my left pocket either—I only pulled out the butt-end of my black beeper, stuffing it back inside quickly.

"Daniel O'Dwyer, Information Services, Pharmacy Unit," I growled, thinking of nothing else to say. The man's face had turned red, he was sweating. I'm not sure any of my words registered. "This hallway needs to remain clear. Make sure you tell the others in your department." He looked at me blankly, fear in his eyes. "Stay out of the hallway," I added gruffly. I walked away from him with a masculine, Eliot Ness type stride.

I heard the door slam behind me, loud, frantic words and the sound of scraping furniture. Strange, but I kept going.

The stairway at the end of the hallway led me directly down to the surgery department. I found Greg at the start of his shift and he let me use the male showers in the surgery locker room for a second time. Greg's t-shirt was available again; instead I chose to remain in my crumpled work clothes from yesterday. Even though Pickles had mellowed somewhat, I didn't think she would approve of a "Got Naloxone?" t-shirt in her department. I also explained to Greg my transportation troubles ("Oh man, you're Cubeless!" Greg said, laughing) and he agreed to let me use his car at lunch to get Willie something organic to eat. I felt like I was taking advantage of Greg when I submitted a third request, a ride to the Southport Ferry Terminal after work. I explained I didn't know when the Cube would be ready once I had it towed to Extreme Tires along Route 133 in Southport (*Extreme Tires* for an extremely ugly car seemed fitting). He went above and beyond by offering to take me all the way to Fort Fisher and Kure Beach. What a pal.

After sprucing up, I ascended the same stairs and retraced my steps down the hall, passing the Financial Services door. The door opened a few centimeters and I could make out the large, bloodshot eye of the rotund man staring out. He slammed the door, crying, "Code Silver! Code Silver!" I could see a large shadow moving behind the frosted glass; sounded like a desk was being scooted. I heard shouts and women screaming.

I scanned the hallway but I seemed to be the only one around. Code Silver? Is that code for a missing geriatric patient? I should have paid more attention at orientation. Oh well, it seemed like a strange time for a drill, but accountants were kind of odd. Maybe this sort of activity kept them going, got them through their day after countless hours of looking at boring numbers.

I pounded the spacebar, bringing my computer back to life. Might as well test the thirteen drugs that were finally set up in the limited test environment of Medi-Soit. The representatives claimed the full test system would be up and functioning by the end of the week. Whoop de doo. They also said all the previous work had definitely been lost when the test system crashed and would have to be redone. Double whoop de doo.

By ten thirty, I had tested all the drugs in the database backwards, forwards and sideways. At least they worked as designed and I didn't have to report any "Medi-Bugs" as the company affectionately called them on their test scripts (complete with a drawing of an insect head with antennae, a computer monitor as its thorax with six legs sprouting out). I was supposed to validate the test script by initialing each step (which I did) and signing at the bottom of the last page. I hesitated signing my name to the document, instead picking up the small toy drum that had been delivered to each member of the I.S. team this morning as well as all the "volunteers" (uh…yeah, right) in each department, the Change Beaters.

Todd Rundgren's primitive song suddenly popped into my head; I banged my tiny drum with my tiny drum stick and couldn't help singing.

"I don't want to work,
I want to bang on the drum all day.
I don't want to play,
I want to bang on the drum all day."

I paused singing, still banging the drum. I unfolded the paper with one hand that had been packaged with the drum and read it. Change Beaters would be responsible for "reverberating the river of change" throughout the facility, for "guiding the employees through the *rhythm* of change". Sounded to me like we would be drubbing change into our senseless victims by any means necessary (Mafioso came to mind), whether they wanted it or not. I threw the paper over my shoulder and continued wailing:

"Every day when I get home from work,
I feel so frustrated; the boss is a jerk.
And I get my sticks and go out to the shed.
And I pound on that drum like it's my boss's head."

I was making so much noise I didn't hear Edwina Pickles come up behind me. With a thwack of a rolled up Medi-Soit Installation Guide to the back of my head, she banged my drum.

Just before noon, Willie was irritable, hungry and vocal. He threw the mystery meat from his tray across the room like a petulant child. Welcome back, my friend. I promised to go to Lowe's Foods and bring back all things organic.

Carl had called my office right after Edwina Pickles had whapped me in the back of the head (setting my mind right). It wasn't stars I saw as I signed the bottom of the test script—it looked more like broken glass shards. When I shook my head, it rattled. Carl seemed excited about something, insisting we meet. I invited him along on "Mission: Organic" since that would take my whole lunch hour, meeting him in the hospital lobby.

Carl came clomping up to me on his huge feet, swinging his arms excitedly. I stifled a laugh. He could give Monty Python's John Cleese a run for his money at the Ministry of Silly Walks.

"It's been the best day of my life!" Carl shouted, his words echoing off the lobby walls. Heads turned, but Carl was oblivious. "First—first—" He paused, panting like a dog, unable to get out the next word.

I placed my hands on his shoulders, calmly giving Carl directions. "Breathe. Deep breaths." Carl looked me in the eye and followed my lead as we both inhaled deeply and exhaled slowly. "And again," I directed.

Even his sudden respiratory problems, however, couldn't wipe the huge smile from Carl's face.

"Do you need to sit down?" I asked, motioning to the same lobby couch I had taken him to after he had bowled me over at our first meeting.

"No, no. I'm okay." Carl went through one more round of breathing, before suddenly roaring, "Dr. Pearson gave me a compliment!"

Carl jumped in the air and landed on his giant flipper feet. "Yes!" he shouted.

"On rounds he asked me for a diagnosis. I thought, here we go again. Always asking me for a diagnosis. So, I pretended he was the unfunny *Robot Chicken* episode and I looked at all the signs and symptoms and answered 'lupus'. Dr. Pearson looked at me, smiled, and said…" Carl straightened himself, puffed out his cheeks and dropped his voice. "Good job, Dr. Rodriguez."

Carl squealed and spun around. I couldn't help clapping my hands, giving him a rousing round of applause.

"Good job, Dr. Rodriguez," Carl repeated in a deep voice.

"That's awesome, my man! I knew you could do it!"

"He's never, ever called me doctor. And then, this other resident, Brian—Brian Gitchey, asked me if I wanted to join the other residents to study for the boards. Can you believe it?"

I clapped him on the back. "That's great Carl. I'm so happy you had a banner day. Come on." I led him out the door into the sunshine. I dangled Greg's car keys in my hand; he said his car was a silver Ford Focus. I gazed across the sea of white and silver cars in all three employee parking areas. Dang, wished I had thought to ask him where he parked. I sent Carl to one area to search while I walked to another, weaving in and out of the cars, peering at makes and models. Greg told me he had nicknamed his car "Lackof" to go along with Focus, but that did me no good in my search. I didn't think the car would come running if I called out its name.

Bending over, trying to make out the model on a silver car, a large slap on my behind caused me to bump my head into the trunk. I stood up, rubbing my cranium and turned right into the dangerous décolletage of Sparkle.

"Eye Candy! I thought that was you skulking around the cars! You looking to steal one? Need me to be the lookout?" She put her hand above her eyes and scanned the parking lot comically.

Sparkle laughed and grabbed me in a big bear hug, smashing me into her bosom. I couldn't breathe; the only parts of my face free were one eye and one ear so I listened and searched the parking lot for help. From the depths of her chest I heard the beginning of a yodel. I saw two women coming at me and I waved weakly, with the last of my strength. My oxygen was depleting fast. After waving weakly back, the two women stopped. *Save me,*

I tried to cry, but the only effect was some of my last, precious air leaked out. The world was going fuzzy. What a way to go.

Just like that, the yodel ended and I was released, gasping, coughing and gulping the wonderful North Carolina air. When my eyes focused and I could quit weaving like a punch-drunk boxer, I expected the male hardhat to walk by and say, "You've been triple-yodeled, man. You're doomed!" but instead I saw the two women still standing there, ten yards away.

"Hello Daniel," Jill Comer, Emergency Room Physician Assistant extraordinaire said. Beside her, Nurse Nancy gave me a little wave.

I have eyes everywhere, Daniel. Jaclyn's words echoed through my muddled mind.

"Going out to lunch?" I asked feebly.

Jill ignored my question, instead turning her attention to Sparkle. "Are you a roller girl?"

"You got it!" Sparkle said enthusiastically. "Cape Fear Roller Girls." She made what I can only assume was a roller derby program pose.

Clumsily, I made the introductions. When the two left, Jill looked at me sadly, making a slight clucking sound with her tongue.

"Look, Sparkle," I started. "Those two are friends of—"

A loud shout interrupted my attempt at admonishment. It came from the direction of the construction area and the parking lot where I had sent Carl. We took off running and I had a hard time keeping pace with Sparkle (in my defense, her powerful legs were used to short bursts of roller sprints; I'm more of a distance runner). She reached the edge of the pit a few seconds before me. We stood there staring down at an incredible sight.

A compact, powerful looking man in a hardhat was grappling with a tall, gangly kid (with big feet). They both had their hands on something white between them, pulling back and forth like overgrown kids at a preschool shouting, "Mine!"

"Carl!" I cried, jumping down in the pit.

"Tank!" Sparkle yelled, following me.

Although I suspected it was not a white volleyball they were arguing over, when we reached them I was still shocked to see the distinct nasal bone and mandible of a skull.

Carl saw me and cried, "He was trying to hide it!"

"You little shit!" Tank yelled. He let loose of the skull and Carl went tumbling backwards to the dirt. Tank charged and jumped on top of him, pummeling him with his fists.

Sparkle and I hit Tank about the same time, knocking him off Carl. He came up swinging, saw Sparkle and directed his punches at me. He punched with his right and I sidestepped left, feeling the air from his fist as it missed. A bear-like growl and he threw another punch at my head; I ducked just in time. When his steel toed boot shot up, I caught it with both hands before it could connect with my groin. Fool me once, shame on you. Fool me twice...

While I had Tank hopping on one leg, Sparkle calmly kicked his other leg out from under him. Tank hit the ground on his back with a thud, knocking the air out of him.

"Damn it, Tank! I'm writing you up this time!" Sparkle looked like she wanted to give him another kick while he was down.

I went to Carl. He was lying on his back, crying and "neeping" and "acking", clutching the skull to his chest. So much for his banner day.

I knelt down beside him. "Carl, are you okay?"

He stopped sobbing when he heard my voice, no doubt realizing the danger had passed. With one last "neep", he lifted the skull from his chest and gazed into the indented eye sockets. A look of wonder crossed his face.

Sparkle had disappeared but returned quickly with an evidence bag. "You got to put it in here," Sparkle told Carl. "That's what they told me to do if we found any other bones. And I have to call them, too," she added, sighing.

Carl was mesmerized by the skull, as if it spoke to him, telling him a story.

"Carl, you have to put it in the bag," I told him, gently. He had a strange, determined look and a weird half-smile as the skull disappeared into the plastic.

By the time I made sure Carl was okay (after we got him checked for cuts and dusted off, he was strangely quiet and calm, saying he needed to go do some research), I didn't have time to look for Greg's car, let alone organic shop for Willie. I rushed to the cafeteria, found a sealed fruit cup in a vending machine, a multi-grain roll from the cafeteria line and hurried back to Willie's room. I made a quick stop at the nurses' station and asked around until I found a nursing assistant with a permanent marker and good penmanship.

Willie was sitting up in bed when I arrived and handed him his lunch. Throwing the multi-grain roll aside, he asked, "What's this?"

"Organic fruit cup." He was studying the label. The nursing assistant had done a good job modifying the label but I didn't want Willie looking at it for long. "The Big O," I added. "I'm sorry I didn't have time to get anything else, but if you like it, I can get more." Shoot! I forgot to get the name of the artistic nursing assistant in case I needed her later.

"It doesn't matter," Willie said sadly. "I am *not* eating any of the toxic material they bring me on those trays." He peeled the cellophane off the fruit cup and I hurried over to take it, lest he see the word "organic" carefully written on the outer wrapper in Sharpie.

Willie lifted his fork but before sticking it in the fruit cup, I could see his eyes drifting to the label again. I was desperately trying to figure out a distraction when Willie's resident doctor walked in.

"I'm Dr. Gitchey, Mr. Welch. Dr. Olfend's surgery resident. How's lunch?" Brian Gitchey asked Willie.

Willie stuck his fork in the cup, removing several pieces of fruit (sorry, *organic* fruit) and put them in his mouth, chewing slowly. He made a "not bad" shrug and I relaxed. Apparently, he would not turn into The Incredible Hulk if something non-organic touched his lips.

"When can I go home?" Willie asked, a little fruit cup syrup dribbling from the corner of his lip.

"Mr. Welch," Dr. Gitchey said confidently. "We need to keep you *at least* a couple more days."

I was making the slashing gesture across my throat but Brian Gitchey did not see me.

"You need to have intravenous antibiotics for forty-eight hours before we can switch you to oral," he continued.

I made the slashing sign as hard as I could across my throat but "Surgery Resident Malibu Ken" still didn't notice. It was too late now.

"Antibiotics!" Willie shrieked. He glanced frantically at the IV piggyback containing the cephalosporin antibiotic dripping into the tubing chamber, which gave me just enough time to pin his left arm down before he tried to rip the IV line out of his right.

Brian Gitchey was noticeably shaken. "Mr. Welch, you've—got to have the antibiotic. Your appendix ruptured."

"Antibiotics are dangerous!" Willie was nearly foaming at the mouth (fruit cup foam, the worst kind), trying to break his left arm free. "They increase the risk of cancer, heart disease, cause problems in your stomach!" I was starting to break a sweat holding his arm down.

"I don't understand." The resident was red in the face and sweating as well, although he wasn't helping me a bit. "If we don't give you antibiotics, you could get an infection which could be fatal." He looked at me, asking, "What did he think we were going to treat him with?"

"Natural antibiotics!" Willie screamed. "Like raw garlic, oil of oregano, even colloidal silver."

"Is he serious?" Brian Gitchey whispered to me.

"Yes," I said. "Willie is a time traveler from the past, the mid-fourteenth century to be exact. He survived the bubonic plague on nothing but natural ingredients."

Brian Gitchey stood there looking at both of us like we were crazy. He had a long career ahead of him and I didn't think he'd even scratched the surface of crazy patients, although dealing with Willie put him a leg up in that category. Willie began thrashing in bed and the resident just stood there, helpless.

"Dr. Gitchey," I said calmly. "Would you please get me a nurse."

Pickles glared at me. She was giving me "The Look". I could imagine young children bawling if caught in her yard or flower garden, dogs running away from her yowling. Girl Scouts would not venture to her door to sell cookies. For me, the look was standard. I had gotten used to it. I had only been ten minutes late from my lunch break and you would have thought I had broken every rule in the BGCH Employee Handbook (some twice). I promised her I'd retest the thirteen drugs in the limited test database that I'd already tested and retested. She plopped a clean copy of the same test script I had already completed in front of me. For some reason, my delightful personality and upbeat attitude seemed to rub her the wrong way.

Edwina Pickles left, picking another victim, screaming about the inability to reach Accounting all day. (Accounting? Financial Services?)

I peered over my cubicle wall, finding Stanley at his desk. "Hey Stanley, what's Code Silver."

"Huh?" he said, looking up at me. "It's on the back of your ID badge."

Dropping back down in my chair, I turned over my ID badge: Code Red-Fire; Code Blue-Cardiopulmonary Arrest; Code Amber-Infant/child abduction; Code Silver—"

"Active shooter!" I cried. I replayed the scene in my mind. Surely the rotund accountant hadn't thought I had a gun. I stood, intending to go over there immediately and straighten out the misunderstanding.

Pickles returned to the room, growled at me and pointed to the test script.

I sat down. Oh well. The last time I turned in an expense report, Financial Services did make me wait four weeks for the reimbursement check—I guess they can wait a little longer for the "all clear".

Absentmindedly, I started testing a ciprofloxacin 500mg tablet, emulating the physician ordering it on his or her side (on test patient Seymour, Butts—at least someone in the department had a sense of humor, even if a bit infantile), through pharmacy verification including allergy/interaction checking and scheduling, and finally the nursing electronic medication record system where I pretended to administer it to the patient (skipping the barcode scanning step since I didn't actually have the drug). Strangely, it did not test any different than the five other times I had tested the drug.

I thought of Willie. It hurt my heart to leave him in that kind of state. One nurse had taken my place holding him down so he wouldn't pull out his IV line and the other ran out of the room to get an order for lorazepam and restraints from Dr. Olfend. Willie didn't even get to finish his fruit cup.

I changed the ciprofloxacin order, testing the "modify" function, by switching the physician name to Dr. Pearson. My mind drifted to Carl. For the first time, I wondered how to get in touch with him. He had always been the one to find me, even paging me that one time. I looked down at the blasted beeper attached to my pocket. The only page I had received was from Carl (although I'm surprised Edwina Pickles hadn't started paging me, to torture me for my transgressions). I unclipped the beeper and started pressing buttons—Carl's earlier message magically appeared. I wasn't sure how to erase it (maybe I should have read the instruction pamphlet Scott had given me). I pressed the buttons again, this time faster in case that made a difference. I wondered if it would give me the number Carl had called from, hoping it was his cell phone, but nothing of the sort came up on the screen. I guess I would have to wait to hear from him, hoping he was okay and not experiencing any aftereffects from his tussle with Tank.

Starting to nod off, I took another slug from the blue, silver and red can nearby. It made me feel like china in a bull shop (I'm not sure what that means, other than I've had far too much Red Bull these last two days). My thoughts were slurred. I needed sleep. I missed Jaclyn. I continued testing the same drugs. Even though my eyes were open, I was technically sleeping on the job (breaking yet another rule in the BGCH Employee Handbook).

Edwina Pickles reentered the room. "O'Dwyer!"

19 - (BIKINI) BOTTOM FEEDER

A few misguided gulls and seabirds followed the ferry, in search of a handout. Rather than following a large boat with thirty or so automobiles on it, the birds would be better pressed to use their sixth sense and find a shrimp boat. Later, when I walked to the stern and saw kids throwing bread to the birds, I realized I was the one misguided. Never underestimate the intelligence of our fine feathered friends (I thought of Edgar Allan Crow and my stolen sunflower seeds and shivered).

Greg exited the driver's side of his silver Ford Focus (it had a large Narcotics Anonymous bumper sticker, "NA Just for Today" on the back, so I probably could have found it in the hospital parking lot if I hadn't been delayed by Sparkle and the skull). He joined me at the railing, watching the ferry pull away from the Southport terminal.

To drive to Kure Beach without using the North Carolina Department of Transportation Ferry Division would mean driving thirty-five miles to Wilmington, through all the stop lights in the town (at least twenty more minutes, depending on traffic), taking U.S. 421 down the coast to Pleasure Island (beware Pinocchio!), the barrier island that contains Carolina Beach and farther south, Kure Beach. Taking the ferry, it's just a skip over to Southport, drive onto the boat, travel four miles across the scenic Cape Fear River and land at Fort Fisher, just below Kure Beach. All for five dollars a carload. Best bargain of the twenty-first century.

Greg's longer hair was whipping in the wind like the blue and white North Carolina Ferry System flag on the bridge. Some of the passengers had climbed the stairs to the second deck to get a better (and windier view).

"Whew, man!" Greg deadpanned. "Are you ever going to change that shirt? Can you stand downwind?"

I mimed a laugh. (But just to be sure, I smelled my right pit.)

Greg watched the other passengers ascend the second deck stairway with great interest. I followed his gaze to see three twenty-something blondes in too-short shorts (Daisy Dukes!) disappear up the stairway. When they were out of sight, he turned back to me.

"How's Wild Willie doing?" he asked, shouting over the wind, pausing to spit out a few strands of hair that had danced into his mouth.

I sighed long and loud (reminding me of Jaclyn). "Surgically, everything was repaired," I said, raising my voice to be heard. "Medically, he needs at least a seven-day course of antibiotics because of the rupture. Mentally...well, he's Willie."

I was still really worried about my friend. But under the influence of lorazepam, at least the nurses had been able to remove his restraints. I hated seeing him tied down like Frankenstein's monster or Quasimodo on the whipping wheel. I didn't want him going on a hunger strike like Gandhi, so I had cashed in my favor to Dr. Neutre. Valaree promised she would go to Lowes Foods; "All natural," she had said (I thought she said "au naturel", a stunning vision but not legal in Brunswick County, not even in the produce section). Willie would have a fine dinner tonight with good company.

"When I left," I said. "Willie was lobbying Dr. Olfend for an olive oil drip instead of antibiotics."

"Good luck on swaying Olfend. He's as stubborn as a mule," Greg said.

"And spits like a camel," I couldn't help adding.

Greg laughed, turned his back to the rail and looked up to the second deck. He let out a little mewling cry, kind of like a kitten stuck up in a tree for the first time. When I turned around, he had a big goofy grin on his face and was giving a little wave. I looked up to see the three blondes smiling down at us. Yowzah! (For the first time, I understood the phrase "the image was seared into my retinas".)

Greg turned to the rail again; I continued watching while the girls leaned in, whispering in each other's ear, like someone could hear them over the roar of the wind. It wasn't like my friend to turn his back on such a show.

"Are you feeling alright?" I asked Greg, twisting my body back to him. (My head stayed focused on the second deck—I had to take my hand, place it on my cheek and force it back to look at him.)

"Yeah—I don't know." He looked at me, a pained expression on his face. "Obviously I have an addictive personality. I've always known that. Since NA, the only addictions I enjoy are women and Mountain Dew/Code Red."

I looked back at the three blondes. "So, you want to go talk to them?"

He shook his head sadly. "Naw."

I made the exaggerated gesture of grabbing his wrist and checking his pulse.

"I know, I know," he said. "I don't know what it is. I don't get the same pleasure from my exploits as I used to."

Greg looked so sad. I didn't know what else to do but joke. "What? Are you going to WA now?"

He didn't laugh, but he did smile weakly. "Where the motto is 'One Woman at a Time'? Yeah, I guess it is kind of like that."

I had never heard him talk in such a manner. Women were the one thing that caused his eyes to sparkle, put the giddyup in his step. Without them, I was truly worried about him.

I guess he saw the look in my eye, because he chuckled, putting his hand on my shoulder. "It's okay, man. It's not that bad. I think I'm just bored. I don't have anything in common with young chicks anymore, kind of like that Steely Dan song where he sings, 'Hey nineteen, that's Aretha Franklin. She don't remember the Queen of Soul'."

Our heart-to-heart was interrupted by the sister ferry boat going the other direction, from Fort Fisher to Southport. We stopped to wave at the other passengers, as excited to see us as we were them.

When the other ferry was out of sight, Greg continued: "I think I'd just like to meet an interesting woman. She doesn't necessarily have to be my age, but someone who would knock my socks off. Make me say *wow*."

I thought long and hard, looking at him for at least a minute or two. "How do you feel about roller derby and yodeling?"

Greg drove slowly in the line of cars unloading from the ferry, pulling out onto the Fort Fisher terminal. I had always planned on making a trip to Fort Fisher to explore, but had only used the ferry to pass through on my way to and from Wilmington.

The whole area was a living monument to the early Southern United States. Wilmington, the grand dame with historic mansions, brick streets, old cemeteries. Fort Fisher, the reminder of more troubling times. No parties; no dinners; no stained glass windows or silverware—the fort was a place where the future of the United States had actually been decided.

Fort Fisher, a confederate fort during the Civil War, today a National Historic Landmark, was unusual since it wasn't a brick and mortar fort. It was made of earth and sand mounds and because of its location, the sea on one side and land on the other, could be easily defended, earning the fort the nickname "Gibraltar of the South". I had read where a restored thirty-two-pound seacoast cannon was on display at Shepherd's Battery at the site. As we drove by and I gazed at the earthen mounds outside the visitor's center, I vowed to return. Until the last few months of the Civil War, the soldiers and the fort had kept the port of Wilmington open to blockade runners supplying necessary goods to the Confederate armies inland. Fascinating stuff. After the two Battles of Fort Fisher in late 1864 and early 1865, the fort fell and the trading route to Wilmington was cut, as was the supply line to General Robert E. Lee's Army of Northern Virginia. The Union army occupied Wilmington a month later and the war officially ended in another two months.

My thoughts returned to the reason for our visit, Dr. Mantellus at Mendle's Mental Health and Convalescent Center. When I had googled it at work, it was on Kure Beach, not too far from the North Carolina Aquarium at Fort Fisher. Kure Beach was a throwback beach, kind of like Oak Island. Small mom-and-pop motels and restaurants dotted the area—no chains. The Kure Beach Pier seemed to be the biggest draw around. Mendle's Mental Health and Convalescent Center was located on a quiet side street, two blocks from downtown Kure Beach. A rusted metal sign, with the last word "Center" nearly obliterated, was the only indication the white, three story wooden building was anything besides a large house. I looked to the top floor; the residents might be able to catch a glimpse of the Atlantic Ocean since three stories seemed to be as high as the zoning of Kure Beach allowed.

We climbed the creaking wooden steps to the front door and I realized I didn't know Dr. Mantellus' first name. It would be a shame to be turned away at the front desk. Before I could decide how to handle it, Greg pulled back the screen door with a long squeak. It wasn't much of a door, with chipped paint and barely any screen.

I had given Greg a little background on the way and we stepped to the front desk together. A middle-aged woman built like a Carolina Panthers' linebacker looked up at us through her cat eye glasses. She was reading a Star Magazine (which had "Stars Without Makeup" on the cover—that can't be Julia Roberts, say it ain't so!)

"May I help you?" she asked in a deep voice. (In my mind, I wanted to ask if her name was "Anna-bolic" but I thought that might get me escorted out the front door instead of up the stairs.)

"Yes ma'am. I was hoping I…we could visit one of your patients."

Her bushy eyebrows shot up. "Name?"

"Mantellus." I didn't think it possible, but her caterpillar eyebrows moved farther up her forehead.

"I see," she said ominously. "Are you related?"

I opened my mouth to speak, without really knowing what to say. Greg placed his hand on the desk and leaned forward, looking at her nametag. "Miss…oh, I see you are a nurse. Nurse Mendle—"

Mendle? Just our luck to get one of the owners at the front desk. I'm pretty good at sweet-talking underlings, but persons of authority don't usually warm to me. Our chances of seeing Dr. Mantellus were blowing away like inside-out beach umbrellas in a stiff ocean breeze.

She saw the look on our faces. "The Center was named in memory of my father, Sam." She nodded her head in the direction of a man's portrait on the wall opposite the front door. "Daddy was injured in a fishing boat accident. My mother survived the accident, too. But daddy, he was never the same afterwards—mentally. My mother had to bring him here and eventually he passed away." She glanced up the stairs, sadly.

She put the Star Magazine in a desk drawer, before continuing. "The nurses were so good to him. And so kind to me, as a kid. Eventually it helped me decide to become a nurse. The people who ran this home took as good care of him as they were able. His mind was just never right afterwards." She paused to look around the room. "This place was going to close in the early 90s and my mom gave them a substantial monetary gift to keep the place open. The board voted to change the name in memory of my father at the time."

Just as suddenly her face cleared, the caring nurse gone and the bouncer returned; she was all business again. "Now, what is your relationship to the patient?"

Greg looked at me quickly before speaking. "Nephew."

She eyed him suspiciously. "I have been instructed to call the family if there are visitors. Excuse me."

We watched her broad shoulders disappear into a glass walled office and pick up the telephone. "Not good, *nephew*," I said to Greg. I took the opportunity to look around the lobby, such as it was. It had the look of a psychiatric facility from the mid-twentieth century trying hard to look like it belonged in the twenty-first century. The new furnishings couldn't hide the cracks in the ceiling, the smell of mold, the muffled sounds of anguish from above. I walked over to the picture on the wall, reading the gold plate below it: Sam Mendle - 1925 to 1989. The picture showed a smiling Sam Mendle beneath a fishing hat decorated with lures, holding up a fishing rod with one hand and displaying a fancy, shiny fishing lure in the other. Looking at his face, it was hard to believe the man went insane. Sometimes the truth *was* stranger than fishin'.

Sam Mendle's daughter returned to the desk slowly. "I wasn't able to reach either one of his sons," she said, sitting down and putting both her hands on the desk.

Greg reached over and patted one of her hands and I couldn't help noticing he left it there as he spoke. "I understand your position. It's just—we've come a long way to see my uncle. I give you my solemn word we will not upset him. I haven't seen him in—well, it seems like forever."

Nurse Mendle frowned at Greg (but didn't remove her hand from beneath his). "Well...I guess it can't hurt," she said. "The truth is Mr. Mantellus's dementia is getting worse." She called to a tall oriental youth coming down the stairs. "Phil, how's Mr. Mantellus today?"

Phil, dressed in the white shirt and white pants of an orderly, stopped at the bottom of the stairs and shrugged. "He's back in his pineapple under the sea."

Nurse Mendle removed her hand from beneath Greg's. "I'm afraid he's not going to know you. Most of the time he thinks he's somewhere else…"

We followed Phil up the stairs. Once we turned the corner from the lobby, the stairwell became narrow and dark; the wooden steps moaned and cracked under our weight. I felt like I was ascending to the Addams Family attic. A bald-headed man popped his head around the door frame of the second-floor landing and for a minute I thought it was Uncle Fester. He crowed like a rooster and quickly disappeared. The sound echoed eerily throughout the stairwell. Phil continued to lead us up the stairs to the third floor.

"Man, how do you deal with this every day?" Greg asked him.

Phil shrugged again. "You get used to it. They're human beings. Most were good people, I think—most of them."

"How long have you been taking care of Mantellus?" I asked.

"Two or three years—maybe longer."

"Is he one of the good ones?" After I asked the question, a dark look came over Phil's face as he turned back to us.

Phil stopped at the third-floor landing and lowered his voice. "I don't want to talk bad about anyone. But sometimes when he's lucid, he scares the hell out of me. One time, when he was mad at me for bathing him, he reached up and tapped my head, right between the eyes." Phil tapped his own fingers to his head to illustrate. "In his spooky, foreign voice he said, 'Change ze mind, change ze life.'" Phil shivered. "I've had patients say all kinds of weird things to me and I usually laugh them off, but that time— well, it felt like the devil himself talking to me."

Phil led us down the hallway to the third room. "What did you mean when you said he was back in his pineapple under the sea?" Greg asked before we entered.

Phil chuckled. "I'm afraid it's my fault. I'm a big fan and whenever I am in his room taking care of him, I turn on the television. I didn't think cartoons would hurt, but in his case, it seems to add to his delusions. You may have to roll play if you want to talk to him." Phil walked into the room, waved at the old man slumped in a wheelchair by the bed and continued on to the bathroom. Greg and I hesitated at the threshold.

"I still don't understand," Greg said. "Who lives in a pineapple under the sea?"

"*Sponge-Bob—Square-Pants*," I sang.

"Yes?" The old man had perked up and was looking at us. "Who calls out to me?"

Greg gave me a crazy look. "At least there's nothing wrong with his hearing," I whispered as we walked into the room.

The man sitting before us looked like he had once been a hulking figure and that hulk had now settled into other places—unsightly and uncomfortable places. His complexion was pasty and yellow. If I didn't know better, it looked like the Pillsbury Doughboy had collapsed and fallen into a vat of yellow food dye.

"Dr. Mantellus—" I started.

"Who?" the old man asked in a deep voice, clearly confused.

Phil walked out of the bathroom with a hairbrush and carefully brushed the old man's thin white hair from his eyes.

"What you got there?" the old man demanded.

"It's just Gary, your pet snail," Phil told him cheerily, following with a "meow" sound. Strangely, this seemed to comfort the old man.

"Dr. Mantellus—" I started again.

"Who are zeese strange people?" the old man cried.

Phil turned to us. "Gentlemen, this is SpongeBob. Mr. Mantellus is...out right now. And SpongeBob," he said, addressing the yellowed old man. "This is—" He paused to look at us. "Mermaid Man and Barnacle Boy."

The old man sat up straighter, obviously impressed.

"What the heck," Greg whispered. "I'm totally lost."

"Bikini Bottom," I whispered back. "We're aging superheroes. SpongeBob and Patrick are big fans."

"Patrick? Is that you Patrick?" the old man asked.

"Yes, SpongeBob," said Phil slowly, imitating Patrick's voice from the show.

Greg shook his head and walked over to sit on a wooden chair by the wall. I didn't know whether to feel sorry for him or applaud the fact he had never watched *SpongeBob SquarePants*.

The old man pointed to Greg. "What iz wrong with him?"

"Barnacle Boy is just worn-out," I answered. "You remember we are both retired now."

"Barnacle Boy? Why am I the sidekick?" Greg muttered, figuring out at least that much.

Phil moved toward the door. "I've got to go take care of Mrs. Wydell. She turned one-hundred and one last week and I think she's finally starting to go downhill. I'll be back shortly."

I kneeled in front of the old man so I was at eye level. "Mr.— Squarepants. Do you like games?"

The old man nodded his head slightly as a thin line of spittle dribbled down his chin.

"Okay," I said. "I'm going to say a word or phrase and you say the first thing that comes to mind."

I thought for a minute. "Octopus."

"Squidward," he said without hesitation.

"Good. Good." I hesitated to think of the best way to approach the subject. "School," I said, with added emphasis.

Without missing a beat, the old man said, "Mrs. Puff's Boating School."

Crap! I had forgotten about the school SpongeBob attended.

I took a minute to look around the room. Completely devoid of knick-knacks, family pictures, books, magazines, newspapers, it looked like Dr. Mantellus had just moved in, instead of having lived there several years. Didn't Nurse Mendle mention sons? The only visible decoration was on the end table by the lamp, a small figurine of Plankton, SpongeBob's arch nemesis. I had no doubt Phil brought it in for the old man, just for kicks.

"I'm aware of Mrs. Puff's Boating School, but how about the Foulmire School for Boys?" I asked. As I waited for the old man's reaction, I realized I was holding my breath.

The old man's wrinkled brow furrowed even more. There appeared to be a spark of life in his eyes.

I leaned in closer. "You were a doctor there. You...took care of the boys."

Suddenly his eyes narrowed. His right hand shot out and a gnarled finger tapped me between the eyes. "Change ze mind, change ze life," he said in a deep, sinister voice.

In spite of the fact the hairs on the back of my neck were standing up and I had broken into a sweat above the spot where he touched me, I felt hope. I decided it was time to play my ace in the hole.

"Silo," I said loudly.

The old man rocked in his wheelchair like he was trying to stand. Visibly irritated, his face became red as he grunted with exertion. He collapsed back into the wheelchair with a wheeze.

I tried to feel sorry for him, but if the things Driftwood claimed about a doctor in dark goggles experimenting on his cousin Owen and other boys were true... "Silo," I repeated, louder than before.

The old man's head lolled back, his eyes rolling back in his head. He muttered something that sounded like, "Free man."

Greg stood up and walked over to my side, intrigued. I bent down by the old man's large and hairy ear. "Silo," I whispered.

His whole body fell forward into a slump, his right arm extended out. Slowly he lifted his left arm, which I originally thought might be paralyzed. He seemed to be reaching for me so I stepped back, partly, I have to admit, out of fear. With his left palm facing outward, his fingers toward the ceiling, he moved his thumb upward, like he was lifting something small. His right hand shot forward in the direction of his left, his fist closed like he was holding a tool or weapon; it stopped just short of his left hand. He moved his right hand slowly from side to side, like he was searching for an imaginary opening. When he seemed to find it, he thrust his right hand forward, like he was brandishing a knife, stabbing.

"What the hell?" Greg mumbled. The old man had raised his head off his chest and I looked back at his face. Although his eyes seemed to have clouded over, there was an unmistakable look of rapture. Barely audible was the chant of, "Free man. Free man. Free man," coming from his lips.

Returning my attention to his hands, the old man used his left hand to take the imaginary weapon, holding it in place in the air. His right hand went down bedside his thigh in the wheelchair where he got another imaginary tool and raised it back up to his left hand. He jerked his right hand forward twice.

"It's like he's hammering something," Greg said.

"Free man. Free man…"

If it was indeed a hammer he was pretending to use, the old man put it back in its place beside his thigh. For no reason I can explain, the next thing he did chilled me to the bone. With his right hand, he took the "tool" from his left and plunged it forward. Then he moved it laterally, back halfway and plunged it forward again. For some reason, I thought of pumpkin carving as a kid where my dad let me clean out the "brains" inside the pumpkin, as I called them.

"What the heck did you do?" cried Phil, appearing beside Greg.

"Free man. Free man," chanted the old man, still going through the hand motions, like he was doing a psychotic version of the Macarena.

"Daniel broke him," Greg said.

Phil had a handful of pills. "It's time for his medicine. Maybe that will help." Phil ran off to the bathroom, returning quickly with a glass of water.

We watched him try to get the old man to take the pills in between chants. "I don't know what those are," Greg said, referring to the pills. "But I'm guessing the dosage is too low."

Phil got one capsule into the old man's mouth, but before he could get the water glass to his lips, the capsule slipped out the other side, sticking to his chin.

"Is there anything I can do?" I asked.

Phil pointed to the end table. "Get Plankton!"

I quickly retrieved the villain of *SpongeBob SquarePants* and handed the figurine to Phil. The young orderly held it in front of the old man's face, imitating the character's voice as he said, "Give me the secret formula to the Krabby Patties, SquarePants!"

The old man stopped, his hands dropped to his lap. One last "Free man," died on his lips. Phil put Plankton in one of the old man's hands; the gnarled fingers gripped it and he brought it lovingly to his breast.

"Whew!" Phil exclaimed, getting the old man to take his pills finally. "Plankton seems to calm him down. To tell the truth, he seems to associate with that character more than SpongeBob. I think he used to be devious in his previous life as opposed to happy-go-lucky."

I thought about that statement later, when Greg and I were having a late dinner at Big Daddy's Restaurant, not too far from the mental health center. *Devious.* What an interesting choice of words. I poked my fork through my scallop and spinach fettuccini, moving it around on the plate. The food was excellent but I was not hungry. I couldn't stop thinking about the hand motions of Dr. Mantellus. What was he doing? Something from his past, something *devious?* Or was it just the repetitive movements, tremors, the dyskinesia of old age? Whatever it was, it was creepy as hell and Greg agreed.

"I didn't like the old dude," was all he said.

I took a long drink from my Fat Tire. It was new—a special release, Fat Tire Belgian White. Just because I wasn't hungry didn't mean I didn't thirst. The new beer was exceptional and I drained it.

Phil had told us to call him at any time, if we needed anything. Without embarrassment, he said to ask for "Oriental Phil" (he explained there was an "American Phil" that worked there, too). I gave him my work number and he promised to call me if the old man said anything of interest (in other words, non-SpongeBob related).

When we were back on the ferry, I realized how close I was to total exhaustion. My mind played tricks on me (telling me things like, if I didn't get some sleep, I wouldn't be able to function well at work tomorrow— God forbid the thirteen drugs in the test database not get retested adequately). I think I fell asleep standing up at the boat railing.

Back on the mainland, Extreme Tires was long closed, so Greg offered to take me home. Another day without a car I could take, but another night of staying at the hospital might just send me over the edge. I needed my own shower, my own toothbrush, and new clothes (and some might say a new outlook on life). Greg dropped me off in my driveway, promising to pick me up in the morning to take me to work. What a great friend. As I watched him back out of my driveway, the headlights flashed over what passed for my "lawn". It was actually a collection of weeds with a few strands of zoysia grass trying to take hold in the sandy soil. I noticed some of the weeds were knee-high. It had been several weeks since I had "mowed" (or what I called rearranging the sand). The last time I had let it get that high, a "concerned" anonymous neighbor stuck a sheet of paper in my screen door. It was a copy of the Town of Oak Island Ordinances and highlighted with a yellow marker was Section 14-31 Certain Conditions

Declared Public Nuisances. The first bullet point was highlighted as well: Growth of weeds and grass. *The uncontrolled growth of noxious weeds or grass over the height of one foot causing or threatening to cause a hazard detrimental to the public health or safety.* I lovingly touched the top of the highest weed. Weren't weeds one of God's creations, too? Oh well, I would get to it when I had the time. I had been called worse than detrimental, noxious and a nuisance.

Fairbanks and Pickford about bowled me over going in the front door, becoming their own kind of nuisances. I gave them Big Daddy's leftovers, and while they twitched their whiskers at the spinach and fettuccini, they gave four paws up to the scallops.

"Hey guys," I told the cats. "You should chew those first." My pager went off at that moment and the shrill alarm caused both cats to jump and back away from the food, their backs arched. They were okay when AC/DC's "Highway to Hell" started, apparently fans of Angus Young and the gang.

The text message on the pager stated simply: *Call me. Carl.* I called the number provided. Carl was so excited I could barely understand him.

"Slow down, Carl," I told him. I could tell he was talking about the skull but nothing else made sense.

"Neep," he said when he stopped his long stream of words. He took a deep breath, then said, "The eye sockets, the orbits. There were holes in the top of them!" He was getting excited again and talking faster.

"Yeah. So? Those skulls have probably been buried a long time," I reasoned.

"No! I noticed it in the first skull but didn't get to look at that one close. The holes are not something that would have happened posthumously."

"What do you mean?"

He took another deep breath. "Those children were lobotomized."

20 - TURN YOUR HEAD AND YAWP

Before the day went to shit, I sat at my cubicle desk yawning, drinking a Red Bull and surfing the internet. I had every intention of conducting the search the night before, but after talking with Carl, my mother had Jitterbug butt-dialed me. I called her on her house phone and we talked for forty minutes. She sounded good and when I told her I had been thinking of my grandfather lately, she had gone off on her usual stories about Finnian O'Dwyer (he never thought she was the right bride for dad; he farted in his sleep; he once saw FDR in an open-air car drive through the streets of Charleston). We discussed the fact that Finnian told me stories of his days on movie sets, but, being young and movie naïve at the time, I actually didn't know which movies he had worked on. Mom didn't know either. After the call to Mom, I had gone to the bedroom extension and picked up the phone to call Jaclyn. That was the way I woke up in the morning—laying on top of the bedspread in my grimy clothes, still clutching the phone handset.

Jaclyn. I sure missed her, regardless of whether life was like a Hallmark movie or not.

I typed "lobotomy children" into the search engine. I was appalled at the findings. Most children who were "treated" with lobotomies were diagnosed (or misdiagnosed) with schizophrenia. Brutal tantrums and withdrawal were often labeled schizophrenia in the early days.

One site singled out a six-year old in the first half of the twentieth century, chronicling her horrors. Linda, pre-lobotomy, was active and agile, although often smashing her dolls and using her toys as weapons. When she became mute and began rocking to and fro, reacting violently to attempts to control her, her parents had her institutionalized. Eight months after a lobotomy, Linda chewed her clothing and fingers, became incontinent, sat alone gazing into space, rocking back and forth, hallucinating—her smile changing at a moment's notice to a look of stark terror.

When I saw the name of Linda's physician, I displayed my own look of stark terror.

My face was so close to the computer screen when Edwina Pickles shoved my chair (with me in it) toward the desk, I smacked my head on it; dazed, gravity caused me to crash into my keyboard, teeth first. When I finally raised my head and was able to see one screen instead of two, I had typed this: *ft6 4s ky7ku.*

"And why aren't we testing, Mr. O'Dwyer?" Pickles demanded.

"ft6 4s ky7ku," I mumbled, holding my head.

"Let's get to it!"

"Yes, Mrs. Connor," I answered. (Mrs. Connor had been my four-foot-tall, fourth grade teacher—one time when I was trying to get my friend, Ed to laugh by placing a pencil between my lip and nose, she had walked up behind me, smacked me in the back of the head and sent the pencil flying across the room.)

My phone rang as soon as Pickles had disappeared into her office.

"Stapling machine," I answered, staring at—you know, one of those machines that fastens paper together with a little metal doohickey.

"O'Dwyer? Is that you?" The booming voice on the line sounded familiar.

"I think I chipped a tooth," I answered, trying not to whine.

"What?"

I knew that voice. Some kind of doctor, but I couldn't place the name.

"Are you still there?" the voice yelled, causing me to wince.

A picture was forming in my mind as I tried to think of the doctor's name. Long, gray (hairy) ears...a little black mane on top of the head...a swayed back suspended on four legs...a thin tail with coarse, switching hair on the end. Suddenly the animal turned its hindquarters to my mind's eye—

"Dr. Pearson," I replied, drunkenly.

"Have you been drinking this early in the morning?" he asked.

"Only Red Bull." *You jackass.*

His voice softened. "Have you got my date lined up with Nurse McCall yet?"

"Yes, Saturday night. Joseph's Italian Bistro in Southport." The only problem was my keyboard addled brain couldn't remember if I had actually made the reservation yet.

"Time?"

I looked down at the little clock in the lower right corner of my computer screen. "Ten-forty-five."

"No! What time is the reservation?"

"Seven," I guessed.

"Fine. Fine." He sounded nervous. "I suppose I ought to call her. *Gulp.*" (I had never heard a gulp on the phone and it sound just like…well, a gulp.) "Do you have her phone number?"

"Me?"

"No! That silly resident," he replied sarcastically. "Who I've been being nice to, by the way."

"I don't have her number. Sorry."

I was seeing two computer screens again, so I shook my head, hard.

"That's okay," Dr. Pearson said. "I appreciate you getting the reservation." (*Reservation? What's he talking about?*) "I will call her tonight on the unit. *Gulp.*"

"That sounds good, Forrest Gulp," I said. For some reason, I was holding the receiver out in front of my face and staring at it.

"What? What did you say—"

The phone seemed to flop out of my hand and land back on the base. I gave both cheeks a slap with my right hand. After a long drink of Red Bull, I began to feel a little better. After ten minutes in the restroom, splashing water on my face, I began to feel more like myself. By lunchtime (and another Red Bull), I was ready to take on the world. Unfortunately, the feeling wouldn't last.

I decided to visit Willie and take my lunch break in his room. After a quick trip to the cafeteria (Try the Superfood of the Month—Legumes!), I carried my handy, Styrofoam lunch container to the stairwell. I balanced my Red Bull can on top the container and started to open the door, but paused when I heard a loud clatter coming from the stairs. I put my ear to the door, hearing loud shouts, before the door exploded outward, knocking me on my arse. A patient jumped over me, his arse exposed by a gap in his hospital gown. He began to run away and stopped, turning back to me.

"Daniel?"

I was looking forlornly at the precious liquid seeping onto the tile floor. "You made me spill my Red Bull."

"Why are you drinking that? That stuff is toxic."

I looked up into the bloodshot eyes of Willie.

He had a point. "I don't know. I think I'm hooked."

The door to the stairwell slammed open and out jumped Greg, dressed in green scrubs. He leaped over me, taking Willie by the arm. "The little bugger sure can run," Greg said, breathing heavily. "He shot the moon all the way down the hall, past the nursing station and down the stairs." He took a deep breath, holding on tightly to Willie's arm. "It's a sight I hope to never see again."

I looked at Willie's arm. He still had a heparin lock inserted with IV tubing hanging out of it. Blood dripped down his forearm. "Willie," I said.

"We've talked about this a hundred times."

"I want to go home to the *Silent Cow*," Willie moaned. Greg rolled his eyes at the name of Willie's houseboat, no doubt thinking about ole Silent Cal Coolidge.

"Did you forget about the ghost pirates?" I asked.

"I don't care," Willie answered childishly. "They would be better than the bloodsucking leeches around here. Plus it would be a whole lot cleaner."

"You gonna walk all the way home, with your pale moon hanging out?" I asked. "Look, I couldn't take you home now even if I wasn't working. The Cube is still in the shop. Greg's going to take me there after work to pick it up."

Willie physically deflated. The haggard appearance of his face, dark circles under both eyes, it looked like he hadn't slept since he had been at the hospital. I felt a sudden sympathy.

"Willie, I promise you. If you go back to your room, I will see if you can be discharged a day early. If your doctor agrees—and I'm sure your nurses will do everything in their power to convince him—then I will come back after I get the Cube and pick you up."

"Home?" Willie asked pitifully.

We led Willie back through the door, Greg in front and me behind on the steps (holding my Styrofoam container with one hand and trying to hold together the flaps of Willie's gown with the other).

"Thanks for checking on him, Greg," I said.

Greg laughed. "Not a problem. Willie my man, you are one of a kind."

We were slowly making our way up the stairs. Willie turned back to look at me. "You know, Daniel. Styrofoam is dangerous. Chemicals leach out into your food and drink. Not to mention the environment where polystyrene clogs the landfills, small pieces ending up in the ocean, where sea birds and marine animals swallow it."

He had a point, but it made me mad nonetheless. If there was such a thing as a Q-Tip with the end made of Styrofoam, I would have purposely inserted it into my ear in front of him.

We passed the nursing station on the way back to Willie's room. The nurses gave us a sideways glance and I noticed a few rolling their eyes. One followed us back to the room and helped get Willie into bed.

"Thank you so much for bringing him back," the nurse said in monotone. "I don't know what I'd do if we lost the delightful Mr. Welch."

"Do you think we could get him discharged today," I asked her. "I will take him home after I get off."

The nurse visibly brightened. "I'll see what I can do," she said, as she charged from the room.

I looked around Willie's room in amazement. Boxes of organic food were stacked on every surface, making it look like a Natural Products Trade Show.

"Wow! Valaree did it up right," I commented.

"There's plenty. Have some for lunch," Willie said.

"And miss out on hot dogs, legumes and leached polystyrene? No way," I said, opening the deadly container. Just to prove my point, I picked up the first hot dog, scooped some legumes and mixed them in with the chili, and as a final insult, rubbed the bun on the Styrofoam bottom. "Mm! Mm! Good!" I exclaimed, after taking a big bite.

Ignoring me, Willie said, "Speaking of your pretty vet friend, she called this morning."

"Yeah? What'd she want?" I asked through a mouthful of my "Bean Me Up Scottie" dog I had just named. I wasn't paying total attention because I was wondering if I could market it to restaurants, or at least hospital cafeterias. (Or perhaps the next big Star Trek Convention.)

"Something about the work Moses did for her. She didn't seem happy."

I had suggested Moses for the work on the drug storage cabinets and locks. Being the ultimate handyman, I couldn't imagine him doing subpar work.

"Hey, I have to get back to work," Greg said.

"Cool legumes," I said, picking up the bedside phone and dialing the vet office.

The party on the other end, to whom I was speaking, declared the situation at the office as "chaos". Prior to opening, someone had tried to pry the door off the new metal cabinet Moses had installed for fentanyl storage. The police were there and I could actually hear Hands speaking loudly in the background. I asked if I could speak to the police, telling the woman on the line my name. Hands came on the phone immediately and I told him all I knew about the fentanyl saga at the Neutre Veterinary Clinic.

"Hey Hands," I said, before letting him go. "Carl was right. There's some crazy shit going on with the skulls of the children found here." Someone at the vet clinic hollered for him—it sounded like his partner Sphinx. "I'll tell you more about it later," I added quickly, before hanging up.

Willie had been listening and he looked at me closely; I could almost see the old sparkle in his eye. Just as quickly it was gone. The whiny baby look reappeared. "You promise to take me home tonight, Daniel? Promise?"

When I got back to my desk (with a new Red Bull), the first thing I noticed was I had an email in my Inbox. It wasn't that I didn't normally receive emails, it was just I didn't receive any emails of substance. I had routed most of them to automatically go to a Junk folder (the ones about Russian and Asian women offering me their bodies, the Penis Enlargement Network Information System—brilliant use of an acronym there, and all Human Resource updates from Scott) and the other emails about the new computer system I had routed to a folder named "To Dream the Impossible Dream".

The email was from Greg: "Hey, forgot to tell you I called the nursing home or whatever it's called. Can't get that creepy old man off my mind. Oriental Phil told me the old man hadn't said anything else but he's still been agitated and doing the hand motions. He did tell me that nurse finally got hold of one of the two sons to tell them about our visit. He said he could hear the son yelling through the phone all the way across the room. She gave our descriptions to him. Anyway, see you at five in the lobby. Hopefully we can get your Cube today."

Taking a drink of Red Bull, I replied back: "Thanks buddy. By the way, I may need your expertise in helping me get off Red Bull."

I heard Pickle's office door open, so I began furiously testing the thirteen drugs again. I had done it so many times, I could do it in my sleep. Forty-five minutes later, I realized I *had* been doing it in my sleep. I had appeased my boss and managed to refresh myself in the bargain.

Mid-afternoon break time—next best thing to quitting time. Thanks to Red Bull, I made a beeline to the bathroom. Throwing open the door, I nearly mowed down a man washing his hands in the sink.

"Father Spinelli!" I cried. Not sure how I missed his flowing robe at first.

The priest turned to me, frowning a little, obviously trying to place me. "Daniel O'Dwyer," I said. When he still didn't respond, I added, "You came into Willie Welch's room by mistake the other night. You did a little swimming practice through the turkey and giblets."

"Oh yes! The *Silent Cow* and the spectral disturbances," he said, smiling. "I'm glad I ran into you. I've been meaning to call you. I've talked to my colleagues and I've written down some possibilities for you."

"Great!" I looked at him standing there in his floor length cassock. "Father, since I've seen you in here—I just have to ask. How do priests...you know...go, in that thing." I motioned toward his robe. "I mean, there's no zipper."

Father Spinelli smiled. "My son, just as the rosary has its mysteries, so do us priests. It would be best not to meditate on this particular mystery, though."

I laughed. "Fair enough."

On the way out of the restroom, the priest tripped over the metal threshold at the bottom of the doorway and gave me a sheepish look.

"It's okay, Father. I had a basketball coach in high school who yelled at me for tripping over the painted lines on the court."

He told me he had his written notes for the *Silent Cow* in the chaplain's office, which just happened to be across the hall from Human Resources, so I followed the clumsy priest to the elevator.

When the elevator opened on the third floor, it was like a scene from *Godzilla* (no offense to Oriental Phil). Men and women were screaming and running right at us. Father Spinelli quickly made the sign of the cross. At least fifteen people crushed us to the back of the elevator car before we could exit.

"Let us out!" Father Spinelli cried, pushing his way through the sea of people. Dang, his bravery, in spite of the obvious danger, inspired me. I shoved my way out too, before the elevator doors closed. Standing on the other side, breathing hard, I told the priest, "You are one courageous man of the cloth."

"Not at all," the father confessor confessed. "I'm claustrophobic."

People were still running down the hall, seemingly in slow motion, screaming. I expected them to be crying, "Godzilla!" or "Mothra!" or "Rodan!" or "Ghidorah, the Three-Headed Monster!" or the name of the enormous, fire-breathing, fanged turtle, Gamera (forget Michael's small bite radius, Bobby's turtle Tito wouldn't stand a chance with Gamera— CHOMP!) When I saw a young candy-striper run out of the Human Resources' office door, I jumped in her way. She stopped momentarily, her eyes wide. She was panting. "What's wrong? What is it?" I asked her. She said one word and ran past me. *Mantis.*

Mantis? What kind of name is that for a Japanese movie monster?

I fought my way through the oncoming rush of hallway humanity to the Human Resources' office door. "Come on!" I shouted to Father Spinelli who was pinned against the far wall.

"I'll never make it!" he cried. "You must go on without me!"

I plunged through the HR office door without looking back. God be with you, Father Spinelli.

The secretarial desk was empty. "Bertha, where are you?" I called. I heard a squeak from the next room. I ran through the open doorway. Bertha, in all her girth-a, was standing on top the conference room table. She screamed at me to join her on the table. I jumped up on the table, in spite of my worry that the maximum weight limit for table balancing on this particular piece of furniture had been exceeded long before my weight was added to the mix.

"What's wrong, Bertha?"

She pointed out the open door. "Ebenezer!"

Ebenezer? What's an Ebenezer? It took me at least a minute to figure it out.

"You mean the mantis shrimp?"

Bertha nodded her head in the affirmative, obviously terrified.

"You mean the mantis *shrimp*?" I couldn't help repeating. "Emphasis on shrimp." It was bigger than the average shrimp (and probably smarter than the average bear), but the keyword was still shrimp.

I moved down the tabletop and peered out the open door. I could just make out the aquarium. There was a large outward crack in the glass, with a gaping hole.

"You mean Ebenezer escaped?" I asked.

Bertha nodded her head quickly, too many times in fact, making her look like a Bertha bobblehead. I couldn't help but think of the mass of humanity running down the hall, screaming. Ebenezer? How is that possible?

"Did someone drop a radioactive isotope in Ebenezer's water?" I asked Bertha. "Some kind of atomic accident making the marine crustacean huge?" (I imagined a ten-foot tall Ebenezer terrorizing the people running down the hallway. At first, an unsuspecting human would stop in front of the peacock mantis shrimp, mesmerized by the beautiful colors. Ebenezer's antennae would twitch and slowly, a red feeler would move forward, until it touched the prey's face. Then—BAM! The club-like appendages would shoot forward and knock the person's block off. Rock'em Sock'em Mantis Shrimp-Bot.)

The table started to tilt beneath my feet so I moved back to the middle. "Where's Scott?" I asked.

Bertha snuffled. "He's barricaded in his office. I heard him move his desk in front of the door. He abandoned me out here—left me to die at the hands of that...that...bully!" She started sobbing.

"Technically," I said, not really knowing what to say. "The mantis shrimp doesn't have hands—" For some reason, that made her cry harder. "There, there," I said, patting her clumsily on the back.

Bertha stopped crying suddenly and pulled up the hem of her dress to dry her eyes (thank goodness she was wearing a petticoat). She clutched my arm. "If you get me out of this alive," she promised. "I will be nice to you for the rest of my days."

I was touched. There was an awkward silence. In a movie (say *The Poseidon Adventure* or *Earthquake*) where two souls are thrown together in survival mode, usually they embrace at this point. I moved a half-step toward Bertha and she backed up two steps; her red puffy eyes narrowed, shooting arrows through me that would have best been saved for Ebenezer.

"Bertha," I said, reaching over and patting her lightly on the arm. "Let's not go making promises neither one of us would enjoy. I *will* get you out of here, but I wouldn't want you to change one bit."

Bertha gave me a genuine look of gratitude.

"And now," I said proudly, pounding my chest. "For my battle cry." I let out a howl to weaken the knees of my enemy. (Does a mantis shrimp have knees?)

"I sound my barbaric yawp over the roofs of the world!" I cried. "Or at least this tabletop."

Bertha looked at me cockeyed and shook her head. "You're still not funny."

"Fear not, large damsel. I will save thee." I jumped down from the table and ran into the deadly room.

I stopped just inside, out of Bertha's sight, suddenly feeling vulnerable. I had no weapon. I picked up a chair by the wall and brandished it, holding it in front of me, poking the air like a lion tamer.

"Do you see it?" Bertha yelled from the other room. I scanned the floor and didn't see anything, except several dropped Doritos around Bertha's desk. Would a mantis shrimp eat Doritos? Would eating Doritos cause a mantis shrimp to grow a hundred times its normal size? Were those Cool Ranch, Nacho Cheese or Spicier Nacho? Could a mantis shrimp's stomach endure Spicier Nacho? Does a mantis shrimp have a stomach? I shook my head—so many questions, so little time.

I cautiously walked over to the far wall where the bookshelf ended, the corner covered in shadow. "Ebenezer may be in the corner," I yelled over my shoulder. "It's dark. I can't really tell."

A muffled voice from behind the office door closest to me: "Daniel, is that you?"

"Scott?"

"Yes?"

"Um, Scott. You seem to have a bit of a Human Resources emergency out here. Employees are terrified, running haphazardly through the hallways. Haphazardly, I tell you. It's a Code Ebenezer."

Silence from the other side of the door.

"Scott?"

"Yes?"

"Are you coming out?"

There was a long pause. "Do you think I should?"

"Well, despite the fact that he is neither fuzzy nor cuddly, Ebenezer *is* your pet."

I heard some shuffling of paper. "I don't know…I've got a lot of work to do."

My gaze returned to the dark corner. I guess this was something I was going to have to do myself. I had the chair in my left hand and waved it menacingly, but it did not feel like enough protection. I recalled the sudden strike of the mantis shrimp against the glass of the aquarium—*bam!* Remembered what Bertha had claimed—"*They can strike at the speed of a .22 caliber bullet.*" I looked over to the bookshelf for another weapon. There was nothing but pictures and a bunch of cheap plastic BGCH swag. I didn't think I could hold off an attacking mantis shrimp with a BGCH multi-function pedometer (with built-in clock).

I looked closer at the aquarium. The huge crack in the glass seemed large enough for Ebenezer to escape, of that there was no doubt. But it was right in the middle of the glass, leaving a couple of inches of water in the bottom of the aquarium. The bottom of the coral outcropping, with the dark hole in the middle, was mostly underwater. I walked toward the aquarium to get a better look when Bertha screamed from the other room.

I ran over quickly. "Bertha, what's wrong?"

"The table about flipped over," she said breathlessly.

"Bertha, were you near the aquarium when it cracked?"

"Yes! There was a huge crash and I got sprayed with water!"

"Did you see Ebenezer escape?"

"Yes! Well, I think so. I ran in here and jumped on the table. I think I saw something crawl across the floor."

I thought about this for a minute. "Bertha, you said you looked up mantis shrimp on the internet, did you not?"

"Yes."

"This is very important," I said. "So take your time."

"Okay."

"Can mantis shrimp live out of the water?"

She frowned. Her upper lip twitched. "I...I...don't remember."

I was still standing there thinking, when she screamed, "You said you would get me out of here!"

"Okay, okay," I said, my ears ringing. "I'm going to go hold off Ebenezer while you run out the door. Deal?"

She did her Bertha bobblehead impression again.

I crept back in the room, keeping my eye on the shaded corner. I didn't think anything was there—but I really liked this pair of pants. If a freaky-eyed peacock mantis shrimp came flying out of the dark at me, it would be soil city.

Passing by his door, I said, "Scott, you there?"

I heard a slight movement and heavy breathing.

"Scott, I know you're in there. Do you want me to believe you jumped out the window to your death? At the very worst, if you landed on your feet, you would have broken enough bones to really appreciate Randy Newman's song 'Short People'."

"I'm sorry," he said. I could hear him fumbling a phone receiver. "I'm on a conference call."

"C'mon Scott. I need your help out here."

"What do you need?"

I looked around, grabbing the chair again. "I need another weapon." Before I could add, *and another body to run interference*, I could hear a desk being moved away from the door on the other side. The door opened a crack.

"Thanks, Scott—"

He threw something at me which struck my leg. The door slammed shut and I could hear him grunting and the sound of the desk sliding in front of the door again. I looked down at my feet.

"Um, Scott. Why do you have a whip in your office?" It wasn't a black, cheap plastic toy whip like I used to have as a kid ("Dance, Billy. Dance!"), it was a quality leather bullwhip with a long, braided handle. "Scott, are you into something kinky?"

"What? No," the muffled voice from the other side replied.

"You've been hanging out with Derica, haven't you?" I asked, thinking of the dominatrix from my computer.

"No. No! I got that from CrocodileDundee.com. It's made with the highest quality 'Grade A' kangaroo hide."

I cracked the whip. In a feminine, steroid-deep German accent I said, "You have been vewy, vewy bad and must be punished, Scott-ee."

"What's going on out there?" Bertha cried from the other room. "Are you trying to be funny or are you going to get me out of here?"

"I'm sorry, Bertha dear," I yelled back. I snapped the whip hard, brandished the chair in front of me and moved toward the shadows. "When I count to three, run!"

I heard her shifting on the tabletop.

"Ready?"

"Yes."

I couldn't help myself. "Three!" I cried.

I heard her grunt, hit the floor and the sound of the table crashing against the wall. I looked back over my shoulder as I used my chair and whip to tame the wild (yet invisible) mantis shrimp. All I saw was a Bertha-blur pass through the room and out the front door. And they say big women can't sprint.

"You better take some ibuprofen in the morning," I called after her. (Sometimes I just can't suppress my inner pharmacist.)

I returned my attention to the dark corner, sliding the whip along the floor toward it and using the chair to block any flying crustaceans. Quickly I probed the corner with the end of the whip, when a sound behind caused me to jump. I turned, expecting a ten-foot tall Ebenezer bearing down on me, simultaneously crushing me and pounding me with those pesky club-like appendages. Instead, it was a six-foot-six Human Resource Director with a giraffe neck bearing down on me.

"Save me Daniel!" Scott cried, jumping on my back before I could turn all the way around. It felt like I had the weight of the world on my back, or at least the weight of all the employees of Boiling Grove. I heard a pop which could have been my L2 vertebrae.

"Holy cow, Scott," I grumbled. "You really have to lay off those Mai Tais."

"Get me out of here alive and you can have anything you want!"

"Anything?"

"Anything."

"Even a meeting with the CEO about Medi-Soit?"

After a slight hesitation. "Yes."

"And I can get rid of the beeper," I added.

"Yes. Yes! Get me out of here!"

"You got it, big guy," I said, and started toward the front door. Scott was so heavy, and so tall, I moved at a snail's pace. He was draped over me like a shawl, his feet dragging the floor.

"Scott," I said, as we passed the busted aquarium going approximately 0.2 miles per hour. "Can mantis shrimp live out of water?" I was eying the dark grotto in the tank, still mostly underwater.

"I don't know," he whimpered. "I was just trying to be cool."

As I passed the threshold out into the swarming sea of humanity in the hallway, I told him, "Scott, you may not be cool, but you *will* be remembered."

He jumped off my back and into the flow before I could tell him to stay close to the wall. I watched as he was swept along backwards down the hallway, his long arms waving above the crowd. His giraffe neck tensed as he screamed something unintelligible towards me. The swarm moved toward the stairwell, and the last thing I saw was Scott's head thumping off the top of the doorframe.

A shrill alarm sounded, followed by AC/DC's "Highway to Hell". My hand automatically went to the beeper on my belt, unclipping it. The tiny pager screen displayed a single word. Did I mention earlier the day had gone to shit?

21 - SILO-NARA, DANIEL-SAN

I writhed, shimmied and squirmed, trying to get comfortable. A sharp pain in my shoulder was my reward. The zip-tie around my wrists was pulled really tight, my arms wrapped back around a large pole. Sitting in the dirt with legs out flat in front of me, I wriggled my wrists but only managed to poke the body on the other side of the pole.

A weak, "Ack" was followed by an almost inaudible, "Neep."

"Carl! You're alive!" I whispered, tasting blood from my busted lip.

During what would later become known as the "Ebenezer Affair" or the "Nightmare *Way* Before Christmas", most of the people exited the building in front, but I had chosen the back. I made my way along the side of the hospital, past the construction site and into the woods at the back of the property. There was only one person who knew my beeper number and could have texted me. The single word had chilled me to the bone: *Silo*.

On a large platform above, I could hear two men walking and arguing. I had made the mistake of charging into the old silo, and one of the men had tackled me, punched me in the face and dragged me to the pole while the other secured my wrists behind me. I didn't see my attackers but I could make out Carl's head lolled over on his shoulder behind me.

"Talk to me, Carl. What is happening?"

Carl didn't move or make a sound. (My stomach rumbled—no doubt from the legumes at lunch—and I tried not to make a sound on my end…er, from my other end.)

"Carl! Who are these men? What do they want?" I tried to poke him hard with my tied wrists.

"Neep."

I gave up trying to communicate with Carl, and tried to use my aching shoulder to probe my injured nose. Obviously not as limber as I used to be (my hands behind me didn't help), I couldn't reach my nose with my shoulder. My schnoz ached and felt like it had been rearranged when I took the punch. My mind drifted and I wondered if Jaclyn would still love me if I looked like De Niro after that fight in *Raging Bull.*

I heard footsteps on the platform above moving toward us, until they seemed directly overhead.

I could just make out their words. "What the hell are we going to do with them? The kid knows about the skulls and the other son of a bitch definitely fits the description of the guy who visited Pop."

"I don't know. Shut up and let me think."

Guy who visited Pop? Fits the description? My mind swirled. The sons of Dr. Mantellus? How did they know where to find me? How did they know about Carl and his research on the skulls? It didn't make sense.

"Let me use *this* on them?" It sounded like one of the men was patting something.

I held my breath. What kind of weapon did they have? Were they professional killers?

"You idiot! You brought your paintball gun!"

Nope. Not professionals, thank goodness.

"It could still kill them—maybe."

I heard a derisive laugh. "At the worst, it would stain them for a few days."

"It wouldn't kill them?"

"I guess maybe if you held it directly over their carotid artery, there might be a slight chance of mortality. But I doubt it."

It seemed the second son was the voice of reason, as well as possessing some degree of medical knowledge.

"Ah, come on! Let me try!" the other man whined.

The other son was definitely the loose cannon, the one I would need to watch carefully.

The mind drifts into strange waters under dire circumstances and, at the thought of loose cannon, mine decided to go in the direction of pirates. I remembered a nasty, pirate-themed t-shirt I had seen at a Myrtle Beach shop: *I'd like to fire my cannon into your treasure chest!* And what of the ghost pirates? Would I be around to help rid the *Silent Cow* of the phantom privateers? What would happen to Willie? (A little voice inside my head answered, "He'd just move into your house, stupid.")

I shifted my legs in the dirt, looking around. It was nothing but an old grain silo, but I couldn't stop myself from shivering. I lifted my shoe, as if to shake the dirt from it. I thought of Driftwood's tale of his Cousin Owen tortured in this exact spot, his blood no doubt soaked into this very soil. I tried to recall Driftwood's exact words— "...man with dark goggles performed experiments on unruly boys in The Silo. Mantis. All us boys called him Mantis. He was the bogeyman."

I heard the two men move across to the end of the platform, their feet and backsides soon visible as they climbed down the metal rungs attached to the inside of the silo wall. I pretended to be dazed from the punch, but kept one eye open, studying the backs of the men as they descended. When the first one reached the bottom and turned, I had to swallow a gasp. Tank! The belligerent worker from the construction crew—the one who seemed hellbent on hiding the skulls. Tank was holding the paintball gun so there was no doubt he was the loose cannon; I watched him carefully. When the other man turned, I didn't recognize him, but the dark, malevolent scowl made me forget about Tank. Frightened and a bit queasy, I realized Tank may be the least of my troubles.

"I knew when that nurse described the guy who went to Pop's room, it was this son of a bitch." Tank walked over to me and stopped. "He's been a thorn in my side since I been here." He took a step, drew back a work boot and kicked me in the ribs.

I fell over awkwardly on my side, my hands still behind me; the pain intense, as I coughed and sputtered into the dirt.

Carl seemed to awaken on the other side, no doubt to defend me. "Neep!" he cried.

"Shut up, you freak!" Tank yelled at him. "You gonna let me shoot 'em?" he asked his brother. I could hear him patting the paintball gun again.

"I got a better idea," the other man said. "They're okay tied up here— no one around to hear them if they yell. Let's walk back to the truck. I think one of dad's instruments is in there somewhere. Help me look for it. By the time we get back, it will be dark."

The tears were streaming down my face into the dirt when I heard them walk away. At the strange angle I was laying, my breathing was labored. It felt like my rib wanted to poke through my skin, kind of like that alien baby that popped out of actor John Hurt's chest in the aptly named *Alien*. If something nasty did pop out of me, Carl would be toast.

In order to sit up, I had to scooch in the dirt until my arms were taut behind me, so I could use them to pull my body upright. And, like my dad used to say, it hurt like "blue blazes" (whatever that is). I guess that would be more G-rated than the words I wanted to scream.

"Carl, you there?"

"Neep."

"If an alien baby shoots out of me, you have to find a way to get out of here."

"Ack?"

"An alien baby."

With Tank and his brother gone, it gave me time to look around the silo.

The pole we were secured to led up into the platform above. The platform, made of wood, appeared to be rickety from below, but must have been pretty stable to hold the weight of the two men. It covered about a third of the interior of the silo. Ignoring the pain, I leaned forward, looking up past the end of the platform and could just make out a dim shaft of light coming through the dome.

I concentrated on the zip-tie again, twisting my hands and wrists, trying to free myself. Damn! Who came up with using zip-ties in place of loose, unravelling rope (you know, with that one little cord left in the middle)? Heroes and cowboys these days could never free themselves in time to save the girl tied to the railroad tracks (with good ole rope, not zip-ties, thank you). What evil scriptwriter came up with the idea to tie someone to the railroad tracks, anyway? (Perhaps he had a friend like Willie.)

I quit trying to free my hands when my side and shoulder cried out, *No más!* (I did feel somewhat like Roberto Duran after getting pounded by Sugar Ray Leonard in the boxing ring.) I focused my attention on Carl. I had to find some way to get him to come back down to earth. Maybe together we could figure a way out.

I poked Carl hard, instantly regretting it when the pain returned. A weak, "Neep" was all I received back.

"Carl, I know the one guy is Tank from the construction crew. And I think they are brothers, the sons of Dr. Mantellus. There used to be a boys' reform school on the property many years ago." No response from Carl, but I kept going. "I think their father is the one who performed experiments on the boys. In this silo. The boys called him the Mantis."

Carl gasped, straightening his body, but still did not speak.

"The experiments," I continued. "Were possibly lobotomies."

Carl came alive. "They *were* lobotomized! More specifically, transorbital lobotomies."

"Transorbital?"

"Yes! That's why the skulls had a hole in the orbital cavity. Transorbital lobotomy was developed in the 1940s by Dr. Walter Freeman—"

Freeman! There was that name again. The same doctor who performed the lobotomy on six-year-old Linda in the case study I had read on the internet. I thought of Mantellus, sitting in his wheelchair, half out of his mind, chanting, *"Free man. Free man."*

"How are transorbital lobotomies performed?" I asked, not sure I really wanted to know.

Carl seemed to pull himself straighter. "You won't believe this, but there is actually an instructional film from 1950 that Dr. Freeman made and you can watch it on YouTube!"

I was not surprised. YouTube, where the motto should be "From crap to talent and everything in between".

"First, as an anesthetic, Dr. Freeman gives his patient an electroshock until they convulse."

My mouth dropped open.

"Then he lifts the upper eyelid and inserts the leucotome—that's the instrument Dr. Freeman and his partner, Dr. James Watts invented which looks like an ice pick—into the tear duct. Then he gives the end of the instrument two sharp strikes with a hammer—well, it looks more like a mallet—which breaches the transorbital bone."

I winced at the thought of hammering an ice pick into someone's eye. Brutality, in the name of medicine.

"Then Dr. Freeman would pull the handle of the instrument as far laterally as the rim of the orbit would allow in order to sever the fibers at the base of the frontal lobe. Another hammer strike, and he would move it around again to sever more fibers. Finally, he would twist the instrument out of the skull."

"Holy shit," escaped my lips. Sickened, I thought of the hand motions of the old man in the wheelchair, hammering, moving the invisible tool back and forth and plunging it deeper.

"And then he would proceed with the opposite side," Carl said.

"He would do it twice?" I squeaked, out of breath or I would be screaming in horror.

"Each eye."

"You are kidding," I muttered. Carl didn't answer, leaving me to visualize the horrific procedure and aftereffects.

I leaned forward again, looking to the dome of the silo. The light filtering in now was noticeably dimmer.

"Carl, we've got to figure out how to get out of here." I could hear him start to struggle with his zip-tied hands. He grunted and neeped and awked.

"Won't...budge," he finally said. I was twisting my hands again and had come to the same conclusion.

"What about this pole?" I asked. "If we move our bodies around and use our legs to push, we might be able to topple the pole."

"I don't know," he said hesitantly. "Won't the platform come down on our heads?"

I looked up. "Maybe somehow we could move out of the way, shield ourselves."

"I don't know—"

Carl was interrupted before he could add a "Neep" by the return of the brothers. They were arguing.

"Let me kill them!" Tank raised the paintball gun above his head. "If it won't work, I'll take the butt of the gun to the side of their heads." He feigned the maneuver in the air.

"We can't kill them. They would be missed and maybe someone would trace them to us. We just need to render them…docile." I noticed the other brother was holding some kind of weapon in one hand and a box-like machine under his arm. I could see dials and wires on it. They walked over to the other end of the silo and I couldn't make out the rest of their conversation.

"Carl," I whispered. "The other guy scares me more than Tank—"

"M.E." Carl said clearly.

I couldn't tell if Carl had lost it, reverted back to his childhood and started spelling words again, or if he had given me a clue to the brother's identity.

"Is that his initials?" I asked.

"M.E.—Medical Examiner."

What?

Totally lost in my thoughts, I didn't realize the brothers had walked back to us. In a split second, I decided the best course (actually the only course) of action. "So, you're the Medical Examiner."

That stopped the man in his tracks. He was carrying the box-like apparatus with both hands—the sharp weapon balanced on top.

"Tank—lovely human being that he is—is your brother," I continued, trying to reason it out.

"See!" cried Tank. "I told you he was an ass. Let me kill him!"

"Shut up," replied his brother evenly.

"Your father, Dr. Mantellus," I said. "Performed experiments in this very silo on the poor boys from the reform school."

"Poor boys, hah!" the Medical Examiner spat. "Brats, degenerates…wicked, wicked children. They deserved it."

Deserved it? Neither son could have been there at the time, they would have been too young. Obviously they had been brainwashed by their father.

Tank grabbed me by the throat. "Our father's name will not be tarnished!"

In spite of the lack of air, I managed to put it all together in my mind. His brother made Tank let go of my throat, leaving me coughing and sputtering.

"Tarnished is such—a big word for you—Tank," I rasped. Tank growled at me. "So, you managed to get yourself on the construction crew at the hospital, just in case something got *dug up* that might *tarnish* your good and decent father. So you could try to hide it. And you—" I pointed at the other one. "I don't even know your name."

"I am named for my father," he said proudly.

"Okay. And you, Lobotomist Junior—" This time they both growled at me. "As the Medical Examiner, could make sure anything found was covered up. Mistakenly identified as Native American."

"See!" Tank yelled. "We got to kill them now!"

His brother (I never knew his father's first name, so I would just have to call him Lob, Jr.) held up the box, removing the sharp weapon from the top and pointing it at me. "We do not...have to *kill* them." I gasped when I realized the weapon looked like an ice pick. "We just have to make them *forget*."

My bravado had suddenly vaporized. "Neep," I said weakly.

"This," Lob, Jr. said, holding up the instrument. "Is a leucotome. It was invented by Dr. Walter Freeman for transorbital lobotomies. Isn't it beautiful." He held it before his eyes and smiled lovingly. I saw a glorified ice pick with a handle, monstrous and grotesque. "Our father was on the medical staff at the Trans-Allegheny Lunatic Asylum in West Virginia when Dr. Freeman visited and showed the physicians how to perform transorbital lobotomies." His dark eyes sparkled. "Oh, how wonderful that must have been," he added reverently.

"And now you get to have your very own lobotomy, Daniel O'Dwyer."

That chilled me to the bone. I was very fond of my orbital bone and did not care to have a hole punched through it. As a matter of fact, I liked all my neural fibers exactly where they were. Unlike some parts of my life, my neural fibers did not need rearranging.

"Hell yes!" Tank added "You probably won't be able to say your last name when we're done with you."

Lob, Jr. placed the leucotome down on the dirt floor, which worried me a little, as I thought maybe, just maybe, the sterility of the instrument might be compromised. "Oh boy," he said. "I haven't done this in a long time."

What did that mean? Had he actually performed the procedure? I couldn't believe this was happening. Would Jaclyn still love me if I had a lobotomy? Would I even recognize Jaclyn? Would Hallmark movies even play into the equation?

He set the black box down beside me. It had two small, white windows near the top with little needle indicators visible. There were four black dials of various sizes on the top as well as a silver on-off switch. A wire ran out the side and when Lob, Jr. held up what was attached to the end, I couldn't help but think of the clunky stereo headphones I had when I was a teenager (yes, the ones I used to listen to Pink Floyd's "Shine on You Crazy Diamond"). He put the pads on the end of the wire frame over my temples, next to my eyes. *Hey*, I wanted to shout. *I can't listen to Pink Floyd that way!* He tightened some kind of screw on the frame above my head. Carl's words came back to me in a rush: *As an anesthetic, Dr. Freeman gives his patient an electroshock until they convulse.*

I began shaking my head violently from side to side, trying to throw the headgear. Tank grabbed me by the throat again and held my head still.

Lob, Jr. turned each of the dials on top of the box. (I had a vision of Bela Lugosi as a mad scientist in *The Devil Bat*.) Then he flipped the silver switch…

White light. Intense pain. I thought I heard Jerry Lee Lewis singing "Whole Lotta Shakin' Goin' On". I definitely heard him banging on the piano keys with his hands, his feet, his head (maybe with my head). *Whose barn? What barn? My barn.* What the hell was Jerry Lee singing about. We were in a silo, not the barn. Ouch! I think I bit my tongue! My eyes felt like they had "gone back in my head", as my grandfather Finnian used to say.

I heard a sound like a thousand bug zappers fighting their way through an insect infestation. In spite of the pain, my mind focused on the noise, wondering if that's what it would sound like if all the Justin Beiber songs were thrown in a pot and stirred. (Now I'm a Belieber, yeah, yeah, yeah, yeah, yeah.) A blinding burst of white light put The Bieb out of my mind (thankfully).

My head felt like that time in college when I drank too much grain alcohol mixed with Mountain Dew at a party (I'm not sure which ingredient did me in). I was struggling to open my eyes when a large crash was followed by another jolt to the head.

"Daniel. Daniel, are you okay?"

The voice seemed far away and sounded familiar. "A penny saved is a penny wasted" came to mind. The voice did sound somewhat like my grandfather, Finnian's, although it was a bit stronger than I remembered it.

"Daniel! Up and atom, boy!"

I opened my eyes, expecting to be in my childhood bed with my aged grandfather standing over me, his bloodshot eyes staring at me, a slight tremor from his neck up. I did not expect to open my eyes and find myself in the great hall of a gothic castle—the walls gray and cracked, cobwebs littering the room and staircase, everything bathed in shadow.

My grandfather, Finnian *was* standing there, but only the grandfather I knew from old, faded black and white photographs. He seemed to be in his twenties or maybe even younger. I started to reach out and touch him, see if he was really there, when out of the corner of my eye, I saw a shadow move and disappear behind the staircase.

"Is this place real?" I asked, looking around again.

"Yes and no," Finnian answered. I recognized the mischievous gleam in his eye, although it was much brighter than I had ever seen it.

"'Splain," I answered, reverting back to my childhood when I asked my grandfather to 'splain everything.

"You are in a castle in Transylvania," he said in a spooky voice.

"Really?" I looked around again with interest.

As he did so often when I was a kid, he froze his face in a look of alarm, eyes wide and mouth "O-shaped". I saw the figure in the shadows move again and thought I saw a black cape flutter.

"Transylvania," I said mystically.

Finnian's face broke and he laughed. "No. Not really. California—on a Universal backlot."

"Not Castle Dracula?" I asked, crestfallen.

"Yes and no," he answered again. I remembered it seemed to be his favorite way to answer my questions. "It's a movie set."

I saw the figure in the shadows move again and I cried out a little (okay, a lot). Finnian looked back over his shoulder. "It may be a movie set, but there are still things you should fear."

"Is that—" And before I could say the name of the most famous actor to play the part, a giant, black bat flew out of the shadows. I cringed as it came toward me, its huge wings flapping gracefully. Terrified, I looked up in time to get a close-up of the pointy ears, black beady eyes and snarling fangs as it descended. (I may have screamed and wet myself, but I'll deny it except in a court of law.) An almost inaudible screech filled the air, causing me to put my hands over my ears.

"Don't be such a baby, Danny Boy," my grandfather said as the giant bat landed on his shoulder. The bat chittered into his ear. It was my turn to look at Finnian with alarm, eyes wide and mouth "O-shaped".

"Yes, yes," Finnian said, turning his face to the bat. He turned back to me. "Bela wants to know why you are so obsessed with him?"

I forgot my fear for a moment. "Me? He's the one that keeps showing up in my out-of-body experiences!"

Finnian clucked his tongue several times and shook his head. It was a weird experience as he acted as my grandfather did in his declining years, but stood before me (with a giant bat on his shoulder) in the springtime of his youth. And then he said something he had told me a hundred times. "Daniel, many a time a man's mouth broke his nose."

I sighed. "Back then…um, in the future…I don't really know what I mean. I guess what I'm trying to say is I always tried to take those words, your words to heart, but my mouth wouldn't let me. I'm sorry Grandfather Finnian."

He laughed, a laugh that obviously stayed the same through the years. "It's okay, Danny Boy. You can't help it—you're Irish." He laughed so hard the giant bat on his shoulder jiggled.

I smiled and couldn't help adding another of his favorite sayings. "Bottoms up or bottoms down. Either way no one will frown."

He stopped laughing and looked at me. "I like that one. I'll have to remember it to use later."

The giant bat flapped its wings and chittered loudly, apparently growing bored with the conversation.

"What did Bela say?" I asked breathlessly, not surprised any more that Grandfather Finnian could speak Bat-uguease (Bat-ish? Bat-enese?)

Finnian repeated what Bela said, in a voice I can only describe as Hungarian hillbilly. "He said, 'You got a pur-ty neck'."

I immediately hunched my shoulders, covering my throat. The giant bat's chittering was different this time, kind of like laughter.

"LOL, Bela," I said, keeping my shoulders hunched and head down.

All at once, the bat stopped making noise and wrapped its wings around it, like Bela did with his cape in many of his movies. A single noise escaped the bat.

"Bela says it's time to get serious," Finnian interpreted. "He doesn't want to see you leaving in a meat wagon."

"O-kay," I answered, trying to remember the lingo of the times. (It didn't matter—it sounded ominous.)

Bela the bat emitted a long, sonic sound. "First," Finnian said, turning from looking at the bat to me. "You need to drop and roll back. Drop and roll back. Bela said it's very important."

"Drop and roll back," I repeated.

"And pull the sap with you," Finnian added, after another sound from the giant bat.

"Pull the sap?"

"Hey, I just call them as I hear them," Finnian said. Next, the giant bat chittered the loudest of all.

"What did Bela say?" I asked, before the noise had subsided.

Grandfather Finnian's eyes grew wide while he listened. "He said the poor little fellows need to go home. You can find them at five-hundred and fifty paces southeast, between the tree with bumps and the giant rock."

22 - A SPARKLY RIDE THROUGH THE FOREST

Splintering wood, a man crying out, the distinct sound of metal wrenching free. I drew in a sharp intake of air and opened my eyes. Had I died and returned?

I was stunned, on my knees in the dirt, my hands still zip-tied behind me. Tank and his brother were backing away with looks of horror on their faces. I could see the splintered post behind me. The sounds intensified, echoing off the walls. It seemed the whole silo was folding in on itself, preparing to crash down in a heap. Suddenly the words of Bela came to me: *Drop and roll back.*

I dropped (okay, it was more like falling over) and rolled a half turn, before remembering, *pull the sap with you.* With my hands behind me, I managed to grab Carl by his shirt and pull him to the dirt in front of me. "Roll, Carl! Roll!" I cried. Frantically, I rolled, pushing Carl along with me until we reached the back wall of the silo where we huddled together and neeped.

The wrenching metal exploded, deafening like a bomb blast, and the platform crashed to the ground. Without the aid of the pole, the end had initially tilted downward and gravity caused the heavy, wooden platform to fall toward the middle of the silo, instead of straight down. The crash caused a great cloud of dust to rise, blinding us. I buried my face in my shirt, trying to cover my mouth and nose. I could hear Carl coughing beside me, but couldn't see him.

As the dust settled, I noticed I had developed a facial tic on the left side, as I couldn't stop winking my eye. A side effect from the electro-shock? Thinking the eye-winking may be permanent, I started worrying if other parts of my body were intact (i.e. nothing had shriveled up and dropped off). I wouldn't want Jaclyn to return to a drooling, eye-winking eunuch. (The only upside—there would no longer be a target there for jellyfish.)

Pushing against the silo wall, I rose to a standing position on wobbly legs, my hands still tied behind me. I shook my pelvis. Everything *seemed* to be okay down there.

"Carl. Carl! Carl?"

He answered with a soft, "Neep."

"Carl, are you injured? Neep once for yes, two for no."

"Neep."

I breathed a sigh of relief. "Thanks for pulling the pole out, buddy. That was quick thinking."

"Ack?"

"You saved us."

Carl cleared his throat and spoke. "It wasn't me. You did it. Your convulsion was so intense after the shock, you were writhing all over the place and you splintered the pole."

There was a sound from the other side of the silo. "Shh," I shushed. "We're still in danger."

The edge of the platform was a mere five feet away. We were lucky to have survived and I wasn't about to let that change now. Slowly I stepped onto the platform and began walking across. The surface was uneven and it was hard to balance with my hands behind me. When I was halfway, I could just make out the tips of work boots at the far edge. They seemed to be at a strange angle. I stepped near that edge and heard a moan beneath my feet. They were Tank's boots! The platform must have fallen on him, trapping him. His boots were sticking out like the Wicked Witch of the East's ruby slippers when Dorothy's house fell on her. I wondered if Tank's boots would shrivel, curl up and disappear. That thought made me start to worry about my nether region again.

I had just stepped off the end of the platform, bending to check out the degree of Tank's squishiness, when the cry of a banshee sounded. I looked up just in time to see Lob, Jr. charging at me, screaming, brandishing a weapon. Nowhere to run, I sat down hard on the platform (causing Tank to moan again). With no hands to hold him off, I bent my knees, raising my feet just as he reached me and shoved him backwards with a thrust of my legs. He landed with an "oomph" on his butt in the dirt. Unfortunately, it only made him madder.

"I'm going to kill you!" he screamed, standing and running at me again. This time I could only hold him away with straight legs when I couldn't get enough force to shove him back. Using his size, he leaned into me, slowly pushing his way toward me as my legs weakened. He raised his arm and I gasped—the leucotome! Snarling and spitting at me, he was hell-bent on lobotomizing me!

The medical ice pick gradually moved toward my eye as my legs started to bend and give out. My quads were burning. I tried to keep my back straight and locked, but it was starting to curl. A crazed man with a leucotome, only inches from my face! I moved my head to the side, although I wasn't sure if I would fare any better with an ice pick to the back of the head.

Amidst my grunting and his snarling, I heard the door to the silo slam open. Half delirious, I wondered if it was Bela and Finnian coming to save me. I opened one eye and saw three angels, instead of two. One dressed in scrubs with a white lab coat, another the tallest woman on earth (a circus angel?) and the third the strangest of all. In a loose hospital gown that swirled with movement, I could have sworn it was my bare-assed guardian angel.

The next part happened so fast, I was surprised I had time to recognize my saviors. Greg kicked the leucotome out of the crazy man's hand, Sparkle picked him up like a rag doll and threw him across the dirt floor and Willie sat on him, pinning him down with his exposed lily-white buttocks.

I let my head fall back to the platform, laughing, then crying, followed by more laughing when I looked up at Willie again. By this time, Carl had stumbled his way across the platform to the group. Like any good surgery employee, Greg had a pair of bandage scissors in his lab coat pocket and quickly cut through our zip-ties. Oh man, my shoulders seemed locked in place. Greg and Sparkle sat me up, each taking a forearm and guiding my arms back to the front of my body.

"Castle Dracula!" I yelled. "That hurt!" Greg and Sparkle exchanged a look of concern. As the powerful feeling of relief spread over me, my head began to throb. The spastic intensity of my pulsating cranium rivaled anything by the best screamo band (was there such a thing as the *best* screamo band?) It felt like the lead singer—I mean screamer—was right there in my head screeching out unintelligible lyrics. (Lyrics, no doubt, that would make "Louie Louie" seem like the most articulate song ever recorded.)

What? Greg was slapping my cheeks with an open palm.

"I think we need to get him back to the hospital," Greg said. "I tried my cell and service is sketchy here."

"I left mine back at the site," Sparkle answered.

Greg looked in Willie's direction. "I don't think our friend Willie has anywhere to hide a phone."

Greg slapped me again. "Daniel, do you think you can walk?"

Walk? Of course I can walk. That's what I meant to say—what came out was: "Finnian...on set of Hallmark movie."

"He seems to be delirious."

"He should be," Carl said. "He had a shock."

Greg put his hand on Carl's shoulder. "I imagine you both did."

"No, you don't understand," answered Carl. "An electro-shock from an old ECT device that was used in psychiatric facilities."

"What?" Greg and Sparkle responded simultaneously.

I was following the conversation, but also trying to remember something Bela the bat had told me. What was it?

"Giant bat!" I blurted. Greg, Sparkle and Carl hunkered down, looking at the top of the silo. Willie shifted uneasily on top of Lob, Jr. "Giant rock!" I added, hoping they could figure out my clues.

"Whew," Greg said. "We have got to get him to the hospital. He's talking more nonsense than usual."

Greg and Sparkle left me sitting there while they walked over to Willie. I noticed Greg had found an unused zip-tie in the dirt and he bound Lob, Jr.'s wrists behind him. Good. (I'm not one to wish pain on another human being, but I hope it hurts like hell.) Greg gave Sparkle his cell phone and she came back to stand in front of me.

"Spar-kill, Spar-kill," I chanted.

"I'm touched you remembered my roller-derby nickname, Daniel," she said.

Daniel? Had she ever called me by my name before? I wasn't even sure she knew my real name. "Thought I eye-shandy," I slurred. My eyes felt heavy and I started to drift off.

The voices seemed far away. "Got to get him to hospital."; "I'll stay here with Willie. We'll watch these clowns until you can call 9-1-1."; "He doesn't look good. Keep him awake."; "You sure you can handle him alone?"; "Wow! Those are the largest biceps I've ever seen on a female—I guess you *can* handle him!"; "I'd rather have a bottle in front of me, than a frontal lobotomy."

I don't think anyone said that last one out loud, but I heard it in my head nonetheless. I tried to repeat the old joke but it started me thinking about a nice frosty bottle of Fat Tire which led me to flat tire—which led me to address the two Gregs standing in front of me. "Hey! We gotta go get the Cube!"

"Yeah," Greg said. "The Cube's got four brand new tires and it will wait another day."

Thinking of the Cube, its beautiful box symmetry and remembering reading that Nissan designers said the interior was inspired by the "enveloping curves of a Jacuzzi to promote a comfortable and social atmosphere", seemed to bring me out of my funk. (Wonder what *would* happen if I filled the inside of the Cube with water? Did those forward thinking Nissan designers put secret jets in the doors? Would the cup holders be above or below the waterline?) I took a deep breath, but before I could say "I'm feeling better", Sparkle lifted me and threw me over her shoulder. My view of her anatomy was pretty much the same as her view of mine, if she turned her head slightly to the right.

"Call the cops as soon as you have reception," Greg reminded her.

Holding on to my legs so I didn't flip over her back, Sparkle turned her head to the right and gave my bottom a light smack. "Don't worry, boys. I won't let anything happen to my little Eye Candy."

As Sparkle walked out the silo door (nearly banging my head on the frame), I heard Greg ask, "You know the way back to the hospital, right?"

Even upside down with the blood rushing to my head, it seemed Sparkle turned left when she should have turned right outside the silo. She was taking long strides, trouncing my face against her back with each step. At first the full moon provided a bright light through the foliage, but as we traipsed onward (okay, Sparkle traipsed and I trounced), the trees seemed to get thicker and the light thinner.

With each trounce, my head felt like it would explode. My thoughts became jumbled again. Opening my eyes between trounces, I was convinced we were being followed. At first, I saw a man in a black cape, but after a few more trounces, the shape transformed into something much more hideous.

Every so often Sparkle would stop to try the cell phone (and yodel-cuss when there was no signal), allowing me time to breathe. It was on one of these stops, in a wide clearing, when I got a good look at the creature following us.

"Pooka!" I cried.

"Yes, darling?" Sparkle replied affectionately.

Grandfather Finnian wasn't fibbing! Pookas were real! He had often told me bedtime stories about the malevolent Irish goblins. The pooka snarled, drifting in and out of the nearby trees, its green, deformed face made even more hideous by five horns on top of its head and a smaller horn on its chin.

I closed my eyes, anticipating the attack. When it didn't come, I opened one eye, looking to the trees. The pooka had been replaced by a smiling German/American bandleader, from television's golden days, dressed in a spiffy white suit with shiny white shoes.

I managed to get out two words. "What the—"

"Wunnerful, wunnerful," Lawrence Welk replied.

Finally able to get out a complete sentence, I cried, "What's Lawrence Welk, the TV maestro of champagne music doing in this forest?"

I can't be sure, but I believe Sparkle's concern for me ratcheted up a notch.

"Hey Lawrence! Can you play a nice polka or waltz for me?"

Sparkle placed two hands on my hips and carefully lifted me off her shoulder. Laying me on a bed of leaves, she looked down at me anxiously. I looked to the side of the clearing; Lawrence Welk had disappeared into the shadows.

"You okay?" Sparkle asked.

"Yeah, I thought I saw—" I stopped when the baldheaded dome of Paul Shaffer emerged from the trees (in keeping with the bandleader theme). I could just make out David Letterman lurking behind him, that big, goofy, gap-toothed grin on his face.

Amazed, I rolled over on my side and started prying up a piece of brown moss near my feet.

"What are you doing?" asked Sparkle.

"Looking for Doc Severinsen."

She quickly pulled the cell phone out of her pocket and tried again. "Damn!" I could tell she was worried about something. Maybe, like most of the world's citizens, she was stressed by spotty coverage, terrible reception, dropped calls and dead zones. Perhaps we were in a dead zone because I could see deceased bandleaders Tommy Dorsey and Benny Goodman peeking at me through the tree limbs.

Sparkle gently lifted me and started to throw me over her shoulder again; I whimpered like an unhappy baby, an abandoned puppy.

"You don't like that?" Sparkle asked, in as close to a tender, motherly voice as she possessed.

With my lower lip pooched out, I shook my head.

"How about a piggyback ride?" she asked, brightening.

I smiled (and squealed a little).

Sparkle threw me up over her back, where I landed with a gonadal thump (I squealed a lot). She took off through the forest.

"You okay back there?" Sparkle asked.

I had been looking back over my shoulder, spying a worrisome sight. "Hurry!" I cried. "Glenn Miller is following us and he's 'in the mood'!"

Sparkle quickened her pace and trudged on for another five minutes; Glenn Miller peeled off into the forest (he must have needed to catch a train to Pennsylvania or Chattanooga).

The undergrowth thickened, causing Sparkle to slow. I looked in all directions and couldn't see light.

"Sparkle?"

"Yes."

"Are we lost?"

"No, we're not lost!"

"I think we're lost."

"I know exactly where we're going!"

She started battling her way through the thick vegetation.

"Why don't you just pull over and ask directions?" I muttered.

As Sparkle kicked and clawed her way through the brush, I was jostled and pommeled to within an inch of my life. Losing my grip, I finally had to reach around her to hold on.

Sparkle stopped abruptly.

"Um—what you doing, Eye Candy?"

"Holding on for dear life."

"Yeah—you know those aren't grab rails you're holding on to."

Grab rails? Those are way too soft to be— "Oh shoot!" I cried, letting go. I started falling backward until she reached behind and grabbed my shirt and hair, pulling me back. Sparkle laughed huskily.

"It's okay," she said. "I kinda liked it."

Sparkle charged forward again, yodeling as she attacked each new challenge. I carefully held on to her shoulders, riding piggyback badly, like I had flunked out of rodeo school. Had it really been earlier today when I had given Scott a piggyback ride out of his office? Was it National Piggyback Day? International Give a Friend a Piggyback Week?

The light of the full moon barely filtered in through the trees and it seemed we were going deeper into the forest, away from the hospital. I had no doubt Sparkle was lost, but I wasn't about to make a comment. She could flick her wrist and fling me to the top of a tree in a heartbeat.

Sparkle stopped so fast my chin hit the back of her head and I bit my tongue. "Wow! That's a huge rock!" she declared.

I swallowed the salty blood and brushed away the tears from my eyes, looking over her shoulder. Huge rock—it was a giant rock! *Giant rock?* The words of Bela the bat (as translated through Finnian the grandfather) came back to me.

"Sparkle!" I said excitedly. "Look around for a tree with bumps."

"A what?"

"A bumpy tree."

"You mean, like a titty tree?"

The poor little fellows need to go home. You can find them at five-hundred and fifty paces southeast, between the tree with bumps and the giant rock.

"Please, Sparkle," I implored. "Look for the tree."

Five-hundred and fifty paces southeast. Southeast! If we had come southeast from the silo, the hospital would be northwest. Boiling Grove was situated perpendicular to highway 17—south to Myrtle Beach and north to Wilmington. The silo was on the Wilmington side of the property. If we would turn back and retrace our steps, we would eventually get to the hospital.

The area turned into a small clearing as Sparkle tromped around it. "There it is!" Sparkle cried. The full moon shone on the tree with bumps along its upper trunk, which indeed looked like mammalian protuberances.

"This is it," I said in a low voice. I pointed to the rock. "Between the giant rock and…" Still perched on Sparkle's back, I twisted around to look at the tree. "The tit—er, tree with bumps."

"What do you mean?" Sparkle asked.

I took a deep breath. "This is the spot. We need to mark it."

She looked around. "Okay, what did you have in mind?"

"I don't know." I searched for something bright in the trees, on the ground. When I couldn't find anything, I said, "A piece of clothing, maybe."

"I know just the thing," Sparkle said, moving toward the trees. She broke a small limb from a nearby tree and moved back to the center of the clearing. Pointing the sharp end of the limb groundward, she poked it into the soil, like a flagpole.

She turned her head back to look at me. "Undo my bra strap."

"What? No!"

"Oh, come on, Eye Candy. Don't be shy."

"I am *not* going to undo your bra strap."

"It's easy."

"But *I'm* not." I tried to glare at the side of her face. "I wouldn't be able to unhook an industrial strength brassiere anyway," I muttered.

Sparkle hefted up her large ta-tas. "Thank you very much," she said.

"I didn't mean it that way. Don't you have special construction site work clothes?"

Sparkle laughed. "Well, I usually wear my sports bras to work but they are all dirty from derby practice. This baby is a Walmart special." She reached her hands up the back of her shirt.

"Hey! Watch it!" I scooted my package away from the hands snaking upward. Deftly, she unhooked the brassiere in a couple of seconds. "Wow. See, it would've taken me at least an hour to do that. Do you need me to get off your back?"

"Nope." Her sleeves were rolled up, and she stuck her left hand up her right sleeve to the shoulder. In a flash she had removed her hand, holding up her brassiere like she had pulled a rabbit out of her hat. Amazing! Houdini or David Copperfield could never have performed a trick that magical (they didn't have the right equipment). She twisted the strap around the top of the limb; the brassiere hung limp, until it caught a strong breeze, flapping in the wind like a Women's Rights symbol from the 60s.

"Consider the spot marked," Sparkle said proudly. "What's so special about it?"

"The poor little fellows," I said sadly.

"Who?"

"More of the children from the reform school, like the ones you found in the pit. Possibly lobotomized and buried here without their relatives' knowledge."

We were both silent, looking around the clearing, imagining the worst.

Sparkle tried the cell phone again with no luck. "Hey," I said, remembering. "I know the way to the hospital. We need to go back in the direction we came."

Sparkle took a step in that direction, then stopped. She looked around reverently and did something I didn't expect—bowed her head and prayed. The Lord's Prayer, quietly. I closed my eyes, thinking of the children. Before the end of the prayer, I sensed something and opened one eye.

I can't be sure it wasn't my short-circuited brain, but the shimmering souls of children encircled us, watching with sad but grateful eyes.

23 - HOPE YOU LIKE JAMMIN' TOO

Sparkle sprinted toward the bodies blocking her, turned her body, dipped her shoulder and burst through on powerful legs, sending torsos flying.

"Spar-Kill, Spar-Kill, Spar-Kill…" the crowd chanted.

She didn't stop there, circling around so fast the star on her helmet was a blur. Lapping the opposing jammer wasn't enough as she barreled through the remaining members of the Charlotte Roller Girls, making them look like prepubescent girls who just received their first pair of roller skates for Christmas (*I got a brand-new pair of roller skates, you got a brand-new key*).

Sparkle put her hands on her hips and smiled widely as she rolled around the track.

The microphone squelched as the announcer came on: "It's a grand slam for Spar-Kill and the Cape Fear Roller Girls!" The crowd cheered wildly.

This was flat track roller derby—not your parents' roller derby from the 1970s with the banked track and staged confrontations with skaters flying over railings. The skaters in this revival of the sport seemed athletic, but came in all shapes and sizes. I looked around the crowd and saw much the same—grandmas, bikers, parents, college kids and little girls, lots of little girls. One held up a handmade sign: "Support Your Local Roller Derby – We Love You Spar-Kill!" Sparkle skated over and gave the little girl a high-five. The flat track certainly allowed for the athletes to interact with the crowd, and the crowd loved it.

The hand I was holding squeezed my fingers. I smiled, looking down at Jaclyn's hand clasped in mine. She pulled on it to get my attention; when I looked up, she was smiling broadly and nodding her head toward the seat next to her. I leaned forward and glanced that way. Greg stared, openmouthed, his head following the skating form of Sparkle. I nodded, laughed and squeezed Jaclyn's hand.

Things were good with Jaclyn again. She had returned a week ago, relaxed, back to her old self. I didn't get to see her at the hospital since I had to take a week off as a precautionary measure due to my head trauma (in all honesty, I could have gone back to work but the ER physicians couldn't find a protocol that gave them a return-to-work for patients who had undergone electro-shock therapy). I hadn't done much during my week off, besides a vigorous daily workout and going to the rec center to visit the Happy Rummikubers (I had asked them pointblank if they were part of Ken Kesey's Merry Band of Pranksters and they had only smiled). I did manage to have dinner with Jaclyn a couple of times after she got off work, but we had both looked forward to the weekend. And so far it had been glorious. It was Saturday evening and we had spent every waking minute together. Not that we had been alone for much of it. I glanced down the bleacher row at our long line of friends.

Sparkle was not in the next two-minute jam and she rolled over to our seats. Besides black eyeshadow and black lipstick, her uniform consisted of colorful skates, black fishnet stockings, black knee pads, tight black shorts, black elbow pads and a black shirt with white stripes. The Cape Fear Roller Girls' logo on the front of the shirt was a female pirate with pirate hat, eye patch and crossed swords over her head with a red heart pierced on one of them. The back of her shirt had "Spar-Kill" spelled out in white letters. Her helmet was off and her hair looked wild. Sparkle had saved the first bleacher row for us (the sign on it stated: "Reserved for Spar-Kill's friends—kindly set your keister elsewhere") and left us complimentary tickets at the door. I had argued over the free tickets, but Sparkle wouldn't hear of it. As it turned out, I emptied my wallet in the donation jar and I saw several others from our group throw in twenty-dollar bills, so the Cape Fear Roller Girls were about two hundred dollars richer.

"How you like it, Eye Candy!" she exclaimed exuberantly. She looked to Jaclyn. "You don't mind if I call him Eye Candy, do you?"

"As long as you know he's *my* eye candy," Jaclyn said, smiling, yet shooting eye-arrows at Sparkle.

I laughed nervously. To change the subject, I asked, pointing to Sparkle's chest, "Is that a pirate or a privateer?"

Sparkle hunched her shoulders, bringing her arms together, which made the Cape Fear Roller Girls' logo appear to expand and come toward us (if I had on 3-D glasses, I would have screamed). Sparkle gave a whoop and said, "You are *such* a boob man!"

I didn't look at Jaclyn but I could sense her angry glare and the eye-arrows she was shooting into my ear.

Sparkle placed her hand on Greg's knee. "How's my N.A. Stud?" She gave him a kiss on the cheek.

Greg managed to smile (even though his mouth still hung open), but he couldn't get any words to come out.

Sparkle snapped her fingers and pointed to the person to the right of Greg. "Good to see you, hero," she said to Carl.

Carl could only manage a "Neep", but he had still topped Greg by one word. On the left of Carl, his uncle, Officer Hans Rodriguez, who was a hero in his own right, smiled broadly and slapped his nephew on the back (which caused an "Ack" to escape).

(Okay, so maybe, just maybe, I had changed the story a little where Carl and I were alone in the silo with the wacko brothers. Did it really matter who actually knocked the pole over?)

The fans from the stands swarmed Sparkle, and she had to leave us to pose for pictures with young girls, sign autographs and to leave a black kiss imprint on a biker's white helmet.

I gazed around the gymnasium of Cape Fear Community College (home of the Sea Devils). There were Pabst Blue Ribbon banners from one of the Cape Fear Roller Girls' proud sponsors, The Pour House and one huge promotional poster with a fierce looking Spar-Kill and teammates on it proclaiming, "They're Bad...They're Beautiful...THEY'RE BACK!" The mood of the whole gym was electric. This was so much fun. My friends were having fun, the crowd was having fun, the Cape Fear Roller Girls and the Charlotte Roller Girls, even though they were rivals, showed respect for one another and even shared a few laughs. Pure bliss.

Down at the end of our row, I heard Dr. Valaree Neutre give a long whistle, followed by a cheer. She was really getting into the competition, smiling from ear to ear. She put her arm around the person next to her, planting a quick kiss on her cheek. It turned out Valaree was engaged, to Adrienne, the dark haired woman who had seen Valaree and me eating at Duffer's Pub and Grille. One of Jacyln's golf partners—and Jaclyn had known of the engagement all along. We talked about it when she returned from her trip and she seemed to think it was funny, making me eat crow like that on the phone in the Emergency Room (which reminded me of Edgar Allan Crow and my lost pack of sunflower seeds).

Dr. Neutre had shored up all the controlled substance processes at her vet clinic, including encasing the metal cabinet Moses had installed inside of another metal cabinet, so there was a double lock. Dr. Neutre kept the keys on her person at all times. The new paperwork was immaculate (and readable). As in a lot of drug diversion issues, there was no way to prove without a shadow of a doubt that Brad, Angela, or anyone else had stolen the fentanyl. She was disappointed in the outcome of the police investigation, but accepted it, determined to never let it happen at her clinic again. After filing DEA Form 106-Theft or Loss of Controlled Substances and completing the action plan on changes to her processes (with my help), she considered the case closed and was happy to move on.

Valaree pumped and whirled her fist while shouting, "Woof, woof, woof!" Arsenio Hall-style. Adrienne laughed delightedly.

Sparkle was back on the court for another jam, lined up behind the blockers on the jammer line with the opposing jammer. A short whistle blast by the referee and the four blockers from each team and the two jammers began skating counterclockwise, jockeying for position. I marveled at the spectacle. Other than the basic uniform top of each team plus the elbow and knee pads, it was "anything goes". Some wore shorts, some leggings, others skirts. Sparkle's black fish net stockings were pristine, while another skater had black fish net stockings with larger holes ripped throughout. The jammer on the Charlotte team had diamond shaped tattoos up the backs of her legs. A couple of the skaters had fluorescent hair with face paint. As the skaters circled and Sparkle passed through the opposing blockers yet again, I tried to read as many names on the back of the jerseys as I could: Luna Shovegood, Tragedy Ann, Scratcher in the Eye, Tits McVenom, Bloody Holly, and Bethamphetamine (have to be a little concerned about her).

Carl stood up and cheered as Sparkle passed the Charlotte jammer for another point. I laughed and Hands looked over at me, giving me the thumbs up. Hands and I had discussed his nephew's change in behavior since the silo incident (after Hands had bought me several rounds of Fat Tire at No Egrets). Carl had more confidence now, plus the respect of the other residents since the silo story had spread like wildfire on the Stethoscope Telegraph (I had to help it a little by telling the story to Jim and Ora in Housekeeping). I even heard rumors that Carl had been seen having lunch with a certain, shy nursing student on a couple of occasions. I reached across Jaclyn and Greg to give Carl a fist bump. He might just make it to Medical Examiner someday.

The only thing that could keep Sparkle from playing human bowling pins with the other team and scoring another grand slam was the buzzer for the end of the period, which occurred before the end of the jam. Score at the end of the first period: Cape Fear 82 – Charlotte 58. The crowd cheered wildly.

The announcer came on again. "In honor of the total eclipse of the sun happening Monday…"

The eclipse! I had forgotten about it. That must have been why Pickles had given me an extra day off on Monday, instructing me not to come back until Tuesday (either that, or she hoped I would look at it without protection, lose my sight, and therefore have to be transferred out of her department).

"I have a surprise for you," Jaclyn whispered in my ear. Her voice and breath in my ear caused me to tremble. She leaned back when she saw my dreamy look, my eyes starting to roll back. "Not that kind of surprise," she laughed. "I took off Monday so we could watch the eclipse together."

Before I could express my thanks, the overhead loudspeaker started blaring "Total Eclipse of the Heart" by Bonnie Tyler (what that had to do with the solar eclipse, I'll never know). While the rest of the Cape Fear Roller Girls had gone to take a seat on their bench (which had a Bus Stop sign with the "s" in bus marked out and replaced with "tt"), Sparkle appeared in front of the crowd, mouthing the words to the song. We all cheered like she was Steven Tyler instead of Bonnie Tyler.

"Once upon a time I was falling in love,
But now I'm only falling apart.
And there's nothing I can say.
A total eclipse of the heart."

The musical interlude began and Sparkle let fly with a yodel that made my hair stand on end. She was standing right in front of Greg and he just about tumbled backwards off his seat. Jaclyn grabbed him and kept him upright. Sparkle paused to breathe, opened her mouth and the yodel that escaped can only be described as a cross between Austrian folk singer and a Tarzan yell. It shouldn't have worked with a 1980s rock love song, but her voice flowed right along with the music. The crowd, worked into a frenzy, cheered and clapped along.

When the song ended, I noticed Jaclyn taking Greg's pulse.

"Do you think he's going to be alright?" Jaclyn asked me loudly, over the cheering crowd.

Greg's trancelike stare was following Sparkle as she took bows and blew kisses to the audience.

"No," I shouted. "I don't think he's ever going to be the same again."

Greg suddenly came to life. "Did you see—she smelled wonder—her voice—she touched my knee—kissed me..."

It seemed Greg had just suffered a total eclipse of his five senses.

The excitement of Saturday night faded as I settled into a somber Sunday afternoon, trudging through the Old Smithville Burying Ground, alone. Jaclyn had to go to the hospital for a few hours to do payroll and catch up on managerial duties, so I had driven the new and improved Cube to Southport (with the new tires, it drove like a dream—somewhere between the one where you are being chased and the one where you are falling).

I stopped beside a huge, bent and gnarled live oak. Ahead I could see a small group of people where a graveside service was taking place. On closer inspection, it seemed there was a preacher and a few men who could be cemetery workers, all on the left side of the open grave. On the right side there was only one man, in a familiar dirty army jacket.

It didn't take long for the scandal to break and a different Medical Examiner to be brought to the county. Since Driftwood's cousin, Owen was the first name to be tied to the remains, he was identified quickly through dental records. The last I heard on the news, there was a whole line of families coming forward who had missing children from the reform school during that era. The story dominated the local news markets and had now spread nationally. People were fascinated once again with headlines of lobotomy and lobotomist, the terms still producing shock, distress, and discomfort in the general public.

In a strange twist of fate, the senior Dr. Mantellus had slipped into a coma four days ago and was spending his last days in Hospice care in Wilmington. His dirty deeds were quickly overshadowed by his offspring however, so in the end I guess they succeeded in protecting him somewhat. Tank took the least of the outrage (there seemed to be a degree of sympathy since he had a broken spine from the silo platform), even though he had tried to cover up the skeleton finds and was charged with kidnapping and attempted murder. But it was his brother, the junior Dr. Mantellus who garnered the most headlines, especially since the blockbuster revelation of two days ago. It seems he *had* performed a lobotomy in his lifetime—on his estranged, wealthy wife who relatives had to put in an institution for care in Kansas City. They had always had their suspicions about the odd, aloof Dr. Mantellus, but they could never prove anything. The fact that Dr. Mantellus continued to spend his wife's fortune especially goaded them. But after reading about the effects of lobotomy, they became suspicious and hired a distinguished neurologist to examine her. Since transorbital lobotomies left no scars (just two black eyes), it was impossible to tell until the neurologist performed x-rays, a cat scan and a MRI. And lo and behold there were two holes in her orbital cavity, as well as scarring on the prefrontal cortex of the brain. The neurologist proclaimed, without a doubt, she had been subjected to a lobotomy.

The preacher spoke, holding open a bible, but I could only make out a word here or there. Driftwood had his head bowed so I did the same. The community had really come together for Driftwood after the news of his cousin broke. Someone had started a GoFundMe account, but it turned out it wasn't necessary. A rich benefactor in Southport had donated an extra plot in the Old Smithville Burying Ground, another anonymous donor had provided money for the coffin and headstone (some believed it was the famous driftwood artist P.W. Adams).

When I looked up, the dirt was being shoveled into the hole. Driftwood had turned and was walking toward me. He stopped when he reached me;

there were tears streaming down his face, disappearing into his gray beard. He nodded once at me and continued on his way.

24 - SOLAR LUNACY

One of the stipulations of Willie getting released early from the hospital was to return in a week for a blood test (his nurses had thrown a party for Willie when he was discharged, but I think it was more a celebration for them than him). The eclipse wasn't until the afternoon, so early Monday I prepared to take Willie for his blood test. It turned out easier to get Fairbanks in a cat carrier than it was to get Willie back to the hospital. I waited in the lab until the harried phlebotomist brought him back to me.

Afterward, I lugged Willie with me for a quick visit to the I.S. Department to say hello. The first thing I saw was an unopened Red Bull can on my desk and my hands started shaking, the skin on my cheek twitched and I started sweating. No! I will not go back—I'm going to kick this habit cold bovine!

One of my co-workers popped his head above his cubicle and waved. "Hey Daniel, did you hear the news? The project is delayed!"

"What?"

"Dr. Pearson did it! He threw a holy fit, came in here first to rant, then marched right in the CEO's office. The next thing we know, Pickles is telling us Medi-Soit has been put on notice by the hospital and they have one month to fix certain deficiencies. She didn't tell us what the deficiencies were, and to tell you the truth, I'm not sure she knows."

Good ole Dr. P! For once his anger was justified and directed at the right target. And he saved *me* a trip to the CEO's office.

"Oh, by the way, Dr. Pearson let you an envelope on your desk."

There, under the dreaded Red Bull can, was indeed an envelope.

"Willie, can you throw that can in the trash for me?" I asked, not wanting to touch it. He looked at me like it was a can full of maggots.

"Thanks for your help, Willie," I muttered. "You're a real pal." I looked away and grabbed the envelope quickly from under the Red Bull, leaving the can standing. I tore open the envelope to find a note, written on a piece of paper emblazoned with a drug company logo, from Cincinnaticus Pearson, MD:

Daniel,

I wanted to thank you for setting up my date with Dixie. Strangely enough, the restaurant had lost our reservation, but it turned out for the best. I was really nervous and it gave us time to walk around the marina and get to know each other better before the wonderful Italian dinner. Dixie is fantastic and we're going to have another date. I can't thank you enough.

It was signed "Cincy". I could call him a lot of things, but I didn't think I could call him Cincy.

P.S. They wanted me to test the computer, and not only could I not find Lasix, I couldn't find Cipro! What a piece of crap!

I laughed. Good ole Cincy. As Lawrence Welk would say, "Wunnerful, wunnerful."

Next, I hauled Willie to Scott's office. The first thing I noticed was an empty space on the bookshelf, just large enough to hold something rectangular, say, an aquarium.

"Hello, Bertha my dear," I said, walking up to her desk.

Bertha smiled for an instant; I thought she might just jump up and give me a hug.

"You been doing any table dancing lately?" I asked, smiling myself.

Her smile poofed out like a butane lighter that just ran out of lighter fluid. "I have two things to say to you," she said. "One I will only say this one time and never again. Thank you. The other I have a feeling I will be forced to say over and over—you're still not funny."

"Ah, Bertha." I placed my hand on my heart. "I lurv ya, too." I pointed to the empty space. "What happened to Ebenezer?"

"That *thing* is gone, thank goodness. It was just a big misunderstanding. It seems mantis shrimp can't live out of water after all."

I gasped. "Ebenezer didn't pass on to join the ghost shrimp of aquariums past, present and future?"

Bertha snorted. "If only. After the infernal thing broke the glass, it retreated to its cave to hide in what water was left."

"Whew!" I exclaimed. "Where is Eb now?"

Scott had just walked out of his office with another man. "I gave him to an employee who had other mantis shrimp," he said. "I will miss him, but I think it's for the best."

"Gone, but never forgotten," I said, with a forced tinge of sadness. Never, ever forgotten; hospital employees would tell the story for years.

The other man stepped from behind Scott. "Daniel…and Mr. Welch! It's good to see you."

Father Spinelli looked better than the last time I had seen him. "Father!" I cried. "You didn't get crushed by the stampeding horde!" I ran to him, giving him a clumsy hug.

The priest laughed and clapped me on the back. "I am used to such things. It's not much different than the exodus when Mass is over." He put me at arm's length and surveyed me carefully. "And how are you doing? I heard you had quite the scare."

"I'm okay. Not many people these days can say they've had electroshock therapy and came within an icepick's length of a lobotomy. Kind of makes me special."

"Daniel," Scott said, smiling. "You are indeed special. When do you come back to work?"

"Tomorrow. Is there anything I need to do?"

"You need to visit the employee health nurse first thing in the morning and take her Form 597A-HR15." He turned to Bertha. "Can you give Daniel Form 597A-HR15, please?"

Bertha blinked slowly at her boss. "No."

Scott frowned. "Why not?"

"Because you won't let me keep Form 597A-HR15 out here. You said Form 597A-HR15 should only be kept locked in your office drawer."

I wanted to get into the act. "Woe is me! How will I ever get Form 597A-HR15?"

Scott turned to go back to his office. Over his shoulder he said, "I'll go get you Form 597A-HR15."

"Mr. Welch," Father Spinelli said, taking a step closer to Willie, out of Bertha's earshot. "Daniel has told me of the spectral disturbances on your boat, I believe the *Silent Cow?*" Willie nodded. "I have talked to colleagues and was just looking at my notes. It is either luck or divine intervention that I ran into you this morning. May I ask you some questions?" Another nod from Willie. "Spirits most often attach themselves to human beings. First, I would assume you are not possessed—"

"Not with demons of the spirit variety," I answered. "Psychological ones, yes." Willie glared at me.

"How long have you been in your houseboat?" the priest continued, undeterred.

Willie scratched his head. "Sometime over a year, maybe a year and a half."

"When did the spectral disturbances begin?"

Willie looked to me. "A month or two ago," I answered. "Although since Willie's been living in my house instead of the *Silent Cow*, it seems like a year or two."

"I see," said Father Spinelli, rubbing his chin. "I think we can rule out the dwelling…your houseboat being haunted."

"What does that leave, Father?" I asked.

"Have you brought anything new on to your houseboat in the last couple of months?"

Something occurred to me. I moved to Willie and whispered in his ear. "What about Polythene Pam?" I asked, remembering her floating above the bed and her head spinning.

"No," Willie told me. "I've had her for a long time."

"You perv," I whispered back, moving away from him.

"You claim the ghosts are pirates," the priest continued. "It most likely would be a really old object, maybe from that era."

Willie's eyes lit up. "The astrolabe!" he exclaimed, gasping.

Father Spinelli looked at me and I shrugged.

Willie, seeing our reaction, said, "The astrolabe was a navigational instrument used on ships before the sextant. Using celestial bodies, seaman could determine a ship's latitude."

"How did you get one?" I asked.

"eBay."

At least he didn't get it from Amazon and charge it to my account. "I've never seen it. Where do you keep the astrolabe? In your bedroom, under your bed?" I asked, thinking of Polythene Pam.

"No. I intended to hang it near Ian," he answered, referring to the photograph of the Jethro Tull frontman (back before the ghost pirates broke the frame, crinkling the edges of the prized photo). "In the eBay picture, the astrolabe was a beautiful, oval, polished brass piece. But when I opened the box, it was filthy." Willie involuntarily wretched.

"So, where is it now?"

"Foredeck, under a bench."

Father Spinelli made a small clucking noise and we turned to him. "I'm definitely no expert," he said. "But one of my colleagues mentioned the possibility of spirits attached to objects. He personally witnessed the trials of one of his faithful who owned a Pillsbury Doughboy bank. Every time a coin was dropped in the slot of the bank, it would emit that famous Pillsbury Doughboy laugh—you know, like when someone on the TV commercial pokes the Doughboy in the stomach and it tickles him?"

The priest paused and seemed to be waiting on a response, so I answered him. "Yes, I am familiar with the Pillsbury Doughboy laugh; I am intimately acquainted with his cookies, biscuits and crescent rolls as well. Poppin' Fresh forever, man," I finished, giving the Doughboy salute (I don't know if there really is such a thing; I just made it up on the spot).

"Anyway," Father Spinelli continued. "The Pillsbury Doughboy bank was on a shelf in their son's bedroom, and during the day whenever a coin was dropped in the slot, it would laugh normally. But at night, the Doughboy would start laughing, coinless, and wake up the whole household. And not the usual Pillsbury Doughboy laugh…but a slower, demonic version."

"Wow!" I exclaimed. "Sounds like a R. L. Stine 'Goosebumps' story where the kids eat raw cookie dough and hallucinate."

Willie wretched again. "Raw cookie dough can contain E. coli."

I licked my lips theatrically. "I always loved eating raw cookie dough when I was a kid."

Willie scowled. "And how many times did you have abdominal cramps and bloody diarrhea?"

"That, my friend, is none of your business. That's between me and Poppin' Fresh."

Father Spinelli had watched this exchange and was shaking his head. "You guys make my head hurt."

"Sorry, Father," I apologized. "So, it is possible the astrolabe is possessed and needs to be removed from the *Silent Cow*."

Scott had just returned from his office, proudly waving Form 597A-HR15. "Astrolabe? You mean an old nautical instrument? You getting rid of one?"

Willie nodded. "Definitely."

Scott looked sadly over at the bare bookshelf. "I need to make my office interesting again. Maybe a nautical theme." He paused to think it over. "Yeah, old nautical instruments would definitely be an attraction. Employees would be stoked!"

I winced, thinking about telling Scott nobody said "stoked" anymore, but decided against it. You can't teach an old dog new words. Instead, I told him, "Scott, you don't want this particular piece."

"Nonsense. Willie, I'll give you a hundred dollars for it!"

"Are you sure that thing will work?" Jaclyn asked. It was twenty after two in the afternoon and we were walking the road to the beach, hand in hand. The Great American Eclipse (as dubbed by the media) had already started, although the blue sky looked normal at this point.

"Absolutely. Would Bernie Sanders lie?"

"Bernie Sanders?"

"Feel the Bern!" I exclaimed, removing my hand from hers and giving the salute (I didn't know if there really was a salute, so it turned out to be the same as the Pillsbury Doughboy one).

Jaclyn laughed (a good sign).

"For some reason Bernie was on the *Today Show* demonstrating how to make an eclipse viewer out of a cereal box," I said, as we crossed the bridge over the canal on Middleton. "I guess he needed the work."

I proudly held up my handiwork. "Didn't have a cereal box, but had a Ritz Cracker one. You cut the ends off the top, put paper on the inside bottom, cover one of the ends with aluminum foil and poke a pinhole in the foil. Voilà!"

"Well," Jaclyn said, laughing. "If Bernie Sanders says it will work."

"Speaking of work, how is it going?" I hadn't broached the subject since Jaclyn had returned.

"Okay. I think I just needed to get away. Manager duties, budget cuts, staffing issues—they were all piling up and getting me down. I had forgotten the passion I once had for nursing." She squeezed my hand. "But it's a little better now."

"Good."

"By the way, I saw Carl in the cafeteria, surrounded by the other residents *and* sitting next to a pretty, blonde resident. Rumor has it, he is a completely different doctor on rounds these days. One nurse said she heard Dr. Pearson compliment him, not once but twice, at a patient's bedside." Jaclyn gave me a sidelong glance. "What did you do?"

"Me? Nothing. Carl just needed a little push in the right direction. I think he will make an outstanding Medical Examiner someday."

I stopped momentarily on the sidewalk. "Oh wow!" The area at the end of Middleton, the beach access, was a parking lot for golf carts only. On a beautiful day in the summer, there may be eight or nine parked there. It looked like there were at least twenty golf carts parked, two deep. We crossed Beach Drive, marveling at the carts, from ones that had seen better days on the golf course to expensive stretch carts with two rows of seating. One brand new one sported Clemson's colors, paw prints and the school logo.

As awe inspiring as the carts were, it paled in comparison to stepping on the beach. I heard the sharp intake of Jaclyn's breath. There were more people on Oak Island's beach than I had ever seen, in fact about five times as many as I witnessed over the July 4th holiday. I closed my eyes and opened them. Had I been transported to Myrtle Beach? Where did all these people come from?

Jaclyn and I walked through the crowd, amazed. They were seated on beach chairs, laying on towels, propped against coolers, and all doing the same thing—staring at the sky through dark, plastic glasses. There was only one little girl playing in the ocean, oblivious to the behavior of everyone else. It reminded me of a scene from a 1950s Science Fiction movie where everyone looks to the sky as the alien spacecrafts arrive. *Klaatu barada nikto,* indeed.

I held my head high and carried my homemade Ritz Cracker eclipse viewer proudly, like a trophy.

"What's that thing?" someone whispered.

"Will that thing work?"

"Nah, he just waited too long to buy eclipse glasses."

My confidence was starting to waver. The *Today Show* and Bernie Sanders wouldn't let me down, would they?

Jaclyn grabbed my arm and led me through the crowd, toward a somewhat deserted spot fifty yards down the beach toward the water. "When did you ever care what people think?" she asked. Hmm—good point.

I pointed the open end of the Ritz Cracker viewer to the sky (remember those old Andy Griffith commercials, with his signature line, "Mmmmm-mmm—*good* cracker"), closed one eye and looked through the pinhole. Dejected, I told Jaclyn, "I don't see anything."

She took the viewer from me and, looking through the pinhole, started slowly rotating. "There it is!" she said excitedly.

"Lemme see! Lemme see!" I danced around in a circle like a five-year-old.

"It's so cool," she said before handing me the viewer. When I closed one eye and peered through the viewer, she smacked me on the back of the head. "Don't try so hard! Relax your face muscles and look through the hole normally."

Where does she get off treating me like a five-year-old—wait, what's that? The image of the moon passing in front of the sun appeared miraculously on the paper in the bottom of the box. Wow!

I looked up dazed, displaying a big goofy smile. Jaclyn laughed and we embraced.

"I really missed you, Jaclyn," I breathed in her ear. "I didn't think you wanted me anymore."

"I'm...I'm sorry. I felt like I was losing my sense of self. I didn't know what was wrong."

I hugged her closer before continuing. "Your comment about life not being a Hallmark movie really got to me. I watched a bunch of them, trying to figure it out."

She released me, pulling back to look at me. "I said something about a Hallmark movie?"

I nodded.

"And you watched the movies, trying to figure it out?"

Another nod.

"You're either the sweetest boyfriend ever...or the dumbest." When I saw the affectionate way she was looking at me, I decided it didn't matter—

I could play sweet or dumb. As long as Jaclyn was in my arms.

"So, what does it mean?" I asked.

"What?"

"Life is not a Hallmark movie."

Jaclyn laughed. "I have no idea."

Thank goodness. Another mystery of the universe left unsolved. I felt like the weight of the world had been lifted from my shoulders.

"Excuse me." Jaclyn and I turned around to the sound of the voice. "Would you like to borrow my eclipse glasses for a minute?"

A slightly graying middle-aged woman was holding out her dark glasses to us. It turned out she was from Virginia and had traveled to Oak Island specifically for the eclipse.

"Sure!" Jaclyn exclaimed. I started to protest, to warn about non-ISO glasses and going blind, until I saw a man's picture on the side of the glasses. Was that Bill Nye the Science Guy? Surely Bill Nye the Science Guy wouldn't let my girlfriend go blind.

When Jaclyn donned the glasses and looked skyward, she didn't say a word. After several minutes, she handed me the glasses, a rapturous look on her face. I had already seen the eclipse through my Ritz Cracker viewer, why would it be any different through—wow! Amazing! Bill Nye the Science Guy trumps Bernie Sanders!

The lady took her glasses back up the beach, and now it was Jaclyn's turn to dance around me.

"Let's go back to your house, Daniel," she said.

"You want to watch a movie?"

She waggled her eyebrows up and down. "I want to *make* a movie."

"Oh, a Hallmark movie?"

"Nope. R-rated. Maybe triple X."

I took off sprinting back through the crowd, Jaclyn close on my heels.

EPILOGUE

Holding the screen door, I pushed open my front door and stopped, listening. It had been almost two weeks since Willie had returned to the *Silent Cow*, but still I worried the ghost pirates would reappear. I had just finished de-Willie-izing my house (not nearly as complicated or time-consuming as Willie sanitizing the *Silent Cow*, yet not something I cared to repeat). Leading with my ear, I poked my head through the opening. Ah, blessed silence.

I started to step into the house when I heard the scrape of a lounge chair on the front deck, as if someone had just stood up. I turned and got blindsided by two furry projectiles, one calico and one orange. Pickford hit me low and Fairbanks jumped from the deck rail and hit me high; I tumbled backwards into the house, the cats clawing over me. "Chop block!" I cried. "Throw the flag!" Upside down, I watched the cats run to their food bowls in the kitchen.

Pulling myself to a sitting position, I noticed a rigid cardboard mailer in the floor. Too large for my mailbox, the mail carrier must have slipped it between the doors. Holding it up, I noticed "Do Not Bend-Photograph" written in my mother's careful script. Leaning back against the wall, I carefully ripped it open. The first thing I pulled out was a note from my mother:

Daniel,
You've been talking so much about your grandfather lately, I started thinking about the trunk that used to be in his bedroom. I paid the boy next door to go into the attic and bring the trunk back down. I found this picture among the junk and thought you would like to have it.

I love you,
Mom
P.S. Helen's sons came to visit her, and brought all their kids. Helen has the cutest grandchildren! I could just eat them up! Are you still seeing that nurse?

I pulled the picture out of the sleeve. I gasped. It was an 8 x 10 black and white glossy photograph of my grandfather, Finnian, at the young age from my dream (out of body experience?) Finnian was standing on the first step of a gigantic staircase, thick cobwebs blanketing the scene. He was smiling wryly. Slowly, I turned it over and found this inscription:
Finnian O'Dwyer on the set of 'Dracula', 1931.

"Cap'n, what kind of ship is this? It's huge. Look out yon window."
"Not sure, mate. How did we get here?"
"Think the tall deckhand had something to do with it. He keeps running to and fro through that door. Tall as the main mast is he."
"Aye. I've followed him to that room. Something strange hangs on the back of the door. It looks like a coconut, but is cut into two halves and attached with string. I know not the purpose."
"How about the large wench over there at the desk. Want to have some fun? You knock over her glass and I'll whisper in her ear..."

ABOUT THE AUTHOR

Lance Carney is an award winning 30+ year hospital pharmacist (5 year award, 10 year award, 15 ...). He has been writing medical/pharmacy based fiction since the 1980s. He has written three novels, "Ripped Tide: A Daniel O'Dwyer Oak Island Adventure", "No Egrets: A Glenn and Glenda Oak Island Mystery" and "Mantis Preying: A Daniel O'Dwyer Oak Island Adventure".

Lance's short stories have been published in magazines, anthologies and trade paperbacks. He often collaborates with David Moss, a buddy since junior high school. David is mostly grown up now, working for state government and having every holiday off, including Peter Rabbit's birthday. "Truth is Stranger than Fishin'" with David was chosen for publication in The Year's Best Fantastic Fiction. One of Lance's own, "Snare of the Fowler", was published in the trade paperback "Monsters from Memphis" and recognized by a nomination from the Darrell Awards Jury for Best Midsouth Short Story.

Lance lives in West Virginia with his wife and too many cats. His daughter graduated college in 2017 in film studies and is currently in Los Angeles. His son graduates from Mississippi State University College of Veterinary Medicine in 2018 (hallelujah!). And yet, they still manage to throw the empty nest into turmoil at times. He escapes to Oak Island, North Carolina, whenever The Man isn't keeping him down.

NOTE FROM THE AUTHOR

A huge thank you to my readers. If you are reading this, then you made it to the end (or maybe you dropped the book, picked it up backwards and accidentally ended up here). Either way I am grateful; I hope you enjoyed the story. If you decide to go the extra mile and take time from your busy schedule to leave an honest review on Amazon or Goodreads, it would be very helpful. Reviews are extremely important to Indie authors and I appreciate each review I receive. As a special incentive, all those who leave a review will be entered into a drawing to win either a haunted astrolabe or a peacock mantis shrimp named Ebenezer.

Made in the USA
Lexington, KY
25 October 2019